The Afflicted Girls

The Afflicted Girls

A Novel of Salem

SUZY WITTEN

Published in the United States by DREAMWAND) (Books)
An Imprint of DREAMWAND
715 N. Croft Avenue, Los Angeles, California 90069-5303, USA
www.dreamwand.net
www.theafflictedgirls.com

Library of Congress Control Number: 2009937229

Witten, Suzy
The Afflicted Girls *A Novel of Salem* /Suzy Witten—1st ed.
454 p.

ISBN: 978-0-615-32313-8 (pbk.)

Printed in the United States of America

Book & Cover Design by Suzy Witten
Author Photo by Janet Wallace, Art Marks, Los Angeles

10 9 8 7 6 5 4 3 2 1

A Paperback Original

For my parents, Ben and Lee, who are gone now, yet

have taken this journey with me.

FOREWORD

As a librarian, a book reviewer, an avid reader, and a friend, I have had the opportunity to watch and enjoy the evolution of Suzy Witten's novel *The Afflicted Girls* since its inception. Her meticulous research, passion for discovering the truth, and dedication to creating the finest work possible have produced an invaluable addition to the historical canon surrounding the Salem Witch Trials.

Using the actual texts and characters contemporary to that time and place as a foundation, into that seemingly familiar frame this author pours masterful storytelling, complex characterizations, and so many twisting inter-dependent pathways that Salem becomes a new world to explore and now finally to understand. While the motives and behaviors of "the afflicted girls," and those they accused who were executed during that strange and awful time, may seem unfathomable and confusing upon first glance, Suzy Witten presents a scenario that not only makes those events plausible but inevitable, while keeping them heart-wrenching and human. A rich tapestry for any reader, it is this author's unique insight into that infamous community that allows this novel to shine in its examination of the quotidian details of lives struggling for physical and spiritual survival in Salem in 1692, while casting a probative light into the dark corners of our present time.

It has been my honor to read this novel at every stage of its development, and I am so pleased to add a comment to its publication.

Kathleen Sullivan
Malibu, California, September 2009

AUTHOR'S NOTE

This journey began some years ago with a ten-minute stop at a bookstore to gather ideas on my way to a "pitch" meeting with a Hollywood producer. For some reason (now understood) the book, which cried out and caught my attention, concerned the Salem Village witchcraft trials, and the few pages I quickly read described the afflicted girls—in such mysterious terms that this was the story I pitched, and wrote.

The Afflicted Girls found recognition a year later as a finalist in the Walt Disney Studios annual Screenwriting Fellowship Competition.

When I decided to adapt my screen story into a book, I asked to join the professional writers' workshop taught by Los Angeles' most generous resident genius, PEN Lifetime Achievement Award recipient and NEA Fellow, novelist John Rechy. To John, I am indebted for the *crafting* of this book, and for *conjuring* me into a novelist.

I owe a huge debt, of course, to all the historians, researchers and investigators whose thought-provoking works provided me with much information and conjecture about Salem.

I'd also like to thank three dear friends: producer Leslie Embersits for setting me on the yellow book road; writer and editor Katharita Parsons Lamoza for her many insightful edits; and Malibu librarian and book reviewer Kathleen Sullivan for her never-ending support and counsel.

And finally, I wish to thank all the resounding voices of the past still whispering their stories.

The Serpent Horseman **(Clive Wright)**

What danger is the pilgrim in, how many are his foes?
How many ways there are to sin? No living mortal knows.
Some of the ditch shy are, yet can lie tumbling in the mire.
And some though they shun the frying pan do leap into the Fire.

A PILGRIM'S PROGRESS
John Bunyan (1678)

I know not the truth of those happenings. Who it was, God or the Devil, looking down as a group of young girls, streaming life and hope, converged innocently in passing. I know only that a rough and heavy rock, an unforgiving Rock of Ages, was thrown down upon me that day.

PART ONE

Salem Village, Massachusetts
Late winter 1692

JOHN INDIAN THE PARSONAGE MANSLAVE WAS hacking at the frozen ground in the meetinghouse graveyard. Winged death-heads, crudely carved skulls, bird flanked mossy faces stared out from their frost-patched marker stones. Icicles, some with cedar shingles attached, began falling from the eaves of the steeply pitched roof. The sun was breaking through.

A heavy storm had come barreling in two nights ago after a week of early spring weather. No one saw it coming, except his wife. She'd sat up all that night staring into the blank whiteness of it having her visions—it was something she always did when it snowed. Then in the morning she'd have things to tell him. Yesterday was no different. She said somebody in the village had died and he would be digging a grave today. She went quiet for a spell then said: *'Evil spirits hoverin' round that body. Blowin' a storm into it. Don' you be touch'n it.'*

He dropped his shovel, walked to the water barrel at the side of the church, poked through a thin icy veneer and ladled himself a couple of mouthfuls, splashed his sticky face and aching neck, and wiped a winter's worth of dirt off a cracked pane and peered inside. He saw his master, Reverend Samuel Parris, standing at the pulpit behind a miniature casket. A dead baby was inside it, wrapped in its winding sheets. He stared at the tiny thing, listened to the funeral-goers singing their hymn-song. A shiver wrinkled his spine. *Maggot song. Dead song. Thinkin' is alive.* He began folding in his rich sweet baritone, not because he was a believer — he wasn't one — but because he loved to sing:

> *How great His power is none can tell*
> *Nor think how large His grace*
> *Nor men below, nor Saints that dwell*
> *On high before His Face*

Shutting his eyes to the wasteland around him, he was soon back in his warm easy sugarcane fields scything the fragrant stalks, feeling a familiar breeze skim his bare back, lopping off a piece to chew, glad to be alive. Till a devilish shriek from inside the church yanked him back to his frozen ditch. He looked at the screamer, guessed it was the baby's ma. And went back to his digging, and wondering about the evil baby with the storm inside it.

❧

A fire crackled in the oversized hearth, but most funeral-goers kept their sad-colored coats bundled. Numerous windowpanes were fractured or poorly boarded and a chill was seeping through. It had been a winter of violent storms, like the one on the night the baby had died, when he'd gotten more attention than ever he had: washed pure, laid out, prayed over, wept for, read to from Scripture, fasted for; and now today he was being eulogized.

Reverend Parris had entitled his testimonial: "Right Thoughts In Sad Hours." He'd taken it verbatim from an obscure book of published English sermons, knowing no one in his congregation would have read it. Raising his white-silk mourning-gloved hands heavenwards and tilting up his comely chin, he propounded:

> "It was from God that we received them, our children, and it is to God that we return them. We cannot quarrel with God if about these *loans* He says to us, 'Give them up.' A dead child should be a sight no more grievous than a broken pitcher or a crushed dais—"

The shrillest wail, the most piercing one yet from the mother, startled him. It rang so loud that her husband, sitting beside her, had to clap his ear.

On any other day Thomas Putnam, Jr. would have clapped her. But today he wanted his wife to let loose her hysterics, to be the proxy for his rage. His cherished baby son had died in the cradle in the middle of the night without any illness or warning. Sucked into eternity just like that . . . by a Succubus?

Weird thoughts had been passing through his mind for two days now. *Come Satan. Tempt me to trade my wife and daughters for a son. I'll do it. I will.* He glanced across the aisle at his three girls, doubting the eldest, Lucy, at twelve, would live to see her maidenhood taken; frail and sickly, with weak lungs from yearly bouts with winter fever, she was wheezy coughing now. His stony stare silenced her. His youngest two were hardier, but high-strung like their mother. *Useless daughters, wife without hale womb. What profit in any of them?*

Yet thirteen years ago how eagerly he'd hand-fasted petite Ann Carr from Salisbury because she was pretty and promised to augment his pocketbook. Her father, one of that area's wealthiest inhabitants, owned 400 acres of the choicest farmland, a profitable ship-works, and the busiest ferry across the Merrimac. But her prize-worthiness faded the day her father died and her brothers stole her inheritance. In weary wedlock, she'd delivered him nine children. Each time a boy child was born, he'd rejoice and forgive her their cold bed. Then the infant would die, and he'd hate her all over again. Now this one was dead, too. *Why? Why only my sons?* For a surety, he had made a poor choice of wife; but he also knew, no matter what, he could never cross the Serpent's sinister line. *Not even for a healthy son? Not even if Almighty God is as callous and cruel as the Devil himself?* He looked up and saw the minister frowning, as if that man had just read his mind, had seen him standing tempted on the parapet of the Temple. The sleepy hymn filtered back in through his ears. He dropped his eyes to his Psalter, and sang:

> *Let me join this Holy Train*
> *And my first off'rings bring*
> *The eternal God will not disdain*
> *To hear an infant sing*

Spurred by grief his wife again rose, screaming, from their bench, flailing her arms toward the casket. This time he angrily struck her and yanked her back down into her seat.

Ann Putnam buried her stinging cheek inside her quivering hands, and wept.

Better. Better. Reverend Parris abhorred displays of emotion, especially inside his church. It bespoke self-indulgence and lack of humility before God. He took his role as Salem Village's Spiritual Pilot seriously. But it wasn't as if he lacked understanding or sympathy for a grieving mother. He had walked a thorny road himself, had suffered many bouts with vile emotion, before conquering and shuttering himself to it.

His life had begun lavishly, till a chain of bad luck and insidious betrayals drove him to ruin and the great estate he'd inherited at eighteen was lost to him at twenty-two. Not because his plantation had been devastated by that "once in a hundred years" hurricane. But because, in the wake of that deadly storm his two most trusted business partners—one of them his uncle—arranged loans that he never saw against his properties, loans that were called when forged signatures on promissory notes listing his deeds as collateral were upheld by the magistrates. He was left bankrupt within a hairsbreadth of imprisonment. In one cruel blink, his estate was forfeit and he passed from a life of privilege into humiliating indenture, spending the next five years of his early manhood in common labors paying off debts. As a merchant's pecuniary, no less, counting *other* people's money!

Reverend Parris' highborn eyes returned to his flock and settled upon the sobbing woman. *You see . . . I was once as rife with resentment as you are today, Goody Putnam. Till the day I received my revelation.* Now at age thirty-nine, after nine years as an ordained minister and three years leading this parish, he knew utterly that God had shaped his destiny. That God had led him out from earthly bounty into divine responsibility. God had called him.

During the hymn's final refrain, several funeral-goers started shifting in their seats. One barrel-shaped middle-aged gentryman sitting on the front-most bench dropped his Psalter.

Reverend Parris knew the *dropped-Psalter signal*. It meant it was a weekday, a work-morn, and the sky was finally brightening and there were labors waiting. Turning his eyes sidewise to glance into the day, he suddenly felt how his over-starched collar was chafing. And so, he reached up to loosen the button, reflecting that although his minister's garb was oftentimes rigidly uncomfortable, his rigid community was always a perfect fit. He approved that the village selectmen had designed rules for all aspects of daily living and strictly upheld their obedience. He could count at least half in this room who had been at one time "selected" for the pillory, stockade, a public lashing or a fine. He had privately dubbed these village rules his "Ten-Times-Ten Commandments" and committed them to memory. Often, he'd report transgressions according to his judgments:

> *Felled trees cannot be left near roadways*
> *Fences must be kept in good repair*
> *Bitches in heat shall not be turned loose*
> *Mixed public dancings and gamings are banned*
> *Fornicators and onanists shall be whipped, and*
>   *pilloried, and fined ten shillings*

He stifled a smile. *His firm Hand fastens every collar here.*

There was only one thing about Salem Village that he didn't like: the lawsuits. His parishioners sued each other endlessly over everything: land, money, grain, beer, timber, oxen, hay, flax, fences; and now even the minister's salary-tax (though he didn't know this). He frowned. This most righteous community he had ever encountered, his parish, had the broadly publicized ridiculed reputation as the most contentious concord in all of New England.

That same impatient goodman Nathaniel Ingersoll—innkeeper, victualer, ale-maker, Church Deacon, village Head Selectman, scion of a prosperous founding family, and an ally—let his Psalter slip from his knee again. This time as he bent low to pick it up, he flung Reverend Parris a flinty look saying: *Conclude the service! Bury the child!*

Reverend Parris bowed his head respectfully but his thoughts weren't spiritual: *My contract is being voted on for renewal and I need Ingersoll's support for a £4 increase. I must remember to write out my terms tonight. And on Sunday, in particular, remind those who by choice are lately so forgetful, how New England was originally a plantation of religion. Not a plantation of trade!* Hadn't John Calvin taught them that "innate self-interest," the original sin, the "old Adam," even more than *lust*, put souls into their greatest peril?

Casting a final glance at his friend Thomas Putnam, a longsuffering father, and next at Ann Putnam, the inconsolable mother, he waited until he had caught their eyes—because this gesture was for them. He pulled out an only slightly worn miniature-sized Testament from his inner coat pocket and tenderly laid it upon the dead infant's breast. He carefully fitted the coffin lid, wedging it down with the heel of his palm. And, while he knew for certain that this poor un-baptized soul was already condemned to Hell, as are all the unchristian no matter how innocent or pure, still he recited:

> "Precious in the sight of our Lord is the death of each one of His Saints, whom He redeemeth from the power of the grave and receiveth into His Bosom."

2

DIRGEFUL VOICES SANG LOUDLY AS REVEREND Parris led the funerary procession in a somber walk over to the burial ground:

> Here cease thy tears
> Suppress thy fruitless mourn
> His soul – the immortal part – has upward flown
> On wings he soars his rapid way
> To yon bright regions of Eternal Day

As was customary whenever a youngster died, the children, not the adults, were carrying the casket; but not the dead babe's siblings, who were too young and besides were female. These pallbearers were the four eldest boys of one of Thomas' sisters' seven sons.

And now inside the graveyard on his master's nod, John Indian nailed shut that pine box he'd built and thrust it into the hole he'd dug and just as quickly began shoveling in chunks of dirt and mulch, remembering Tituba's warning.

Young Lucy Putnam fought a puking urge and squeezed her sisters' hands too tightly. Four-years old and six-years old, they protested with disruptive squeals. She shushed them with a quick shake of her head and squint toward their father. She often had the responsibility to mind them and correct them. Her mother's frequent maladies demanded it. But, today that parent was in greater pain than she had ever seen. Wracked and rent, bereft of her senses, her mother had to be propped upright by her father to keep her standing. His demeanor was stern, as usual. But she thought she saw him squelch a tear when the minister assured him: "Verily, Thomas, your lad is cradled at this very moment in our Lord's most tender Arms." She winced, closing her eyes.

> *Under these trees and under this sod*
> *The pea is not there; there's only the pod*
> *The pea was shelled out and went up to God*

Glad was she in her sorrow that her baby brother was in sweet Jesus' Arms now instead of her mother's. She watched her father throw in a handful of dirt, and was surprised to see that his hand was shaking. She, too, felt a pang.

The minister had resumed his preaching—cawing really like that big black crow sitting on the meetinghouse roof eyeing them bleakly. She wished she could cover her ears, but that would earn a slap from her father. Instead, she glanced across the gravesite toward the Ingersoll family, whose inn her father visited after every Sunday service, where they'd all be going later for the burial feast. Those gray-haired parents were clutching their daughter's hands tighter than she was her sisters', though that child was *no child*, but a fully-grown person.

On yester eve, nice Mrs. Ingersoll had brought cider and sweet-cakes to the wake, and while she and her sisters nibbled their fills in the kitchen, that goodwife grieved with her mother upstairs, and Mr. Ingersoll consoled her father in the parlor. But that daughter did not condole or attend them. Sapling Ingersoll, as her parents strangely named her, was an odd-kin who never left the village proper. She stared at the spinster. *Why hasn't she married? Didn't she wish for a husband most of all? Children? A house all her own? Her parents would surely build her one.* Maidens, she knew, required only a middling dowry to secure a good marriage. The Ingersoll daughter was an only child of doting, wealthy older parents. Plain, but not homely, she was unmarried and nearly thirty. Her own mother wasn't much older. It was puzzling. She tried to catch the eye of her favorite cousin, Susanna Walcott, who at sixteen was the wisest regarding this subject. But Susanna was listing on one leg, half-asleep. She considered crouching to find a pebble to throw, but then someone blew a nose too loudly earning a glare from the minister. She shifted her gaze to the honker.

Old Rebecca Nurse made the gray-haired Ingersolls look like youngsters, she was that shriveled and bent-over. *Shaped like a pot-hook*, she thought. Her father didn't much like the Nurses. Each time Goosey Nurse waddled into church, followed by her rowdy stomping flock, he'd mutter "self-righteous biddy" or "hypocrite," under his breath. But he disliked old gander Francis Nurse even more. He was a *landgrubber!* She knew what that meant. People from elsewhere who bought up lands they had no rights to, paying pittances, squeezing good folk dry, especially during hard times, like now. Greedy grubbers were a *specially* sore subject with her father.

But now Goody Nurse caught her eye and sent back a well-aimed, well-meant squinty twinkle.

For this ancient *pothook* considered it her duty to console aggrieved church members. She attended every funeral and sickbed, nuptial, bee and christening, invited or not. Although to this sad ceremony she had been invited. A skillful midwife for more than fifty years, she had herself—less than a week ago—delivered the poor Putnam infant.

Lucy was amazed at how many wrinkles Goody Nurse had and started counting them with each new clump of sodden earth John Indian shoveled in.

The Afflicted Girls

3

MERCY LEWIS, A TRAVELER, STARTED AWAKE. IN her dim half-dream, she'd heard a gunshot and felt the coach speed up. Her heart was pounding as she pulled aside the dingy curtain half-expecting to see bloodthirsty savages attacking. There were none. Only skeletal, snow-laden trees standing stiff in the pre-dawn mist. *A dream, only a dream . . .* she felt relief, though not fully. Their coach was moving at its normal pace, bumping along through endless rimed woods. She tied back the curtain, glad that morning was again soon to come and they were a day nearer to their destination. Scanning this landscape, her deep-set azure eyes, though guarded on this gloomy March morn, couldn't hide what was strongest in her: her kindness. She was a good-heart, that rare sort who always puts another's comfort before its own, while expecting no considerations back. And none were ever given; until now, that is. Abigail Williams had given her hope.

Abigail, who was sprawled asleep with her head in Mercy's lap, who was younger by four years to Mercy's nineteen, and by no measure was as pretty, nor kind, although some might count her as clever. They'd just left behind years of orphan life to begin their adult lives with the help of Abigail's newly discovered distant relation. He'd sent the invitation through a lawyer. But it wasn't because they were particular friends that they were companions today in this coach. Rather, it was because one drudgery-filled morning while they were scrubbing a mud and soot-caked almshouse floor side by side, a sudden cold insecurity shunted through Abigail. She blurted the invitation without even thinking; afterward, she decided her traveling companion might as well be Mercy Lewis as anyone. Mercy's life hid in a murky past, and she, herself, was wildly intrigued by secrets. So she lied to the proctor to gain Mercy's freedom, insisting 'twas her uncle's wish and warrant.' A long, unfamiliar journey was the perfect opportunity for prying.

Mercy accepted the invitation without hesitation. She knew what her prospects were. She'd observed degraded women in the back alleys of their harbor town, and gutters where abandoned, hungry pockmarked urchins sat and begged. As often as she'd brought a sick child back to the almshouse, she was beaten for it. But it was a small price to pay, for the child was usually nursed and kept. Like she and Abigail had been once through other persons' kindnesses.

She stroked her companion's thick matted curls with affection. *You have saved my life, Abby Williams. Do you know it?* (Abigail sighed just then in her sleep.) *But where do you put your torments? Tell me. I will do the same.* She was amazed her young friend could sleep so soundly. Long-range coaches, like this one, were commonly attacked by highwaymen, and on occasion by renegade savage bands. She, herself, had barely slept an uninterrupted hour since leaving Falmouth four nights before. And when she did, she had nightmares. But then, she'd always had nightmares.

Another gunshot rang out louder, seeming much closer. Her hands fisted on her friend's locks. She heard lashes of the whip and a horse' terror as the driver yelled down: "Hold on! Hold on!" She grasped at the side rail, wishing she held a gun. The coach began to rattle and pitch. It was lumbering too fast for this uneven terrain. There came an intense shaking then a hard bump with a lurch to the side as the carriage careened. A wheel rolled away, smashing into trees. In her next gasp, she was thrown sharply forward and then sideways, scraping her cheek on the rough wall of the coach.

Except for that companion's scream, Abigail would not have woken in time to view their coach tipping over. After it settled, unhurt but livid, she vaulted from that now sidewise coach and screamed at the driver: "Damn you, stupid man! Damn you down to Hell!" She stomped her foot beside his stunned face, not caring a farthing that he'd been thrown from his seat and was lying injured, half-senseless, and that his coach horse—one of a reliable team—was fallen too, its life draining, tangled in bloodied straps and bellowing in agony.

Struggling to rise on his pained leg, the man ignored this young passenger, and pulled himself up to the top of his wreckage to retrieve his bayonet. Not yet to defend them—first, to jab his loyal beast through its neck. As soon as he did it, blood gushed soaking his boots. He stared down at them.

Abigail had sauntered up to glimpse the gore. He sternly ordered her back to the coach. And when she refused, he grabbed and dragged her, wincing and limping and with less than his usual muscle. However, she had been made strong-armed herself through years of forced sculleries, floor scrubbings and wringing out of miles of sodden cloths, and easily broke his grip. "Let go of me, you filthy man! All is spoiled now because of you!" He pushed and pinched her harder. "Inside the cab, miss! Do what I say, and keep yourself silent!"

"You dare order *me*? A minister's niece!" And she shoved him off hard as she could, and was pleased to see that as he fell his limping leg twisted in its descent. He suppressed a great yowl of pain, because there *was* still *somewhere* an unseen enemy. In a more urgent voice, he appealed to Mercy now: "Make her lie low, miss.

Make her hold her tongue. We're in danger here." But he couldn't look that passenger in her eye, because his compass had been thieved at their two nights' past way-stop, after he'd imbibed excessive hard spirits while playing cards. This girl had urged him to park in the yard, sensibly offered for them to sleep in the cabin. Instead he drunkenly, pigheadedly forged on into this unrecognized wilderness . . . possibly to death.

Mercy reached out to Abigail. "It's no one's fault, Abby. Come inside. Be with me. I will protect you. I will shield you. I promise . . . whatever foul fate comes." Abigail reluctantly took that proffered hand and climbed up inside the coach to huddle behind the slanted seat next to Mercy. But unlike her friend, she was neither prayerful, nor fearful . . . only furious.

The Afflicted Girls

4

A DISTANCE AWAY, HUNTER BEN NURSE HEARD gunshots. Relieved, he began stomping through the woods in search of his hunting companion, Joseph Putnam. It was before dawn that they'd gotten parted in a fog and one of them had been lost ever since. He'd searched the wood, fearing for his friend. But there he was now, up ahead, safe enough. He almost waved and called out. But then didn't. Because the scene, of a sudden, looked eerie odd: Joseph standing frozen as a wood block, staring fixedly at something (or at nothing—one never could tell) with his very valuable gold-filigreed ivory-handled flintlock musket lying half-buried in a mound and powder horn spilled out and blackening the snow.

Detecting a movement hardly more than a quiver, his tense eyes winched sideways picturing a stalking bear or boar. Instead, he saw the most magnificent black-tailed deer standing motionless behind thick foliage, a doe bigger than a stag, staring mirrors back at his friend. He wrenched off his useless mittens and raised his musket with numbed fingers, and slowly inched forward, while moistening two painfully cracked chapped lips and picturing a thick, juicy cut of roast venison on a trencher. He steadied and took aim. But then didn't shoot. Because Joseph had spied it first, and their handshake on this sorry hunt was whoever spotted the quarry took the shot. *Here we are famished. What is he doing? Nothing! Bloody eyes nothing! Grab up your gun, man! Fire it, before it rusts!* Unthinkingly, he lowered his own gun and instantly the creature bolted. By instinct he gave it chase and the militia drill practiced hundreds of times with his bandsmen on the green came rushing into his mind:

> *Unshoulder your piece; poise your piece;*
> *Take up your piece; prime your piece;*
> *Handle your charge; charge your piece —*

Sprinting hell-bent through frozen snow crust after a zigzagging giant deer, nonetheless, somehow he managed to keep pace, because his stubby legs held power. Cast in quicksilver, if anything, they could outrun all of his kin and anyone who ever bet against him. Once at a faire, he even outran a horse, albeit a lazy wagon nag. But he would usually come in last in other prowess contests, and on this hunt had shown no improvement since his slingshot days. When as a boy he managed to hit one out of five—frogs, birds, rabbits, knotholes—or sometimes two, when the stars were willing.

The deer was heading for a wide gully. It meant to jump across. So what if he couldn't shoot? He could barter for game any time with farm spoils. Besides, guns were costly. Equal in price to a wooded acre or a third of a cleared lot. He wasn't even that fond of venison. But at the furthest possible range, just as the creature was springing over holly thickets, he took aim and fired. The animal expired mid-leap.

The most agreeable grin knit across his ruddy cheeks, and broadened more on his sprint back to boast of his success to Joseph. Until he spied his friend standing dumbstruck in that same place and posture as before, still lost in some unknowable oblivion. He shuddered. *He's befuddled. Not bedeviled. Befuddled.* Like everyone their age, which was twenty, he knew all the tales of weird creatures and unholy spirits one might encounter in the deep woods, that could take on the form of a beautiful maid—*or a deer*—to seduce a man and suck out his marrow. Surging up, he blubbered, "Was a deer, that's all, nothing weirder than that, and I killed it! Dead!" He wrenched Joseph's shoulders around in his oversized paws and eyeball-to-eyeball affirmed: "Starved, you are! Like me! You've eaten only half a bony rabbit in two days!" (By luck during that weird blizzard they'd found a cave with a starving rabbit inside it; they put a quick end to its shivering. And exactly this drew them close in boyhood: he was always so earthy and good-natured, so relentless in his affection, he could usually summon Joseph from a mood.)

Joseph shook his head. "It looked at me not with eyes," he said, strangely, "but with blue watery pools. Which felt unearthly. They drew me in."

Chilling words. Were they meant to put him to spooks? Was it a trick? Ben wondered. Had his friend been snow-blinded? He delved Joseph's glassy eyes for the truth of it. Then shrugged. "Well, I'm still going to eat it. I'm not given to superstitions like I used to be." But he did look over his shoulder now, not in the willies, only to imprint into his memory that remarkable feat lest he forget any small detail, ruing how there'd been no witness and that anyone he'd tell would never believe him. And with a final forlorn punctuating sigh, he picked up Joseph's musket by its carved ivory handle and slung it onto his shoulder next to his borrowed champion, saying cheerily to his boyhood friend, "No oceans to cross. No more watery pools. Or as many miles as a deer runs."

Ten minutes later, a dollop of sun confirmed it, and he sighed with relief. Seeing clearly now that the deer's eyes were brown, not *blue,* as he was securing its carcass to a roughshod litter of hide and poles hitched behind his horse. The creature barely fit. He had trounced a giant! And he felt equally relieved that Joseph was recovered, having nearly returned to his normal senses. So to help that leaden spirit stay risen — at least till they reached the first road — he figured he'd reel out silly prattle, as much local gossip as he could remember, because Joseph had been gone for four years getting educated and wouldn't have heard most of it, if any. He began with a mention of the central figure in a looming local controversy: "Have you heard about our village minister, Reverend Rides-an-ass?"

Joseph seriously pondered. "A trumpeting bare-threaded strut who wears the same charred suit every Sunday, pours over-baked hellfire from his oven-sized maw, and calls other kettles black?"

Ben laughed, "What else did your mother tell you?"

"How he's sued half the parish claiming arrears, beginning with the poorest most in need of his charity."

Ben nodded. "It's why there's such loud cluck for getting rid of him."

"Loud enough that I heard it in Old England . . . so, are you sued, Ben?"

"Are you?"

"Would he dare?"

Ben shrugged and said he doubted it; and now related all that he knew of the minister's secret maneuverings, all of which Joseph already knew. Next, he described, Goodman Louder's latest complaint of lewdness against bawdy Bridget Bishop and her counter-suits of trespass against him, whose less than neighborly brawls had been going on for years, ever since they were eavesdropping snickering boys. Though, personally, he was only curious about the contentious Putnam family feud. A sizeable fortune was at stake. He casually hinted and waited for a comment, but his friend shared no secrets now. When he ran out of lawsuits, he shifted to maladies. Described a pox contagion, which had swept through the bailiwick three winters past. He named casualties, lost relations and friends, all lamented with sighs and winces—for he was a sensitive man. He made mention also of this year's high summer fever, which although it had felled many and even he had suffered a bout: "Thankfully, no one died from it—"

No one? One did. My father . . . Joseph's face darkened. He spurred his horse ahead.

Ben yelled out about the deer he was dragging, demanding Joseph wait up. Only realizing his error when they were side-by-side again and that heartbroken friend couldn't look at him; he gave a heartfelt apology and a condolence, which though late and inadequate, was accepted. And now, to reignite his friend's failed interest, "fornication" was the next chosen topic, starting with adulteries. He spooled out transgressors and punishments, described confessions in pilloried tears, and who yet protested innocence, even though "a dozen baseborn with sire-ships unknown bore uncanny resemblances." He guffawed, couldn't help it, but then his cheeks flushed pink as he turned to which first-blooms had been plucked and by whom—two by himself he admitted without naming names. He would never stain a pure maid's reputation. No babe emerged from it, he assured his sullen friend. But had there been, he'd have married either girl.

"And what if there'd been two babes? What then?"

Never having considered this, Ben flustered. Then whiffing scorn, and to avoid the ridicule he knew would be striking him next, he began sourly badgering to hear scandals, instead, from Old England, claiming his mouth was dry and tongue needed rest. Joseph held out his water-skin, announcing he had nothing but water to share.

He hadn't even finished his first gulp when that laughing braggart's endless yarn began: about jaunts to brothels, seductions of schoolmates' sisters in dormitory trundles, of his own by the spouse of one of his college masters, of numberless other trysts with pub maids in hired rooms, and even a months'-long affair with a famed Drury Lane actress. Conquests all begrudged with another long gulp and a grunt. Nevertheless, he wondered: "But were *you* ever smitten? Did any of them conquer *you*?"

Joseph shrugged, stating cheerlessly: "Well, they were surely lost in it. Weeping, begging me to keep them . . . but no, I scorned them all."

Ben's shoulders slumped. He'd twice been speared through his hopeful heart, gutted, and thrown back. And this was the purpose for their hunt. For these best boyhood friends to grow reacquainted, to turn forward their hourglasses. Four years ago, when Joseph sailed to Old England they were boys. Now they were grown men. "Here ride two freemen!" Ben shouted suddenly, zealously to the treetops, rising up in his stirrups, a sun ablaze inside him. "With modern ideas and high ambitions standing at the cusp of a new century!" He flung up his arms to receive his bounty.

Joseph groaned, not unkindly, just unable to picture his farmer friend rousing anyone to passion, not through oration or with his body, or in any way gaining prominence in the world. He began propounding his new cynical view: how no one was or ever could be free in this world, or even content with his life. "The human heart is corrupt to its core. Bound to fail, whatever its high aim."

Ben parried with a bawdy ballad commonly sung at Bridget Bishop's tavern. And soon they were both singing loudly and lustfully:

> *A big-breasted maid down to Boston had strayed*
> *And with her the young blades made free.*
> *She wept and she sighed and she bitterly cried,*
> *'Any one would've courted me,*
> *And I'd now a married lady be,*
> *But for off'ring me titties to see,*
> *And to thrust in and out of me.*

The Afflicted Girls

5

ABIGAIL, THE FIRST TO HEAR THEM, THREW OPEN the coach door and cried out: "Englishmen!" The driver's face poked from behind the wreckage; when he saw them, he began limping as swiftly as his wounded leg allowed, using his musket for a cane. Gratefulness gushed when he reached them: "Providence stems a calamity . . . musket-fire grazed my horses. When they panicked, God's own Hand could not have stopped that rampage. But thankfully He protected, by misdirecting the savages. They never appeared at all." He glanced nervously in the four directions, lowering his tone, "Be vigilant, sirs. They may still be lurking."

The hunters, dismounting, exchanged a slippery glance. This region's woods, both knew since boyhood, were devoid of *redskins*. Since it had been more than a generation since all local tribes had been killed off, driven northward, or beaten down into Christianized domicile thralls, with the untrustworthy remainder resettled onto militia-guarded islets in Boston Harbor. There were none living wild here now. Their *part* in this calamity they knew. But neither was honest enough to admit his fault or generous enough to offer recompense. They merely listened, nodded, glanced aside at each other, sometimes at the spilled coach, and at the end of the coachman's sorry tale, offered to accompany him and his passengers back to their village, where succor might be obtained — from others.

The driver gave prayerful thanks, and returned to announce to his charges: "A miracle has saved you. These men are from Salem Village."

Abigail leapt jubilantly from the coach, racing toward the hunters to breathlessly inquire: "Do you know Reverend Parris, the minister?" Ben was behind the horse checking on his deer, so Joseph answered for him: "My friend knows a man called Parris, who ministers to himself. I haven't had that good fortune."

The driver was amazed. "Twofold Providence, fourfold luck. He's the very man I'm to see for payment."

"Such luck that more likely he'll sue you," Joseph warned.

Abigail glared at Joseph Putnam. *I shall loathe you forever, and cause you misery however I can, for insulting my uncle.*

When the men first appeared, Mercy had suffered a weakening, not relief, as an old choking dread rose up within her. The contradiction was confusing. So she secreted herself behind the coach, and then needing some visible purpose, awkwardly reached up to the rack and began to untie their coffers. She strained to pull Abigail's free, which was only slightly larger than her own chest but three times its weight. She wondered what her friend kept inside it. *Books?* But she'd never seen Abigail read any book although she knew her friend was literate. At the almshouse Abigail would recite daily all the banns and notices nailed to the courthouse, church, and constabulary doors. *Skillets? Crockery?* (No. It was andirons. Huge, tarred bronze and copper andirons, over one hundred years old, snarling dogs' heads with bared teeth and sooty faces—Abigail's dowry, her only family heirloom.)

Footsteps behind her, and now eyes searing her back, branding her, not for the first time . . . she tugged harder, but moved that heavy coffer not even an inch. A hunter's knife cut through the thickest knot and then the man's other hand settled on her forearm, and she heard: "I'm sorry but you'll have to leave them." His touch was soothing. She hadn't expected that. She took a moment to compose, then turned to face him. She instantly lost herself in Joseph Putnam's eyes. At that same moment, he saw that hers were beautiful. They were that same deep miraculous blue the deer's had been, but even more forgiving. They rushed into him. He hadn't known his soul was so empty. He heard her say, *"But it's everything, everything we own, sir."* Yet, she hadn't spoken. Her lips hadn't moved. When he realized that, he let go of her arm in wonderment.

In the next blink as their eyes shifted askance, the darkness returned to each with the warning: *Get thy heart weaned from the Creature. The Creature is empty. It's not able to satisfy thee fully. Nor ever make thee happy.*

The other young man was the bullish sort Abigail usually favored. She was watching him dump from his pallet the hugest deer she'd ever seen, which he dragged now with only one hand by its stiffened hind-leg over to the dead horse. Both would be left to rot. She pondered that image till a putrid maggot pile was all that was left. *Dead horse, dead deer and dead duck . . .* and now conjuring coyness out of ruin, she sauntered nearer, suggesting in a well-practiced lilt: "We've spoiled your hunt . . . haven't we, sir?"

"No, miss, only my supper."

She wanted to laugh. She'd expected him to politely deny it. She was suddenly taken by his toothsome grin. *His face is common, but his body is thick with muscle . . . and his teeth, though mulish, glint white.* "I'll make it up to you, sir," she offered, sidling nearer, brushing two fingertips atop his hand. He took an awkward step back, and nearly tripped over the carrion. "No need of that, miss. I can make do with mutton." For as modern as Ben Nurse was, and as fond as he was of lusty songs, ribald gossip, and rosy-cheeked plump pretty maids, he held firm as an anvil that in courtship only the male should do the chasing and choosing. Even dumb beasts followed that rule. This girl was too bold for her age, too young for his, and had a face that was nothing to boast of to his brothers. So he mumbled an excuse and bumbled away.

Abigail frowned. Mercy Lewis—that *nothing and nobody*—stood between both young men now. While she, Abigail Williams, a minister's niece, stood alone. *No! Not alone! With carcasses meant for maggots!* She kicked the deer in frustration.

Later, she openly sneered when that hateful young man walked up to them—and did not address her or even glance at her, for his eyes were fixed only on Mercy—bringing them two lengths of rope cut from the trunk tethers. He said for tying up their skirts into britches. At once Mercy, acting the superior, seized both strings and only then passed one to her. But then her friend removed to behind a tree for lack of a door or curtain—Mercy always turned the dormouse if men were present. Well, she wasn't falsely modest. She could lift her skirts in plain view, not caring if anyone saw her; rather, hoping *someone* would. Hadn't she adorned this traveling petticoat and her other one with the proctor's lace scraps? Wasn't it worthy of admiration? It was! *It is!*

But the only eyes that viewed Abigail's beveled bottom were the driver's, till she spied his lurid eying. She scowled and hissed and threw a fist-sized rock at him, which he ably dodged, but just barely with his impediment.

He hurled back a grimy wink.

When the girls' coffers were secured onto the litter and all skirts were modestly tucked and tied, Ben Nurse stared forlornly at his lost prize—no, not at the deer . . . at her. The pretty girl; because without prior discussion or agreement, his trustless friend had just taken that girl's hand and led her over to his horse—when it was he who'd spied her first! Joseph lifted her up onto his saddle and mounted behind her, his thigh against hers, threading his arms underneath her cape to grab up his reins. Then that cheat shifted

The Afflicted Girls

closer! And it wasn't the first time he felt like punching that rich nose. But all he did then—was the opposite with Abigail: did not take her by her hand, waved her over after he'd already mounted his nag. Yanked her up by her forearm onto his beast's bony rump, to a seat cushioned-pillion only with a folded-up filthy waistcoat. Riding out, there were inches separating them because of the litter-poles and it was a seat that Abigail took no comfort in, rather suffered, but she did not complain of it. She could endure this hardship for his sake. He had chosen her over Mercy.

Several times that injured driver had failed to mount his Hobby; the unusual hoist and hurl of a plank-stiff leg, accompanied by bellows and curses confused the beast. When he managed, finally, to gain his seat, that spooked animal attempted to dislodge him. It had never before been ridden as a mount, nor taken to any road without its pulling mate. Holding tight to its neck and mane while it reared and kicked and whinnied, he cursed it until it settled. Now he praised God for that miracle and spurred out with a hand-slap after the others, following hoof scuffles in the wet earth and melting snow. Twice now, the horse had tried to run back. While he, who wasn't used to horseback, held on to his makeshift reins the one young fellow had made him and turned it, staring back also in disbelief; and he still turned to look, long after his regret—a coach fully owned, not owed a penny upon—was swallowed up by trees.

6

BIRD SCREECHES, CLOPS AND HEAVY DRAGGING sounds echoed off the stiff inner silences of the riders. Till Ben Nurse broke from his sulk, reached up to an overhanging branch, snapped off a twig and informed his rider: "Cinnamon wood . . . good for cleaning teeth." He bit off a chunk of the sassafras, and gave the rest to Abigail.

Pleasant she thought, as she tasted it. Nearly as fresh as the mint she normally chewed. She looked over her shoulder to tell Mercy to pick some, and instead saw how close the two of them were sitting, pressing even. She frowned.

Moments ago, when a long strand of Mercy's pale hair had slipped from beneath her cap and dangled in front of Joseph's face, without thinking he had twirled that wayward strand round his fingers playing with it; and Abigail saw. But then he let it go in the next moment, realizing, and leaned forward to ask with seeming interest: "I know where you're destined. Not where you began," though this was untrue; the driver had mentioned Falmouth, Maine, that edge of civilization. As she half-turned to answer, she also tucked that strand back up. Only then did he notice how the cap was torn and her cheek was scraped and bruising. He touched her injury, admonishing: "I would judge it too dangerous a distance for maids to travel alone."

"We are of an age, sir," she informed, politely.

26

"But it would have been wiser to sail. Even in winter squalls sea routes are safer. You keep to settled coastlines and spare yourself much peril."

"It was arranged for us, sir. We had no say in it."

"Yes, I suppose a small hired coach *is* the cheaper passage, however uncivilized and unsafe."

He means to provoke me thought Mercy. "The driver was told to see to our safety, sir. But neither Abigail nor I are unschooled in danger. We both hail from the northernmost part of the Commonwealth. From Casco Bay."

"Famed for the brutal Indian wars?"

"Yes, sir, that same place."

He glanced up at the girl riding with Ben. Could picture her amid a firestorm of heathens; there was an air of the savage about her. But nothing of that ilk was in this one. "Most Casco settlers did not survive the massacres."

"Too many, sir."

"Fortunately, you did."

Mercy heavily sighed, "I've often wished I had not . . . but one's fate is not one's to decide."

Her gloomy confession intrigued him. He could understand it. He had wished for death—not often, but more than once in his moods. *Her thoughts run dark. There is the kinship.* "The voyage of their lives is bound in shallows and miseries—"

"Swirled from the spout of a famed Bard's inky storm-pot." She had recognized the quote, and had cleverly re-made it.

He marveled at her quick mind and rare education. "So you've seen this play performed?"

"Oh no, sir, no. I was never privileged in that way. I've read Master Shakespeare's words . . . not many, but a few. Truly aloft were they above the page." Good quips always impressed him, but hers surpassed even his. "And yet that quill is banned here in the Commonwealth. So you must have been flung abroad, like I was, to be properly schooled."

She hesitated. "No, sir. This wood is the farthest I've been from my birthplace."

Riddles or quips, whatever she was playing at, had met its match in him. "Such loftiness was not beyond your grasp?"

"At first, sir, yes. But a poet speaks to hearts . . . mine somehow understood." She fell silent, then deeply rued it, understanding only now, how that master of the pen abused his purest maids, and gave them all sad, wasteful endings.

While he was intrigued how this provincial, un-traveled maid in a filthy torn head-rail cap could trump him with such ease. "But surely, you must have found your lessons arduous? If not, your teacher must be praised. Was it your father?" He was prying.

A shiver passed through Mercy before she answered. "I was ward to a minister once, who was a copyist. I read all that I could in his absence. I was never schooled, sir, but have taught myself to read and to think . . . for my own mind's civilization."

He laughed and gave the contest to her. "Uneducated, yet you quip on the cuff, quash me as I might a lowly guttersnipe. You recognize authors by phrase, when I can barely muddle through their sentences. I concede. My four forced years at Cambridge are today, by you, proven worthless."

"Forced to a fate I would have chosen for myself, sir."

Backwoods trails fed into lanes, which led to cart-ways, and then one widened into a wagon-way, which finally merged onto that broad well-traveled thoroughfare, the Ipswich High Road, traversing a string of counties and connecting Boston Town with Salem Town and villages in between. They rode at a faster pace now, passing an occasional side road marker, farmhouse, or fellow traveler. From the first, Mercy had been sitting slanted forward in an uncomfortable posture, an attempt at propriety. Till Joseph eased her back against his chest, saying: "This will be more comfortable for us both." *It will be more than that* she knew, even before his arms had wrapped around her and they were breathing in unison as if their lungs were a single bellow.

But later, upon entering the civilized world, he let her go and sat apart, and held only his tongue and unfriendly distance. They soon halted beside the Frost Fish River, where he offered no explanations again, only led his horse away to a watering pond to drink, leaving her standing by herself, disquieted.

But Mercy knew that as soon as Abigail arrived even this troubled tranquility would end. So she made her way down the embankment to stand at the mossy edge of that great rushing flow, perched amid knee-high ferns and skunk lilies, sorting her thoughts—and there were many—but also taking in that wide sweep of thundering water. Breathing in its wet clean scent, marveling at the great size and numbers of bright red salmon jumping to joyful heights—a few of which tried scaling finger-like cascades on the opposite shore; in truth, she understood their plight. So when one finally succeeded, she clapped her hands and awakened a happy echo—though happy only in this nature, not inside herself. Meanwhile, the others were riding in above her.

Ben Nurse had yanked Abigail down from his horse when she couldn't manage it by herself. But instead of paying attention, his eyes began wandering elsewhere. So her leg was scraped against the litter pole and her stocking tore. Abigail cursed his inattention. He begged forgiveness for his flub, and then tried to give her his full ear—she'd just asked him what distance remained.

He knew exactly. "We follow this river to the point our creek feeds it. Then veer inland a scotch hop."

"But how far *exactly* is that, sir?" She detested vagueness.

He scratched his mop. Even more than manners, sums were not his aptitude, not even in counting bales, barrels, bundles or sacks, all of which were of consequence to a farmer. Left on his own at market, he was usually gypped. He knew it, of course, but would never admit it to his brothers; when half of them couldn't count any better. "Well, not as far as we've already ridden. More or less depends on our pace."

Abigail judged him to be a bumpkin.

Mercy had begun wending in careful footfalls along the slippery bank, clinging to brush, while formulating her feelings, not realizing that Joseph Putnam had only returned and come down to the river's edge to drink and refill his water-skin. He bristled at her intrusion, even more when she shared:

"This land is more an Eden than I imagined or expected, sir. It is a pearl in God's Creation, a place perfectly true to its name."

He answered coldly, without looking up: "Its name belies it. Words are rarely truthful. Words, in fact, charmed Adam *out* of Paradise, not into it." He capped his water-skin and left her.

If Ben Nurse had been watching her then, like before, he could have explained his friend's insulting manner, for dark moods struck Joseph most often under calm skies in quiet moments. But he was currently too distracted watching Abigail shimmy off her layers of dust, and undo her *britches* and fan out her skirts in front of him, and then lift them higher to rub her sore bottom. She complained of numerous blisters and, of course, offered to show one.

"Nay," he neighed, putting up a hand to shield his eyes, silently vowing to improve her seat. He felt other urges, too. So he left to go fiddle with the litter.

She had almost caught him she knew, and would yet, she decided, as she sauntered off toward the watering pond—she preferred ponds to noisy rivers—and then knelt at the edge to brood; and also to untie her bodice laces and expose part of her plump girlish bosom to a splash of icy water.

Ben Nurse stared at those scones, while his own began to bake, and the words of another dirty ditty came lurching up into his mind:

Oh, her breasts and her thighs and her cunny between.
They beckon you sir. They're the finest you've seen.

Any rake would have pounced and ravaged. Not being one, he hurried off opposite in search of a thickset tree trunk to lean behind and finish his business. Before being shamed in his pants.

When the party rode on, within minutes the sky had changed from wintry to welcoming as strong morning sunbeams pierced through the last thin wash of gray. Both girls undid their cloaks.

Abigail flung hers onto the litter, feeling dozy in this sudden warmth. Of course, she would have liked to lean up and lay her cheek upon her young man's broad-beam back. But instead, she forced herself to sit upright. There was too much to see in this new land of civilized cottages, cultivated farmlands, pretty pastures, beaver brooks, covered bridges, stone fences, and webs of roadway, each sporting signage with curious names— destinations with tantalizing histories to learn.

They turned onto a lane, and soon had traversed a covered bridge, and then cut through a leafless grove of white birch, and now were approaching a rich-looking homestead set upon a sloping hill. A bright-painted plaque reading "Orchard Farm" was nailed to a latched gate at the bottom.

Here, her young man dismounted. She grew alarmed when his dobbin began to neigh and strain against its straps. But the mule held onto his horse, unlocking and swinging wide the gate for them. He led them up that incline set between two lining arms of trees. Which he said were lilacs, which would be a purple wonderment in spring. Of the handful of dwellings that sat upon the summit, he pointed only to one—the topmost—informing her: "That's the earliest construction in Essex County. The first house ever built in this settlement."

The dwelling he'd pointed to was a large saltbox, three stories at the front sloping down to two at the rear. She could tell it had been recently painted, because it sparkled green and white. It was a pretty house, although not the best or even largest in this enclave. Four were superior, in her opinion. But, by now, she was more interested in the two hundred or so thick-coated sheep bleating in a walled in pasture to one side—so much mutton to eat, soft fleece to wear, and sheepskins to sleep upon! Beyond it sheepfold lay fruit orchards almost as far as her eye could see, and foraging underneath them was a rich man's herd of fat milk cows—with so much fresh cheese and butter and cream inside them, her mouth began watering; for it had been years since she'd tasted any not rancid.

Rounding to the hill's other side, she spied a number of men and lads oxen plowing and hoe stubbing in dark-soiled, snow-dotted fields below. Her young man whistled and waved down to them, but they didn't hear him.

"What place is this? Why have we come here?" she asked, hoping he'd say that her uncle's parsonage sat among these fine dwellings.

"Us Nurses abide here. Forty-one at last count. Two more due mid-spring . . . another at summer's-end." He was grinning.

"You're married then, sir," she mumbled with dampened spirits.

He answered that he wasn't, but aimed to be by year's end.

Well, sir, I will not marry you, to number among such multitudes. Though sport with you I might. You are not too bad looking. "You Nurses must be very rich, sir. To own such a glorious property."

"Oh we are, surely we are, miss . . . but not as rich as we will be. We partly own and partly lease, but aim to own it all."

She leaned forward and let her hand brush his privates, as she feigned an embarrassed gasp. "Oh, beg pardon, sir, for my witless hand. I only meant to stretch it." *A bull in your britches . . . no wonder you Nurses propagate like rabbits.*

Reaching a yard, they halted. And when her young man brought her down from his horse—more carefully this time—Abigail flung herself against him, pressing her cheek to his stubble, coiling her arms tight round his thick middle, vowing in a rush of whispered sentiment: "I know you are modest, sir. If not today, know you shall soon be properly thanked by me." She expected him to kiss her and her eyes fluttered shut.

Instead, he rudely set her at arm's length, telling her bluntly: "No point in it, miss. I do not wish it." Bolting away, Ben Nurse cursed himself for his fickleness. Till he strode near that pale haired pretty girl Joseph kept ignoring and thought how, if she'd have just done that—wrapped two wanting arms around him—he'd have offered her more than a kiss: *A hand-fast. Then a nuptial!* And she should have been his rider. He'd spied her first. He'd been robbed of his quarry. Robbed of his chance for happiness in a mate.

He irritably yanked open the door to the parking barn where the carriages were kept. But didn't see the Sunday cart, or even their second best one; saw *no* carriages or carts or work wagons, only one old broke wheelbarrow no one ever bothered to fix. So there was nothing to offer these maids for a proper conveyance to the village. Now he was glad he'd only thought of the gesture, not spoken it aloud. The door creaked behind him and he bristled before he turned. But it was not his pursuer, only the coach driver coming to ask where to find a local wheelwright, and a horse monger with cheap but sturdy stock and an honest handshake. *Well, Joseph Putnam used to be that!*

Long years before Joseph Putnam sailed away to Old England for his education, or turned sixteen, he was already counted Essex County's premier breeder and trader in horse flesh—a career begun for him at the age of four after his mother sent his father down to Virginia Colony to purchase Quarter horses for their new stable (Virginia being the only place in the New World where that rare fast breed was then known). She'd learned how the aristocracy in Europe raced these steeds for prizes, and realizing that since no one in New England had, as yet, attempted the sport, it as an opportunity for easy profits. On that point, she convinced her husband.

The breeding pair his father brought back in early autumn produced a foal the following spring, which his mother gave to him—her own "little foal"—to nurture. Barely a month passed after that birth, however, before her own lack of foresight hampered her plan. Realized only when too many pairs of her expensive Boston-cobbled shoes met filthy ruin on her twice-daily trudges on manure-strewn lanes just to glimpse her little son. She had turned her only child into a stable boy not into the foxhunting son of gentry she'd intended.

When Joseph turned eight, she brought him a playmate—her new tenant farmer's son—hoping that simple farm boy of similar age would distract him from his obsession; but in truth, she'd only delivered Joseph a willing assistant and ally, named Ben Nurse, for his ever-increasing stable-tasks. She'd also failed in that common course of using her womanly ploys to persuade her old husband to curb their son's hobby. Because Putnam Sr. already judged his youngest as too attached to his mother's kirtle, and insisted it was respectable time spent in a manly occupation, arguing that their stable was successful only because of the boy's talent with the beasts. He liked that buyers were coming from as far afoot as Boston to purchase from their herds. He refused to interfere. And barred her from it, too.

But as that business prospered and grew beyond bounds, so did her resolve grow not to leave a horse-trader in her wake. Eight years more she bided her time until her spouse grew too feeble to oppose her. Following Joseph's sixteenth birthday, she sent her son away from hearth and stable, friend and father to Old England for his education. She had purchased his entrance into Cambridge College for a sizeable sum, and also obtained excellent introductions, knowing her son's good looks and generous stipend would open other doors. She even secured his seat for meals at the High Table at Cambridge among noblemen's sons, where he could sit close enough to overhear the tabletop debates of college masters like Isaac Newton.

Unfortunately, he never listened, nor learned diddlysquat in any room. Preferring instead to roister his time with sopped fellows, or rut with willing housemaids, or wallow alone in locked-in moods, but rarely to sit amid books or college masters in drafty lecture halls and libraries.

Then two months ago, during his fourth term at Cambridge, he received word from his mother that his father had succumbed. He sailed home with a heavy heart, and with lusterless letters in every science and art—logic, rhetoric, arithmetic, geometry, astronomy, history, metaphysics, ethics, natural science, Latin, Greek, and philosophy. And also, with a sublime pair of Arabian horses, over fourteen hands tall, corn-silk colored, a stallion and mare perfectly matched, which he planned to breed and cross-breed with his Quarters and Hobbies.

They were a gift for his mother he said, knowing a pearl brooch, carved ivory comb, or gold-threaded velvet-tasseled belt would have pleased her so much more.

7

THE COACH DRIVER HAD OFFERED HER A FOOT up. But he smelled so foul and was so encrusted and rank with body stink and dried blood that Abigail covered her nose and mouth, mumbling: "I'll walk the two miles." And before that indifferent man could shrug, before Mercy might offer her own seat, or any of them could thwart her, she had dashed back down that winding farmstead lane relieved to finally be on her own. Exiting the gate she walked a brisk pace back to the High Road, where she hurried along past numerous farmsteads, fields, hedges, fences, woodlots, and even one busy tavern—a popular way-stop obviously from the numbers of carts parked outside and riding mounts tethered by the trough. The sign read: "Bishop's Ordinary."

Normally, she would have stopped and peered in at those drunken lazybones, but not today. *Today is too glorious for "ordinary" distractions!* She laughed at her clever pun.

Following signposts, eventually she spied the village up ahead. A Union Jack fluttered above its treetops. She spurred into a trot and nearly stomped on a wood toad, but instead bounded over it . . . for today was a day for loving all of God's creatures. *Even His most hideous!* Soon she was running in through the Salem Village gate, grinning and breathless, until she spied the handful of rundown wood-frame structures squaring the green. *What a coarse and ugly place this is.* She sat down on the log bench underneath the flagpole, not to await her companion really, only her clean best apron and cap. Villagers walked past her, but gave her no acknowledgments, no welcomes, no nods or smiles—not even when she attempted one. She thought they were coarse and ugly, too.

A black-crested meadowlark sat trilling atop the gate as Mercy and Joseph rode underneath it into Salem Village. A smile burst upon her face. "Wonderful, wonderful . . . music in my heart, music also in Heaven. For joy that I am here." Joseph recognized the quote as from <u>The Pilgrim's Progress</u>. And because Bunyan's allegory was still the most popular book in Old England and he had read it, like all of his school chums, numerous times, he remembered the text well enough parry: "Our joys to *tears*, our faith to *fears* are turned. Thus we see, our Beginning shows just what our *End* will be." He meant it as a warning.

No sir . . . no. My tears will turn to joy now, like the young Pilgrim's, and my years of fears to faith shall return. It was a hope, not a surety; Mercy understood this. But in this long-awaited moment of renewal and beginning, she allowed herself to believe that her sought-for happiness would be found. "I am so grateful to be arrived safely, I fear neither grim prophecies, nor Bunyan misquoted by opinionated young men, sir."

Now Joseph had deliberately quoted Bunyan in the reverse, intending to trip her. But again she had topped him, which might have piqued a less-modern man. He steered toward the inn yard. After dismounting and helping her down, he held her hand longer than he should have, interlacing his fingers and gazing into her eyes, repeating the same words with a different purpose: "Our beginning shows just what our end will be."

Abigail frowned. She'd been watching them from her bench. *He wants her. Men always want her! Never me!* Her lips had turned up recalling how on the journey south she told Mercy she'd dreamed her friend would find a husband in Salem Village. But it wasn't really a "husband" she saw. It was an arrogant lout like him, who after taking his lustful pleasures gave her coins in payment. *She is a penniless and an orphan. She will never be a wife. But I shall! I shall! I now have an uncle to endow me!*

≈✦≈

The Putnam funeral had concluded. The earth had been patted flat as each adult male took a turn hammering the mound with the back of the shovel. A temporary wood marker had been set. The procession was now wending slowly across the green toward Ingersoll's Inn for the burial feast.

Thomas Putnam was helping his wife Ann to walk, who was unsteady on her feet, but at least was calmer. That is, until she saw Joseph Putnam, her enemy, standing in the inn-yard. She began shrieking worse than the banshee, flailing her hands up to her head, tearing wildly till her black coif fell off and her mourning-bun unraveled.

Thomas handed her off to his upset sisters, bolting the rest of the way across the green into that yard to scream at his half-brother, "How dare you show yourself here on this day! Hellfire take you! You and your devil-spawned mother!" He spat in Joseph's face, and grabbed him readying his fist for a bruising blow. But Joseph broke the grip, reached his horse and leapt up into the saddle, and without wiping off the spittle spurred his horse into a gallop.

Mercy stared after him, also spattered with venom. Thomas Putnam shoved past her, pushing her out of his way.

Abigail was intrigued. The procession was moving past her now. So she cast a wry grin at a bosomy girl about her own age, and the girl, Susanna Walcott, smiled back. *She'll be an apt source for tattles;* but in her very next blink, she gasped. Her heart pounded in sheer jubilee. There, at the rear of the procession, walked a figure in minister's garb. It was he! Her Uncle Parris! "Uncle Parris!" she cried, madly running toward him.

Reverend Parris spun around, baffled.

"It's me!" she pealed, crunching his crisp-ironed coat in a drowning hug. "Your long-lost niece! Abigail Williams!"

He broke away stiffly, saying tartly, "You were not to arrive for two months more. I stated so in my letter. Who altered the arrangement without my consent?"

Crushed, Abigail pulled a crumpled page from her pocket.

He read it, grumbling, "Lawyers, a mercenary lot." He gave his niece a long cold stare then ordered her to the parsonage to his wife.

The coach driver, hauling the litter, reached Salem Village later, and seeing none of his party waiting, he asked a passerby regarding the minister. He was directed across the green to Ingersoll's Inn. He tethered the horse in the inn yard, hoping the luggage would keep secure. He calculated his fee incorporating his travails: the damage to his coach, cost of a new pulling horse, recompense for his own bodily damage; likely, he'd need to consult a physician about his torn knee. Entering the premises, at once he whiffed the heady malt and spied salvers with roasted meat. He was pleased. He had bumbled into a feast. He noted the minister at a corner table, and now decided to mention he was hungry and especially *thirsty*, before settling their account.

Reverend Parris saw a shabby person he didn't know standing just inside the doorway, who was waving his cap at him specifically. He arose to usher the stranger out. Stepping onto the stoop, he informed him that here was a private gathering and a sad occasion. As he turned to go that ruffian grabbed his arm and forced him to listen to a lecture about how an uncle should be grateful for the safe delivery of a niece.

"When she was not to be delivered for two months more?" Reverend Parris was growing upset now, too, because the driver was still pinching and thwarting.

"Whether or not you thank me, sir, you still need to pay me!" The man held out his opened hand.

Reverend Parris shook his head. "No, sir. I knew nothing about this arrangement. Therefore I have no responsibility or liability for it. If you knew anything at all, you'd know the law directs you to collect your fee from the person who hires you."

"I'll lower my fee then. But you, sir, must pay me!"

"No, do not lower it. Compromise is a sign of weakness." And to show his decision, Reverend Parris elbowed that man out of his way and quickly returned to his table. To again sit with Ingersoll, Putnam, and Putnam's in-laws Trask and Walcott (who also was Ingersoll's nephew). Noticing at once how Ingersoll had filled his glass to only half, while other glasses on the table were filled to the rim, refilled rather; he could smell it on their breaths. But he also knew that this had not been done out of parsimony on the innkeeper's part. Rather, from respect. Extolling moderation always, he generally directed Nathaniel Ingersoll to fill his glass only to half. Agreeing with Massachusetts' most famous divine, Reverend Increase Mather, his former mentor at Harvard who had written:

> Drink is itself a good creature of God and is to be received with thankfulness. But the drunkard is from the Devil.

With one exception: if that drunkard was a friend or supporter, like these men all were, he received them also with thankfulness.

He gulped down his half shot of rye, was considering asking for another when that filthy outlander limped across the hall up to his table, and announced loudly—so that everyone here would hear—without removing his cap: "Just so you know I'm no thief, but an honest man just like you, Reverend Parris, I come to inform you — without compromise — how I'll be taking those heavy coffers of your kin, with all that's inside them, as my payment. You can count our account as settled.

Though thrown to a boil, Reverend Parris allowed no further bile to rise. It was too tragic a day, for his friend Thomas Putnam especially. So he calmly replied: "My meal was interrupted, sir. Perhaps I spoke too hastily because of it. But let us conclude our business in private later."

He instructed the man to take a seat at another table. The rest was up to Ingersoll. But he did make sure to tell his inn-keep friend to get the bugbear sopped.

≈✦✥

Abigail and Mercy trudged past the graveyard and meetinghouse to the last structure on the green, a small two-storey, weather-beaten frame house: the parsonage. Abigail tried peering in through a window at the front, but its shutter was tight-closed. So were other windows at the side. She spied a clothesline tied to posts, but which displayed no fine garments. A fenced-in pen was rife with smelly muck from a stunted skimpy pig. Some chickens were pecking about. A stumpy woodlot sat at the property's rear, where there was also a small barn, which hopefully held her uncle's cow, for this weedy pasture did not. It held only one wormy crabapple tree, which she was sure gave only sour fruit.

Doffing her bonnet, she finger-combed her tangles into ringlets and splashed her face with trough water, wiping it dry on her dirty apron. She pinched her cheeks till they hurt, and now walked up to the door (with Mercy following), paused on the threshold, and stood a moment ignoring her pattering heart, and then knocked.

SUZY WITTEN

A flat-chest woman in a gray, shapeless dress answered promptly. This person's thin lips pointed downward, and her sallow cheeks caved into furrows. *Coarse and ugly! Uncle's spinster servant. No doubt.* Abigail asked to see the minister's wife.

"But I am she. I am Mrs. Parris."

Uncle Parris is handsome. Why would he marry her? She curtsied and forced a smile. "Aunt Parris."

The Afflicted Girls

The Lord God said, "It is not good that man shall be alone. I will make a help meet for him."

Genesis 2:18

8

ESPITE HER BOUNTEOUS PLAINNESS, ELIZABETH Parris considered herself the perfect "helpmeet" for Reverend Parris. They had met during his student years at Harvard Divinity, introduced by her father, a prelate there. At the time, she was the remaining unmarried daughter in one of Boston's most prominent families, the Eldridges, who were closely related to the influential and political Sewalls; and not, as yet, having entertained any suitor, she anticipated spinsterhood more than marriage. Thus, she was not indifferent to the attentions—or good looks—that set Samuel Parris apart from the other young men who visited her father's popular discursive parlor . . . who all cordially overlooked her.

His fashionably coiled tresses were the same color as the Barbados sand that sifted down through the small hourglass he'd gifted her. She turned it over numerous times for no reason, picturing her suitor's handsome visage, musing how his deep-set green eyes, with glinting specks of gold, were honestly and truly the most penetrating and discerning eyes she had ever seen. But while her young man was gifted, indeed, with a beauty that rose to any portrait master's standard, it was Samuel Parris' burning passion for God, which actually won her heart.

For his part, Sam Parris considered Elizabeth Eldridge a fortuitous match, as well. He'd been praying to God for a lifelong companion and she—no other—had been sent. So he courted her ardently to awaken her baser urges, but even then her walls of dignity would not crumble. So he decided: *As she is unworldly, let me be that, too.* He bridled in his wilder nature, and they were wed soon after his ordination.

Through this marriage, he re-made himself, was rooted now in Boston's foremost society, superior to the best in Barbados. His wife's father helped him secure his first ministry, and generously bought them a small house; he, of course, picked out a prestigious street. The following year, their daughter Betty was born. Inspired in his new vocation he would boast, often, how his modest parish was equal in spirit to that of the Reverends Mather. Because although set in an unsavory outskirt of Boston amidst a laboring immigrant population, his congregation, though poor, was as Christian as was theirs at that famed North Church, although he was invited to fewer suppers and parlors, and never to theirs.

But then after three years of preaching selflessly to God's humblest, he was crucified like the Savior. His minister's contract wasn't renewed; no reason was ever given. No additional help was forthcoming from his wife's father, who had suffered a stroke in the interim, losing his ability to walk, speak, or even to wipe his sore-covered bottom, no less to convince another congregation to hire a foreign son-in-law. Throughout, nevertheless, his goodwife fulfilled all of her daughterly duties without complaint until that good father met his end; but thereupon, they received hardly any of his worldly effects, and certainly no items of value, because her sisters' richer husbands were the ones who arranged.

Difficult times grew worse. By the fourth year of his marriage, his wife's dowry was spent, while demands for payments crammed the nooks of his desk. He already had tried his hand at various commercial ventures but failed at them all, falling deeper into debt. He took out loans against the household property, dispensing his wife's heirlooms till there was nothing left to pawn. He did odd jobs whenever he could, and always beneath his station. But the day he lost his house was the day he lost his faith. He feared his little family would starve, and began praying hours on end, weeping behind a locked door.

Then one day in this midst, after serving as jury foreman in Boston's Court of Attaints and Appeals, after that suit was decided in defendant Thomas Putnam, Sr.'s favor, he received an invitation from that village Head Selectman to come and serve as his parish's resident minister. God had heard him, again had saved him. And because of it, he took a sacred vow. In Salem Village, he would set the world to right.

❧✦❧

Her Aunt Parris led them down a narrow passageway into a steamy kitchen hall, where a household drudge, an Indian slave, was stirring laundry in an iron cauldron hanging from a lugpole over the hearth-fire. That feral half-person was soaked with reeking sweat, despite that the kitchen door was propped open, and cool breezy air was wafting in. Abigail detested savages for good reason, but at the same time she was pleased to see that her uncle owned one—because she also hated scullery.

Her aunt eyed the Indian skeptically, ordering: "Fetch a jug from the damp cellar, Tituba. Serve them cider. One cup, each."

The slave grunted and put down her stirring stick and sauntered past to go downstairs through a half-sized door. While her aunt instructed them to sit at the table and went to get two cups from her larder. Both were chipped Abigail noticed, when her aunt set them down. Now the woman brought over the heel of a knobby dark rye loaf on a breadboard, but gave them no jam or apple-butter to spread. Worse, when she reached across the table to grab for the knife, she heard that scold's correction: "You will learn to wait until food is offered, Niece Williams. Manners govern in this house, not impulse, or passion. You are now to wait until my slave returns and serves you. I am going to speak with my husband." Her aunt took down her cloak, ignoring her bonnet but complaining of the blinding sun in her eyes when she stepped out of doors. She didn't see Abigail's equally blinding glower.

The slave's easy sensuality was apparent to Abigail at once when that half-person reappeared from the damp cellar with an uncorked jug of apple cider perched on her ample hip, which was swiveling side to side like a large smirking grin. She had droplets peppering her dark full lips. *Fat unbound teats . . . bodily scent of a goat. Were I my ugly aunt, I'd be jealous of her.* (But that thought would have been unthinkable to Mrs. Parris, who knew utterly that her husband was faithful. *Had he not Covenant-ed himself Eternally unto her as she had to him?*) Because Mrs. Parris did not know—nor ever would—how Reverend Parris in his profligate youth had purchased an Indian child to be both servant and concubine. Or that in the years of his youthful manhood, he'd fathered offspring with his slave girl then sold the babes at market to avoid a scandal and to feather his purse. Only Reverend Parris, Tituba, and John Indian knew that.)

The slave poured them cider then returned to her chair, but not to her stirring. Instead, her slanted eyes closed.

Abigail picked up the bread knife and sawed off a piece from her aunt's stale unfriendly refreshment.

Gazing about this parsonage kitchen, its best feature, Mercy decided, was a handsome cherry wood court-cupboard standing cater-corner to the table. So she got up to go and examine it. Earthenware filled two bottom shelves with items neatly sorted by function: porringers, saucers, bowls, four of each, and two cups. Wood trenchers were stacked underneath the apron. A third shelf held some scant pewter-ware, and two dented items of brassware: an oil pitcher and small tub. The top shelf stood empty of aught but dust. (There was no fine English-made Eldridge family silver anymore on display in this Jacobean court-cupboard, where it had resided for half a century — this family's handful had been sold or bartered for necessities during the lean years.)

A brightly painted castor was wall-hinged to one side of the cupboard. Mercy took note of the assortment of variegated condiments, more than were common in a New Englander's kitchen: small blown-glass bottles filled with vinegar, catsup, molasses, colored peppers, cloves, nutmeg, and salt. Red threads, she did not recognize. But a muddy brown paste looked familiar — was its use as a poultice? (No, this was a fiery-hot island pepper-mustard that was the minister's particular favorite.) There were empty bottles, too, that the slave would soon fill with pickings from woods, riverbanks, and waysides. Tituba was only waiting for the weather to turn, for she knew better than anyone how to please her master's spicy palate.

Lastly, a large wooden cullender was hanging underneath the castor, and on the shelf above it, a beaker, tumbler, tureen, and tin tub sat. Stirring utensils were hanging from hooks. Also there were side-by-side canisters that she guessed were filled with salt, tea, flour and yeast, staples every parsonage house was provided. (But in fact, they sat empty. For there'd been no tithes of such goods, or even much grain here of late.) But all of it for Abigail . . . *a kitchen well ordered as any. May it be for you also, a nourishing, happy home.* She came back to the table and sat down beside her friend and dipped her bread into cider. She was hungry to the point of weakness but ate leisurely so this one small piece would satiate.

The slave jumped up suddenly from her chair — startling them both when she threw a heavy log on the fender and grabbed her leather bellows and began fiercely pumping up the floundering flames. The water had stopped boiling, and Tituba knew how her mistress, if she saw that, would make her boil and mash the laundry again. And she could feel her mistress approaching, clomping back in heavy strides across the green.

"You're to share my daughter's bed," said Mrs. Parris upon walking in and crushing underfoot the crumbs scattered on her clean swept floor. She clearly wasn't pleased seeing this, or by having to tap that messy person's shoulder, and gesture for the other girl to follow, and lead them both back down the narrow passageway into her furnished parlor. But that was her husband's command.

Abigail frowned. This parsonage house was spare, dark and small-quartered, not the fine home she'd imagined; not even half the size of the bumpkin's saltbox on the hill. Her spirits lifted a little, though, when they entered the adjacent chamber, which even in darkness she could tell was seemly furnished. It was a gentleman's room, filled with books and a writing desk. But it reeked worse than the slave did! She and Mercy had to cover their noses till her aunt had thrown open the shutters and window sash. And now that human stick stuck out her head! (By explanation, the air in this room stank foul because Reverend Parris smoked tobacco leaves whenever he could obtain them—which was whenever Nathaniel Ingersoll got in an Indies shipment and felt generous enough to share some. Last night, because of sad circumstance, a leaf was given which Reverend Parris brought home to smoke with his window and shutters closed while he was composing the infant's eulogy. It was a devilish habit forged in his youth in Barbados, that he couldn't forego, even now. During their years together, Mrs. Parris had learned to tolerate this defilement of her home. Whenever her husband smoked, by habit she would immediately afterward open his chamber window and fan out the stench using the blotter from his desk. But for some reason this morning she'd forgotten to do it.)

It thrilled Mercy to behold so many books. It had been years since she'd viewed any. Against three walls stood august bookshelves crammed from bottom to top, not only with bound volumes, also with pamphlets and handwritten journals, likely containing the minister's innumerable sermons and lectures. She read some titles on spines, only some of which pleased her for Abigail's sake, whose intelligence needed moral steering; because, others of them might steer wrong. There were also vellum-bound books, old ones, and a few which sported gilded leather covers. Those were rare, she knew. She'd never before beheld a gilded cover.

(For even in his direst poverty, when Reverend Parris sold off most of his household possessions, he never sold any portion of this collection. Instead, he hid his cherished books away from his creditors, but also buried them from his wife. And afterward, didn't have the heart to tell her what he'd done — to confess that only her treasures had been sacrificed. It was later, after they'd resettled in Salem Village and begun their second life that she discovered this betrayal while unpacking and was wounded in her heart. He offered the slightest of fibs: "Through my benefactor's aid, I was able to repurchase my library, wife . . . but alas, not your silver. The stipend was too meager." She believed him, of course. And although he had lied, perhaps broken a covenant, it had been with the highest purpose. Because a true spiritual archive must be preserved at any cost.)

And now that her aunt was standing by the window fanning out the fouled air and wafting in the fresh, with her spiny back turned to them, Abigail approached her uncle's desk and laid her palm tenderly upon it. It was a small French walnut wood *escritoire*, belonging permanently to this house, not to the current occupant. Of course, she didn't know the name for such a furnishing, or its history, but thought it rich-looking and that it suited her uncle well — with its curled ornate flourishes and little scrolls for feet. She glanced underneath at the place where his feet would rest, and beheld a large wooden box with a shiny brass bat-shaped keyhole, but lacking its key. It was locked, she discovered, when she tried to open it for a peek. It was obviously where her uncle kept his important papers, and sums of money. That he had money to lock was a comforting thought.

But now something more exquisite caught her eye. Atop his desk, behind his glass inkwell, sat an oval gold-framed miniature portrait painted on eggshell, under which was written in his elegant hand: *My Own Picture.* Her uncle's splendid beauty in his youth took her breath away. He was dressed in a courtly coat of royal blue satin with pouf sleeves, and wore around his neck a white knotted cravat, obviously of spun silk, for it formed billowy soft folds around his face. He sported a halo of tresses too, ringlets just like hers, and of almost the same hue, which fell in fullness past his shoulders. But today his hair was stringy, long and straight, and was thinning on top. *Is this painting of a periwig? Had her minister uncle once been a very rich wigged gentleman?* She looked up and frowned at her aunt, still vigorously fanning, convinced that this whey-faced praying mantis was the unlucky cause of her uncle's diminishment. *My uncle was wealthy once. His ugly wife, no doubt, has brought him down to mediocrity.*

Mercy had just strolled up to the desk to join her friend and happed to glance down at the oversized, hand-engraved Geneva Bible sitting open upon the desktop to *Psalms, 58.* The words made her shudder:

> The wicked are estranged from the womb: they go astray as soon as they are born, speaking lies. Their poison is like the poison of a serpent.

Mrs. Parris turned and caught them snooping. She waved them aside with her blotter, telling the companion: "My husband instructs you wait in here until he returns. Stand in quietude in that corner. Do not touch or look upon any of his things." To Abigail, she coolly said, "Come." Abigail followed her aunt out, through the parlor and now up a narrow staircase to a second floor landing.

The Afflicted Girls

When her mother opened the door, nine-year-old Betty Parris pricked her finger on her embroidery needle and the hoop she was sewing on clattered noisily to the floor. Mrs. Parris walked over to pick it up and seeing a bloodstain on the crisp bleached linen, she scolded: "Look what you've done, Betty. You've ruined this collar now with your clumsiness." The little girl's thumb flew into her mouth, which her mother directly pulled out. "Manners, child. You're in no cradle. Now go wash your hands properly in the bowl. Then greet your father's niece, a cousin, Abigail Williams. She is to lodge with us until arrangements can be made."

Mrs. Parris turned to face that *lodger*, blind to the gaping wound she'd just inflicted. "I suspect you are tired. So I will permit you to rest until supper. But at first light upon the morrow, you will begin to shoulder your share of our daily burden here." She left, closing the door behind her.

There will be no arrangement! Aunt Ugly! Abigail struggled against exhaustion and this crushing disappointment.

Betty Parris timidly approached. Thin, like her mother, pale and stringy-haired, like her father, by no account was she a pretty child; nonetheless, she was sweetly innocent in this moment that she reached for that fisted hand and gazed fondly and curiously up at her new cousin.

Abigail tore her hand away and lunged for Betty's bed, and collapsed upon it in a tearful release.

❧❦❧

It was hours more before Mercy learned her fate. By now the candelabrum was lit, a curtain was drawn and the shutters were latched. Also, Reverend Parris was pacing back and forth in front of her, with his hands clasped at the small of his back:

51

"I've arranged for you to serve in the house of Thomas Putnam. His wife has just suffered a terrible strain. Whatever your new master bids you do, do it gladly. For Christ commands servants to obey their masters, and nothing is hidden from Him. You will be indentured for seven years, not the usual five . . . your debts are in excess of five. I will collect your wage at each month's end and will forward an appropriate sum to the almshouse. There will be a small stipend held out for you, from which you may tithe to your church." He stopped pacing and looked at her. "I will expect you to be grateful for my charity."

Mercy lowered her eyes, "I am grateful, sir. It is by God's Grace . . . and yours of course . . . that I am here."

"Have you anything to ask me?" She shook her head. She had so many questions, but none for him.

He pulled aside the curtain, unlatched the shutter, and tapped on the glass pane, calling out loudly with a booming voice: "John Indian!" When his manslave appeared, he ordered him: "Take this girl out to Putnam Farm."

Mercy trudged for miles behind the parsonage manslave, a brown skinned giant who carried her trunk on one shoulder or sometimes on his head, and sang as he walked in long easy strides.

She should have found peace on this clear moonlit night. She was arrived safe, and tonight would sleep under the roof of a good family, and on the morrow there'd be children to serve; also, this man's voice was as sweet-toned as any she'd ever heard. Yet she couldn't listen, or think, or even gaze up at the starry firmament, which for years had been her one enduring comfort. Despite being wrapped in her thickest-wool winter cape, which had buttressed her well enough on the frozen journey southward, in this salty, civilized, balmy night air of Salem Village, she felt bone-chilled walking out to Putnam Farm.

The Afflicted Girls

But at the parsonage, it was the opposite. Abigail felt bathed in warmth after finishing the grandest meal she'd eaten in years at her own family table: something tasty stewed in gravy (not dried fish) with fresh baked bean bread and moist curds with a spoonful of jam—was it *blackcurrant?* And then even Indian pudding. And now she was going to learn how her aunt wanted the wicks to be braided. Candle making was to be her nightly chore.

When earlier she'd awakened from a dreamless slumber in the softest bed imaginable in a room red-cast with ember, she hurried first to the window to gaze outside. Darkness had descended on the village, but there were flickers of light in every small window. She wondered which house would welcome her first. There was much clattering and clanging, ordinary cooking sounds floating up inside the chimney flue. *Was that what had woken her?* She lit the standing torch on an ember and opened her coffer, which now sat on the floor delivered. *Had her uncle brought it in while she slept? Had he gazed upon her in her slumber?* She felt a surge of sweetness.

Her two other dresses had been deliberately folded and set above the sooty andirons. But then the coffer was tumbled when the coach overturned. So now they were covered with smudges from soot; a speck of char flew into her eye when she flapped one out. She sponged them both off with lye suds and brought them to the fireplace chair to dry. She washed her face and hands in the bowl, and chewed the rest of her cinnamon wood. She combed her tangles using her cousin's comb. She didn't possess one herself; such items were always common-shared at the almshouse.

No one at the supper table looked prettier or smelled fresher, or was wittier or more thankful than was she this eve. And when her uncle interviewed her later in the parlor, and said the word "welcome," all turned right in her world again.

(Now all souls at the parsonage had a nightly chore to perform before a day was called "lived well and ended." For

Abigail, it would now be to make candles. For Mrs. Parris, it was her embroidery. For her daughter, learning—because for Reverend Parris, it was his child's spiritual instruction after supper in the parlor, which tonight included both girls.) He was surprised by one: not Betty; never Betty, whom he'd always presumed had suffered a mishap at birth; it had been a difficult and prolonged labor for an unready, fearful new mother. There was no other explanation for his child's plodding mind and her inability to recall anything he taught her. However his niece, he saw at once, was naturally inclined to learn, was as eager for a Godly education as he was to give one.

Later, after both girls went up to bed and his goodwife likewise retired, Reverend Parris commenced his most pressing chore yet—the care of this newly enlarged family. At the top of a blank page, he scribed "My Terms":

First—*an annual salary of £66 from all inhabitants, proportionate to the lands they hold. When money shall be more plenteous, my wage shall be raised accordingly.*

Second—*though corn, rye or any such like provision may reach a higher price at market, for my own family's use I am to have whatever is needed at the fixed price of today.*

Third—*no provision is to be brought to the parsonage without first asking whether or not it is needed with only myself to make the choice of what (unless a person is unable to pay in any other sort but one).*

Fourth—*firewood is to be given freely, and continuously, as the parsonage woodlot is nearly spent.*

Fifth—*two goodmen of my choosing shall be appointed yearly to ensure that my minister's salary is promptly paid month by month.*

Sixth—*contributions are to be given each Sabbath Day in an envelope or a pouch with the donor's name written clearly or stitched upon it. Contributions from*

> *visitors will be considered a perquisite for the minister,*
> *not for the general fund.*

Doubtless, there were additional needs. But he was too fatigued now to recall them.

He left sufficient space on the page and signed his name at the bottom. He powdered the ink and placed small weights at the edges to curb the parchment's curl. He rubbed his eyes. This had been a difficult day, a day of unwelcome events. But the Lord, he knew, would help him to sort it.

9

P EASOUP FOG WASHED OVER JOHN INDIAN AS HE was hurrying home from his errand through neighbors' woodlots to avoid the village byways, because somewhere about were two suspicious watchmen keeping their eyes out, and his master's private business was private; although a certain handful of men usually knew it, and were allowed to make use of him for theirs. Tonight four had: from Putnam Farm he was sent to Walcott Farm with a note, and from there to Goodman Trask's house in the village, and then to Deacon Ingersoll, who put him to labors cleaning out stable stalls, cutting a bale open and forking hay, and then watering all troughs for his morrow's business. Aching in his overtired bones, John Indian finally descended to the damp cellar eager for his own hay-strewn stall, and wife-hold, and heavy sleep. Yet with taking in so much moist crisp air into his lungs, their hovel smelled foul as a crapper. Tomorrow he'd fetch fresh straw for it, he decided. He would have done it tonight if he could have thought forward—a big armful of sweet inn hay. But he had no ability to think forward. And now he stood naked, squinting down at Tituba in the dark till he could just make out her shifting shape in that narrow space that was theirs between the shelves. He crouched down.

For three days, she'd been suffering a night terror, which wasn't right for his wife. And it worried him again seeing her writhing so wild in her sleep. Because never once before had she ever left her calm, not even when they were sailing away from their island in that rickety boat and met with a sea-rage that nearly gulped them down. She calmed him then, and even the master. So what was she dreaming? Well, he wasn't good at guessing, and she wouldn't tell him in her Indian way. But if she was scared it was fearsome.

Everyone judged them an odd-match. There he was, tall and muscular, with skin the color of charred tea of an African-European blend, while she was a red-skinned melon squaw, lighter cast than him, but darker than those sad Sagamores one saw traipsing on local roads behind masters. She hailed from a world away from him, but also from them, and also not from Barbados. Her bloodline was savage Arawak, a Carib tribe more savage and older than was his by his African root. But so were those white-skinned slavers savages, who tore Tituba out from her ancient jungle. While he hated them for that, he wouldn't have met her otherwise, so he hated them mostly for the rest, but not as much as he hated the master. That was a hate without end. They'd been their master's slaves since childhood, but he wasn't a minister then. He was a planter, a planter of sorrows, and a bad rotten man. So when their peacock got plucked of his rich feathers, they were glad. Also later, when he escaped to cold Boston and turned the black rooster and married a sharp-pecking hen, and allowed them to Christian-marry, though they'd been growing on one heart stalk for such a long time.

John pulled off the coverlet and spread his wife's restless legs and put his mouth onto her opening to suck the demon out. (Nakedness was a habit they'd forged in humid, sticky Barbados. And never once had they worn any cast-off flannels to bed that the mistress had given, not even on the most blood-freezing nights. They'd set each other on fire instead.) That's what he was doing to her now: wooing in between with licks because his fingers were too calloused. He didn't want to wake her, only to shift her away from wherever she was. He teased some with his hanger, and now slipped it inside her. At once, he felt that dark thing flee. But then it was himself writhing in a body frenzied. That wily demon had fled into him!

Tituba awoke to her husband's fevered thrusting. She longed to clasp him, but instead pushed him off, squinting up through clamshell eyes: "No, John, cants. I's in my babe-time 'n I got no weeds." So they quickly put their mouths on one another. Their way, when there were no abortifacients left in Tituba's gathering basket. Because they'd long ago decided not to make babies. Even though it broke their one heart.

≈✿≈

Upstairs, Abigail awoke in a shiver in an unfamiliar cold. Confused at first, then she remembered she was in bed beside her mousy cousin, who'd grabbed off the quilt when the embers died. She considered lighting a fire, but that would mean full waking up; while just now she'd been dreaming of the forbidden fruit, and was still filled with the delicious sensations of her bodily self, her earthly creature. So she ignored that selfish bedmate, and despite the cold, raised her gown up into nakedness. She stroked her nipples and rubbed and probed her privates with increasing fervor till her mortal coil unwound into waves of aching need. That burly farmer of her dream wasn't pictured — but him: *Uncle Parris,* while experiencing more perfection than ever she had before.

Afterward, while lying in a contented half-sleep with only herself now under the coverlet, she heard a rustle out of doors. Something moved underneath her bedchamber window. Too curious, she forced herself up this time, and struck the flint and lit the candle stub. She took the stick to the window and pressed her nose to the pane hoping to catch a glimpse of her uncle heading to the privy, thinking how if he looked up at the window he'd see her face and would know her heart's contentedness.

But no one was in the yard. Nothing was astir. And yet, something *was* on the move. A shadow had just slunk across the barn wall. *A ghoul? A walking-spirit?* Her window overlooked a graveyard after all!

She flew down the stairs, flung open the kitchen door but then stood very still on the threshold peering out. And as she stared, a cold wind rushed in on her snuffing her candle.

SUZY WITTEN

Give me a Call
To dwell
Where no foot hath
A path
There will I spend
And End
My wearied years
In tears

Reverend Increase Mather
(His Diary's Title Page)

PART TWO

10

PUTNAM FARM WAS SITUATED ON A WESTERN branching off the Topsfield Road and its farmhouse clearly bespoke its age. Two stories with no cellar, it had been built early and cheaply, in 1637, by the original Putnam forebear, grandfather Tobias Putnam, a founding settler who'd put all of his money into land and farming profits into building his house, which now sat decayed and mite-ridden.

The present occupant, Thomas Putnam, firstborn grandson, firstborn son, had been given this property when he married. He had planned to do repairs before winter: to replace loose weatherboards, missing shingles, smoke out termites, patch the leaky ceilings, and perhaps paint. But unfortunately he failed to earn enough from his harvest to finance any endeavor. Unusually heavy summer rains had caused most of his rye crop to rot on the stalk. He couldn't afford to hire a house-wright or joiner, or even a carpenter's apprentice. He had no sons to assist him and his strapping nephews, a sister's sons, helped only their own. So he told his wife to make due when the spring rains came by putting pails and pots underneath the leaks. Their next harvest would be better he assured her, although neither of them believed it.

The house started out as a typical *hall-and-parlor:* a timber frame construction with a central chimney fireplace, three feet deep and tall enough for a man of Thomas' middling stature to walk through, set between two bottom floor rooms, a kitchen hall and a parlor, above which on the second storey sat two equal proportioned bedchambers. Years ago when Thomas was rich, young and newly wed, he also built a gabled and latticed sitting porch (which his bride never used) and also began building an additional wing on the parlor-side for sleeping chambers in anticipation of the large brood of sons he was expecting to father. Ten years now had that wing sat unfinished. Not from his wife's empty womb, only from her empty cradles afterward.

So was the soil here deficient. Fertile in his father and grandfather's times, it was sterile now, nearly gravel from years of overuse. The best that could be grown in his wife's dooryard garden (which first had to be fertilized mightily with dung to produce even meager results) were carrots no bigger than the length of his hand and turnips the size of his big toe.

His riding mount and plough horse were adequate, for now, and so were his less than a handful of milk cows, which all sheltered at night in the barn. Other livestock—a ram and twenty ewes, a few goats—lived up in a fold and grazed on wild grasses. But he had no shepherd to guard them, only a half-crazed mongrel that couldn't be trusted but luckily knew his boot. His chicken coop was thriving. But not near enough did he have of any creature to keep a family of five rightly nourished for long. And now here was a sixth mouth to feed. He'd never raised swine here—however cheap they were to keep and despite his constant craving for that meat—because his wife couldn't abide the stench. It had been over a month since he'd last tasted pork and that was at his Sister Trask's table, and counting in beef it would have been longer if not for the burial feast at Ingersoll's.

The most prominent feature on this farm, which he felt bestowed distinction, were the twelve tall matched wineglass elms his ancestor had planted, betokening the Apostles, which stood sentinel over his family, house and yard. But he wished they'd do their job better. And at the end of the yard, by the well, was that dreaded monument: a three-hundred-ringed oak stump, carved with the initials of three generations of Putnam males. His sons, had any survived, would have done the same. But all that rooted, rotted monument did now was remind him of his affliction, of his stumped bloodline, his cut-down family tree, and of the empty chairs for sons at his table.

He had other wounds festering, too. About five years ago, he'd obtained a loan to purchase additional acreage; but not from his skinflint father, who'd refused to lend him the money. From a greedy Salem Town usurer, who charged him uncommonly high interest, and raised it every year. And although that loan was half-paid back, a court lien had been filed against his fields for the sake of two recent missed payments. He would have to counter-sue now to delay, when time was precious and he had less of it to spare than money. And even though those particular fields lay an inconvenient distance away—as far as the crow flies as his farmhouse was from the village—and his daily haul out and back was irksome—especially since they'd been overpriced to begin with and were the result of landgrubbers, like Francis Nurse, overbidding him on the closer, choicer lots—it would ruin him to lose them.

He was burdened not only by ill luck and by grief, but also suffered humiliation. During his wife's last childbed, his eldest girl had to take up her mother's chores. But they proved too taxing for her weak constitution. Straw dust set Lucy to rasping or wheezing, morning air chilled her lungs, and she began to suffer nosebleeds, which were difficult to stanch. Barely could she lug two empty buckets up to the barn, no less carry back a full one to the kitchen. So he'd been forced to do the milking himself before he went to his fields. Forced to do a woman's work.

But then recently at the burial feast, the minister offered to hire him a servant. He declined, of course. Spring was near and he needed all of his money to buy seed. Then the minister brought the price down to an almost charitable level. He felt humiliated; his impoverishment was something he resented, and he didn't like it pointed out, especially when in public. But Sam Parris insisted that the gesture was being made on behalf of the church, and not from him personally. That it was "an investment by God in a good man's goodness," reminding Thomas how he was a Covenanter and churchgoer who resiliently tithed, and that this was a way to keep him solvent. So in the end, lured by *that* holy harpoon, he agreed to hire himself the servant.

But in truth, Reverend Parris was only offering the wench to ensure that his minister's "Terms" would be approved by at least one village selectman who had two other votes in his pocket. So he gave away that bright penny of a scullion Mercy Lewis for an oak-tree tuppence when he could have gotten four pine-tree shillings for her. Thomas Putnam and his in-laws would have approved his "Terms" anyway. They supported their minister, without any questions or complaints.

11

THE PUTNAMS SLEPT BENEATH PAINT-CHIPPED eaves but the farmhouse itself was not at rest. Spirits moved through it. On her first night here, uneasiness seeped into Mercy's soul and she still couldn't dispel it even after four days. Lying on her kitchen settle, her hard bed in front of the hearth-fire, hours after midnight and still watching fading embers lick the logs, which usually wooed her to sleep, tonight it was taking longer for her mind to let go of its last drifting image.

She heard a creak on a stair and raised her head thinking one of the children was coming down to find her. Instead, she saw her master in his night shift standing in the doorway staring at her strangely, with his hand clamped at the front of his gown. He was rubbing himself rigid. Wrapping her quilt, she flew to the kitchen door, reminding this new master in a voice loud enough that her mistress might hear: "Reverend Parris is my benefactor, sir."

"Be quiet, wench! You're no innocent. Seven years under this roof you're now bound." He recited scripture while moving closer: "'Show your servants all paths of the Destroyer whereto they may be inclining.' I mean to show you only one."

She was bold. "I'll accuse you of sodomy which is punishable by death, sir."

"I'll say you're a liar and trouble-maker, for you are one," he shot, lifting up his flannel and dangling his half-hard prick. "I'll vow I never touched you. And I'll be believed, temptress, not you. Now wrap your flap-mouth around *this* nightly chore."

Mercy turned away, crouched against the wall, waiting for the inevitable violation. Yet this wasn't sodomy Thomas knew, and it wasn't forbidden to him. Rape, adultery, fornication, fellatio were all regarded as pardonable human weaknesses. So whatever the wench might say (and he doubted she'd say anything for the shame of it), he'd only be punished with a fine. It always came down to money in the end.

Log remnants crumbled to ash. Mercy's tight-shut eyes opened. Saw that the kitchen was vacant. She rushed back to her settle, and lay down upon it and wept. She soon sank into a fitful slumber, and a fearful familiar dream:

> A child stands in a circle of candles. A man puts a hand
> at the back of her neck. Forces her to drink from a flask. A
> vile dark liquid trickles down her chin, staining her white
> bodice and apron. Her limbs turn spindly. The lights
> around her begin to spin.

And now, ever since, anxious alertness filled Mercy whenever she arose from that unlucky bench to perform her burdens of indenture. Prior to first light till her sleeping hour, she labored hard at this ill-favored farm, tending a cloistered mistress, three neglected youngsters and neglected household, undernourished livestock, a fallow garden. Her tasks were numberless but constantly increasing: cooking, cleaning, mending, milking, weeding, foddering, pumping well-water, refilling barrels and troughs, cleaning stalls, coop, fold, collecting manure, teaching tykes how to wash their bottoms, and scrubbing everything from waxy ears and grimy nails to encrusted chamber pots and a privy, which hadn't seen ash or lye in a month. Exhausted, dejected always, she also suffered dread when she saw her master approaching. Though he would always turn and change course to avoid the encounter, then would also deliberately look away when she served him his food.

Thomas had his reasons. After suffering a slew of shameful, penitential thoughts on the night of his transgression, he had vowed to keep himself clean for the sake of the son he wanted, lest God forsake him entirely. Because on that sinful night after spurting his virile seed into the chamber pot and viewing it wasted, and then later lying in bed beside his uncaring spouse, he reflected how everything he'd ever done in his life had brought him only misery and famine: first, by marrying a wife, frigid and unstable, who was his continuing torment, who although she may have delivered all the sons he ever wanted, it was to Death not to him; and also his years-long estrangement from his father and the numberless petty lawsuits he'd brought, which won him only more rancor, and in the end disinheritance. And now here was the Devil Himself, not God, tempting him with a fertile bondmaid unasked for, a pretty Hagar for unhappy Abraham. But if he planted her with a bastard—and it would be a boy he knew, he was sure of it—he would be that much more ruined. He was just that unlucky.

For Mercy, the oppression lifted a little when her master's eldest daughter befriended her. Lucy Putnam, an unusually sensitive child, became enthralled one day watching their new household servant clear cobwebs from the ceiling corners, and then put the spiders to work in the dooryard garden, instead of squashing them with the broom or her shoe like her mother always did. It was a spiritual awakening, a brand new understanding of the value of even God's tiniest creature:

> *There is a Garden in her face*
> *Where roses and white lilies grow.*
> *A Heavenly Paradise is that place*
> *Where all pleasant fruits do stow.*

The Afflicted Girls

Clear to Lucy now was her favorite song's secret meaning: the face in that marvelous Garden was Mercy Lewis'! She formed a strong attachment to the servant after that. And soon, in one another's near-constant company, the loneliness receded for each.

These days, Lucy always kept out a watchful eye for useful spiders. She also began to hide humble gifts, tucking some special item between the layers of Mercy's quilt, or hiding it in her dress-pocket, or inside her shoe, and then keenly watching till it was found. A pretty quartz pebble she'd found by the brook, a knotted hairnet she'd crocheted, the gold ribbon her mother had bestowed on her last Easter. And even her most prized possession, difficult to part with—God's perfect shell painted with rainbows, which her father had found along the bays-water and given her on her eleventh birthday. Each gift earned a kiss.

12

ONE MORNING SUSANNA WALCOTT DECLARED A need to visit her grieving aunt. After her chores were done, permission was granted by her mother for an overnight stay—which would be her first since her cousin babe's death. Along the way, she picked a bouquet of early wildflowers to add to the gifts she already carried: a small sack of flour, a jar of preserves, and a book of consoling poems—that popular volume by Anne Bradstreet, New England's only poetess—which her mother had thought to lend.

And now some hours later, while sitting on that creaky rocker beside her poor Aunt Ann's bed, she read aloud that poem which was her mother's particular favorite:

> *Tho husband dear be from me gone*
> *Whom I do love so well,*
> *I have a more beloved one*
> *Whose comforts far excel.*

Pondering that sentiment, her brow furrowed—*dare she ask?* Susanna knew the family history: how her in-law aunt had brought a rich dowry into her marriage and that her Uncle Thomas was also then quite rich. *And look where those two have ended!* So she had dire reason to fret, because she herself had nothing to offer a suitor, no dowry at all. No comforts were lying packed inside her coffer. And she didn't even know if there'd be a plot of Walcott land for her father to bestow, if their family lawsuit wasn't won. *Dare she ask her aunt of its progress?* But now, the invalid cried fatigue. So the book was closed, and the rocker swung forward to its tips, and two frustrated talkative lips pecked an uninterested cheek.

At dusk, Mercy brought the milk cows down from pasture, and roped them into their places inside the darkening barn and gave them their hay. Outside she split two sawed logs and carried that firewood back to the kitchen for the supper fire; but found it already built, and utilized. An oven kettle was hanging from the lugpole. The Walcott cousin had decided to bake and was already mixing dough, which meant that her pottage would have to wait. *No matter.* A respite was always welcome to a servant, as were sweet-cakes made with jam, whether or not she would get one. But at least the children would. She set down the wood, noting how her three charges were engaged in a counting game, sitting all together on the floor. Seeing no reason to disturb them, she sat down quietly herself at the table and picked up the book lying atop it, and began leafing through it.

"Put that down!" barked Susanna, truly perturbed that this inferior person would dare touch a possession of hers without asking permission; not that she would have shared it, even were it really hers.

Mercy looked up, and teased: "'Put that down' came a voice like a pin . . . from a girl with flour on her nose and chin."

The two youngest stopped playing their *beans in a cup*. Seeing Susanna's floury face, they succumbed to silly giggles, and soon were holding their bellies, rolling about the floor. Lucy desperately wanted to laugh, but didn't want to offend her favorite cousin. So she held in her mirth until Susanna had wiped her face on her apron, which only made that white mask spread. For she was a messy cook and flour had spattered her apron.

Susanna gave Mercy her version of the evil eye, and barked at them all who were laughing, warning of spankings next. But Mercy wasn't laughing, only thinking how this girl wasn't her mistress, nor had any authority here and was younger than her by three years; if anything they were peers. Likelier than not, Susanna Walcott would be five years indentured to a household she might not like. Nonetheless, she chose to make peace and closed the book. "I have no need to read your volume, Susanna. I already know these pages by heart." And now she recited a Bradstreet poem appropriate to that cousin's visit:

> *Farewell dear babe, my heart's too much content,*
> *Farewell sweet babe, the pleasure of mine eye,*
> *Farewell fair flower that for a space was lent*
> *Then ta'en away unto eternity . . .*
> *Blest babe, why should I once bewail thy fate*
> *Or sigh thy days so soon were terminate,*
> *Sith thou art settled in an everlasting state.*

Susanna stared agape, wondering how anyone could remember so many grand words so flawlessly. But more, that it was an orphaned scullion doing it. Not only that, but who was doing it with grace.

But one here took that sad reminder to heart. For Mercy in her boastfulness had not considered this specific poem's effect on sensitive Lucy. She continued reciting that lyric until she noticed the child's distress, and understood its cause. She stopped her recitation, and went over and sat on the floor beside the bean counters. She took Lucy's hand in hers, as looked into that girl's struggling eyes. She smiled, and now began reciting a happier poem, also by Anne Bradstreet:

> *I had eight birds hatch'd in the nest,*
> *Four cocks there were, and hens the rest;*
> *I nurs'd them up with pain and care,*
> *For cost nor labour did I spare,*

The Afflicted Girls

Till at last they felt their wing,
Mounted the trees, and learned to sing.

The little ones began chirping in another made-up game. While their sister, comforted by Mercy, tried her best not to sniffle.

Susanna was so impressed with the servant's erudition that she confessed to Mercy now—without envy—how much she admired verse. And how wonderful it was that a woman had dared write poems, which men saw fit to publish. Mercy heartily agreed. Soon they were chatting amiably, Mercy even admitting to having tried penning verses herself but which were too forlorn to ever share. Though Susanna, of course, kept needling.

Later that evening, after Mercy had herded her cousins up to bed, Susanna, while serving her uncle his pottage, bragged about his servant's erudition. Thomas rose abruptly from his chair and stomped out to the parlor, shutting the door behind him. Susanna began to brood because the four remaining sweet-cakes were his, and she was wondering if he'd return to claim them. But then she decided that since he didn't yet know of their existence, did it matter? Nonetheless, she would bake him more tomorrow. So she gobbled down his cakes, and then thought no more about it, neither tonight nor on the morrow.

Now Salem Village had no dame school or writing school. Mothers and grandmothers were expected to educate their children, who were meant to master the hornbook, speller, first reader, and New England Primer before the age of eight, and then move on to more complicated subjects. That sore had been festering on Thomas' brain. Because his youngsters' instructions ceased the day his wife's last morning sickness began, and had continued for nearly a year now in that neglect. He'd done nothing to address it, because he couldn't . . . till today. And while he desired a son above all else, and his rightful inheritance second, among the other life necessities in life was to get his daughters educated; for that would ensure them a dowry of sorts should he fail to fill their hope chests with clover. So he knelt in the parlor, with his hands clasped to his heart, appealing to God to uproot and pluck out the remainder of his lust, because the Almighty hadn't been fooled. And when he felt washed clean enough of that sedition, he thanked God for the gift of a teacher.

The next day yet another chore was added to Mercy's long list—to teach her younger charges their alphabets and catechism, and Lucy more complicated subjects: sums, natural science, history, poesy, anything that eager child wished to learn . . . except spirituality. Only their father was allowed to teach them religion.

The unwritten law in every Puritan household was that father was minister at home.

The Afflicted Girls

13

NOT ONLY A NIGHTLY CHORE, TWO DAILY RULES were also observed at the parsonage: first, for life to be as orderly as its kitchen. Second, that each week begun anew on the Sabbath be better lived than the last. Today was that Day of Renewal.

Prior to first light, John Indian went to Ingersoll's barn to milk that man's two fattest-udder cows. Rich gleanings for Tituba's butter churn. But before she churned, she ladled him out his Sunday gruel, steaming and with a thick slop of clotted sweet cream on top, but which he had to gulp down quickly, hardly savoring, because on Sundays the master came early to the kitchen, while the lanterns were still lit.

Reverend Parris' Sabbath Day morning meal was usually a filling one. Today it was two pan-fried eggs on a thick slice of rye, a bowl of oat gruel steamed with dried apples, not cream. Like always, he took his trencher to his study and ate at his desk, hardly tasting a morsel, while he whittled more on his sermon. Which in *every* first light on *every* Sabbath morn seemed too lengthy, defective, and unfinished.

Also today, like on every other Sunday, Mrs. Parris stomped down to the kitchen promptly following the sun's first true ray and would be wearing her dun-colored dress, Nature's "humblest color." (It didn't matter which garment she put on, because all of her dresses were the self-same dun gray or brown, any muddy mixture.) She proceeded to sip her tea, for only on the rare occasion was island coffee, her favorite, ever tithed to the tin. But this week no tea had been tithed either, so she was drinking a bark or leaf that Tituba had brewed for John. Normally, she sipped that kind without pleasure, while waiting for her child—now children—to appear before partaking of sustenance, as it was a mother's duty to set the table example (although sometimes she'd allow herself to nibble). Today, she downed her beverage in one formidable gulp and ordered Tituba to come over and pour her another. Her stomach was uncommonly queasy and her mouth was unnaturally dry. And although bread was a stomach settler, her sore gums combined with the staleness of this loaf barely allowed for mastication. Something was amiss in her body.

But it was the slave who earned her loudest complaint: "Haven't we a fresher loaf?"

Tituba went to the bread bin and looked, and shook her head.

"Is this what you served the Master?"

The slave shrugged.

And now Mrs. Parris frowned, thinking how although her husband never complained, he must be weary of her poor table-fare: *stale loaves, salt-dried meats, fish chowders, mishmash pottages . . . nothing ever pleasing or truly tasty, no, not at this table anymore.* She felt a sudden sharp cramp, which bent her at the waist, and then up came an oink of a belch, which left a bilious taste in her mouth, but also relieved her gut's discomfort. Strangely, it brought an inspiration with it, as well. She made haste to the doorway and called out to her manslave, who was lazing in a sunny patch out back by the barn: "Slaughter the pig today, John!"

Hearing that, John Indian grew alarmed. Because, while lugging the milk back from Ingersoll's, he'd seen a pen-rail broke and no pig inside it. He told Tituba, who sent him searching in the midden-heaps. He didn't find the runt. 'It'll come back for its slop,' she said. But it hadn't. Not yet. And likely wouldn't. After that worrying thought, Tituba's voice filled his ears: *'Oh well, John, oh well, if it don' juz go look fer 'nother runt. Steal't while these folks is at church.'*

Stomping over to the churn now, Mrs. Parris took a large finger-lick of butter. Turning to the cheese rack, she palmed the two hanging whey-dripping, linen-wrapped globes of curd to test their firmness. Squeezing them, white whey juices trickled through her fingers. She looked up and saw her slave's subtle smirk, but didn't catch its meaning as she pursed her parched thin lips and dried her hands on Tituba's apron, instructing:

"You and John are to say your prayers at home today. I want Reverend Parris to have a special Sabbath Day dinner. Roast the pig with parsnips and potatoes, fry up winter peas and onions with its liver in the lard. Bake biscuits, and make a treacle pudding. Make sure to save some clotted cream for it. Fetch flour and syrup at the Inn. And-and--" she looked about her kitchen trying to recall.

Tituba squinted toward the breadbox.

"Oh, yes . . . bake bread. Two loaves. No, three."

Upstairs, the cousins finished dressing.

Betty Parris' Sunday dress was identical to her mother's in style, but wasn't dull or dun, having been cut from a quarter bolt of shiny blue English twill, which someone had tithed to the parsonage in lieu of money. This pretty dress sported white linen cuffs and had a crewel lace collar (both made by her mother), and her shoes were of good cobble, too. Whereas Abigail's "Sunday best" was so faded one couldn't tell its original color. There were moth holes in its folds, which she had done her diligent best to darn but the threads didn't match.

Noticing, however innocently, Betty asked: "Don't you have a better dress, cousin?"

Abigail frowned. This *was* her *better dress*, the one she'd sewn from cloth found behind a Falmouth tailor's shop. And it was the second best one she owned, which had been kept unworn for months to wear to her uncle's first sermon, like the other one had been for her first night's supper. She was in the midst of combing Betty's straggly mop readying that insulting child for church. As she hit a knot, she yanked the comb through anyway and the child bleated. She warned: "Squeak again, ugly mouse," forcing the comb through another knot, "and I'll never do plaits for you again."

Downstairs, Reverend Parris stopped pacing and returned to his desk. He leaned over to reread what he'd lastly written. Then he dipped his quill into his inkwell to add a short foreword to the message already scribed inside his large black Sermon Book: *There are devils as well as Saints here in our little church.*

The Afflicted Girls

14

T HE CHURCH MEETINGHOUSE WAS HARDLY HALF full, fewer than were present at last week's Sunday sermon. Reverend Parris tallied empty seats, considering who was newly truant. Yet a hundredfold of the Faithful were still in accord with God. Only a few were still looking for better seats, as most were already seated in their usual Sabbath Day alertness on the thirty roughhewn split-pine log benches set on either side of his center aisle: goodmen, farmers, tradesmen, goodwives, children, indentures, a few visitors. Latecomers were to stand at the back he reminded Deacon Ingersoll, despite the surfeit of seats, because he'd brook no interruptions, clattering, whisperings, or turning of heads during his Sermon.

But there were always interruptions. Mid-way through the opening hymn, the village lads would always angle away from their family rows to stand together by the windows, so they could stare outside if bored, or ogle their future wives in profile. Of course then all those young downy swans would ease back their shoulders and tilt up their chins, thrusting out their budding breasts to best advantage, aching to see who in particular stared at them, but not daring to turn round to look, lest they signal to their watchful parents—or to him—any unspiritual awakenings. And now he, too, had one of these in his house!

Reverend Parris glanced toward his Williams niece and caught her staring inappropriately. At him! He looked away, because his wife, not he, was the person to correct her. But he made a mental note to mention it.

No gentryman besides Nathaniel Ingersoll was present, nor ever attended this church. Although a score of well-heeled freemen, landholders and merchants (two score, if one counted widows) lived and prospered within his parish fold, they all conspired to worship—and to tithe—at Salem Town Church, or the pariah Beverly Village Church. Yet, they continued to govern cruelly the destiny of *his* church. Wresting control of the Village Committee six months ago when his patron's life was on the wane, they then viciously voted to withhold his minister's salary by suspending its tax. They had taken this vote repeatedly ever since, month by month, forcing him to live on the graces of a faithful few now, like Nathaniel Ingersoll, who by seniority had inherited the hat of Head Selectman, nevertheless held little power.

These church-going men were comprised mostly of poor farmers and tradesmen, who all aspired to a new rising middle class and perhaps dabbled in politics by signing petitions or voicing opinions, but they held no seats as yet on the Village Committee, nor would they till they rose much higher.

Needless to say, they all certainly held tight to their leather purse strings on Sundays!

Abigail was in rapture. Because her Uncle Parris was so fiery and animated as he preached. Standing in his long black minister's coat and white potato-starched collar, cooked by her on yester morn and ironed perfectly last night. He *was* Moses on the Mount, Jesus in the Temple. Of course, she also saw him daily at the parsonage. But today she saw him as he meant himself to be seen, as he saw himself: *Parris of Salem . . . in full Purpose at a Holy Pulpit . . . a pointy sword for God.* She cared not a whit or a dull blade that other preachers could spittle and whittle equally lofty sentiments.

The Afflicted Girls

Because, only her uncle bestowed true Divine Wisdom, only *he* opened the Tabernacle . . . to her.

Reverend Parris *was* an impressive speaker to be sure. His weekly sermons and lectures were always constructed cleverly using themes relating to everyday living. And his parables, though not always of his own invention (many being fished from his volumes), were apropos and instructive, if not aptly construed. Since his words usually fell short of persuasion as his tone was always too accusatory, too stiffly personal and tainted with animus. Because long ago, when first called up to Christ's Pulpit, he chose *fear* over *love*, deciding then to vigorously hawk God's wrathful side.

While his parishioners, the majority at least here, not knowing any better, sought only God's Love.

> "There are devils as well as saints here in our little Church. No one is above suspicion. The person one least suspects is often a devil in disguise."

Mercy, alone, saw him clearly. *He means to raze not raise them,* she thought as her charges and other youngsters in the room shivered underneath his pronouncements. *And he means for them to fear him to better control them.* What a fool she'd been to hope for better here. Ministers were the same in every place: they were men who craved power over others. She noticed now that even the parents sat stone-faced, until he lingered his eyes upon one or another to make sure the point was taken. Then their hazed eyes cleared.

> "Christ said, 'Have I not chosen you twelve and one of you is a devil?'"

Reverend Parris frowned. *Didn't they understand they were his Lost Flock? His Multitude! To guide safely across the Red Sea of Sin!*

Sinners like Betty Parris? That minister's daughter thought that her father was singling her out. She was sure that she would be *corrected* later because her cousin, Abigail Williams, seated beside her, who knew *everything,* kept gloating. And she knew it also because every time she sought her mother's hand for reassurance, her hand was sloughed off and thrust back into her lap. (But, really, this was only because Mrs. Parris felt that a daughter's lapse of decorum during the Sermon was a sign of disrespect for the minister giving it— never mind that he was her own father—a mother's disappointment certainly worthy of a censure: *A penance of no dessert. No proper example in church . . . no treacle pudding.*) And so Betty was right; there was to be a correction.

Whilst that newly arrived cousin, Abigail Williams, had actually been entreating that father: *Look at me! At me! Not at her, Uncle Parris!* And now, his handsome eyes almost settled on hers. But then they darted aside to her mousy cousin's. Yet, he must have heard her calling, for now his eyes came back and met hers!

Ruffled, Reverend Parris lost his place in his Sermon Book. *My niece must be cured of that goggle-eyed mannerism.* His finger quickly retraced on the page. He pretended only to have paused. He put his palms at the corners of the pulpit and shifted forward, looking out presciently as if about to make an even weightier point:

> "Judas betrayed Jesus for only thirty pieces of
> silver. The small mean price in Jerusalem for a
> base female slave—three pounds, fifteen—"

Someone had begun coughing. Irritated, he looked up. Till he realized that the transgressor was Thomas Putnam's sickly daughter, not his silly niece. He allowed that hacking girl a moment to compose, watched while the indenture passed her a kerchief for spitting, a servant he now deemed a responsible sort, and regretted having sold her to Thomas Putnam for such a measly sum. And were he not so smug in temperament or distracted by coughs, flirtatious nieces, or inadequate finances, he might have realized—before bellowing it—that his next example would cause that Putnam family even greater distress. But at least Thomas' goodwife was absent today, or there'd have been an eruption, not merely another interruption, when he said:

> "Our little Church, indeed, has both good and
> bad in it. Just as gardens hold both flowers
> and weeds, and fields produce grain, chaff
> and tares. Even in the best families can be
> found those who drank heresy with their
> mother's milk — "

Lucy Putnam gasped, her siblings cringed, other youngsters in the room tucked in tighter to mothers, grannies and sisters—all wondering, were they the ones corrupted at birth? While Reverend Parris gripped the sides of his pulpit so tight his palms turned white as he named their infection:

> "There is no trust to a rotten-hearted person,
> no matter what piety or loyalty he professes. A
> hypocrite can give an appearance of sanctity
> to deceive God's very angels. Even now, Judas
> sits in our midst, loyal only to Satan. We must
> find him, and find all Judases who sit in our
> midst and weed them out, before they choke
> and destroy our healthy crops--"

By "crops," he meant their children. But these were simple folk to whom "crops" meant "crops," like "pestilence" and "drought" meant "trouble."

Seeing so many darkened faces lowered and slightly turned, and also hearing muffled whispers, Reverend Parris suddenly felt adrift. Should he soften his tone? *Add salve? Be more fatherly?* (For Reverend Parris had a talent, a gift, of which he was wholly unaware, but which in a different world and time, and by a different fate, would have afforded him a much happier life as a playwright and actor; despite that occupation being a corruption of the soul.) Two paragraphs had to be excised, since they would not have been understood. Recovering, he spiraled upward to his conclusion, promising, enlisting, soothing, and stretching out his arms to embrace his feckless flock:

> "Brethren, do not fear, do not be alarmed.
> Together we can conquer Satan. We can defeat
> this insidious plan. Does not God furnish the
> Faithful with *all* necessities for victory? We
> need only to put on *His* armor and stand
> ready. To fight the Serpent, wherever he rears
> his treacherous head."

He uttered his final "Amen" and closed his Sermon Book. And, again, perused faces.

While one perused his, and knew: *You have never seen the Serpent, sir. You know nothing of that Darkness.* Mercy glanced up toward Abigail, and saw how bright-faced her friend was with adulation. *Oh, my poor Abby. You are so deceived.*

The Afflicted Girls

15

I T HAD BEEN A LONG SERMON, OVER AN HOUR.
When the closing hymn began, a handful of folk began putting on coats and capes, canes tapped as knee-locked elders half-stood then sat again, when spied. But when Francis and Rebecca Nurse arose and their clattering clan of forty kinsmen scattered about the room rose with them, Reverend Parris was indignant. He felt wholly disrespected.

Ingrates! Apostates! Those Nurses run only to avoid me on the threshold! He watched that old bent matriarch, Rebecca, be escorted up the aisle by a grandson, remembering how her carrion crotchet of a mate had paid a high enough sum for his committee seat, yet avoided tithing to his minister. And there she was again, like on every Sunday, stretching out her arm, taking sluggish steps deliberately, smiling and nodding to neighbors. *Commanding attention! Insolent hen! I am still standing at my Pulpit! My service has not concluded!* He truly wanted to run up the aisle and slap her proud cheek. Instead, he briskly leafed through his Psalter in search of a second closing hymn. For the benefit of those here who still respected their Spiritual Pilot:

> *And all he doth, shall prosper well,*
> > *The wicked are not so:*
> *But they are like unto the chaff,*
> > *Which wind drives to and fro.*
> *Therefore shall not ungodly man,*

Fail to stand in the Doom,
Nor shall those sinners with the just
In that Assemblie come.
For of the righteous men the Lord
Acknowledgeth the way;
But the way of the ungodly men
Shall utterly decay.

Ben Nurse was assisting his granny in that exit. And as they passed by Mercy's row, he tossed her a cheery grin. She saw him and smiled back with equal warmth, reminded how there were also good souls here.

Meanwhile, behind Ben, standing by a window, one freckly gangly red-haired boy thought this pretty stranger with the Putnams was *flirt-gilling* with him. He sent her back some squinty winks. None of which Mercy noticed.

Abigail did. She'd been scrutinizing that boy gaggle by the window, trying to decide which one to pursue. She locked eyes with this redhead now, and made him turn redder. Unfortunately her chosen, John Doritch, was a poor farmer's son . . . at best a dullard, at worst a twit and nitwit.

After the second hymn concluded, Reverend Parris, with his Sermon Book tucked tightly under his arm, collected his family and led them out in a formal procession up the aisle. Abigail walked proudly behind her uncle, wrapped in her new cloak of sanctity and privilege, and also in a gray cape her aunt had lent her this morning when hers was judged too shabby. She eyed Mercy, but her friend's face was turned. So she threw her gloating glance to the girl sitting just behind, someone she vaguely recognized. Susanna Walcott. Who felt honored to be singled out by the minister's new niece. Polite in church as any maid when observed by elders, she would have gotten up to go greet the newcomer personally. But she was too upset, having just overheard her uncle's servant ask her cousin Lucy this heinous thing:

"The young man your father quarreled with in the inn-yard—does he ever come here to worship?" Before Lucy could answer, she sprang between them like an adder: "Don't speak of that hideous creature to my cousin! Do not ever mention that person again!"

Mercy stammered an apology.

❧ ✦ ❧

Reverend Parris took his customary place on the meetinghouse threshold, where he could best greet the Faithful as they exited and collect their weekly donation—his just dessert for the satisfying meal he'd just served them. "Good Sabbath," he beamed to a thick-bodied fellow.

"Good Sabbath," muttered the village blacksmith, bumbling past.

Reverend Parris looked after that ox, surprised. It was the first time the man had ever failed to tithe. *Perhaps, he has forgotten.* He made a mental note to pay a visit to the smithy later, and now shifted his attention to the next persons to emerge—a well-to-do young couple recently settled here from Connecticut, the new junior constable John Willard and his wife, who each carried a toddler in arm. When one cherub gurgled, Reverend Parris reached out to pat its chubby cheek, informing its father: "It's said that souls entering the world as a matched pair bring a special blessing to the parents." His conscience at once decried this: *No! No! Not according to Calvinist belief!* That was only true in that otherworld, the dark-underneath of Barbados. It was a native superstition that Tituba once had told. But John Willard could comprehend for himself how a twin pair of thriving, handsome sons would indeed be a Grace to any man. He felt no need to share

85

his joy with this one. Rather, he felt the need to nod curtly and escape. He slipped his hand onto his wife's back and ushered her away. Reverend Parris felt insulted.

And the cruel rebuff repeated. Guildsmen and tradesmen, one after another: cooper, gunsmith, carpenter, joiner, mason, wheelwright, even the cobbler whose goodwife he'd ministered to for weeks while she lay suffering in her sickbed and for whom he had prayed and fasted for two days, while unsuccessfully wrestling the Grim Reaper—who all could afford to tithe, and generously, for some reason, today, weren't! *Cheapskates! Scoundrels!*

Nathaniel Ingersoll walked out next, and finally a full tithing pouch was thrust into his hand. But he was so upset he barely noticed or heard this sober sincere comment, while the man was shaking his hand: "Thank you, Samuel. It is one to heed. This call to vigilance." Reverend Parris looked him in the eye. "Not all my parishioners are as steadfast as you, Nathaniel." He was about to make his numerous complaints known when that innkeeper's wife and spinster daughter spilled through the doorway, nodded pleasantly at him as they clasped their mister's arms on either side and marched that happy Church Deacon across the green back to their inn, where patrons were already gathering. Reverend Parris stared after them. For most villagers, the Sabbath Day was a respite from labors. But for that family and for him, it was their longest, busiest, most lucrative workday.

Today, however, there would be no comparison. Their moneybox would be full tonight. His would be empty.

"Good Sabbath," offered Thomas Putnam handing Reverend Parris a tiny coin pouch. "For you and yours, with thanks from me and mine . . . with apologies it can't be more."

Reverend Parris stayed Thomas' arm and quickly guided him out of earshot several few steps, to a place at one side of the meetinghouse cloistered by trees. "Hardly one in ten has tithed today. I don't understand it. This congregation knows it has an obligation. The terms are written clearly in my contract. I am to receive *weekly* offerings of goods *and* money."

Thomas sucked in his breath. Ingersoll was Head Selectman, not him. So he was the right party to inform the minister. But Nathaniel Ingersoll was not standing here right now with an agitated person digging fingers into his arm. He answered what he knew, however reluctantly: "There's trouble in the parish, Sam. Dissenting brethren have been speaking out against you. The din is growing louder. More are beginning to listen."

"To what? What are they saying?"

"Complaints you preach too much about the Devil and not enough about God. Dwell mostly on the low points of our Lord's career. Mind you, I, for one, welcome it." Saying that, Thomas put on his hat signaling a wish to depart. But then couldn't, because the minister still clutched him.

"Who are these traitors? Tell me! I demand to know their names! Do they expect me to work for their salvation free of charge?"

Thomas grew even more uncomfortable. *Why should it fall upon him to name names?*

"Do *you also* wish to humiliate me, Thomas?"

Thomas shook his head. What he wished for was his Sunday drink. "Nurse, Porter, Jacobs for three," he said, hoping those names would satisfy.

But Reverend Parris declared they were ones he already knew. "Who else?"

Thomas considered how it wouldn't be a betrayal because he owed these other men no loyalties. He counted none of them as friends, but neither really as enemies. Some he'd known since childhood, but of that bunch, the ones that counted were mostly dead already, or poor like him, and the minister was his friend. So he answered: "Proctor, Hutchinson, Corey, Cloyce, Wardwell,

Willard, two score and a half more . . . their kinfolk, too. And excepting my two kinsmen, all but one who serves on the Village Committee. Old Bray Wilkins stands solid on your side, as do his sons and some of his brethren. But that other faction numbers over sixty now, and boasts twice as many freemen."

"F-faction?" the minister stammered.

"They've raised a petition to fire you, Sam. That new junior constable Willard is taking it around. Many have signed it. Look there if you want to know names."

"Scofflaws! Hypocrites! I'll sue them!"

"Do it quick. They're next planning to file in the General Court to revoke the parsonage deed."

"They cannot! The parsonage house is legally mine! It's stated so in my contract!"

Thomas answered bluntly what he'd long known as a fact: "What was agreed to when you first arrived was never written down in the Village Book of Record. My father, who hired you, likely carries the blame for it. Knowing him, though, most likely it was deliberate." That same instant he realized his mistake, because a father—even an avaricious, underhanded, vindictive one—must be respected till the end of one's days. *The heavy Curse of God will fall upon those children who make light of their parents and treat them with ungodly contempt.*

Hardly. Reverend Parris was livid at the dead man himself! "Iscariot! Swagman! Devil's spawn!" He punched the clapboard. "Your father is a worm-ridden louse!" But his next bruising blow was thwarted. Thomas had grabbed his wrist and held it firm until his angry fingers had unclenched. And now both men stood embarrassed, as Thomas proffered: "I, for one, have been speaking in your defense, Sam. You're the best minister our village ever had, and there's many of us who'll fight to keep you."

Abigail frowned. She'd been loitering behind a nearby tree gazing upon her uncle, and overheard all that he was suffering.

The Afflicted Girls

❧✦❧

When earlier Tituba returned to the parsonage with her meager bowl of pickings from other dooryard gardens—mostly herbs, roots and salad makings—when she approached the kitchen threshold, she heard a frightening sound. She rushed in and spied John, who was supposed to be cranking the pig round on the spit, sleeping in the hearth chair instead, cranking only snores.

She hurried to turn it. Somebody's chattel runt hardly bigger than a suckling was dark and crispy on its grilled side, but thankfully wasn't yet charred. *Would'a been a foul day t'were it char.* She woke her husband, not angrily, never angrily. "G'wan out, John. Don' needs ya. Take sum bread an' drippins' if yer hungry."

He rubbed his eyes, suddenly remembered the pig, and looked up sheepish.

"Don' matter," she shrugged. "G'wan."

So he broke off the heel of that fresh loaf she kept hidden underneath a loose floorboard, soaked it in rich fat, and exited chewing.

And now she lifted a pot of boiling vinegar water off the fenders and carried it outside to drain. Soon, she was pounding boiled pods with her mallet and scraping out seeds into her mortar, which already held soaked ground rye, pig's blood, and lard. And when her red mixture turned thick and sticky, she patted out cakes and put them into the ashes to bake.

She chanted some heathenish words, smote the backs of her hands together, and spat three times into the fire . . . and once at the pig for not waking John.

SUZY WITTEN

For the love of money is the root of all evil, which, while some coveted after, they have erred from the faith and pierced themselves through with many sorrows.

Timothy 6:10

PART THREE

16

ANOTHER GUTTED BEAST—A FAT CHOICE MILK-fed calf—was roasting on a six foot spit in a kitchen hall fireplace of grandiose size; veal, to celebrate the signing of a contract. This house was almost calf-shaped itself with three wings protruding at right angles from a center block. Unusual, "E"-shaped, and designed by a freemason, it was constructed of expensive brick, which was rare for the Bay colony; since lime, a necessity for making brick, wasn't found in New England and few could afford to import it. The center prong held this formidably equipped kitchen, and crosswise spread a grand hall, and the two outer prongs of the "E" housed both a large dining hall and an equal-sized sitting-parlor.

Rising from the center of the grand hall wound a curving walnut staircase of broad girt up to a second storey, which itself had a furnished landing and where high plaster ceilings edged in geometric bright-painted strap-work framed three opulent bedchambers. Inside the two outer ones were hidden backstairs connecting down to private pipe-fitted unseen bathrooms. And outdoor sheds housed complex water pumps and flushing mechanisms that served them. One bathroom held a man-sized copper tub; the other a tub of baked white porcelain. Each also contained a separate sitting closet for the water-bowled latrine with a comfortable leather seat, which had been patterned after the celebrated "Ajax" built a hundred years prior at Queen Elizabeth's Richmond Palace, and forgotten by all except this manor's architect, who had engineered for all waste to empty into shallow underground metal cisterns, thus protecting the aquifer, which were periodically dug up, and carted away, and emptied at sea.

Less royal, but similarly inventive, was the décor throughout the house: carved lion masks and acanthus scrolls, caryatids and modern parquetry, rich-dyed Chinese silk carpets, wool stuffed pictorial Italian lounging couches, a modern harp and an antique French spinet—both prominently displayed in the parlor, but never played. And each room was so riddled with fine-cast iron fireplaces sporting picaresque hearth-plates and mantles that the rooftop sprouted chimneys.

For two days now, the household staff (comprised of an immigrant English family, previously underlings on an English Dorsetshire estate) had been working their hands to blister preparing the house and commons, even seeding the front carriage way with mica to give the gravel extra sparkle. This father, mother, two young adult sons, a half-pint lad, and a marriageable-aged daughter had been hired here three years ago on a seven-year indenture: the father to oversee the livery, grounds, and stores; the older sons to serve as butlers, boot- and saddle-blacks, grooms, gamekeepers, foremen, drivers—whatever was required—with their little brother of ten a go-between; the mother served as "Cook" and sometimes housekeeper, her daughter was kitchen assistant and the mistress' lady's maid—both were adept seamstresses and flatterers.

Like most of their region's ilk, they put aside all that they earned toward the purchase of a farm of their own. Burning new moon candles thirteen times a year, praying for this current employer to settle a parcel of land on them at the completion of their contract, because Lord Dorset had not, and fertile freeholds in this *new* Essex County were rapidly growing in value.

The cornucopia poured out beyond the lime-brick, as well, into formal Old World gardens lined with braided privet shrubberies, a sitting terrace enclosed by boxwoods sheltered by a vine-latticed roof, an ambulatory leading down to a rose garden (soon to bud) and to numerous other natural bowers that were home to nestling songbirds, and myriad pesky ones. Because these lawns were themselves a rich home to abundant worms and held promise of a dark green velvet carpet come spring from all the imported English grass seed these "gardeners" had recently planted. But the most favorite garden of the mistress were her cultivated flowerbeds encircling the house, which emitted enough scent in spring to enflame a thousand upturned nostrils.

The indentures, although they'd planted the gardens, envied only the farm tracts, fruit and syrup orchards, dairy and double-sized stable with gated paddocks and rolling pastures where superior livestock grazed. Of course, they also admired the large brick carriage house set along the stable lane, where lodged a never-used six-seat four-horse contraption along with smaller agile chariots. And where also, on the second storey, parked this serving family.

A broad bend of the Frost Fish River served as the property's western boundary. There a commercial gristmill had been built the same year as the house; but the brewery beside it was established years later. While on the eastern Salem Town side, the boundary boasted a profitable ironworks. All of the house's fireplaces, festoons, mantles, grates, cisterns, pipes and gates had been designed by its artisans, smelted, forged, cast and hammered there. And there were also numerous day laborers: toilers, drudges, men, women and children, who commuted on foot or by cart from nearby villages and towns, a few came from as far away as Salem Town, a distance of thirty miles, to work the farm and factories. But none came from Salem Village.

Because Mary Veren Putnam, mistress of Putnam Estate, for the sake of large ears, refused to hire any of her workers from Salem Village.

17

THIS MISTRESS OF PUTNAM ESTATE HAD, ABOUT two hours ago along with her son, arrived home from attending spiritual service at Salem Town Church. She came directly to the kitchen to view the meal preparations and to order a hot bath be drawn. She progressed from there up to her chamber to refresh, and later, to exchange that coarse-cloth plain Sabbath Day dress for fancy cavalier attire. Guests were expected.

And now, as she stepped out onto the upstairs landing, she wore an elegant scooped-neck gown of violet-colored silk covered with silver-threaded pillow lace and cinched at the waist by a tight velvet girdle. Her white-poached raven hair, that earlier had been pinned up in a modest bun and capped, was unfurled with the ends curled and frizzed. The rest was raised up in a delicate tulle veil, with two knit-lace lappets hanging down at the sides, skirting her gold dangling earrings. Her lady's maid was as inventive with hairdos as she was with ornaments: and the final touch sat pinned prominently at the powdered crease of her buttressed cleavage. A large obsidian and river-pearl brooch set in Spanish coin gold, which she'd designed to emphasize that her breasts were also still pert and eager for display; but only, of course, in *private* company.

Despite a fair assortment of wrinkles, frown-lines and two dappled farthing-sized spots on one cheek, Mary Veren Putnam knew she still possessed strong remnants of the striking natural beauty that had hooked her late husband.

The Afflicted Girls

A portrait of him was hanging on the wall and as she descended the staircase now she glanced down at it, and suddenly slipped. And if she hadn't been clutching the banister then, she'd have reunited with Thomas Putnam, Sr. in Heaven. Ignoring her heart's palpitations, she lifted up her hoopskirt to observe her injury, and grimaced. One of her brand-new square-toed French shoes, with green ribbon rose-knots sewn to the instep and high spiny-heels, which had clacked so elegantly on the walnut wood just now as she was descending, was ruined. She had broken a heel and almost her neck.

She fled upstairs to exchange the pair; and returning, ordered her husband's portrait be moved to a different wall.

Thomas Putnam, Sr. had been a widower with nearly grown children when he met young Mary Veren while on a business trip to Salem Town. He was past fifty, she was not yet seventeen, but he was the one smitten like a youth. It was love at first sight for him, but love *never* on her part. It was expensive gifts, family entreaties, and her own high ambition that finally persuaded her to marry him, old and unappealing as he was. Through her will's assertion, she knew she could make her body tolerate anything. She'd already had one lover (although her parents didn't know this and gave Putnam assurances that the prize was his). But that handsome neighborhood rogue was poor and she soon lost interest. Her curiosity, at least, had been amply satisfied.

When her rich spouse brought her home to Putnam Farm, his three offspring, hardly older than she, instantly resented her. But they grew to despise her, when she began to rule their father's affection to such a degree he barely noticed them, or ever mentioned their dead mother's name anymore.

For the first eight years of marriage, Mary took the midwifery precaution in secret. But by age twenty-six, when fertility was said to wane, and also out of boredom, she began to long for a child and willingly gave that besotted old goat a son in his late age, a boy as beautiful as his namesake "Joseph," the name reserved by Puritans for late-in-life miracle children. She was smitten now, too.

And now came her insistence that her baby son be raised a gentryman from his first gurgle to his grave, unlike the common farmer her husband's firstborn had been born, and was. She wrote this promissory into a contract and made old Putnam sign it, although he couldn't see the point. Throughout their long years together, she continued exacting promises through contracts. The manor, mill, foundry, brewery, all had been her ideas originally, and later demands. "Too expensive! I'll be bankrupt!" Putnam would bray. She'd simply deny him her wifely favors until he agreed. His lust yielded to her every time. Her lust was for money—she was fonder of wealth than she was of her own husband. But he wasn't so different in type to her. He was more attached to beauty than he was to his own children—the first three, that is. Much like Jacob, patriarch of old, he was wildly devoted to his youngest son, Joseph.

Despite that Mary never possessed real property or money of her own during married life, she never once succumbed to worry. Not even when her husband died and her stepchildren danced on his grave and then sued to reclaim their portions; because she was informed enough to know that Commonwealth laws favored the current wife, the widow, over a prior family. That her twenty-seven years of marriage would weigh more on the scales of inheritance than his first wife's twenty. In fact, would weigh *all* to *naught*.

Manipulative by her nature, Mary was in fine form today, standing in front of her gilt-framed vestibule mirror now, primping with her hair and lappets, while quibbling with her son's reflection: "This betrothal will enhance your status. The Porters have influence in the Commonwealth and prestige abroad."

"No influence in my commons," declared Joseph flatly, from his chair against the wall behind her.

"Their daughter is of good pedigree. She's wealthy, pretty. I see no reason to reject her."

"She's dull, witless, and too young for my taste. I don't love her. I dislike her, in fact. More than I dislike marriage. Are those reasons enough?"

A titter masked displeasure. *Petulant.* Her son didn't even know the Porters really. Nor this persuasive fact: "But it was your father who handpicked the little maid for you, as once he chose me for himself."

"The dead do not choose or pick, Mother."

She suddenly noticed an imperfection and glided back to straighten Joseph's cravat and adjust that one epaulet that was sitting slightly askew. She saw how threads were coming loose. But there wasn't time to call her maid to fix it. Thinking that, she happed to glance back into the mirror at the two of them standing so close, and realized that they could almost be the young couple themselves; her eyes had begun to lose their sharpness. Returning to her perch, she offered her son this: "A girl this young and innocent is usually judged a gift by a man—" she had leaned in to wipe the glass, and discovered that the smudge was on her cheek: a beauty mark her maid had poorly painted, which she'd somehow, in these three minutes, smeared. She frowned, dabbing with the corner of a lace pocket kerchief; sighing, when her effort proved fruitless. She wiped the mark off.

During her husband's final illness, during the deathwatch especially, and continuing on through the stepchildren's rebellion, she'd grown increasingly pale till her cheeks looked drained and bloodless. So she'd taken to wearing a manufactured color. Luckily, she kept some in this drawer. As she dabbed: "Her purity enables us to shape her the way we want. She will be the perfect companion for you. I will see to it myself." She had missed her son's transition from boy into man and was curious to elicit his secrets. "This resistance you feel is natural though. Know that I felt it, too. Discover as I did, long ago, how preference disappears as soon as appetite awakens in a marriage bed . . . I ask only that you consider the girl."

"And I ask for a halt to this annoyance! I've drunk enough good wine to know I will spit this one out!"

Ah . . . she had thought so. So she would need to use a different tact, and chided: "But it is God Himself who has created man to marry. Conjugality is of the natural order, Joseph. Not only is it His Ordinance, it is a duty to one's family. As I am your only parent now, and care only for your happiness, you will acquiesce to my wish."

The Afflicted Girls

18

THE PORTER FAMILY'S ROLL-TOP BRIGHT PAINTED calash drove in through that spiked-iron front-gate, its breezy dappled horse trotting up that pebbly manor drive that glistened especially for them; but no one in the carriage noticed. Pulling to a halt, Israel Porter got down now and handed a manservant his reins. Then quickly proceeded to the other side to help his portly wife down, lest she land wrong and injure an ankle—a not-infrequent mishap. As soon as Lizzie Porter was safely grounded, their pretty slip of a daughter—sixteen years old Elizabeth—hopped out on her own. Still, he caught her up in and twirled her round, delighting in her peeling laughter.

Mary, who was watching them through her front bay window from behind a damask curtain, thought how if her husband had resembled Israel Porter even a mote when they'd first met—graying so handsomely at fifty-three, and so playful— she might have been a more satisfied wife. *Israel would have been happier, too. A pity. The fool should have courted me, not Lizzie.* She called out to Joseph that their guests had arrived.

Coming outside, after greetings were exchanged, Mary suggested an amble down through her gardens because of the pleasant weather. Joseph preferred a hike up to his stables, which Israel Porter readily agreed to because he didn't know this boy as yet, although he'd known the father quite well. He was hoping for a private conversation. Mary made effort to keep up with the men's brisk pace, despite being shod in dainty shoes, but poor overweight Lizzie Porter just could not manage it and grew so winded within minutes, she nearly collapsed. When she begged to rest, the men moved on without them. Mary brought her old friend to a bench, who fanned and caught her breath, while she reached out for the daughter's hands to study her more circumspectly. And she noticed now, where she never had before: "You closely resemble your mother as a girl. Did you know that, Elizabeth?" (The girl blushed and looked at her mother, who nodded.) "And this pretty cornflower blue dress perfectly suits your eyes."

The girl's dull brown eyes lit up. "It's a Parisian style, Mary. Mother had it made for me in Boston."

Lizzie stopped fanning and now whistled through a missing bicuspid, a little shamefaced, "Oh Mary, do not begrudge me. But I have hired a Bosss-ton dress-sssmaker once-sss of the French Court in-ssstead of him you urged for my girl's trousss-seau." She proudly grinned at her frilly daughter.

Mary cared nothing for the history of the dress, but did suddenly consider an old friend's rind-skin, flab, rotted teeth, clumsy carriage, shortness of breath, and annoying lisp of import. *Would this daughter inherit these traits? Even more, would offspring of the match?* She remembered, of course, how her old friend Lizzie Hathorne had once been deemed the foremost beauty in their Salem Town circle, and was even more admired than was she— having been a very pretty maid *with* a fortune. *But weathering the years so badly . . . resembling a barrel, more than the perfume flask she once was?* Mary shuddered. Nonetheless, she had to admit, her girlhood friend was ever as cheerful.

After sipping cordials in the parlor, the families progressed to the dining hall, where overhead candelabras were lit despite the day-brightness of the room.

The Afflicted Girls

Mary tried to hide her irritation that the draperies were not drawn, as she ushered each to a specific chair, her son particularly. Lizzie remarked effusively about this impeccably set damask-covered table decorated with an ornate silver epergne and garniture holding a bouquet of pink silk handmade roses set amid twelve slender foot-long tapers—which weren't yet lit! Excusing herself, Mary went and rang a rope bell to summon her wayward servant. Then she again took her seat beside Lizzie, and resumed listening to babble.

Formal white St. Cloud porcelain, silver goblets, and utensils, were lying beside each plate. A spoon, a knife, and the recently invented curved four-tined fork. Silver toothpicks, the final touch, cast in the shape of a rearing stallion, were meant as a token for Joseph in honor of his betrothal, which she'd designed herself for his Putnam family crest. And although the Porters didn't know this, only Europe's nobility possessed authentic Chinese porcelain, so these plates were imitations but they were not inexpensive, having been purchased through a London fine goods merchant from a famous French factory for a sizeable sum.

When no response came to her summons, Mary left to search the butler herself. And now, following in after her, that awkward liveried fellow carried in a large soup tureen, which he set down on the sideboard. He quickly pulled the draperies closed and lit all twelve tapers, and the room glowed as intended.

Simmering creamy lobster bisque was served, while Mary steamed now because her son was sitting apart from the girl, having moved from where she'd put him. Leaning into Lizzie's ear she whispered loudly enough for that petulant son to hear: "My mind is settled . . . an important minister will perform the marriage blessing . . . one of the Mathers."

Lizzie gazed across the flickering garniture at her daughter's handsome prospect. "Oh, which Mather, Mary?"

Lifting her napkin to her lips, Mary scolded, "My words are meant only for your ears. Be discreet."

"*Sss*-sorry, *sss*-so *sss*-sorry," stuttered the sibilant.

"The father, if he returns before summer begins. Otherwise, the son."

"Oh, either is my choic-*ssse*, also," whistled Lizzie, while chewing on a large knob of lobster. "My husband's, too. We *esss*-teem the Mathers of Boston."

Israel, hearing his name uttered, cast a questioning glance across the table at his wife, who didn't notice because now she was navigating her next overflowing spoonful. He watched a large chunk fall from his wife's spoon. He winced when Lizzie speared it with her toothpick from her lap and popped it into her mouth.

As Lizzie was swallowing, Mary leaned in to that bulbous ear again, and whispered (for this was the purpose for her dinner — these arrangements): "And for the wedding feast, I plan to hold a proper ball in High Anglican fashion, with musicians and dancing. Would *that* be offensive to Israel?"

Lizzie covered her mouth with her napkin — to be discreet. "Oh no, Mary, no, my husband is modern in his thinking. He would not object." She added, "Did I ever tell you my *sss*-secret desire *sss*-since girlhood was to dance ju*ssst* once-*sss* at a ball? And now I shall at my own daughter's wedding!"

"*Sss*-so many times, dear Lizzie, hopefully this will be the end of it."

Meanwhile across the table, that other attempt at conversation was proving equally futile for Israel Porter, despite the stunning news he'd brought, and saved till now for a toast. He cleared his throat and repeated: "John Hathorne of Salem Town, as I said, is the judge appointed to hear your brother's lawsuit. He is also my goodwife's uncle. She is his favorite niece. He has told me there is no need for you to settle. That your sibling's suit is frivolous and will soon be dismissed." Again, he waited for a comment from Joseph. *Doesn't the boy care? The matter could not have concluded any better.* He held up his glass of port. "I drink to your victory and success, Joseph." He drank alone. Then he, too, turned back to his bisque.

All this while, young Elizabeth Porter was quietly sipping her creamy soup, careful not to spill any on her new French frock. No one at the table paid any attention to her, least of all Joseph Putnam.

But a saving grace was near, cantering across a hillside.

After losing his fifth game at stakes and bowls up at the militia camp after church, he was riding home with empty pockets. So either to cheer himself, or because he was starved, Ben Nurse was suddenly seized by a hungry urge to pay a certain Sunday dinner visit. It had been four years since he'd last tasted the excellent table-fare at Putnam Estate. So he swerved his nag in a new direction; because Joseph had promised to sit a Sunday meal at Orchard Farm, and though his friend hadn't yet come, he decided he'd likewise be invited. (This was about the time a final chunk of cream-drenched lobster was being fished out from Lizzie Porter's bowl, correctly this time with her fork.)

He spied the wrought iron manor gate in the distance (about the time Cook finished cleaving her thick cuts of roasted veal off that juicy carcass--cuts, which her artistic daughter then arranged on a great silver salver to be pleasing to her mistress' eye. Where already were assembled a flock of bread-dressed pheasants on a lawn of leafy greens, surrounded by colorful hill mounds of buttery mashed squashes dotted with hothouse trees of green bean and slivered carrot, bushes of braised mushroom, and small white potato boulders, not to mention the perfect miniature-sized animal creatures she'd weaved from straw—food, as a sylvan scene.)

He was, of course, imagining a much poorer feast, albeit a good one, when he yanked open that tall dining hall door, explaining how he'd called out several times from the entranceway but that no one came out to greet him. He forgot to take off his Sunday triangle cap while wishing them all a "Good Sabbath. But at least he did properly wait to be invited to the table, crossing his fingers inside pockets, that it would be to that empty chair beside the pretty girl.

The Afflicted Girls

19

IN SALEM VILLAGE EVERY SUNDAY AFTER SERVICE whenever the weather was mild, like today, villagers would gather on the green to meander and socialize.

The men would immediately head off to Ingersoll's Inn to talk politics and imbibe spirits. Their goodwives would stroll the village byways in arm-linked companies, or sit on park benches, or recline on their spread-out capes on the green to besmirch and besmear a least-favorite neighbor. Their children would cavort and play permitted games (though not too energetically, in respect for the Sabbath): stool ball, wickets, hoops, hide-seek, Scotch-hoppers, squat-tag, leapfrog, London Bridge, and riddles.

> *My house is not quiet, and I am not loud.*
> *God fashioned our fate together. I am the*
> *swifter, and at times the stronger. At other*
> *times, I rest but my dwelling still runs.*
> *Should we two be severed, my death is for*
> *certain. What am I?*

"A fish!" one clever tyke guessed rightly.

And the elder siblings, who were meant to be watching those youngsters, were instead sneaking off in pairs or clusters to flirt gill-fully behind trees, some even to kiss or peck. Sundays were their only chance to intermingle and they took good advantage.

Poor Lucy Putnam wasn't playing or flirting. She was wedged on the flagpole bench between her two lanky aunts, who cited her weak lungs as the reason. In Sister Ann's infirmity, they had volunteered to keep a watchful eye on their brother's children, while he was up at Ingersoll's discussing politics with their husbands. (In truth, Thomas had wanted his wife Ann to attend today's service, and she had seemed almost willing on yester-night. But this morning, she staunchly refused, insisting that a cruel stigma was upon her, not explaining how her breasts were still filled with nursing milk, and she feared folk noticing wet stains on her garment. So her family went to worship without her.)

Mercy was grateful for her Sunday's reprieve, a few free hours each week in which to stroll the village byways to learn better the lay of the place, and to view local wares in shop windows, a favorite pastime. Spying some unusual rush weaves through the basket maker's shop window now, her quick mind began duplicating patterns. And here, Susanna Walcott accosted her.

"What business have you with Joseph Putnam?" that girl was rudely demanding, while peering in also through that pane, but seeing nothing but empty baskets.

Recalling Susanna's temperament, Mercy wove an appropriate response. "After our coach crashed in a wilderness, and we feared for our lives and prayed, by God's protection two strangers appeared. They saved us, and brought us here, Susanna. One was your uncle. I had hoped to thank him for that kindness, that was all."

Susanna considered this. It was a reasonable explanation, one she had no reason to doubt. For all knew that story. And of course, she would much rather be milling on the green with her own friends than correcting an uncle's nettlesome servant. But she had to correct her, since no one else would. "Well you had better *not* thank one of those strangers, nor give him any worth at all. From today my uncle Joseph Putnam is to receive only your scorn!" Seeing Mercy flinch, "Yes, scorn. Scorn, I say! Scorn! He's despicable! Detestable! A cur! But *you* obviously do not think so."

Mercy treaded carefully. "I think nothing about the man. I do not know him. Having met him only once. Could I judge anything?"

"But in that *once*, you judged him to be *kind!* Not only kind, also *handsome!* Deny it, and lie!"

Any words she chose now, Mercy knew, would be twisted against her, and against him. So she turned back to the basket maker's window and resumed twisting straws.

Susanna did not relent: "Handsome is as handsome does! Underneath his is snakeskin . . . inhuman flesh rotted to the core! We curse him and hate him and all want him dead! As you are my uncle's servant now, you must you!"

Mercy shuddered, *to feel so much hatred as to wish death on a person?* Not even—*no.* She turned. "Take back your curse, Susanna. No good can come from hatred ever. A family quarrel can in time be set right. But a life once ended can never be--"

"It was no quarrel! He robbed us! He stabbed us in the heart! You are taking *his* side I see!"

"No side. None. I know nothing of what happened. I spoke only as an orphan, who every day and every night prays her own family was alive again, and all that they suffered only a dream. I've begged Time to go backwards and undo my sorrows, though I know it can never be. I've been robbed, just like you, Susanna. I, too, have been stabbed through the heart." She turned away to press her forehead to the glass, closing her eyes now and succumbing to deep-set sorrow.

Susanna suddenly felt ashamed. Today was the Sabbath Day, a sacred day for making amends and granting forgiveness. She'd followed this orphaned girl here deliberately, intending to provoke her. That was wrong of her, wasn't it? She shuffled foot to foot, trying to think of something appeasing now to say. "Well, I suppose, since you live with my Uncle Thomas, and will for a time, I can tell you what happened."

She related how Joseph Putnam's mother had forged her grandfather's will and made him sign it when his wits were gone and he lay dying. "Uncle Putnam, Aunt Trask, my mother inherited five shillings apiece! Not sovereigns even! Shillings! His own first three children! And the grandchildren got nothing! Nothing!" She winced back her own bitter tears now, and swallowed a throaty sob. "They took the money, the lands, the livestock . . . all the farm tools, carriages and work wagons . . . the finest house in all of Essex County with furnishings from England and foreign places. They left nothing for us. Nothing! Not even a salt spoon! They even kept my granny's pretty pearly hairpins that were promised to me her first granddaughter!"

Mercy set aside her own sorrow now and reached for Susanna's hand. "I'm sorry, Susanna, so sorry to hear this. Truly, I understand." Of course, she understood how crippling a burden of poverty was for a young girl with dreams.

Susanna recoiled, her face twisted and she spat: "Our step-grandmother Mary Veren Putnam is a *witch!* She made a bargain with the Devil to make her son rich! Joseph Putnam is second richest now! But when he marries Elizabeth Porter, as he will, he'll be the richest!" thrusting deep her dagger of family rumor into Mercy's already sore heart.

The Afflicted Girls

Hang up the hooks and shears to scare
The hag who rides the Devil's mare.
Till she be all over wet with
Fright's Mire and sweat.
This observed, your house shall be
Ever free of iniquity.

A witch-warding charm

20

TITUBA WAS CROUCHED, RAKING HER RED CAKES from the ashes, when her ear cocked suddenly. Her hearing, like all of her senses, was keen as a wild beast's. She shoved them back under, plunked herself into the hearth chair, picking up her bowl. And now Mrs. Parris stomped in, followed by her daughter and the ward. The girls undid their capes and caps and hung them onto pegs. But the mistress kept hers tied as she strode up to the hearth to poke the roast pig with a kindling twig. Tituba, nonchalantly shelling peas now, looked up, "Be a juicy one, Missus."

"Crank it round. I want to see if it's evenly crusted."

As the slave did this, Mrs. Parris noticed scores of cloves stuck into that glistening skin. And immediately, she deemed the pig ruined—because while her husband liked his pork sharp-flavored she couldn't tolerate that taste. And Tituba had certainly known how queasy her stomach had been this morning. There'd been no instruction to spice the meat, had there? No, there hadn't.

But now she recalled the instruction that *had* been given— how this pig was being cooked for Reverend Parris, not for her. So with a begrudging sigh, she only ordered the dripping pan emptied.

As Tituba crouched over to pick it up, she was eerily silhouetted by embers and small flames: the thick plait hanging down her back, red burnished skin, high cheekbones and jutting forehead. That unexpected vision evoked in Abigail a horror long buried:

> *A log cabin on the Maine frontier ablaze in a rain of fire arrows, her mother, younger siblings, running from it screaming, with hems, aprons, sleeves ablaze, her father rushing over to the trough to scoop buckets of water to douse them. Nervously pointing a loaded musket as the war-painted brave, hatchet raised and fiercely whooping, rode him down. Him not firing, not defending, but sinking fast to his knees and closing his eyes in cowardly submission, letting that Indian slice his scalp.*

Then, the worst image of all:

> *Her mother scrambling for that dropped firearm. Spearing first her children, then shooting her own self.*

She had been spared. The savages didn't see her high above them in the branches of her favorite climbing tree. She watched the massacre till her house had burnt to cinder. Still stared long after the heathens rode off with "Good Jack" their plough horse, and cow "Moody," and all their sheep and chickens. But she couldn't watch when buzzards and crows came to feast on the bodies. She had just turned seven, was a contented, happy kind-hearted girl, intelligent, dutiful, her mother's most thoughtful, her father's delight. She vomited all that night and cried, but stayed up in her tree for two days longer. On the third morning, after a doe with a fawn ambled by at dawn and no evil thing killed them, she climbed down and drank from the trough. Her father's andirons, stood unscathed. So she dragged them down the familiar lane to the neighbor's farm. But she found only the dead there, too. And ever more she traveled the pathway through life: unfamiliar, unfair, always friendless . . . and forevermore *un-forgiven.*

The Afflicted Girls

A blaring, coarse female voice startled Abigail back to her senses. "Charity! Give me Sabbath Day charity!" She whirled around to see a hag-like beggar of uncertain age standing just outside the door—an unkempt, pockmarked woman, who was smoking a man's pipe and had a dirty ragamuffin child of four with her. She was intrigued.

Mrs. Parris kept her distance for obvious reasons: malodor, infestation, a taint of smallpox, saying coolly from her pinched insect lips: "I didn't see you at service today, Sarah Good. Why didn't you come to church?"

"Need food an' a roof. Don't need no church-going," the beggar mumbled.

The parsonness frowned. *What you need is to clean yourself for pity's sake, and scrub this sore and louse ridden child!* "Forsaking the Covenant of Worship displeases God. Let me remind you of that, Sarah Good, since it's said you were better born."

"Then better *not* to have been born I say! Nobody's business if I say my commandments in private. Alls I'm asking is Christian charity for a hungry tyke. Give it or don't, missus, I need no lectures from you."

Mrs. Parris would have liked to slam her door at such insolence, but instead she instructed Tituba—for this was a duty no parsonness could shirk: "Give her the morning scraps."

Sarah Good frowned. Her mouth was watering for pork! Walking up, she'd whiffed that delicious meat cooking. Instead, she'd be given the pig's slop? *Blood in your bladder, miserly missus! Mouthful o' bile!* These were the same unsavory curses she left at all unfriendly doors. And to add to the insult for good measure here, she spat out a wad of yellow phlegm onto the parsonage threshold.

Mrs. Parris began to gag, her head jerked sideways; she covered her mouth. But she refused to regurgitate in front of such a person. So she swallowed the bitter vomit back down.

Tituba, meanwhile, took the beggar's pail and scraped in the leftover gruel.

When the beggar first appeared, Betty Parris had run over to the mending basket, rummaged through, and came happily toward her mother, wondering: "Can I give this dress to Dorcas Good?"

Mrs. Parris looked the garment over. Worn, faded, frayed, obviously much too small to fit her daughter anymore, yet it was useful as a rag. *Parsimony is a virtue,* she considered, judging the beggar child as also too small for this dress. *But charity is a greater one.* "All right, daughter. But let Tituba hand it."

The beggar's daughter, Dorcas Good, upon receiving her *charity,* sent the minister's daughter a timid smile. At that, an equally shy minister's daughter, Betty Parris, grinned back full. Both were thinking the same thought just then: how nice it would be to play together, for neither played much with other children.

Goody Good pushed her daughter out of her way to receive her pail, because she'd seen just now how when the mistress was examining the dress, the slave sneakily ladled in some pork grease and slipped in a raw potato and an egg then buried them underneath the gruel. (Tituba had intended to give the stale loaf, too, but as she was sidling toward the bread-bin Mrs. Parris looked up and wagged a finger.)

Sunday pail in hand, after sneering at its contents and at the parsonness, when Sarah Good turned to go a bulge in her midriff caused Mrs. Parris to later sputter:

"Did you see that? Did you see? That hussy derelict is with child again, when she can't even feed the one she's got! A widow to boot! Oh I swear, with God as a witness, she's a blight on my husband's parish!" She now informed them that she was going to visit a sick parishioner. "Goody Ruth Osborne, in case Mr. Parris asks." She instructed Tituba: "Have the girls do their Bible lesson. The meal must be ready upon my return. If we're out of port, send

The Afflicted Girls

John to Goody Ingersoll to plead an occasion." She nearly stepped into Sarah Good's spit, but caught herself in time, and hopped over. "And clean up this filth before anything else."

After her mistress stomped off, Tituba kicked up a little dirt on the threshold and then sauntered back to her lazy chair and bowl of winter peas. But Betty clung to the doorjamb, watching until her mother had entirely huffed across the green and exited the village gate, and also disappeared around the first bend. Then she came scooting back to Tituba to climb up into that familiar soft lap to be rocked, cuddled, and cooed to, saying as she snuggled in: "I wish *you* were my mama."

Abigail laughed outright.

Tituba looked pleased though scolded, "Oh, naw. Don' say such'a thing, Bett-pet. I's jus' yer Tituba. Wants 'ta help me shell peas?" Betty nodded; she loved shelling peas. And Tituba loved Betty.

"What about our Bible lesson?" Abigail reminded.

The slave shrugged at the spoilsport. "S'upt to you. Me an' Betty won' say nuthin'."

Needless to say, the girls didn't do their Bible lessons today. Abigail sat cross-legged at Tituba's feet, nibbling soaked peas, bored to perdition, while Betty nested in that loveseat lulled. Until Abigail asked: "You're from Barbados, aren't you?"

"Sorta," mumbled Tituba.

The girl's eyes narrowed, "Well you and John Indian better not try to murther us in our sleep like the slaves there just did to their masters!"

"Who sez?"

"The men were talking about it after service. There's been a revolt in Barbados. They said that a mob of Jamestown slaves rose up and cut their masters' throats." She poked her cousin to get her attention, and when she had it, she drew a finger across her neck.

Tituba scolded, "Hush bad girl, stoppit. You be scarin' my Betty." Tituba lifted that trembling child's chin, and looked her in the eye. "Don' you b'lieve tha' Abby, pet, she juz makin' miz'chief. My Barbados be'a sunny place, a happy place . . . juz like Para'dize. Me an' John be singin' all day long—"

"You be sinnin' not singin'!" Abigail accused, mocking the slave's lazy speech. "Voodoo'n! Wakin' the dead!" She pinched her cousin's leg. "Her an' John be doin' that, too!"

And now, a long tongue of flame shot out from the fire, singeing the back of her hand. She grabbed the iron poker and angrily beat that offending log till, with a final defiant shudder, it crumbled into ember.

Meantime, Tituba's worried eyes darted through the ash. "Don't know nuthin' 'bout such things, me an' John's Christian. We wuz bab'tized by the master."

Now Abigail had long prided herself on being a clever snoop. Through her long lonely years, it had been a matter of survival. She laid down the poker and licked her smarting burn. "Go fetch more firewood, Good Christian. This fire's dying."

"Don't need 'nother log. Pig's done roastin'."

"But you haven't done the baking yet!" Abigail barked. "You'll need wood for that, won't you?"

"John'll get it, miss."

"But I ordered *you* to! An' I is *miz-tress* till my aunt returns!"

Tituba set down her bowl, and pet, got up from her chair and went to the woodlot, with Betty following, because that child was too afraid to remain alone with her cousin.

From the doorway, Abigail watched till they'd reached the barn. Then she ran to the hearth and quickly raked those suspect ashes underneath the fenders. Numerous red patty-cakes were unearthed, but she attempted to take only one, burning her fingertips in the process, but a sting hardly felt in the wake of such a discovery! She wrapped the cake with a rag and stuffed it into her pocket, and now got another one, and wrapped it too. Quickly now, she whisked the hearth clean of ash; of course, raking the other cakes back under until nothing red was visible. "Sure as *Hell* slaves can *spell*. But thank Heaven they *do not count!*" Her rare, three-sided pun spawned a conceited giggle. And then she realized that because both her hand and fingertips *smarted,* it was really the unheard of four-sided pun!

When Tituba and Betty returned with their arms full of chopped wood, Abigail was sitting quietly at the table, scrutinizing her catechism.

But Tituba knew. *"Nother storm comin'."*

21

HOW MANY TIMES DID MRS. PARRIS PRAISE GOD for today's fine weather? Many, very many; and each time the sun, in response, shone brighter on her face.

As usual, rides were offered from parishioners heading home, but she waved all wagons past. Her long walk on Sundays was her cherished "alone-time," and her step usually reflected her mood. Today it was high and bright like sol, and purposeful like her husband's sermon had been. She felt no fear, whatsoever, walking alone on these narrow unguarded lanes, and not merely for the Lord's constant watchfulness. Long before her arrival here three years ago from the city, most of Essex County was widely civilized. Ever since then, a steady stream of immigrant folk had increased their parish count two-fold, although not all were churchgoers to her liking. Nevertheless, because of it, someone was always about on these shady lanes.

But she knew that had she lived even a half-day's distance to the north, she'd not be enjoying solitary Sunday walks. For in those lesser settled parts, angry heathens still lived naked under trees and were often spurred to do evil by their spirits or the Devil's French — to murder, plunder, capture, torture, and even rape . . . devout Christian women. *Thank God there are no Frenchmen here!* She turned her mind from that unpleasantness back to their benefactress. That person she was on her way to see.

The Afflicted Girls

'Goody *Rich* Osborne,' as local Goodwife Sarah Ruth Osborne was snidely renamed by Salem Village youngsters and their envious parents, was one of Reverend Parris' most esteemed parishioners. Not only for her piety in the Covenant, as much for her generosity with the goodly sums she'd inherited from two deceased well-off husbands. Nearly sixty years of age now, husband-less and childless of her loins, she suffered a severe physical affliction. But fortunately, she did not live alone. A manservant—an industrious Irish immigrant jack-of-all-trades with muscled arms, a pleasing smile, and a willing spirit—dwelled with her at her cottage now. And this dowager could not have survived without him.

In years past whenever the air chilled in autumn and the frosty rains began, she would suffer her usual bout of seasonal neuralgia; but this year it progressed into a permanent disability. Pain riddled her limbs whenever she stood her full weight upon them. It was impossible for her to walk more than a few steps, even with two canes, no less sit on a hard church pew for three hours, or a soft carriage cushion for twenty minutes. Thus, she'd been unable to attend Reverend Parris' Sunday services or Thursday lectures for the past four months. And her heart, bedridden at home, was truly sore for it.

So Mrs. Parris made it her particular mission of charity to pay this invalid a regular weekly visit—to bring Ruth Osborne the good news of her husband's Sunday sermon, to provide some sisterly companionship, and of course, to collect the minister's tithe, which otherwise might be forfeit or delayed.

First, she would read aloud from Ruth's well-thumbed Bible propounding the text's inner meaning, grateful for this opportunity to express her own unique insight to another thoughtful soul. For this rare opportunity to enlighten another of like mind had not occurred for her since her girlhood in Boston, where she was encouraged to theologize freely and was regularly invited into her father's popular sitting parlor to debate with the divinity students. But that was more than twenty years ago within the liberal umbra of Harvard Square. At home now, in the parsonage, she was expected only to listen.

She had been visiting Ruth for about an hour, which by the garden sundial was after two o'clock. And she knew that soon Ruth's manservant would be carrying in refreshments, and that after she partook of a few polite sips and bites, she'd be handed the donation for Reverend Parris. "And they brought unto Him all sick people that were taken with divers diseases and torments--"She had been reading this same passage for three weeks, as it was currently Ruth's favorite. "And those which were possessed with devils, and those which were lunatic, and those that had the palsy, and He healed them--"

But after her run-in with the beggar this morning, her stomach had again soured. And even reading these inspiring words didn't heal a single cramp. Dare she ask for the donation now? *Certainly not! Do not even think of it, Elizabeth Parris! Derelicts and barn-dwellers beg. Not ministers' wives. Not ever!* Nor would she ever ask to use the privy.

The teapot tray with its basket of fresh-baked scones spread thick with maple butter was brought in. And as Ruth's manservant set it down atop the small round table where she and Ruth's Bible were sitting, he accidentally brushed her knee. She continued in her recital without pause, though she did scantly blush. All in the village had heard the prurient rumors.

Of course, she had put on her muffs to them, though not her blinders. He wasn't as handsome as Mr. Parris, but he did have a certain type of countenance which was welcome to a woman's eye, even hers. And clearly to Ruth's; that woman positively fawned. He was brawny, somewhat younger than her spouse, about thirty-two years of age she would guess. Not educated or quick-witted, but hard working and respectful. She was pleased that this invalid parishioner had found a reliable man for chores.

And now as they nibbled, Ruth disclosed a secret: "Keep this under your bonnet, Elizabeth. But I allow my Irishman to keep a third share of all proceeds from syrup kegs he sells at market."

Mrs. Parris did a mental calculation. *But that is many times what you tithe to Reverend Parris!* The very thought was unsetting. All the good cheer she'd felt was erased. Yet, she responded warmly, because she had to: "Charity is always rewarded from on High." It was a hint. Yes, a hint! *Stingy Osborne, you hussy!* The market price of syrup was soaring. She, herself, could not afford to purchase any. And rarely, if ever, was that sweetening tithed, certainly never by Ruth. Of course she'd relish a syrup keg for her own kitchen. But could she mention it to Ruth to be embarrassed for its lack? *Never. Never! She was no beggar!* So she nibbled her sweet scone in silence, while her liver churned out sour thoughts.

While the invalid's own thoughts turned to her favorite chore of her servant's, that unmentionable one, which was her *real* reward on Sundays. Superior to sugar maples, inspirational friends, hot buttered scones, and nearly equal to inheritances: her weekly Sunday buttering by him!

Meanwhile, down in the kitchen that Irishman was thinking how for the sake of the extra coinage he got, he could abide this employer a while longer. He'd already picked out a market wench to marry, and given her a few tumbles to try her out, and deciding he liked her, a few trinkets he'd found lying about the cottage.

Sadly, as generous lonely women of withered beauty often do, Ruth was planning to tie the silk knot on him herself.

SUZY WITTEN

They go astray as soon as they are born. They no sooner step than they stray, no sooner lisp than they lie. Satan gets them to be proud, profane, reviling and revengeful, as young as they are.

Instructions to Parents,
Reverend Cotton Mather

22

SUSANNA WALCOTT AND LUCY PUTNAM WERE leaning their backs against Ingersoll's hollow oak. They had escaped the maternal net but still weren't free, having been ordered to guide home their drunken fathers later like they did every Sunday.

By now, the green had emptied. The goodwives had all gone home to prepare their Sunday dinners, taking their cranky, overtired youngsters with them. Despite that liberating fact, Susanna despaired having to stand around for hours more doing nothing but wait with another tedious child. *Unbearable really, with the weather so right!* The best part of her Day of Rest was being wasted . . . in Ingersoll's stable yard with Lucy! "It's only drab old men here. The boys are down at Bridget Bishop's having fun."

"What sort of fun, cousin?" Lucy curiously wondered.

"Shovelboard . . . other games." Susanna glanced away to glimpse the proximity of eavesdroppers. Seeing no one, she added in a whisper: "I have been there."

"You haven't . . . no, you haven't."

"Oh, I have, indeed I have, cousin. Thrice. But if you tell, I'll get a thrashing. Then so will you, from me." Lucy was shocked to learn her cousin had been to that forbidden place.

"But weren't you afraid of the troll who corrupts young people?"

Susanna suffered a giggling fit. "Trollop! Silly-skin! Bridget Bishop is herself why the boys all run there. *She* is their Sunday sport! Parading brazen in her scarlet bodice with her jug-sized trollop tits jiggling. Big as a calving cow's, I've seen them."

Lucy's eyes widened imagining that endowment. "A jug?"

Susanna gazed pensively toward the village gate. "Perhaps, bigger. But you must judge them for yourself, cousin."

Lucy shook her head. "Never shall I see such teats as Bridget Bishop's. I'm forbidden. So are you. If you visit there again, to be right in my conduct, I should have to tell my father, who'll tell yours."

Susanna began picking at the much-picked-at dead bark. "You needn't be a spoiler to be right with God. You need only say you're going for a walk-which we will be in truth, so it won't be a lie. By the time we return, our fathers will be too drunk to remember we even went. Come now. If not, I'll leave you."

"But 'tis a wicked place."

"'Tisn't! 'T'will amaze!" Susanna grabbed her cousin's hand and dragged Lucy up those few stone steps and in through the open tavern doorway. Inside, Ingersoll's Inn was elbow to elbow in hard drinking, loud-mouthed Sunday-suited men, all arguing politics and commerce.

No goodwives were present. That gender entered only on occasion of a sewing bee, marriage supper, burial feast, when lodging on a journey with a spouse, or if visiting Mrs. Ingersoll. Nathaniel Ingersoll, of course, was a member of this company on Sunday, as well as its proprietor. Initially, he'd stroll about his two tavern halls in a carefree jovial manner greeting friends and neighbors, raising an eyebrow at enemies; from them all reeling in gossip while taking orders. Later, he'd tally and collect receipts, but only when his patrons stood on precipitous legs. In between, he'd mingle carefree, because on Sundays his wife and daughter cooked and served all victuals and fetched all bottles and poured all brews, while John Indian did the scullery. He had just now retrieved a bottle of middling rum from his cellar and carried it into the hall. Many hands signaled. But he uncorked it at his own corner table, where a heated discussion was in session: "But none of us were polled," complained Thomas Putnam to his in-laws, "even those of us still with seats on the village committee."

"Because the vote was took behind our backs."

"Not behind, Brother Walcott, boldly in front!" amended Trask, the village tinker, who also informed: "In fact, right here last Sunday underneath our noses."

Thomas frowned at Ingersoll after he sat, "Didn't you hear them scheming in their huddles?"

The innkeeper shrugged, "Aye, but I thought they were drawing lots for my bill."

"They were thumbing their noses at you, and us, like they've done every Sunday since November." Thomas stared down the hall at a certain covey of men.

Of course, all at this table remembered that secret meeting held some months back, which none of them had known of or attended, when most of their faction were voted off the Village Committee shifting the political balance of power in the village. Thomas tapped Ingersoll's arm, "You know the law best, Nathaniel. Can we sue? Can we overturn this new villainy?"

The innkeeper shook his head. "Unfortunately for us, Thomas, we've been caught in a pool of unlucky timing. A new governor hasn't been appointed yet. We're powerless till one is. The General Court is still refusing to overturn the votes of village committees. Which means Sam Parris will be booted for certain and they'll hire some sorry fool to take his place, who'll do up their bootstraps the way they like."

"Lick their boots, you mean," sniffed Trask in that tinny voice which perfectly suited him.

"But we outnumber them two to one," argued Walcott.

"In bodies, nephew, not in influence," sighed the innkeeper.

"Meaning votes," clarified the tinker.

"Meaning the money to buy them," Thomas corrected, bitterly downing the rest of his rum.

To the side, the girls had approached their fathers' table, and were standing quietly by waiting to be acknowledged. Noticing them now, Thomas flinched: "What is it?" When his daughter began coughing, he turned back to his cronies.

"We've come to beg permission for a walk, Uncle Putnam," interrupted Susanna, stepping up.

"Can't you see we're busy?" he snapped.

Her father interjected, "Go ask your mother."

"She's gone home," replied Susanna, with ruefully sad eyes.

Thomas waved them away. "Go for your walk then, but don't wander far. And take the serving wench with you."

Susanna curtsied, grabbed her cousin Lucy's hand, and excitedly dragged her toward the doorway, weaving in and out of drunken old men.

Returning from her spited respite, Mercy had found the green deserted. So she sat on the flagpole bench to await her master. Because her duty as dictated by the aunts was to travel home with him later in his wagon. Those inseparable little sisters had already been taken away by their Walcott aunt, and although no instruction had been given concerning Lucy, she assumed Lucy was left in her care. But because that child was right now idling with Susanna Walcott up in the inn yard, more time was her own to fritter. Mostly she tried *not* to stare at that place where the girls were standing, which was so near to where she'd last herself stood with Joseph Putnam. Because ever since her encounter with

Susanna up at the basket maker's shop, she'd been trying *not* to think about him; despite that this morning she'd awakened with the excited surety she would see him again today—till Susanna threw that troubling damper on it. She'd felt disappointed then, and did still . . . and not only because her yester-night's dream had been a cruel trick and not a prophecy.

"Mercy . . . Mercy!"

Someone was tugging at her arm. Her eyes slowly opened. Had she dozed? The sun was too bright in them now, so she shaded with her hand. Lucy was strangely gibbering, telling her something she didn't understand. She expressed she was suffering a headache and that a walk did not appeal to her right now, and that the master would be calling them soon.

Susanna, grinning large, informed her: "But he has approved our walk and has ordered you to come."

And now because Susanna who had been so glum earlier seemed full of cheer, and because Lucy—a child always in need of a distraction from the melancholy at home—was clearly excited, she conquered her heavy limbs and heart and throbbing head, and stood. She took Lucy's hand, and smiled down at the child, and lied: "Yes, I think I would enjoy a walk after all, but only if you have some interesting sites to show me."

"Oh, you will surely see some interesting sites!" chortled Susanna, puffing out her chest, making Lucy giggle. "We also want you to invite the minister's niece. We wish to meet her properly."

"Could we have a word with Mistress Parris?" asked Mercy of the Indian slave who had opened the parsonage door and then swatted at a horsefly trying to get past her. "Mizzus ain't here," grunted Tituba, killing it with a whack.

"Oh never mind her," interjected Susanna. "It's her niece we wish to invite on a walk. It's such a glorious day, Parsonness

The Afflicted Girls

Parris would *surely* want her niece to make our good acquaintance."

Tituba looked down at the dead fly in the dirt, and reconsidered. *If I gets rid o' th' nastee girl, me n' my Betty'll have some peace.*

(Some while ago, Abigail had announced with a yawn that she desired an "afternoon rest." Actually, she was going upstairs to peep through her uncle's bedchamber: snoop inside his chest drawers, peer underneath his bedstead, search his coat pockets for misplaced secrets, tilt his standing mirror this way and that while trying on his hat and dandily twirling his town walking stick.) She was still twirling, when she heard the slave's coarse yell rise from the bottom of the stairs: "Abeeee! Sum girls be invitin' ya to walks with them! Ya wants'ta go?" She didn't answer. But soon as that caller turned her back, she scooted downstairs and saw *them.*

While Tituba, fooled by nothing, grabbed her shoulder. "Ain't my say if you goes or ya don'. Juz be back 'fore the mizzus or there be trouble."

With the briefest side glance at them, Abigail sniffed, "Slave, fetch my cape and cap from the kitchen peg." Tituba sailed away. She did not return. And as Abigail realized this: how she'd been rudely slapped down by a slave *in front of them* — she called out that she would not fetch them either, that she'd go without to be chilled, and would let her nose burn!

They walked away in twos—Susanna hand in hand with her, Mercy with Lucy. Had any of them thought to glance in through a meetinghouse window as they passed they would have seen a dejected minister kneeling in front of his pulpit, wet streaks lining his cheeks.

Reverend Parris felt utterly cast-off, just like his oaken preacher's stand had once been: discarded and brought low, only rescued from splinter by a thrift-minded Salem Villager who'd seen it on the town church rubbish heap—yes, he'd discovered how it had been obtained. Which was right after that popular Salem Town Church built itself the finest carved, inlaid polished walnut throne an ordained minister could ever hope to preach the Gospel from. This crude crumb of a pulpit was his constant reminder of his inferiority and low worth. *How long shall the wicked triumph over me? How much more, Lord, must I endure?*

The girls made haste to the High Road, which the long-dead village founders built to exclude their farms intentionally, choosing to lock themselves and their progeny away, instead, from worldly influence and taint. In ensuing years, however, they soon realized their mistake, when for lack of a public thoroughfare to Salem Village proper, Essex County's rapid growth in commerce, bringing fourfold rewards of wealth and prosperity to all citizens dwelling on or near the Ipswich High Road, bypassed them entirely. This current generation cursed them for it. The next, to which these girls belonged, was yet blissfully unaware.

Four abreast now, arms happily linked, these new friends flitted along like piping bobolinks. Skipping past wooded lots and verdant pastures, sweet-smelling fresh-plowed farm-tracts, hedgerows and vine-twisted fences. But it was the Sabbath Day, so no farmer was out sowing, and no shepherd was lolling. A number of sheep, goats, cows, an occasional feral cat or mongrel eyed them suspiciously, and one friendly herding dog barked and followed a ways, but no handsome youth was bodily present to hear their wistful song:

> *Thrice toss oaken ashes in the air.*
> *Thrice sit thou mute in this enchanted chair.*
> *Three times thrice tie true love's knot.*
> *And murmur softly: 'He will, or he will not.'*

The Afflicted Girls

23

A PUCK HIT ITS MARK AND SENT ANOTHER PUCK spinning as a band of rowdy teenaged boys played shovelboard in Bridget Bishop's tavern.

Hurrahs sounded louder when that infamous proprietress pushed her way through her gaggle of patrons, holding aloft another tray of mugs to serve. Hands flew up to grab ciders and ales, until that great tray began wobbling and almost spilled on them. Someone had collided with her, nearly causing her to trip—and it was that gawky, gangly red-haired farm boy from church, always running without looking, rushing to take his turn with the shovel. John Doritch shrank to half his height when she scolded him, but he also blushed at having such a close view, for she was beguiling to men of all ages.

A flirt by nature and frequent visitor to their wet dreams at night, by day she sported a pert nose on a luscious face, half-smiling rosebud lips, delving eyes, and a mane of honeycomb hair which hung scandalously loose in waves down her angled back. No one would guess that her age was forty-three, either by her face or physicality. Each morning, she'd lace that exceptional torso into a tight fitting, bright-crimson tailor-made paragon bodice, trimmed at the edges with multi-colored ribbon loops she'd crocheted, to be admired by all except her critics; namely, green-eyed tart-tongued local goodwives who called *her* "the tart," or sometimes the "cinnamon tree" (since the only use for that plant

127

was its bark). They would then bark at their husbands about her trimming her body instead of her soul, insisting that Bridget Bishop kept herself young through sinister means. Nature was not sinister, she would think overhearing such mulch. Not that those spouses ever heeded warnings. Because each morning she'd find somebody's husband snoring out on her stoop, or passed out folded over a table.

But the majority of her patrons were good working folk from the neighboring hamlets of Beverly, her place of birth, Andover, Wenham, Rowley, Reading, Lynn, and even Topsfield to the north. Although lately, for some reason, more customers were appearing from closest-by Salem Village; which surprised her, because she had not set foot in that parish for more than six years, even though her public house sat within its taxable boundaries. Not since the summer of 1686, in fact, when the Trask clan blamed her for a family member's suicide and brought her to trial on a false charge of murder. After her acquittal, she'd filed a countersuit, and won it using that family's own witnesses; which resulted in that deceased goodwife's posthumous conviction for vandalism for setting fire to her shovelboard room.

But despite that one tragedy, she welcomed all to her tavern, even ones named Trask. She held on to no grudges, save one: toward her envious next-door neighbor, Goodman Louder, who continuously assailed and harassed her by filing endless lawsuits accusing her as an unremitting law-breaker.

She was one, of course. She more than intentionally ignored all local Salem Village ordinances against music and mixed dancing, gambling and games, and lusty forays by patrons out back behind her prickly mistletoe, which lined the fence separating their properties—assignations, which that hypocrite could only have learned of by spying on lovers through knotholes.

The Afflicted Girls

"It's six mugs you owe me for. A shilling and a half." Bridget had stopped beside a drunken toothless woodsman to set down another frothy ale in front of his droopy face.

Clambering alert, he fumbled in his pocket till he found a coin. Held it up, and hiccupped: "Alls I gots a ha'penny, Bridget." He swooned back as she reached to take the coin, while his other hand rushed up to tweak her tit. She slammed down her tray and grabbed his puffy red nose and twisted till he bleated for mercy. "Just so you'd know how it feels," she scolded him.

She seized his hunting knife from the table, while he cringed and quavered in fear of what else a furious hussy might do (*cut off a feller's dong . . . carve him a nose-less face*). But Bridget only crouched and cut the buckle from his boot, wiping its crusted muck off on her apron. And when she spied the brass underneath, she put it in her pocket, telling him: "Paid in full, I am. Should you offer your other buckle for another round, I'll refuse it. Now go, get out, be gone, and stay gone till you're sober."

The geezer got up and wobbled across the hall one boot flopping, pushing his way past four wide-eyed young creatures adhered to the jambs of the doorway.

Seeing them John Doritch accidentally sent his puck careening down the tavern hall, instead of down the shovelboard. That wayward divot, made of good local hardwood, smashed into a table leg and bounced up into someone's knee. That poor man clutched at his leg, shouting curses in John's direction: "Gurley-gutted simpleton! Knock-kneed horse's ass!"

Everyone laughed, except John, who wished he could squeeze down through that mouse hole or hide up inside the chimney. Till he saw how the minister's niece was tossing him that same juicy look she'd given him in the meetinghouse. Forgetting his shame, he ran to offer the shovel to Abigail.

Meanwhile, someone had started fiddling and folk were pulling aside tables and benches and picking out dancing partners.

Even the busy proprietress, Bridget Bishop, stopped her serving and clearing to join in a first jig, choosing for her partner her injured patron, who bore his pain bravely. He was from Beverly Village and she knew him. He was a member of her church. She didn't attend often, but had gone to service this morning and had heard its liberal minister encourage his flock to express unfettered joy on Sundays. Advice, she heartily took.

After so many lost years, Mercy was reminded of her childhood in Casco Bay, which had also been a place of merriment on the Sabbath. After Sunday service, her family would join with other families for a communal feast. Come nightfall, they'd build a bonfire and feast again; eagerly awaited by the children all week was that great-sized, crackling peak of flaming wood which lit up the world. But the most nourishing parts for her were always the sung ballads, storytelling, and dances.

She made her way across the room to stand closer to the fiddlers. Counter-pointing with handclaps to their rhythms, her spirit rose higher than it had done in years. Joy filled her. Until she saw *him* and then her smile disappeared. For Joseph Putnam was seated in the next room beyond the fiddlers, shoulder to shoulder with a pretty maid in blue. Both were haughtily dressed in foreign styles resembling a peacock and peahen. While his farmer friend, who was in their company, wore that common plain local garb of sparrows most men wore. And now, unhappy chirping filled her ear: "None of the boys are coming up to me!"

Susanna Walcott rudely stepped in front obstructing her view. "The minister's niece already has a beau! Even horse-faced Felicity Sheldon has suitors!" Susanna pointed at a buck-toothed girl standing amid two attentive youths. "She's not even as rich as I would have been!"

"You have what that girl never will, Susanna . . . fairness of face in full measure. A heart that yearns to love will be loved, and loved well. It's not only money that pleases men. You'll have admirers, do not doubt it."

Susanna frowned. "Hollow words, hollow hopes. It's *only* money that counts here. Even servants want *rich* wives."

Mercy argued as much for herself now, as for the other: "But there is a higher value, which true love's eye will always see."

Susanna shook her head fiercely. "What do you know? You're a servant with no worth at all! You'll never marry! But end up a sluttern like Bridget Bishop! And I'll be a thornback spinster! Oh, I'd rather die of the pox than that!" She bolted away to spill her bitter tears out of doors in a place where no one would observe her. Her bold adventure had suddenly turned against her.

So again, Mercy gazed at *him* thinking how after so many hours of prodding heartache, God had given her His answer : how Joseph Putnam would *never* be hers. That hope had been folly. *Then why had her dreams not warned her? But instead foretold the opposite?* Looking up she saw the proprietress scrutinizing her thoughtfully.

Bridget had overheard that lovesick banter, because not much happened under her rafters without her observance or some consequence. She reached for Mercy's hand and turning up the palm ran her fingers gently upon it. "It's not impossible . . . no, not for you. There are tricks I could teach you, should you ever wish to learn."

Mercy retracted her hand, answering politely not to offend, "It's agreeable here . . . in your tavern."

"Oh, it's many things, lass," smiled the proprietress. And now Bridget continued walking back to her kitchen, brushing shoulders with another young stranger on the move; she scrutinized him, also.

Walking up, Joseph Putnam asked with a sweet flavor: "So have you found your lost pearls on this visit?"

Mercy shook her head, "Excepting this place."

"To that, I would agree."

"But I never was *visiting*, sir," she added so he'd know, as her eyes met his then fell again. "I was coming here to live. I thought you understood that."

"I didn't. Now you have proof that I cannot read minds. So tell me, who has brought you here? Don't your relations shun this place? Most of our village populace does. "

"My master's niece brought me," she answered, forgetting that Susanna Walcott was niece to him, as well. "Over there. Taking her turn at the shovelboard." (Because after washing off her tears at the well, Susanna had rejoined her friends, wanting her full measure of recreation today, if not perpetual happiness.)

But when Joseph looked, he saw a traveling companion, Abigail Williams, who had just seized the shovel from Susanna, and recalled her connection with the minister. He looked back at Mercy. *Parris is her master. She is his jade.* Draining of interest, he glanced back over his shoulder now at his mother's choice, the one he'd been ordered to deliver home after that parent convinced hers to allow it. Clearly, they were all hoping he'd seal the bargain. So to thwart them, he'd invited Ben Nurse to ride along, who suggested they stop here at Bishop's Ordinary. Though he would have preferred to continue down to Boston to snook for whores . . . and said as much in front of the girl with much bawdy innuendo, embarrassing his love-struck friend, though not her, who didn't understand any connotations. *Workhorse judged better than purebred . . . minister's scullion set higher than a virgin. Laughable.* "Reverend Parris is your master then?" he said, stepping back, wishing to extricate from further conversation.

"No, sir." Mercy hesitated. "Thomas Putnam is."

His eyes regained a chilly interest. He set his foot against hers, and leaned in so close to her cheek she heard his steady heartbeat. She hoped he couldn't hear her quickened one.

"Does my brother ever speak about me?"

The Afflicted Girls

She knew what he was really asking. "I don't know, sir."

"But would you tell me if he did? In confidence, I mean."

He is asking me to eavesdrop. "No, sir. Though I am indebted to you for my life, I could not." It crushed her to deny him.

"You misunderstand. You would be doing us both a service. You witnessed a quarrel. Yet, my brother misjudges me. I have no gripe. But wish only to settle matters fairly between us, to find some compromise he'll accept."

His explanation sounded reasonable, more reasonable than Susanna's had been. But which of them was trustworthy? Neither. Susanna Walcott was vengeful; Joseph Putnam concealed . . . and courted recklessly. For he was pressing hard against her bodily now, whispering hotly into her ear: "It will be our reason to meet again."

She feared them both now. Both brothers. Was threatened by one and had no defense to the other, with lies more than truths claiming both sides of their story. *Because only Christ is free of deceit. Yet, when His disciples betrayed Him, He forgave them.* Would He not forgive her one small betrayal? She looked into his eyes, and nodded her consent.

Joseph brushed back that strand of wayward hair from her cheek—this time she let him. *Servant to my brother yet mastered by me.* He delighted in the irony.

When he left her, he collected his companions and they rose to leave. While Mercy stared, ignoring that a cat had been rubbing against her leg, purring for attention. When he was gone, she picked it up and absently stroked its hair. "Begging love is easy for a creature like you."

"Commanding it is even easier . . . for a creature like you."

Mercy turned to see Bridget Bishop again scrutinizing her. Comfort passed from heart to heart. "Come to me tonight, or any night near to midnight, lass. We'll see what we can do."

The cat suddenly hissed. It jumped from Mercy's arms. Abigail, Susanna and Lucy were walking up. Abigail eyed Bridget suspiciously. Lucy gawked at the trollop's scandalous udders, which were big, though not the size of a jug. Susanna tapped Mercy's sleeve, "We're leaving."

The Afflicted Girls

24

REVEREND PARRIS TRIED, BUT JUST COULD NOT muster even a mustard seed of appetite for the fine meal his wife had served him. He picked at his spicy ham-steak — while she devoured hers — then pleaded a roiling stomach, excusing himself to his study. Upset then, Mrs. Parris ate past her fill and forced both girls to do the same: to stuff their gullets till they couldn't eat another morsel. She refused to waste such rich fare on slaves.

Abigail knew she'd guessed rightly that her uncle had not confided his troubles to Aunt Ugly. So interspersed with those endless bites, she would lift her apron to her mouth to hide her sudden jabs of glee. Because it meant that only *she* knew of the petition raised to fire him, which made *her* the only one able to console him tonight. The gluttony continued through two portions of creamy treacle pudding for the insect and for her, with none for the mouse. And finally her aunt excused her from the table and also from her nightly chore and quiz, sending her up to an early bedtime — but carelessly, without a caution against disturbing her uncle. So she hid in the hallway spying until the praying mantis had shoved the mouse over to that stinky block of tallow ordering Betty to boil the wax and braid wicks for two score tapers as a penance; obviously her aunt would sit and watch. So now she rushed upstairs with a different purpose: to retrieve her cherished andirons from her coffer and quickly polish them with spit and suds till their black canine-eyes again reddened. When she deemed them fit, she carried them down quietly, one at a time, and set them outside her uncle's closed study door. She tapped lightly. And when he opened it, she curtsied and presented them.

Reverend Parris, eyes already moist, was moved by this orphan's tender gesture, and only turned his face away for a moment to quickly wipe his eyes. They carried them in together and placed them at opposite sides of his grate. He stepped back to admire them. "These are handiworks worthy of a far richer room than mine. Do not offer them to me, niece, but keep them for your dowry. Let me only borrow them for a time."

Abigail shook her head. "That will not do for me, Uncle Parris. *You* are the richest man I know and *my* most treasured person. No husband could be your equal. They are yours to keep, as am I." Humbled, he accepted her gift, vowing inwardly never to sell them, or to disappoint her or to send her away, whatever ill tide of fortune came next. He invited Abigail to sit in his chair. "Tonight, I will read to *you*, niece," he said, as he picked up his Jerusalem Bible and carried it to the fireside, and stood beside one andiron.

Because to Reverend Parris this was the sign he'd been seeking all day that God had not abandoned him. These wolfish andirons were God's own augur that he would in the end trample the jackals of Judah. He wondered if Abigail knew it. He chose a passage from *Ecclesiastes*. Read it with stirring inflection. When he finished, she requested one from *Song of Songs*. He was embarrassed, of course, but was hard-pressed to deny her. So he searched those pages till he found a text extolling lesser passions, which he judged appropriate for young ears, though just barely:

Deep waters cannot quench love,
Nor floods sweep it away.
Were one to offer all he owns to purchase love
He would be roundly mocked —

The Afflicted Girls

He looked up. "But not you, niece. You would earn only praise."

❧ ✦ ❧

The two youngest Putnams were tucked tight underneath their coverlet, but not into sleepy quietude, rather into raucous whining for the story of Noah—which Lucy grumpily protested.

So Mercy threatened no story at all. But upon seeing three crestfallen faces, she relented. "Keep silent. I will choose," she told them. "But you each must listen carefully, for there will be a lesson in it." *Which parable to teach though? Whose example to set?* They needed so many. She imagined the faces of Esther, Judith, Daniel, Moses, Rachel floating past, beckoning her to follow . . . *who all had stories of suffered travails . . .* not so unlike hers. *Though nevermore would she teach any child the story of Joseph and his kingly coat, not even should that child beg.* Knowing how in the Bible, all travails ended well, and not knowing now what would her ending.

She snuffed the torch and sat on the child-sized chair, stretched out her legs in front of her. The room had turned silvery dim. For tonight no embers burned on the hearth, despite the low-hanging fogbank surrounding the house. The mistress had not allowed a fire to be lit, because the woodpile sat too low. Nor was moonlight shining in, only an eerie glow framed in a misted pane. Yet, she preferred spinning her tales in the dark to spur young minds to riper imaginings. (And so did the house's specters prefer the darkness, which nightly gathered to listen):

> *There once lived a devout and decent man, whom God*
> *afflicted in his old age . . . by taking away both his*
> *fortune and his eyesight--*

"That is the story of Job," protested Lucy. It was a Bible story she intensely disliked for the frequency her father told it. Whenever he read it at morning-worship, it spoiled her entire day, and sometimes brought her a night terror. Mercy explained:

"This forebear's name was 'Tobias' and his story is seldom told. For it's from a Bible older than our Good Book, which only some ministers know of."

"Tobias was my great-grandfather's name," the child marveled.

"A happy coincidence. I didn't know."

"I think it is his spiritual self in Heaven who has whispered in your ear, Mercy. He watches over us, and sometimes looks down at us from the elms while we play."

Mercy shuddered. She did feel an intruding presence, but not a loving or grandfatherly one. "Indeed."

When Tobias' children turned against him shamed by his pitiable condition, he began to pray fervently for death. Only one son, his youngest, remained faithful, recalling a property his father once owned in a distant land, and thought if he could find it and sell it, he might at least repay his father's debts. And in that way, give his father hope.

Mercy's reached over and touched Lucy's foot. "Here is the lesson, Lucy. If Tobit—for that was this good son's name—did not know the way to that village, how could he find it?"

Lucy pondered. By now, her sisters' snores were wafting loudly through the murkiness, while her own mind felt too dull to ponder riddles. "He found a map?"

"There was no map. And we, likewise, have no maps through life. But when a faithful soul is most lost and inconsolable, sometimes God takes pity and leads us. Tobit, that good son, was led."

"Where has God led you, Mercy?" yawned Lucy.

Mercy hesitated. "Here . . . to Putnam Farm." *Another house filled with prayers for death.*

In that far-away village lived an equally unhappy maid, who also prayed for death. Because a curse had been put

The Afflicted Girls

*on her by a rival that on her wedding night a demon
would appear and murder her bridegroom in the
marriage bed.*

"I would never prefer death to spinsterhood," declared
Lucy, "unless my name was 'Susanna Walcott!'" And now she
giggled, knowing she'd made a joke.

"Now is that a kind thing to say of your cousin," scolded
Mercy, " . . . when you've not even met the demon yet?" bettering
the joke, and now they both laughed.

*Tobit always asked other travelers, but none of them knew
of that place. Then one night, while fishing for his supper
from a riverbank he hooked a fish of monstrous size, but
while struggling to land it he slipped and it pulled him
under and would have eaten him had not a mendicant
been hobbling by who saw it happen. The old man hurried
down. He pulled Tobit to safety and then beat the fish
unconscious with his staff. Tobit invited him to share his
meal, but the beggar was fasting – though he did ask for
the fish's innards to use as medicines, which Tobit gladly
gave. The next morning, they journeyed on together and
eventually reached that faraway village. Tobit sold his
father's property with its caretaker's help, who also
offered them lodging. For this man had a beautiful
daughter of marriageable age, who was always so sad that
he thought the company of strangers might cheer her.
That night as Tobit lay on his pallet unable to sleep, he
overheard the maid weeping, begging for death. He was
reminded of his father and his heart opened to her. But
when he asked her to be his bride, she refused because of
the curse.*

"And her name was--"

"Susanna Walcott," the sleepy child offered.

"And what happens next do you suppose?"

"The demon eats him?" Lucy guessed.

Well, that would have been the outcome if the beggar had not taught Tobit to vanquish the demon by putting the fish's heart and liver into the bridal bed instead of his own. The curse was broken. The lovers married. And now Tobit returned home with a bag of gold, a happy wife, and a clever companion. But instead of rejoicing, his father complained that he couldn't see any of them because of his blindness . . . So now the beggar advised?

"Don't be sad, Tobias. Your son will guide you wherever you need to go. His wife will cook you tasty meals and rub your feet. And I will tell you tales," answered Lucy.

"Yes, he was thinking all that, but actually he said: 'Rub the fish's gall into your father's eyes.'"

And when Tobit did this, his father's blindness was cured. The beggar now revealed himself as the Archangel Raphael.

"Oh, how wonderful," sighed Lucy, feeling so content in this magical yarn that she never even knew existed at all.

And now that most beautiful of angels explained how he'd been sent down by God to reward three good hearts.

And saying that, he disappeared like a wisp of tinder-grass in a tongue of Heavenly flame.

Lucy was silent. Then she asked thoughtfully: "Have you ever met an angel on your way, Mercy?"

"No," Mercy whispered from the doorway, *never an angel, only demons.* "But I truly hope that you do, Lucy, on your own life's path. Now be happy in your slumber. And tomorrow be kinder to your sisters."

The Afflicted Girls

PART FOUR

25

SPRINGTIME CAME AT LAST TO SALEM VILLAGE. Days were sunny and growing longer, evenings had turned mild and were tinged with fragrance. Everywhere, such fine durable weather inspired passions in beds, barns, bowers and paddocks, as all creatures, but a handful, heeded Nature's call. An exception was Reverend Parris, for both of his worlds now— spiritual and corporeal—teetered at the brink.

Not that he hadn't attempted to mount his spouse, or that Mrs. Parris, out of wifely concern, didn't try her best to uplift him despite her other midlife assault. Indeed, she would lie upon her side in bed at night staring over at her husband's shift praying for his organ to reawaken for *his* sake, though of course, not for the Spirit of Lust to enter it.

But one in this house rose up and bloomed. In one fertile spurt, Abigail grew thinner, taller, smaller in her waist, and fuller in the parts that mattered. Turning sixteen, she sent back a prettier reflection to herself from her uncle's standing mirror. And last week when her aunt's castoffs no longer fit—well, the petticoats still did, for the praying mantis was a tall thin stick, but no bodice would close round her bosom—her aunt had enviously observed this, and now today had driven down to Salem Town with Mrs.

141

Ingersoll to purchase yardage, taking the mouse along. And prior to that, even more pleasing, was when her uncle instructed her aunt that *her* needs were to come first.

After that, she dallied under the crab apple, shirking all morning chores, at times watching the clouds drift past, or thinking how if she stared hard enough an apple would fall, or perusing the printed Bible her uncle had gifted her. Here, too, he set her above his mouse and spouse. She was the one directing Betty in her useless efforts now, using "An Alphabet of Lessons For Youth" and The New England Primer as texts:

J.   *Job feels the rod, yet blesses God.*

K.   *Proud Korah's troop was swallowed up.*

L.   *Liars shall have their part in the Lake, which burns with fire and brimstone.*

Her own favorite letter was "A":

A.   *Do not the Abominable thing do, which I hate, saith the Lord.*

What abominable thing she had always wondered, imagining the very worst fell thing ever done by an ancient patriarch with a matriarch in a tent; and then leafing through those thousands of pages seeking every forbidden fruit ever written, because all the rest was drivel!

Then later, when her uncle sat her and Betty down to give them his nightly discourse on life's deeper meaning, and after that came his quiz, he would praise her for her spiritual understanding. But to the laggard, he'd say that by her parents naming her "Betty" meant she must try to do "better!" For this was their nightly ritual now: first he would praise her to the sky then he'd whisk the dunce's hand, and Betty would cry.

But tonight, Betty was bawling long before that discourse was sat, or even the supper was cooked—for lack of a new dress. After she, the ward, got yardage for two.

The Afflicted Girls

While Reverend Parris, for his part, desired only to bring both his children as near to Heaven as he could following the dictum Cotton Mather had set for the innocents: *Better whipped, than damned.* Tonight, irritated by one though (and by other things), Betty's bottom — not hand — was whipped.

While his household slept, Reverend Parris stole away to a secret meeting at nearby Ingersoll's Inn — his sheep had decided to bite back. Walking in, and not wanting to waste time, he volunteered to draft the petition himself and listed his reasons: his years of experience as a jury foreperson in Boston, of his having reviewed so many legal instruments and of having filed so many lawsuits himself, not to mention having worked as a "for hire" scribe in other persons' legal matters. He was adept at composing persuasive sermons, was he not? So of anyone here, wasn't he best suited to the task? His cohorts readily agreed. They welcomed it. They'd been dragged from their beds on his account. So while he wrote and pondered, they mingled across the room, drinking, gambling and gossiping in low tones, so as not to distract him.

He incorporated as much of the law as he could remember, mentally propounding both sides of every argument, until one side — his side — won it. Because the plot had thickened this week, and the situation now grown dire: the "anti-Parris faction" had this week filed their complaint for fraudulent conveyance of the parsonage deed, just as Thomas Putnam had predicted. Which meant, they were trying to turn him and his family out from their house. Luckily, Nathaniel Ingersoll had ferreted a copy and had read it aloud.

He felt some relief discovering how its author, Israel Porter — a man generally informed about titles and deeds, being a landlord himself — possessed a deficient understanding of the rights of a legal tenant. Disputes of a nature he'd negotiated more than once while serving his church-mouse poor parish in Boston.

But better was his discovery that this enemy was even worse informed concerning the legal rights of tenancy afforded a contracted, ordained minister—a subject well taught at Harvard. *But hadn't he been just as sure of his title rights in Barbados, when a lesser writ shook him free of his inheritance?* Underneath the table, he gave the lightest tap to the wood to ward that possibility.

After two hours of penning, scratching out, reviewing and revising, he tore his six pages in half, having decided now to change his tact: to rely more on sentiment than logic—although not to use preachment, because men who sat on high benches hated smugness. He called for fresh parchment. Those still awake groaned and grumbled. So more free drinks were poured while Nathaniel Ingersoll groaned and grumbled. Three times more was that weary inn-keep's half-hour glass turned before the petition was declared: "Done!"

His supporters were roused from their stupors; a few stood up for the toast. And now that drying document was passed hand-to-hand most carefully, for signatures.

Thomas Putnam clinked his glass, volunteering to deliver it to Boston on the morrow. As they'd decided tonight to file in Boston's General Court since Salem Town's was now suspect. Thomas asked only for a pinch of coin from each purse to cover his lodging expense. They all knew his situation, of course, and so begrudgingly gave it, except for the minister. But none of them knew how all this night he'd been sitting here worrying, not about Reverend Parris' security but about his own—his pending lien, his lawsuits, his rising debts. So this collection was really for that.

The Afflicted Girls

26

ANN PUTNAM HAD MOSTLY RECOVERED FROM her grief and rarely thought about her dead babe now, and meanwhile had discovered that having a household drudge perform all chores meant she no longer had a reason to dress for a life she hated. Robbed twice of a better fate—once by two thieving brothers then by a husband's half-kin—she had earned the right to wallow. So she mostly napped, read, stared out her chamber window while she rocked, ate but little and hardly went out of doors, except to use the privy. She'd attend morning service down in the parlor—it couldn't be avoided; but after that she wouldn't need to descend again till dusk, prior to her husband's arrival home from his fields, to await him in the parlor or kitchen with her children at her feet. Then at supper, she'd plead faintness, nausea, a throbbing head, fatigue—whatever condition came to mind—and without partaking of much, she'd return upstairs to her bedchamber.

Today was different. Thomas was gone to Boston, her eldest was visiting a relation, and her other two were not yet sinners and were easily ignored, and they also had each other and an indenture to attend them. She'd been invited, of course, to Walcott Farm for her niece's sixteenth birthday and the giving of the dower coffer, but she sent Lucy in her stead, granting that daughter permission for a two-night stay. So today, locked inside her room, she reveled in her freedom.

Today Mercy was giving the younger Putnams their morning lesson using Mother Nature as teacher. She'd gotten them to help her push the wheelbarrow uphill hauling fodder to the sheep, with a promise of letting them play with those creatures. At the stream afterward, she showed them how to net a fish, and they also picked wild onions. They all gathered mushrooms next filling a basket. While the children learned a valuable lesson—one she prayed they'd remember all of their days: how to distinguish edible from poisoning ones. Those content but tired tykes rode home just now in a wheelbarrow filled with squeals.

She sent them upstairs for their nap, although she didn't rest. She boned the fishes and added them to yesterday's pottage and set the cauldron to boil. When those cranky sisters awoke ten minutes later and refused a second *nap*, she sat them at the table and gave them whey and fetched their hornbook and slates, while she went to kill a hen by the mistress' order.

The bird badly pecked her before she snapped its neck. So she washed off the blood from her hand using the watering can, and then picked stanching herbs in the garden. Returning to the kitchen, she found those tykes in a hen-fight of their own. Scratching, pinching, pulling each other's braid. Both glasses of whey had been spilt and one glass was shattered. The youngest was bawling. Scooping her up, Mercy demanded an explanation.

"This is my plaything! My father made it for me!" the older sister claimed, clutching a small, whittled horse in her fist.

"But couldn't it be both yours and a shared plaything?" Mercy gently corrected.

"No!" she scowled, stamping her foot, which made her sister cry louder.

Mercy was stern. "Go up to the barnyard then. Play there by yourself. Lest you wake your mother with your selfishness."

The Afflicted Girls

As that girl scooted out, happy to be free of both hornbook and sister, Mercy asked the little one in her arms: "If I made you a toy of your own, do you think you could thank me with a smile?" The little girl sniffled then nodded. So she set her down and searched the mending basket for a partially unraveled flax sock she used for darning thread. She stuffed it with kindling straw and wound a strand of burlap to separate a head from the body, she plucked chicken feathers—the downiest ones—to sew on at the back, making sure they fluttered when she blew on them. Taking a piece of char, she drew on eyes and a nose, and had the child draw the mouth: *a smile*, which she quickly cross-stitched. She pulled down a cob of dried winter corn from a rafter, peeled it and dropped it into the pot. The husk she sewed on, and trimmed round it with scissors.

She held up the sock-poppet now, which sported pale corn-silk hair (like hers) under a zigzagged leafy crown, and which flew fluttery through the air to those outstretched excited small hands.

Beaming now, that child ran outside to show off her prize to her selfish sister, intending to gloat. But in the end, only sharing her marvelous new toy. Not to be generous as Mercy had coaxed, but so her *angel* could ride her sister's *horse* into Jerusalem.

After the fish chowder thickened, Mercy slid the cauldron off the lugpole and set it on the fender to keep warm. She hung a baking kettle oven in its place, and inside sat a plucked chicken, stuffed not with fighting spirit anymore, but seared savory innards of egg, wild onion, herb and mushroom.

She'd found no molasses in the pantry—only one small jar that had long ago been licked. So instead of the promised sweet-cakes, it would have to be biscuits now. But then the flour sack was empty, too. All she could find was one cornmeal sack that had fallen behind a shelf: but which held only enough moldy meal to thicken gravy.

So she thought about *him* who never had to scrounge. Ever since that day they'd crossed paths at Bishop's Ordinary, her hunger to love had increased; but at the same time she was glad Joseph Putnam had not come here to test her. Hopefully he'd realized that folly, as had she. So while the gravy simmered and chicken baked, she lay down on the kitchen settle to breathe in the savory aromas, closing her eyes for a moment's dream, which lasted hardly a blink. Bolting upright, having just seen her rare opportunity: the master was gone to Boston. Lucy, her watchdog and shadow, would be absent another full day. And with only the mistress and tykes to observe her, were she to mix into the gravy a certain plant she'd picked on this morning's walk, those three lethargic creatures would be hard-pressed to rise before midday on the morrow. Her unhappy mistress might even be grateful she'd slumbered well.

Twelve hours later, she was peering into two moonlit chambers.

She came back downstairs now and put a dose of sleep-inducing skullcap—more potent than what she'd fed the family—into a bowl of fish dregs for the dog, because at night, that half-wolf creature roamed and also was a barker. She had nearly forgotten. She pulled on her hood at the first hard salty gust as she hurried down the yard to the gate. She set down the bowl and used her usual soft whistle. The mongrel came running, of course devoured her offering in gulps and when it finished, she petted its coat to ensure favor later; because she had no knowledge, really, of the workings of skullcap in canines.

The sky was clear, the wind cleansing the night, and the moon gibbous and high. Not of particular significance, but shedding enough light to illumine the pathway. The mongrel followed a ways, till it spied some skulking creature in the grass.

She kept her mind on what she chased.

The Afflicted Girls

*Yea, this is she that hath bought off many a man from a pilgrim's
life. She is a bold and impudent slut who will talk with any man. She
has given it out in some places that she is a goddess, and therefore
some do worship her.*

The Pilgrim's Progress
John Bunyan (on *"Madam Bubble"*)

27

AT UNGODLY HOURS, THE DOOR TO BISHOP'S
Ordinary was always locked; because, somewhere
inside was hidden a full money-box. So High Road sojourners
needing a way-stop would have to hope their knocks rattled
someone's ears, which weren't often Bridget's (who plugged hers,
unless a certain knock was invited). But tonight that downstairs
door had been left ajar by a local bibber, coincidentally named
Bibber, whose homeward stumbling after midnight after rousing
from a stupor in a pool of slobber proved fateful for one troubled
girl. Mercy ascended the dark house stair, not sure which sleeping
chamber housed Bridget Bishop among the handful in this two-
winged two-storied public house. Then the cat padded past and
showed her — scratching at its mistress' door.

Wrapping her shawl, lighting her lantern, Bridget led her
visitor downstairs. But with a handful of drunkards snoring in her
halls, and two sprawled on the floor of her kitchen, to protect their
private business she took Mercy down to her cellar, with the gray
cat following. The room below was a true chamber of scents, a
storage equal in size to the shovelboard room atop it. But

crammed twice as full as that room ever was on Sundays. Everywhere, without exception, sat disorganized stores: on shelves, the floor, hanging hooks from beams, all of which now had to be navigated around or under: crates, iron-ringed hickory barrels, kegs, casks, jugs of applejack and hops, syrup, molasses, tea tins, bean, grain, apple and meal sacks, salt, waxed rounds of moldy cheeses of differing stinks, jellies, tallow, dried pork, fish, pickles, a slab of honeycomb with flytraps set around, and so many herbs hanging from beams that the room was canopied.

In a solitary clearing sat a small square table with two stools, where Bridget did her inventories, kept account ledgers, quibbled with merchants or farmers—sometimes flirted to get a better price. She set down her lantern on it, motioning for Mercy to sit. And now the cat jumped into Mercy's lap and began more affectionate purring.

Bridget didn't need to inquire. She knew why this girl had come. "Children, fortune, bedevilment, love. There are simple charms for each."

"But he is promised to another . . . a vow was taken. Or if not, soon will be. It is too late for a charm, I think."

"Have you woken me for nothing?" chided the proprietress.

Mercy sighed, "I came for that purpose, Goody Bishop, and held firm to it till now. But I am not ignorant of what a charm can do. It can rot kernels on healthy stalks, turn milk sour inside an udder—they harm as well as heal. And I do not wish to harm him, or do anyone any harm." She pictured that peahen maid, wishing her no unhappiness, only a different suitor.

Bridget viewed an unsure heart, which beat quicker than it should; but she saw no selfishness in it. "You believe as I do, lass. Neither could I do another person harm or teach anyone else to do that. So you can empty yourself of that fear."

"But are charms holy or unholy? Will they count against us in Heaven on the Judgment Day?"

The Afflicted Girls

Bridget was too tired to wrestle down a vacillating mind. She frowned. "Charms are an understanding of Nature . . . nothing more, or less. And despite that the Lord's own miracles were performed by this same *understanding* does it mean you'll not be deemed profane on the Judgment Day if you use one? How can I know that, when Christ Himself was *crucified* for it? A creature like me can only say that He knows we do it, and lets us. That He is the One who put the gift in us to use as we see fit. But first we must search our true intention. For this is the rule: 'Use a charm, if thy will be pure. Abandon it, if it is not.' . . . What shall it be then? What do you hope to accomplish here? Tell me. For I am weary of discussion."

Mercy stroked the cat's soft coat. "To love and be loved as an equal. That is what I wish for—with a selfish will, I suppose."

"There is no fault in wishing happiness for oneself as long as it does not ruin another's."

Mercy sighed that she truly hoped not. "But there is more, Goody Bishop. Night after night, he visits my dreams. I want to visit his. And have tried, but the way remains hidden."

Bridget raised an eyebrow. Few would even know such a thing was possible.

A mouse suddenly scampered across their feet, startling them up from their stools. The cat pounced from Mercy's lap and gave it chase. Bridget frowned, wondering which of her stores that rodent had defiled. She carried her lantern round the cellar till she observed white tracks leading from a fresh-milled sack of flour. But she didn't curse the creature, which had a right to survive. Instead, she returned to watch her cat futilely scratch at the mouse hole. "Pursuer and pursued—which shall you be?"

A long silence before the reply, "Teach me the charm."

Bridget nodded. It was the same answer she always got from lovesick maids even after her *caution*. "In Old England grows a rare root called *Mandrake*, which we transformed into *Mayapple*.

"I know it."

"But do you know its use?"

"I was taught."

"What were you taught?"

"How it can bring wealth, children, love to empty folds . . . also, that bay and mugwort prevent evil from entering a house, rue and verbena are good for sores, other remedies--"

"Which other remedies?" This was no game, Bridget reminded.

"'Trefoil, vervain, John's wort and dill hinder witches from their will' and if you anoint your eyes for three days with their juices, the spirits of the air become visible to you."

"And who taught you to see spirits?" This was a rare discussion for Bridget.

A startling cold blast suddenly blew across the tabletop, flickering the lantern candle under its glass. It sputtered and extinguished. Mercy had cried out at that wind, and jumped to her feet, and now she said with a trembling voice: "I shouldn't have come, Goody Bishop. I beg your pardon for having woken you."

Bridget caught her arm in the dark. "'Twas a whorl blowing down through splintered floorboards. Common enough in a drafty cellar underneath a dance hall . . . obviously some snorer has opened a window." She felt for a taper behind her on a shelf, lit it with a flint, and saw more than a young girl's doubt. *Better to let her cry on your shoulder than fight her terror with words.* She embraced Mercy full, her curiosity prodding gently: "What is it that frightens you so?" For she could see clearly that this was no broken heart. "Tell me. It's the reason you've come. The charm was the excuse."

Now Mercy had never revealed her torments to anyone, but had kept her shame deep buried. It came up now, not of her volition, but summoned to the light by Bridget. "I-I've . . . I've held it secret for so long, I shudder to remember."

"Remembering it will break its hold. Forgetting it again will break its mold."

"You cannot understand, Goody Bishop."

"Nor will you if you do not try to now."

Mercy shook her head.

"Spin a new course," urged Bridget. "If you falter, I will show you how to spin even faster."

So at the urging of her new mentor, Mercy did . . . by traveling to her past:

> *My family came from Bury in Suffolk in Old England. My grandsire, Father's father, was a county squire fair in all his dealings. He was prosperous, and well loved by all . . . till the day he turned Puritan. Then he was outcast. Lands and livery seized, debts falsified, he was carted away in chains to a pauper's prison, where he died a broken man. Father would have suffered that same fate, but for fleeing with his sister at his own dying mother's urging, setting sail with like-minded pilgrims to settle Casco Bay in this new world. He met my mother on that sea crossing. I was born the second summer of their happiness, the firstborn of five, no, six. Mother was giving birth that day, that day—*

The old grief poured in. She wept softly for a time. While Bridget sat in heart-sore silence, with her eyes respectfully lowered.

> *The babe lay wrong and her birth agonies increased. I saw it was beyond the bearing. Father did what he could to ease her. But he was angry that my aunt never came. When Mother bled through the stanching cloths, he sent me on his horse to fetch a goodwife, any goodwife now, not knowing that our settlement was burnt and all but us lay dead. I returned to find my family also slain.*

Bridget understood this story. Massacres in the northern regions were a common happening. Her late husband, Edwin Bishop, before they married, had served two years in a militia in the north and had evil tales to tell about it. Even now, sometimes, she'd hear mention at her tables of vengeful sorties done by relations of murdered folk. *"World's cruelest savages"* was what her Edwin had called them. She reached out and touched her arm. "I know enough now. You needn't tell me more."

Mercy looked up with eyes cold as gravestones, no longer blue, or any color of this world. "But I must, Goody Bishop, for you have summoned it." And now Bridget felt an even *icier* chill, which was no wind seeping down through her planks but one penetrating her own cornerstone. "A ward of the Commonwealth, I was sent to live in a minister's house. I believed I had found a safe and holy haven. I thanked God. I was seven."

A pretty child in a starched white linen dress stands in the center of a circle of candles. Her guardian, a wiry man of short stature in a black minister's coat and white collar, stands beside her. He puts a hand of iron at the back of her neck and now tilts up her chin. He forces her to drink from a flask of bitters. The dark liquid trickles down from her mouth, staining her bodice and apron. The lights around her begin to spin.

"Aware, but unable to move any limb, I collapsed at his feet. He kneeled and removed my garments, then his own, and holding me open, in between, he pierced and rammed inside me with a husband's organ, uttering words I did not know: *exubitores, in nomine Luciferus, fas mihi tengere, limini illa, effusus labor, defuncta vita, fiat nunc voluntas mea.* Emptying his juices, he arose as if in a trance and stood above my crushed frame: *refectus, particeps ritus sacri, scio desiderium animae ac voluntatem labiorum, meoreum perfecta esse.* Waving his arm to the right, one by one the candles went out, moving it back to the left, again the circle flamed."

"A black minister!" cried Bridget. "Maleficium of the worst ilk! Oh, you poor, poor ruined child!"

The Afflicted Girls

Mercy's voice was barely audible now. "I lived without hope under his roof for six more shameful years, till entering my first moon—no longer a child—I ended my use. Outwardly he was a man of God. He preached in church on Sundays. But in private, in private—" she was violently shaking.

Bridget begged, "Stop! End it here! I cannot bear to hear more!"

"But it will never end, Goody Bishop. For on that first night, when my senses were my own again, he made me swear a covenant with him signed in my virgin's blood, that I would never reveal his secrets. Now that I have, worse will come."

Bridget was adamant. "Nothing will come of it, nothing! Nothing! Your covenant with that evil man is broken! Hear me! You are a woman now, no longer a child, who has a friend who can show her how to weave a new destiny! Who will teach her lore to protect herself! From this day forth, you will never, *never again* be under any man's rule! Upon my own life, I swear it!"

28

ABIGAIL RUSHED TO THE WINDOW. GENERALLY when she heard midnight rustlings, she was too thick with sleep to relinquish her bed. On the rare occasions when she did, it was mostly a roaming mongrel, coon or weasel, owl, once ta porcupine, never yet a wild boar—creatures that foraged at night on midden-heaps. But tonight it might be her uncle hurrying to the privy. He'd suffered stomach cramps after eating Aunt Ugly's offal. So had she.

But no, she saw Tituba on the move, striding out past the woodpile and barn with a basket looped over her arm, heading toward the woodland beyond the fence. She scurried downstairs, out into the yard, squinted hardly a moment before deciding to tramp and follow—despite wearing a nightdress and bare feet.

Leaves moaned in the overhead thickness of trees and barely a footpath was visible, yet she'd long believed savages could navigate woodlands with their eyes closed and wanted to believe that she would not lose her own way now as long as she kept the slave in her sight. Which was difficult, because tonight that lazy Indian was skimming the ground so fast she truly might be flying. She soon spied a curious thing: Tituba setting down her basket beside a vast thorny vine patch and plucking prickly pods. What use had prickly pods? Except to prick.

But to this Carib Indian the plant was a "journeying weed" with no other name for it. And it had been put into the world by

The Afflicted Girls

Ya-Ya in his first breath. While here, three years ago, she had also planted a satchel of seeds gathered long ago by her in Barbados and kept alive with whisperings when her master had no Boston garden. Not knowing then that her jungle-tribe's sacrament grew wild in New England, next to almost every roadway in fact. Her mother had taught how the blossoms in autumn held most of the plant's hidden power. But that seeds in spring pods contained some of the plant's living spirit as well, and its blue wintry leaves also some, though less. (This wild New England weed possessed a plenitude of names as well as attributes, although none were known tonight by either slave or spy, and depended upon place. For this plant grew in all climes in the hemisphere, and had many names for itself: *mad-apple, stinkwort, Devil's Trumpet, datura, Jimson* (after Jamestown). Every tribe called it something else.

Abigail recognized it as a common pest weed, with no purpose other than prickling, except when it blossomed into bells. Then, at least, it looked pretty. And so, she was puzzled by Tituba's gathering . . . until an eerie sensation arose which unburied another memory, and she recalled one use: how in Casco Bay, she and her sisters had gone searching wildflowers to put in hair crowns for the harvest bonfire. But all they could find—that hadn't been plucked by other girls—were this plant's white trumpet bells. So they used those blooms and blue stems to braid themselves pretty hair wreaths. Not pretty enough for their mother though. She grabbed them off their heads and tossed them into the fire, ordering them never to touch this poisonous plant again. Indeed, even the smoke made them sick. Her toddling brother succumbed to a fit. Her two older sisters squirmed on the floor like wriggling worms. While her own vision skewed— instead of one hand, she saw four. Her father was spared. He'd been out scything in the hayfields and nursed them through their miseries . . . their madness of bonfires inside.

Now she knew! Tituba was planning to poison their food on the morrow! Or plug up the chimney while they slept and burn pods to smoke them to death! How she wished now that she had never mentioned the slave uprising in Barbados. It had turned their slave too bold. Or so she believed, until Tituba had cracked open a pod with her teeth and used a twig to scrape the seeds into her palm and ate them. Abigail smothered a gasp. *No! 'Tisn't us! 'Tis her own self wants to die! Her own self she means to murther!* She had never before encountered a suicide, but could understand it. To be owned, as well as hated, would be a misery for anybody, even a *no-body* belonging to her uncle.

That doomed person was gliding past her now, disappearing back into forest. She followed at her same twenty paces to prevent any brushings of her gown or snaps of a twig to alert that ever-listening slave to her presence; and thus, she failed to notice when Tituba spit out the seeds, or observe when a spiny pod fell out from the slave's basket into her path before she stepped on it with her bare foot. She held in that great stabbed yowl, lest she be the one *murthered*. Sinking to the dirt into misery, she began pulling out painful thorns; while truly gruesome, bloodcurdling sounds arose up ahead—death-throes, obviously— which chilled her to the bone. And then, despite a few remaining splinters in her heel, she got up and hurried on her toes to go watch the Indian die.

But Tituba was not in agony. Rather, she was yelping and whelping and thrusting her squat naked torso about in a wild wicked hexing dance. Wrapping her savage witch-limbs around an old oak, sexing . . . *with the tree? Or were spirits of dead warriors present in this wood? Shades that only another Indian can see?*

Abigail watched that erotic ritual dance in breathless astonishment through eyes that kept playing tricks, while her own loins began to ache. So she imagined her self brutally ravaged by wild heathens, though she fought hard for her honor.

The Afflicted Girls

≈✦≈

In moist, mossy undergrowth near brooks, marshes, and wetlands, another wild plant was known to grow, but was only found when one sensed it. Unless it was being searched for in the season when it produced a small waxy visible white flower from its gnarled, tuberous underground root. That root was being sought by blindly digging fingers in mud beside a thin trickle of stream. Each time none was found, the hunt continued downstream until a nosy morning lark began singing and Mercy knew that the cock would soon crow in answer. So she abandoned her quest, rushing back down the hillside to the house.

The sleeping mongrel was sprawled on its side on the kitchen threshold. She carefully stepped over it, opening the door she'd earlier left unbolted. Her caution was in vain. Her livered mistress snapped from the kitchen settle, waking the dog, and now they both barked.

"Hours I've been calling you! Where were you, you sly sneak?"

Her prepared explanation: "I-I was restless, Mistress Putnam . . . unable to sleep. So I went for a walk, hoping to tire myself. I sat and gazed at the stars, while leaning back against a tree. I must have been lulled by crickets for I awoke just now soaked with dew." *The lie begins here.*

Ann's eyes flared. She saw her servant's muddy hands and her damp filthy dress. "Who gave you permission to go on night-walks? My children were crying out for you! Screaming in my ear! Robbing *me* of sleep! You should have been here to go to them!" Mercy went to her now.

"Forgive me, mistress. I will not do it again." She helped that agitated woman back up to her chamber. Then looked in on the little ones—both sound asleep with pacified faces—their night terrors had clearly passed, if night terrors there ever were.

Nonetheless, skullcap had not felled her wakeful mistress and she was nearly caught.

She returned to the kitchen hearth to build up the fire and hang the kettle. Morning was nigh. She made herself some Dyers Broom tea to prop up her weary bones, and tied on her milking apron. She hurried up to the barn, with those empty pails swinging from the heavy wood neck yoke that gave her shoulders constant blisters, to begin another long work-day of the thousands that lay before her.

.

The Afflicted Girls

29

THIS WAS THE DAY IT BEGAN TO RAIN. VIOLENT thunderstorms assaulted the land for nearly a week drowning a wide swath of counties, as far south as Boston. And today, on the fifth day of that weather, during another fierce downpour, Thomas Putnam began his journey home. By mid-morning, he was forced to take shelter when the river overflowed up to his horse's fetlocks. Losing the road and his bearings, he forded across fast-moving rising water to get to higher ground. Eventually, he found an inn in which to shelter. But it was a pricey place, pricier than it had been only two days prior on the way down. Being the sole way-stop at this mile mark.

He squeezed in close to the fire, next to some other stranded folk also soaked and chilblained, while others more comfortable were seated at tables enjoying hot victuals and warming drinks. He partook of no refreshment, nor conversation, only fought off that cavernous compulsion to drink, because he had no money left to spend. He'd used most of the coin he'd connived from his faction to pay a pittance more on his lien. Then forsaken two meals for three days, though not, of course, his whisky. But the bottle he'd brought from the village was emptied. And today, like in his Boston lodgings when eventually his will caved, he bartered: his boiled leather belt for two ales, a blade for a tankard of rye, which in time became the rest of an overpriced bottle for a saddlebag. By nightfall, the innkeeper's wife took pity and served him a free dollop of stew. But she would not let her husband take his other saddlebag, or his saddle, for more drink, no matter how hard he begged them.

Despite Thomas' frustrations, his spirits remained hopeful. Because while filing his faction's petition at the General Court in Boston Town, he'd crossed paths with an Englishman, a lawyer now by profession, but who had once been a judge at England's Old Bailey till a gambling scandal uprooted him. That educated man now dwelt in Boston, and shared a free opinion—a favorable one pertinent to an inheritance case. Additionally, April showers, even violent tempests like this one, which caused delays for travelers were always welcome to a farmer. *Crops need watering* ... "But houses do not!"

Thomas slammed down his mug and teetered to his feet, screaming to all present, how he should have forged ahead and risked the flooded roads and the peril. And for the remainder of this sodden night all those other stranded folk continued ignoring his rants and mug slams, table-leg kicks and curses, and some even applauded when Thomas Putnam of Salem Village passed out.

❧✝❧

The rain ended at midday. After the sun emerged, all drowned places, including Salem Village, took to the task of drying out. Goodwives, daughters, and servants mopped puddles, aired out chambers, boiled musty linens and hung them out to dry, with their own sodden selves soaking in that first sunny dose of warmth, as well.

But at Putnam Farm, oddly, Ann Putnam requested her first *bath* in months and sent her servant down to prepare the neighborhood bathing shed. Not because the neighbor's stream was overflowing its banks now, or for the sake of the stench or grime, which both could claim her, nor was it that her joints and

The Afflicted Girls

muscles ached from so much screaming at her servant about the endless vessels full of water that needed to be carried down to empty. No! This bath was to rid her body of the *thousands of sea-born mites*, which had dribbled onto her person through the leaky ceiling rafters of her sleeping chamber, that were creeping all over her skin now. Her bedclothes were infested, she insisted, and ordered them hard-boiled. (Which Mercy did, but found no spiders or mites in them.)

Left alone in the wake of their mother's bath, those two little Putnam sisters, without elders to overlook them, or a sister, did what wild children normally do after being five days penned in: ran boisterously through the house clanging pan-lids, banging pot-bottoms with tin ladles, marching outside to bang and clang even louder and chase a terrified canine around a muddy yard up past the hen house, and there to also scare waterlogged chickens and a few waylaid geese.

In this clamoring midst Lucy was delivered home by her Uncle Walcott, who didn't want his wagon getting stuck in mud, so he deposited her where the Topsfield Road met his in-law's lane. Sloshing up to the farm gate, she heard and then spied her sisters circling the barn. She ran to them to claim the job of "Sergeant," seizing a small wooden mallet her father used for thumping hides — a baton to lead her parade of "Bandsmen on the Green" in celebration of her homecoming.

Her visit with her cousins had been mostly bright-faced. For Susanna in her best birthday humor had invited her into every game. But then on that sunny first day, Aunt Walcott sourly overruled and barred her from most of their frolics, especially the most enjoyable ones like stickball and leapfrog. "To avoid exertions," her aunt explained. Nor was she permitted to ride with her cousins at eventide in the hay wagon that first night after a drizzle turned the straw barely damp.

So in high-kneed joyful marching strides now, she led her band on parade, wondering where her good friend Mercy Lewis was, who always made life into lessons and lessons into games, because she wished to complain to that sympathetic ear about those missed enjoyments. Also, she wanted a kiss. And now while leading and looking about, she recalled a lovely lesson Mercy had taught them, a made-up song with countless verses with one verse invented by her sisters. To test them, she sang it:

Be you to others kind and true,
As you'd have others be to you.

And when they joined in every verse without reminders, although they'd only just learned it, she marveled how in less than two moons her silly sisters had learned to read—*and* to be good—without even realizing.

Still searching, she marched her noisy soldiers into the house to circle the kitchen table and weave in and out of the parlor, upstairs to circle their beds, and lastly into their mother's chamber, where her bandsmen stopped their clanging now, deciding to see who could jump the higher.

But she sang on, ignoring that she was wheezing—because no one was present to forbid her. Except her self of a sudden—because in this room, in this very spot where she stood waving her baton, her baby brother had died. She thought about that wee boy now, that poor sweet cradling infant who once was tucked and tenderly rocked in her arms and cooed to by her. While those squealers kept holding hands while jumping up and down in muddy slippers on their parents' mat of horsehair.

Instead of scolding them, she grabbed an abandoned pot lid and loudly drummed her disturbing thought away.

The Afflicted Girls

Most of the Evils that abound amongst us proceed from defects as to Family Government.

Massachusetts General Court Synod (1679)

30

ON THE DAY AFTER HIS WIFE'S REVIVING BATH, Thomas Putnam arrived home prior to supper. He lumbered through the open kitchen doorway, hound nipping his heels, and had just begun to unbutton his overcoat when he tripped over his youngest sitting in the middle of the floor. He snatched from her hand the object she was clutching, and his eyes flashed wild. "What bitch-witch gave you a poppet?" The dog barked at the child now in an escalating frenzy. He gave it a mean kick and sent it yelping, tail between its legs.

"I-I did, Mr. Putnam—as a plaything," confessed Mercy as that little one ran over to cringe behind her skirt, fearful that her father would kick her next. And he might have. But instead, he only violently flung her doll into the fire. And now that little girl stared helpless, too afraid to cry, despite the sadness that filled her seeing her beloved angel's silken hair gobbled up by flames, and its white wings of fluff burn to cinder. Her middle sister had run over to hide behind Mercy, too. But poor Lucy, trying so hard now not to cough, was cut off from safety on the other side of the room. She was now grabbed by him and shoved out toward the stairs. "Bring me your mother!"

Thomas sat on the settle to wait.

When Ann came down, although scrubbed of her *vermin*, she was wearing the same reeking gown she'd been living in for weeks. Because after her bath, she'd fetched it out from the unwashed linens having forgotten about *mites*. Thomas caught a whiff of it. "You smell like a crapper! I'll not abide your slovenly ways any longer! Go up and put on a dress and fix your hair. Then come down and greet me properly. My news merits it." So Ann retreated to her room. But then turned the key in the lock, while he waited, and waited. And when she didn't return, Thomas angered and grabbed his gun.

All this while, Mercy had been keeping a protective hand on each small child's back, while at the same time she was silently urging Lucy to move away from him. But her young friend stood paralyzed, because she didn't know what her father meant to do; nor did Mercy. But both guessed, and fear was thick.

But all that Thomas did when his wife didn't return was burst from the kitchen in an increased boil and whip his exhausted mount into a gallop. Because coming home just now, he'd passed his sprouting fields and saw how rabbits had invaded them. The mongrel ran behind at a length. It, too, was hungry for a kill.

⋙✦⋘

Tonight's excursion was more dangerous than her last, with both her master and mistress in such foul tempers inside one bed. But the moon was new on this night only, and wouldn't be again for another month hence. So Mercy gave the dog a portion of the rabbit stew she'd fed to the family earlier. She'd ingested none herself, nor taken anything to stem her hunger for two days. Instead, she'd begged permission to fast for a penance—for the poppet, she had said, planning for this night. Which Thomas welcomed. It meant one less mouth to feed.

Of course, she knew enough not to put any child into harm's way. And although wormwood a more powerful sedative than was skullcap, and this oil she'd made was a stronger concentration than she'd ever administered to the dying or sick at the almshouse, there were wet-nurses, knowing less than she did, who daubed their nipples with its tincture before feeding colicky newborns; although never would they have used it on wasting babes. For as knotted up in her lungs as Lucy was, she was a girl full-grown, and her lazy sisters were hardy hearts that sometimes loved their bed best, and the parents were tormented souls who needed to dream. Wormwood would ease them all.

Hastening on the lane, she suffered a sudden fright fending off an airy creature, which skimmed too close to her face. Not a bat, an omen creature — an owl — swooping down into her path to seize a field mouse in its talons to take up into branches and feed to a nestling. She reflected how this was the season for nurturing mothers, save a few who walked upright. She glanced back toward Putnam farmhouse, sorry for the lack of care in that nest.

In time, she reached the village gate. She hid just inside and scanned for night watchmen, but saw no moving lights. She proceeded quickly to the burial ground now. Entering stealthily and skirting marker stones by rows, reading inscriptions till she found the one she sought:

Thomas Putnam, Sr.

b. 1614 d. 1691

On wings he soars his rapid way

To yon bright regions of eternal day

She began to dig the unsavory earth, just as Bridget had directed:

*Carve the mandrake into your lover's shape. Bury it in
his father's grave with one part milk, three parts water,
and as many drops of your own blood as the years you
wish to keep him.*

❧

Abigail was utterly exhausted and unhappy, but she couldn't fall asleep—in fact, it had been hours now that her restless mind kept churning out resentments about Aunt Ugly. *Why couldn't she lie wakeful at least from something pleasant!* She blamed it on the moon. New moons, in particular smug upturned crescents, always caused her unease. And there that sliver was now, framed in her windowpane, smirking at her just like an ugly aunt.

She bound from the bed to slam the shutter, and happed to glance outside. A skirted figure was moving through the graveyard. *Was Tituba planning to rouse the village dead to dance with her?* And now she blessed the crescent moon, or for the sake of ordinary sleep, she might have missed that ghoulish spectacle.

Abigail looked ghostly herself flying across her uncle's pasture in her new white muslin, while all around swelled the usual noisy chorus of crickets and spade-foot frogs. *Music for Tituba's dance!* Tonight she might dance herself! *But if she did, would the dead know she was yet living?* Crouching behind the fence, she spied that person kneeling. It was a woman reedy and tall. Not squashed, like the Indian. *Was it the mason's wife? Whose husband was crushed to mash in the quarry landslide during the storm?* Snaking down the fence for a closer view, her sleeve caught on a headless nail, and ripped.

A flagon dropped, spilling potion into Mercy's skirt. She jumped hastily to her feet . . . for Abigail was already bounding toward her. "What are you doing? What damnable thing are you doing, Mercy?"

Mercy's hem hid the flagon, yet she didn't know how long Abigail had been spying or what her friend had seen. "Nothing," she stammered.

"In the middle of the night? In a graveyard?"

The Afflicted Girls

Be quick--give an answer, any answer. "I was sent hither by my mistress to offer a new moon prayer for her dead babe. Her mind is unseemly disturbed tonight.

"Mistress Putnam sent you?" Abigail repeated dubiously.

Had the owl been her warning? "Yes," Mercy affirmed. "She is sometimes strangely confused. Night becomes day to her. Death lives on. I cannot explain how she perceives things. But my master has ordered me never to refuse her. So I came hither to do her unwholesome bidding. Even your own uncle has instructed me to obey her."

But Abigail had observed that more than a prayer had been offered. There'd been a libation as well as a supplication; a potion had been poured. She knew this because she had seen her holding a bottle, and also could faintly sniff the scent of milk. And what purpose had milk in a graveyard? Except to feed an infant's ghost. But now she saw how the inscription on this marker was not an infant's, but a patriarch's. She uncovered further proof when she raked her bare toes through this loosened earth, and felt the soil's dampness.

She accused: "You were casting a spell--I heard you. Heard it all, Mercy Lewis. Don't deny it. I always thought you clever, but you're cleverer than I thought." It was hardly more than a guess. Because from her vantage by the fence, while she did overhear some muttering because of those noisy crickets, she'd gleaned no clear or precise words; so she would have to use fluster to learn what was said. "Yes, indeed, this is a Putnam's grave, but no wee bones lie inside it . . . only the bones of your master's father, who wears the same name as him!" Her guess: "You desire a husband and had hoped to bend your master's will toward loving you. You came not to serve your mistress, Mercy, but to conjure her demise, to cast a midnight spell for the grave to take her, since her toes are dipped in anyway!"

Mercy should have kept silent, she should have walked away leaving Abigail with only guesses, but this accusation was so abhorrent to her, she couldn't let it stand. So without sharpening her wit, she crafted an answer, which held drops of the truth, for such was her nature: "Nothing was bent here but my own unhappy heart. I came at my mistress' bidding for the reason I told you, Abigail, but you have cleverly cornered my other frustration. It isn't my master I crave, but a man he mentioned as seeking a wife. I said a prayer for that, too."

Abigail was unmoved. "You have done a terrible thing nevertheless, a sinful thing, Mercy, and I'm obligated to tell."

With Abigail, Mercy knew, it was best not to press against, rather, to flatter and agree, or they'd duel until Abigail won the point or she surrendered it. "Compared to you, I am weak. You have always kept yourself spotless, while I blame God for my every sorrow. That's why you've been rewarded with a good life here, and I've been punished with the worst."

Again the words rang true, but it was a half-truth Abigail decided, and likely spoken deceitfully, because the important half was concealed. She prodded: "Where did you learn your love spell? Did your mad mistress teach it?"

"There was no spell, only a rhyme.

"Indeed . . . but someone has taught it—"

"No one, Abby. It was in a book, yes, a book of tales I read as a child. Does it matter? The truth is that I'm lonely here. As if words could win me a husband. But if you tell, I'll win only lashings. Then I'll be sore in body as well as heart, when my master picks up a strap and beats me for my foolishness."

Abigail's face lit up, "It was a conjurer's book. What other sorcery was in it? Tell me, Mercy! I want to learn!"

Now both orphans in their struggles to survive had mastered the art of dissembling.

The Afflicted Girls

"You already know the rhyme, Abigail: *Thrice toss oaken ashes in the air. Thrice sit thou mute in this enchanted chair. Three times thrice tie true love's knot. And murmur softly: 'He will, or he will not.'* Can we not just say 'good morrow' and part as friends?"

Abigail scrutinized her companion. And also the grotesque warding mask peering out from the patriarch's gravestone. "Unlike you, Mercy Lewis, I remember no rhymes from books. But I do recall how pagan charms are always set to rhyme." She looked up at the smirking moon, now her ally. "And how their power is said to be strongest under a moon that's new, and wax even stronger on a burial mound. By the bye, Mercy, you'll teach me your spells. Vow it now, or on the morrow, I'll tell my uncle what you did."

A long silence . . . a fear-filled sigh: "Please, Abigail . . . you cannot tell your uncle."

"Then you'll teach me?"

Mercy nodded.

One stretch of the Topsfield Road cut through a grove of old willow with low hanging branches. It was a very dark spot, especially on new moon nights when creeping roots often caught up feet. But tonight in that blackness, it was a deep wheel-rut that caught Mercy, and her ankle twisted as she fell.

She limped on with the aid of a crutch—a long branch. But first she chewed some wild thyme to make a poultice for the swelling. She stopped again, taking shelter when a sudden storm arose and sprayed nettles of ocean in her face. She could barely see the road for the rain or tramp it for the mud. So she wondered if this was real—this storm, this walk. Or was it all a mystical imagining? She tried to awaken. Then quick as it started that unnatural rain ceased. The sky cleared. Her ankle still throbbed. She plodded on.

Finally, she beheld Putnam Farm gate, but sitting low above the house's chimney was a sliver of upturned moon turned red, like a Devil's hideous grin. She shuddered, remembering another olden rhyme: *Mis-for-tune . . . roots in the shadows of a liar's moon.*

❧✦❧

Tonight, as on other nights of late, the object of Mercy's pursuit, Joseph Putnam, slept poorly. Not because of her midnight folly, but from his own. He'd just suffered through another dream in which his mother won their argument. Taunting with delight how his impulses had undone him. Saying his marriage banns were now stuck onto posts for everyone to view. Setting his lifelong course in her choice of direction.

Even in dreams, he blamed Ben Nurse for it. For waffling at that last minute about snooking for whores in Boston, going home instead, leaving him alone with that mindless tit. He'd been aroused by the bawdy discussion, so it wasn't a leap to lead Elizabeth Porter into the woods and coax up her skirts and without a whit of desire take her, take her whoring hard. How could he have guessed she'd run to tell her mother of her ruin, who'd run to his, along with the father, with all of them forcing him into this marriage? Or, that when he refused, his mother would take advantage in private. Threatening to leave him with nothing. Reminding how she'd done the same to another, promising he'd end up just like Thomas. He told her he'd kill himself first. That certainly sobered her.

But he knew he'd treat the Porter girl bad always. And that this would be their married pattern: he would ignore her; she'd seek a mother's consolation—hers, or his—and he'd hear about it later with threats. Bringing the scullion into his dreams was hardly a consolation. Nonetheless, he desired her. For her perfectly sculpted body and face, willingness, obvious experience, not to mention useful knowledge of his brother. But the bigger lure was that clear knowledge of *him* she somehow possessed: that deep unfathomable blue knowing, the opposite of degradation he'd glimpsed just once in her eyes, but in no one else's, ever—which in dreams, only of her, had he ever fallen through into joy.

31

TODAY WAS THURSDAY, THIRD THURSDAY IN April. After delivering his usual fustian lecture, Reverend Parris walked Thomas Putnam back to the parsonage to settle their account of the bondmaid. He sat down at his desk and opened his receipt book. He was handed a coin. But not the one previously given, which both of them knew was the price. Immediately, he felt abused, ill used by someone he'd trusted as a friend, who had only to pay the cheapest amount, a pittance—a flea. Nevertheless, he took that coin and wrote that measly sum into his ledger. While his false friend, beside him, blurted: "My wife's not improving, Sam. But sinking lower."

He lowered his eyes to that greedy scribbled sum, and in two blinks dared not look up again. Having just realized how it was himself who was the abuser. For not once in over a month had he inquired after that poor woman's health. *Had he grown so selfishly unfeeling? Yes . . . clearly, he had. The Village Committee's wicked assault on his house had robbed him of his charitable thinking.* He surged to his feet, clasped Thomas' shoulder, saying heartfelt and sincere: "I'll visit Ann today, Thomas. I'll go to God for her. I'll do whatever I can."

So after Thomas Putnam departed, Reverend Parris went directly to the kitchen to inform his wife of his plan. She looked up from her stitching and asked to accompany him, saying she'd been much concerned about Ann Putnam lately herself, though in truth she'd not been thinking of that goodwife at all. But like everyone in the village, she was curious.

Out of necessity, he sent his manslave to borrow a cart from Nathaniel Ingersoll because he owned no formal conveyance himself, a mule only, and his wife was too genteel for that. (Despite that young Mary, Mother of Jesus, when impregnated by God, rode a similar beast to Egypt, and also the Lord rode on one entering Jerusalem.) Because among the populace of *this* place, in this present day of scrutiny and back-stabbings, an educated man's wife—particularly the village minister's—perched in the curve of a mangy mule, while her husband walked beside her, was a parable only for ridicule.

Nathaniel Ingersoll obliged. But predictably, requested tit for tat, asked that John Indian be spared for the rest of the day for inn labors.

Why is it never charity? Only sculduddery? Reverend Parris vexed, deciding he would speak to that failing on Sunday.

≈✦≥

Ann Putnam's unwelcome visitors performed for two hours with the minister kneeling at one side of her bed and his wife at the other side holding her hand, both praying for her restoration. All the while, she prayed for them to leave. And when they did, she finally slept.

Strange, she thought upon awaking. She did feel somewhat healed. She looked into her hand mirror and saw a different face. So she got up to brush out her matted locks and pin up that abundance of hair into a neat bun using Thomas' unction and capping it with a doily. She even put a pinky-tip of his boot polish onto each cheek. She fetched out a garment from the wardrobe, which smelled of mint and was ironed crisp—her servant's usual method of laundering. The dress was ill-fitting, but never mind that, because she still felt healed. She dragged her rocker into the solitary umbra of sunlight left by the window, and sat and rocked while she read to herself from *Song of Songs*:

> *Hark! My lover, here he comes springing across*
> *the mountains, leaping across the hills —*

She grew giddy at that unlikely picture, as she continued reading, skipping unnecessary parts.

> *His fruit is sweet to my mouth . . . I am faint with*
> *love. His left hand is under my head and his right*
> *arm embraces me . . . Let him kiss me with kisses*
> *of his mouth —*

Opening to those yearnings best she could.

> *I rose to open to my lover, with my hands*
> *dripping with myrrh upon the fittings of the*
> *lock —*

Closing her eyes, she imagined her lover's dripping key fitting into her lock, and then turning her, as the sun dipped beneath the horizon. When her sighs ceased and eyes opened, the room was dark. So she closed the Book, fetched her slippers, and went down to cosset her youngsters and await her husband's arrival in the parlor. She planned to greet Thomas with an open-mouthed kiss. Then later in bed, she would let him kiss her other parts, even that place of "dripping myrrh."

But only after she told him to give her another son.

Unfortunately, Thomas Putnam never arrived home today nor planted any seeds in any fertile fields. Because after departing the parsonage this morning, while walking back across the green to where his work wagon was tied, a person he knew stopped him and told him a rumor of concern. Instead of proceeding to his fields, he went into the inn to fish for further details, which he reeled in by the bucketful, since by now everyone had heard.

The Afflicted Girls

He sat in low spirits at the corner table till a short while ago, when the innkeeper snuffed his lantern and bid him goodnight. He said the same, before stumbling out and through the dark up to Sister Trask's house, where he presently slept.

Sadly, he had missed his chance for happiness today and never even knew it. All because the hilly acreage adjacent to Putnam Farm on which his sheep, few goats, and milk cows grazed — which legally was in the possession of his stepmother still, but which he expected to win back through his probate appeal — had just been sold to the new junior constable, John Willard, that landgrubber from Connecticut, who'd purchased the farmstead up the road.

That witch, Mary Veren, had done it intentionally to spite him. Knowing, as she did, how the source of both his stream and drinking well was the aquifer on that property. A battle with a rich man over water rights was coming, and he didn't have the money to win it.

32

ANN PUTNAM'S HEART HAD OPENED WIDE, AND now it clamped shut again—as attested by two sleepy-eyed youngsters who had happily skipped into their mother's chamber this morn seeking kisses, like the ones they'd gotten on yester eve. She was her usual cold self, scolding how there'd be no more waking her or bothering her, or making noise in her house, or wasting of her time. "From today you'll do chores, or I'll bond you out as chars to cold-hearted crones to learn better manners."

They ran.

Awakening so abruptly soured her mood. So she decided to make herself a comforting wine posset for breakfast, despite the lack of wine. Without dressing, she went out to the henhouse to collect eggs. Crawling inside it, she counted half as many layers as she remembered. So she agitated about her sheep. Their herd best she remembered numbered near to forty and by now there would be lambs. But at least she knew the exact number of milk cows she had, since day in and day out for years she'd done the milking herself. Forgetting eggs, she crawled out and sniffed the air. The drunkard didn't keep pigs. But her nearest neighbors bred them, and the air this morning was fouled with the stench of butchered swine. Covering her nose with her sleeve, she continued to the barn, having turned away from her craving for wine posset.

The Afflicted Girls

It was yet an early hour, only a little after dawn. Mercy had not finished milking when her mistress walked in, surprising her, but then stood silent, vacantly staring at a knothole. "Is there something you need, Mistress Putnam?" she asked.

Ann picked up the one bucket already full, swigged cream from its lip and set it down again. "When you take the cows to pasture, count my sheep." *But why couldn't she recall her other fine idea?* She looked about the barn, but nothing jogged her memory. Though the walls were beginning to tilt. While behind her, Thomas' mongrel had skulked up to lap milk from that same pail. Seeing its white snout, she kicked it, and remembered:

"Pick out a lamb, the smallest we have. Take it to the parsonage. Tell the minister's wife it's a gift from me—not from my husband. Say it's in thanks for my healing. Dress proper. Wear your Sunday bonnet." *But was that really what she wanted to recall?*

❧✿☙

Despite its diminutive size, the creature Mercy picked possessed its herd's strongest will. During her five-mile trek to the village, it continuously bleated, pulling against its tether and quieted only when she carried it. She'd been carrying it a little while ago when a work wagon came rumbling up behind and the creature bolted, and its rear hoof struck her breastbone with a painful jab. Rushing sideways out of the way, her weight came down upon her weakened ankle, injuring it again. Upset, in pain and limping, she dragged that balking animal in through the village gate, in a mood so fallen no lark's song overhead could uplift it.

The village was abuzz; hordes of folk were congregated on the green. Mercy overheard bits of their animated conversations: "Phips . . . new Governor . . . Royal Charter." To her, the chatter meant little. But to the villagers it meant their disputes could now be pled to an ultimate authority. Most had lawsuits pending.

In the center of one huddle stood Nathaniel Ingersoll, who, seeing her lamb as she passed, was reminded—and began relating the tale—of William Phips beginning his career as a penniless ship's carpenter, who'd seduced his captain's widow and then married her, turning his booty toward high-seas piracy in the Indies. How off Baileys Reef in the Bahamas, with a crew of only twenty cutthroats, he sank then raised again a royal Spanish galleon with a treasure worth £300,000. How, while the lion's portion went to the Crown "the *lamb's* portion, namely £16,000 in pieces of eight, and a title, *Knight of the Golden Fleece*" went to him. And now by King William's decree, that most coveted appointment of Massachusetts Governor. "Here's to that lucky lamb's luck spilling over on us!"

Meanwhile, Mercy was giving the unlucky lamb its final taste of freedom, letting it romp freely in Parris' pasture . . . but only for her own peace of mind. To avoid having to knock at the parsonage door and encounter Abigail. This hadn't been a welcome errand, but a dreaded one. When she saw the minister's manslave exit the parsonage barn, she called to him. And when John Indian walked up, she delivered her mistress' message. He pinned the animal under his arm and carried it bleating to the animal pen. Then he went into the kitchen.

She was nearly across the pasture when John Indian came running after her.

Mrs. Parris gestured for her to sit. She poured Mercy a cup of whey, querying with an upraised brow and a solemn tone: "How fares your mistress, Ann Putnam?"

Mercy hesitated. "Better, Mistress Parris . . . her eldest says she is much like before."

The parsonness clasped her hands and chirruped: "Such gladsome news. It will greatly please my husband . . . and the lamb was such a thoughtful gift. Tell her it will be fattened up for

The Afflicted Girls

Reverend Parris' Easter feast. Also, that I am inviting her to tea next Sunday . . . that is, if she feels enough in her cups."

Mercy nodded, gulping her beverage quickly. She stood up: "Thank you for the refreshment, mistress. I was exceedingly thirsty." As she curtseyed she was tying on her bonnet, and that's when Abigail entered. Surprise perched on both their lips.

"I have finished my lesson, Aunt Parris," announced Abigail. "Betty is still contemplating hers. May I accompany my friend to the village gate?"

"Are your sums done as well, niece?"

"Yes, Aunt (*Ugly*)." Abigail waited for what she knew was coming next.

"What is man's chief end?"

"Man's chief end is to glorify God and enjoy Him forever."

"What is God?"

"God is a spirit, infinite, eternal, and unchangeable; in His being, wisdom, power, holiness, justice, goodness and truth." Uttered, of course, with suitable awe.

"What is sin?"

"Sin is any want of conformity unto, or *transgression* of the law of God." She looked at Mercy when she said this.

"You've recited the catechism perfectly, niece. Yes, you may walk with your friend to the village gate. But no farther."

Embroidering that walk into a roundabout meander, Abigail kept Mercy's arm tight-threaded, as she snatched as much village gossip as she could to tell to her uncle later. Because he'd gone visiting northwest farms on Solomon's Hill today, and wouldn't have heard this news. And then, as they eventually reached the village gate, Abigail blurted her own important news:

"Susanna Walcott and John Doritch want to learn to cast spells, too."

Mercy was aghast, "But you promised. You promised me you wouldn't tell."

"Falser than false. Twisted are your ears. That isn't what I said at all. Unwind the spool, you'll see. I only promised I wouldn't tell my uncle."

"You betrayed and tricked me. I won't soon forget it."

Abigail cast a flinty eye toward the graveyard. "Nor will I soon forget how you betrayed and tricked God."

The Afflicted Girls

33

J OSEPH PUTNAM HAD BEEN FORCED TO TRAVEL TO
Topsfield this morning on a financial matter relating to
his mother's forge and ironworks, which didn't conclude in her
favor. Yet he didn't really care, because he knew nothing about
mining metals or metal ventures, and if she had truly wanted a
favorable outcome then, he decided, she should have gone herself.
But the errand, at least, brought him two surprising diversions
while it wasted his time.

First was when he came face to face with Salem Village's
unpopular minister in (of all places) the center of a narrow
covered bridge. It wasn't too hard to guess the man's identity, not
only from the snide prickly resemblance he bore to one girl from
Maine, or his pompous though threadbare minister's garb, which
precisely fit Ben Nurse's description. It was more a matter of his
unremitting arrogance. Reverend Parris had ordered him to
withdraw, claiming to have entered the bridge first. Which wasn't
true, but nevertheless was irrelevant. Since normally he would
yield the right of way to any man, even this village idiot.

But then, as he began to turn his horse inside that narrow
passageway, the minister rudely threatened: "Back out of my way,
stable boy! Let your superior pass, or receive his stripe," and
actually held aloft his crop. (Because Reverend Parris didn't know
that his vexation was his own patron's heir, a newly elected
selectman, whose support was crucial to obtain, but who wasn't

recognized by virtue of soiled stable clothes worn deliberately to peeve a nettlesome mother.) "Out of my way, you filthy boy!" swiped Reverend Parris.

"To a thread we are evenly matched, sir. But I'm willing to throw a coin for it--that is, *if* you can find one," Joseph laughed.

Reverend Parris snorted, "Profligate!" his face flushing pink when he caught the intended meaning. He judged this to be an enemy's son, worthy of a brutal lashing. But each time he tried to land a stripe, Joseph deftly deflected — and in that stalemate of bad manners they continued till a noisy ox cart came clacking up.

Reverend Parris shot a hasty glance behind him. Then cropped his mule and quickly trotted it out the way he'd come, because this was the village blacksmith, who hadn't tithed in a month, and the entrance to a narrow covered bridge was the perfect place to accost a debtor.

And now Joseph cantered past them on his way north to Topsfield. The village blacksmith, grinning large, rose to his feat and tipped his cap.

Reverend Parris, confused, inquired the boy's identity and was informed: "Oh, young Joseph Putnam that is, newly returned from England," which the blacksmith knew from doing business with the Putnam Forge and Ironworks. And without tipping his cap to the minister, or any further ado, that ox sat again and lashed his ox and drove his cart across the bridge.

And now, three hours later, as Joseph was returning home from his unsuccessful errand, after emerging from that same narrow transit, he met a second surprise, a far prettier one, who was so distracted she didn't notice him till he was nearly upon her. And then Mercy grew so unnerved seeing him that she forgot to smile or even offer a curtsey. But shuddered, instead, that the charm had worked, and now Abigail's intrusion felt so much more ominous.

The Afflicted Girls

"I cannot converse with you, sir. Beg pardon, but I must hurry home." *Hurry?* She was limping, limping slowly. And the farm was yet two miles.

Just before she reached the bridge, he cantered past and halted his horse, blocking her entry. He dismounted and sent the animal to shamble where it wanted. For this was a creature trained to his whistle. Like she was to his whisper. Taking Mercy's hand without asking, he reminded her: "This is the third time we've met by chance, but the first time no one else is present to observe us."

She didn't resist when he led her away from the road, across a field and down a slope, because she loved him too well. That was the truth of it. Her heart was saying, it too. Even though in her mind's eye, she could see Abigail taunting how they were both now the Devil's daughters. And then, after she stumbled and he caught her and pulled her close into his arms to kiss her, she would have let him. But then he didn't kiss her, instead abruptly let her go and looked away. For he'd just had a second thought that this was a person prone to mishap, and that mishaps bled over, and lest some future accident or mistake of hers affect him, it might be better to keep her at an arm's length.

A grassy bower, conveniently surrounded by trees, was the perfect setting for natural appetites, if two ever wished to lie together unnoticed. He led Mercy into that copse and laid her bodily down, unlaced her bodice and pulled off her bloomers, and sucked hungrily at her nipples as heavy unbridled passions aroused. But he gave no kisses to her lips. Even now. Only drew her legs up around him and drove his full length inside her — before she was ready — and took her hard.

Mercy tried to give her self to him, she tried to offer him love, but her body was recoiling. "Please, sir, you're hurting me."

His fingers curled over her mouth, and now he turned her over to take her from behind, like he always did with his wenches and whores. *Too soon, too soon,* he trembled, and pulled out, rolling

185

onto his back, squeezing the swollen member, trying to force back down its powerful urges. But he couldn't, and expelled.

Her flesh inside was torn. Her petticoat was stained with spots of red. Mercy lowered it, ashamed of her abusing, but accepting that she'd been the cause of it. How could she blame him for the violence of a graveyard charm? *This wasn't a rape. It wasn't!* The Devil had fanned him into a heat. At the same time, cooling her. She sat up. "It-it's late, sir. I must go."

"Not yet-no." He took her face in his hands. She thought he meant to kiss her; and she needed that kiss. Instead, he forced her mouth to his prick. It was hardening against her unwillingness. He said: "More delights first. Then to matters concerning my brother."

The Afflicted Girls

34

TWO WEEKS PRIOR ON THE MORNING OF THE NEW moon at the seven o'clock hour, Bridget Bishop began teaching a local lad she'd hired the proper way to turn up soil with respect for the tiny lives within it. Though he was a neighboring farmer's son, he hadn't as yet been taught olden skills and had been treating her soil rudely. The time had come to plant her yearly garden in the quarter acre behind her kitchen. After a good day's toil, she sent him home before dusk, for tonight the moon was full. And at evenfall, standing alone at exactly the seven o'clock hour, she performed her ritual of *beginning*.

The next day she had the boy lace her rows with dung— dung, that she had collected on the prior full moon's evenfall from her own most fertile milk cows, manure that she had let simmer and bake under sun and wind and stars for a month. This morning, exactly at sun-break, she took those seeds and seedlings milled from last year's bountiful crop and planted them in this Mother's lap. Mid-morning, she commenced the ablution of *watering*.

She had just walked away to refill her sprinkling can at the well pump on the other side of her house, when three of her neighbor's chickens squeezed through a hole in the fence, strutted into her dooryard garden, and began pecking up the newly planted seeds. And now that ever-vigilant gray cat moved down from an open doorway on stealthy paws alongside that fence, then stopped and eyed those brainless birds from behind the scarecrow, waiting for the hens to separate.

Frenzied clucking summoned Bridget back to her garden. She beheld a wildly pecking, flapping, fevered bird trapped in her feline's claws, while two hysterical birds ran in circles through her rows. She caught those two and flung them back over the fence. Then tried to save the bloodied third bird and got both pecked and scratched in the process. Eventually she freed it, though now it was limp. She heaved it, too, over the fence, yelling: "Goodman Louder! Fix this fence or your hens will all end up with their necks broke!"

A gruff voice responded, "Hurt a one and I'll sue you, Bridget!"

"Sue me and you'll lose more than a chicken! This fence with the hole in it is yours, not mine!"

"More's mine here than just a fence!"

Bridget waited till that familiar bloodshot eye appeared in the usual knothole. Then she picked up her watering can and walked over to water the fence.

This bickering with her neighbor had been going on for ten years, ever since her husband Edwin Bishop died and she inherited his property.

Twenty-five years prior, when young Bishop first arrived in these parts in a second wave of English immigrants and decided to settle in Beverly Village, at the end of a seven-year indenture, he purchased a small house-lot on an unsettled part of the Ipswich High Road. By luck, a few years later, he married a girl of wealth from Salem Village, who had a dowry large enough to build them a two-storey, two-winged dwelling; and then also through bribes obtain a coveted license for a High Road public house. When that wife died, he took another, a widow, who wasn't rich but cooked well and worked hard in Bishop's Ordinary. When she died, he married a beauty, Bridget Oliver of Beverly, a young widow, who was the one who reaped her predecessors' rewards.

Their closest neighbor, Goodman Louder, who dwelt on the house-lot behind had, early on in his acquaintanceship with Goodman Bishop lent him a sum of money—a modest amount to be sure, that was used to purchase the original furnishings and sundries for a bachelor's first dwelling. Repayment took the form of years of generosity in free victuals and drink. But after the Grim Reaper claimed his friend, Goodman Louder claimed otherwise. Fortunately for Bridget, inheritance laws in the Commonwealth were generally straightforward: wills were stringently followed, and when there wasn't one—as had happened here since Goodman Bishop died when his heart unwillingly stopped—the surviving spouse inherited her husband's property. Regarding Goodman Louder's loan, she had no further obligation, since a man's debts from before a marriage were buried with him.

Because her husband had fathered no offspring with either prior wife or with her, nor had any living relations that she could locate, she inherited it all. But her husband did have one envious next-door neighbor named Louder, who filed a lawsuit on the day of the burial claiming half of Bishop's property was his.

Bridget searched through her husband's papers, but found no proof of a partnership with Louder: no promissory notes or scribbled IOUs. Nor could she find his name written into any of her husband's ledgers, account books or diaries. Neither could Louder produce any contract written in Goodman Bishop's hand. And while Bridget had, in the ensuing years, paid Goodman Louder back in full all the inflated sums he'd ever stated in his numerous petitions, just to stop his pestering, it never did stop. He was a sore loser who refused to be bettered by a woman, especially one of such dubious moral reputation as Bridget Bishop of Beverly, a harlot really, who didn't deserve to be rich, and who should be wearing black widows-weeds, not red.

PART FIVE

35

THE PRO-PARRIS FACTION GATHERED TONIGHT, this time in the west, at Putnam Farm. Although meetings like this had been taking place on both sides of the cleavage for months, tonight's was the most crucial one yet for the minister's supporters. Because news had reached them yesterday that the English ship, *the Nonesuch*, carrying their new governor, had just docked in Boston.

As always, the meeting began with Reverend Parris reciting an opening prayer, which he'd aptly chosen:

> *Behold, God rejects the obstinate in heart,*
> *He preserves not the life of the wicked,*
> *He withholds not the just man's rights,*
> *But grants vindication to the oppressed.*

Their side would triumph he assured them when he finished, because their cause was just.

"Even if those rots are at Porter's table right now drafting their own petition? For I've heard they are," someone advised. "What if it's a better one?"

Reverend Parris dismissed the naysayer. "Is anyone here acquainted with Phips?" No one spoke up. "Are any of Porter's?"

The Afflicted Girls

Ingersoll answered thoughtfully: "Not that I know this for a fact, Sam. But certain of our foes conduct commerce in London, and with their coffers always so full, and knowing this new governor was twenty years a pirate, who also spent years at that corrupt royal court, should we discount the use of a bribe?"

Hearing this speculation, Reverend Parris' eyes hazed with worry, but only for a moment. Trusting in God, he returned to the matter at hand: to introduce his own inspired idea for redrawing the village boundaries and make his opposition into Salem Town dwellers, since most of them lived in the eastern parts anyway; and in that way extricate from their power over this parish, and also over him. Because, while a privateer might not stamp his approval on a map were he bribed, were he not bribed, or dishonest, a new map which brought an end to the bitter discontent in one village, especially when those presenting it were its minister and Head Selectman, would likely be approved.

So all said aye to it, for they had no better strategies.

But when Reverend Parris picked up his quill to sketch them this new map, the tax collector nixed him: "We'll only be casting out our most productive lands and lucrative waterways. And why do that, when every tide eventually turns by itself?"

Now they decided this was the *better* logic, and they voted against Reverend Parris. The village boundaries would not be changed. They drafted an inferior petition following Ingersoll's advice, asking only that Governor Phips settle the dispute of the minister's salary tax by ordering a compromise between the parties. And when that document was written and signed, Ingersoll announced he was taking it personally to Boston to present to the new governor himself. And when it had dried, he rolled it up and tied it round with a bright purple velvet ribbon, which he'd found, he said, in his wife's sampling basket.

Chuckles weren't stifled, and elbows jabbed into sides. Ingersoll batted back that the ribbon was meant to catch the governor's eye, like honey lures a bear to a trap. "With so many piles of petitions sitting on his desk by tomorrow, ours will be the one noticed and read. Phips may have been a fearsome freebooter once, but thanks to King William now he's a feathered fop. This expensive velvet riband will no doubt end its life on the new governor's hat."

All praised their leader's sagacity. All, that is, except Reverend Parris, who had more at stake in this than Ingersoll, and besides, his idea was the better one. It should have been his map tied with purple.

After the meeting finished, after everyone but his in-laws were gone, Thomas unlocked his parlor chest and took out a legal document he'd purchased in Boston with an IOU. He spread two elegantly scribed pages on the tabletop and told Walcott and Trask to read them.

Both men read slowly, for the language was high and judicial and also interspersed with Latin terms. Also, the lamp oil was low and flickering, and had been of poor quality to begin with. All of them were suffering eyestrain. And even though Trask usually wore reading spectacles, he'd forgotten to bring them tonight. So he, too, squinted.

Mercy had already laid her head down on the settle and closed her eyes. Now she heard her master yelling for his portion, and knew what he meant. Earlier, when Deacon Ingersoll first arrived, he'd set down a large keg of ale outside the kitchen door from which she'd served them, and of which her master had instructed her to siphon off two jugs worth and hide them in the pantry. But in the constant flurry of serving, she'd forgotten to do it. Knowing she'd be beaten for her mistake, an image of *mead* came to mind.

She took down an empty pitcher and ran outside to drain the keg. She mixed into the dregs cold chamomile from the kettle, vinegar and yeast, rainwater from the standing barrel—her concoction tasted wretched, but did have a small bite. She crushed in allspice and mint; there was nothing sweeter in this kitchen. It was still barely drinkable. But was all that could be done. She carried in the pitcher.

As she poured deception into their mugs, she happed to glance down at the pages the in-laws were reading. Her mind swiftly absorbed the text, with Latin no impediment. (Always, she'd been able to read whole pages at a single glance, though wisely kept the ability secret, lest she be accused of possessing impossible powers. While Latin was a language she'd long ago learned.) Her master swilled and now grabbed the pitcher from her hands. Wiping his mouth, he ordered her out, and followed her to the doorway, and locked the door behind her.

He sat and gave his in-laws the explanation now: "The man once sat in a magistrate's chair and knows better law than our enemies. This writ names me legal executor in place of the usurpers. It's based on a little-known statute in English common law, which under our new Commonwealth Charter will be the overriding one, he says. As soon as we file it, we'll be able to take a legal inventory."

"Fen-sucked by a rogue," surmised Trask. "Our remedies were exhausted when our probate suit failed."

"Because Hathorne's seat is in Israel Porter's pocket, who himself is in Mary Veren's. But none of them knows it's possible to overturn contested wills when second or third wives are named in place of a first-born son. Nor do they need to know it, until after our writ is filed in Boston's High Court and the Englishman argues our case there . . . for a price. "

"What price?" Trask wondered, his tired eyes growing alert.

Thomas hesitated. "Ten, ten only . . . and your wife, and Brother Walcott's . . . will get their fair portions."

"Ten shillings? Why that toad-spotted thief! He's lucky to get a ten-pence!"

"Sovereigns, William. Ten sovereigns. Thirty, in all . . . which you'll have to lend us."

"A bleeding, bat-fowled pustule on his anus!" It was the worst insult Trask knew.

Walcott said nothing, but thought how this amount exceeded his yearly income.

Thomas saw his face, and knew what he was thinking, because he thought much the same himself. For although Brother Walcott had strapping sons to work his farmland, and daughters to keep his house, he also had to feed and clothe them, and get his seven and four married—while Trask was middle-aged and childless, and had a thriving business to boot. He hid money under his mattress. Not that his sister was the barren one. That miser had had barren wives before her.

But as much as the tinker lacked in generosity, and despite the poor opinion Thomas held of him, he was a skinflint with one handy tool—his underhandedness. His motto always: *What's the best way to win the purse of a cheat? Cheat better. Rob the robber.*

Trask grinned. "The Englishman thinks we're gudgeons? Let's play that part. We'll wear hapless faces down to Boston to consult him. When he marks my spectacles, I'll offer to write it all down, while you two scratch your heads and seek further opinions and clarifications . . . particularly regarding appeals. We'll grin large and agree to hire him. We'll each shake his hand. After he pleads our case and we exit the courthouse victorious, we'll thank him and sing his praises. And then, when he requests his fee, we'll turn out our empty pockets and tell him he can sue us for thirty sovereigns. "Sue us," we'll say, "and if you win, Brother Putnam will write you another IOU." And now he laughed.

Thomas laughed, too, but still thought the tinker cheap.

The Afflicted Girls

Later, they decided to postpone their trip to Boston until Nathaniel Ingersoll arrived home; and he returned home yesterday. Mostly to avoid encountering him in the government-quarter, where he'd try to sniff out their business. The man was a nosy jabber, who always spilled other people's uncooked beans. Not even their wives knew their purpose in going. Two thought their husbands would be purchasing seed, the third thought rolls of tin.

36

SEEING HER MASTER'S PACKED SADDLE BAG sitting at the bottom of the stair, Mercy prepared her lie: if caught tonight, she would tell the mistress how her friend took ill at the parsonage and that the minister's manslave was sent to fetch her in a wee hour. That she did not want to wake her but had meant to write a message on the slate, and in worry and haste had forgotten to do it.

And now in that actual wee hour, as she swept down the High Road once again, it was through a thick fogbank in which no world at all was visible. She had missed the public house sign going half a mile past, because no candle flickered or fire glowed at Bishop's Ordinary. When she realized, and returned, she also found a chalked sign on the door reading: "*closed.*"

She used the knocker. No one answered. So she came round to the other side and considered ringing the cast-iron bell on a man-sized frame. But then the chime warned her how it was an alarm to be used only for fires, tempests and heathen assaults, that its cry was so formidable, it would summon all within miles, who then would see her. She let go of the rope and instead gathered pebbles to fling willy-nilly up into the fog, hoping one would hit Bridget's chamber window, because she had to see her tonight.

Something must have guided her hand rightly, for a pebble did strike Bridget's pane, and soon that perturbed sleepy face appeared in it.

The Afflicted Girls

Bridget supposed that a stranger had come, possibly a foreigner who couldn't read the King's English. Not caring, she tucked back into bed. Then another pebble struck, and another and lest this annoyance continue the nightlong, or tomorrow's sun greet her exhaustion with so much work left to be done, she lit her candlestick and went down, and opened the door, and growled with displeasure: "This is the week I see no one. Go away. Leave me be."

"You would turn me out without knowing my purpose in coming? Knowing my difficulty in—"

"I would, indeed, aye, I am. Go away."

"Even though—"

"Even though you rob me of my precious sleep!"

Mercy was taken aback. Where was the protective mother she'd risked her safety to see? This was not the woman who'd given her iron promises. She stepped away from the door. "I understand, Goody Bishop. I am unwelcome now and am not to bother you—"

"Now-now, I didn't say *that*. You are free to return to me next week, or whenever else you choose in any other week, just not this week." Bridget had just remembered how this girl was a newcomer who wouldn't know that her yearly pattern was to close the tavern for one full week each year, seeing no one during that time—from Sabbath dawn to Sabbath dawn after spring's first new moon. But all others in these parts knew, and respected it. "So you see, I will not forego my yearly respite for anyone, not even for you, Mercy Lewis. But if you must have words with me—and I can see by that vigorous nod you think you must—then return here on Sunday, at the soonest."

"But tonight my master is in Boston. He will have returned by then."

"Then we'll both suppose it's not meant to be."

As Bridget was closing the door, Mercy begged a humble favor, but not to be difficult: "Might I sit for a moment by your fire in silence? My cloth is damp from the fog. I'm chilled."

"I've lit none tonight. No. Scurry home, back to your own hearth. Which you'll reach soon enough if you run."

Bridget closed her door, and bolted it, and then began to climb the stair, because whatever was this girl's problem, while it wouldn't solve itself she would learn of it eventually. But on the third step, she began to think how since she was already past her annoyance, and was curious about the circumstance, she might as well build a fire for them both—tonight's dank had seeped into her bones, as well. She came back into the doorway and yelled out into the mist, making one rare exception.

Myriad items were messily strewn about in all corners of her kitchen, heaped into unsorted piles for spring-cleaning. Mercy was ordered to a chair to sit, while she kindled a fire. Then she wandered the room search of her kettle, which she found underneath a cauldron. She fished in piles for cups, in another heap for a particular leaf tea, but found it in another mess. "Rattlewood tea, good for unrattling nerves."

Now they both sipped tea and warmed by the fire, and Bridget did try to listen. But what assaulted her ears was such a confusing gurgitation her drowsy mind couldn't cohere any of it. So instead, she began pondering that riddle of how bitterness in the mouth can summon sweetness to the mind: for although rattlewood was a bitter brew, it always spawned dreams that were pleasant. By the time Mercy's narration ended, she'd heard nothing she could recall. So she gave her typical pat answer: "Trust in God first, then in your own self. Clarity will come in time."

Mercy shook her head vehemently. "But I'm not the innocent I was when I met you, Goody Bishop. Nor am I with God like before. But I've been caught in a web of evil deceit . . . which you yourself have spun for me." There, she had said it.

Bridget's mettle flew up. Had she invited this person inside her house to be insulted? "A web? What I taught you was a parlor trick . . . and at who's urging? Nonetheless love is every woman's right. But never did I make a man what he is nor deceive any woman, let alone spin a devious web or a trap for either. And now you will take back those unworthy words or our acquaintanceship ends tonight."

But Mercy persisted. "Threats will not stifle this fact. When you learned I was forced as a child you called it evil. Now that I've done the same to him, you claim it's a right? How can one be evil and the other not? Why can you not just admit you deceived me?" Her voice was strident and she held her cup tipped, and now rattlewood spilled into her lap. She set the teacup on the floor.

"How can they be the same? I will tell you. You were a child then, whose will had already been broken long before her innocence was stolen, and not by magical means but by sinful means. When as a child you were scorched on life's cruelest anvil, even then you never crumbled. So why are you crumbling now?"

"Ask instead why, thanks to you, Goody Bishop, I have sunk even lower than that."

Foolish creature, Bridget thought, *to suffer so for a man.* Love was as predictable, and broken hearts as common, as tempests born in placid waters. "This is the point. A charm will not work unless Fate stands behind it, even then, only if the man's will meets yours halfway . . . or he'd be blind and unmoved as ever."

And what if he is only half-blind, what then? For if anything, Joseph Putnam was that: divided, like she was. It had been useless seeking counsel from this know-it-all woman. They would never see eye to eye. Mercy picked up her cup. She would finish her tea in silence and then go. Bridget's brew would at least warm her, if not cure her. She felt so cold now sitting beside this friendless fire.

Bridget's chin had slumped to her chest; but it lifted up again when her arm was lightly jostled. She mumbled that she didn't know the minister's niece. But upon receiving a description of Abigail Williams, she remembered seeing that Cimmerian girl once at her tavern. Rubbing out the crick in her neck, she observed how the fog between them seemed to have lifted. So she answered: "Girls like her are nuisances, pesks, flies that need to be swatted. I suppose I might show you some fortune-telling tricks to teach her, let her whip as much froth as she likes. But only if you refrain from further insult should your new game turn sour. Mark my next words as final, Mercy Lewis, for I wish to return to my bed: men can improve in time. And maids, even envious ones you're your friend, will soon forget you, when they snare one of their own."

"Abigail doesn't soon forget."

Bridget raised an eyebrow. She had just glimpsed something else. She reached for Mercy's cup and stared thoughtfully at the rattlewood leaves at the bottom. "What troubles me more is the spying. Not hers. Yours. Hatred divides those Putnams. Wherever brother is against brother, evil enters uninvited. I should have given more thought to your circumstance before teaching you the charm. I caution you now . . . be wary."

Something felt wrong to her suddenly, but she couldn't put her finger on it, or read it—like she usually could—in leaves at the bottom of a cup.

The Afflicted Girls

37

I T WAS A PERFECT SPRING DAY, THE FIRST SHORT
sleeve weather in a year. Though no one at church today
would be wearing the cut and slashed sleeves currently in fashion
in other parts of the Commonwealth. Vain, lewd displays were
forbidden here by ordinance, especially on Sundays.

But pleasant weather was not the reason Ann Putnam
decided to go to church, which would be her first public outing
since bereavement struck her down. Yesterday, when the idea
came to mind, she sent her servant to Walcott Farm to arrange a
ride, because Thomas had taken their wagon, and never would she
beg favors from any neighbor.

Meanwhile, she found her Sunday dress clean and starched
and that confirmed it. Till slipping it on later, she discovered how
it hung loose and unbecoming on her frame. For she'd grown so
thin in these two months of her unhappiness that the parish wives
would deem her wasted. Of course, they'd all walk up and inquire
about her health, and say consoling friendly words. But then later,
they'd make her the first topic of their gossip on the green. So
there could be no churchgoing till her garment was suitably
altered, which meant next Sunday at the soonest—but by then, the
drunkard would be home.

But then later she recalled how in an old dower cedar chest,
which hadn't been opened in years—since the key to it was lost—
was a dress which might fit, since she'd weighed a stone less when

it was sewn for her. She fetched the stool from the children's chamber and set it underneath the nook in her own, and climbed up to pull down that dusty box. She banged its rusty hinges with one of Thomas' shoes till the lid nails had loosened. And now she found that old dress amid other forgotten things. That ornamented green thin-spun summer wool dress she had worn long ago for her bridal. Seeing it summoned a vision of Thomas standing across from her with a full head of chestnut hair and confident eyes. But she couldn't quite remember if she loved him, since he wasn't her first choice, or any choice but her father's. But at least she was no longer thinking about ruined things.

Clad in it the next morning, and bright in spirit, she came downstairs and found her girls devouring their Sunday gruel, while the servant finished iron-pressing their aprons and caps for church. Then that nitpicker noticed moth-holes on her hem, and also on her skirt at the back, and offered to quickly darn them. While she pictured all those matronly snickering rats standing behind her back, pointing out her shabbiness to each other. The sickly feeling began worming its way through her again.

When the Walcott wagon pulled in, she went out to inform Thomas' sister that she would not be attending church after all. And she could not be dissuaded no matter how hard her niece begged. Then her youngsters emerged from the house and scampered across the yard and squealed when their older boy cousins lifted them up heels-over-heads into the wagon-bed. Her servant had followed them out and was lugging a picnic hamper.

The sight made her recall a day much like today. Before her womb grew heavy this last time. Before she even knew she was carrying that tadpole. When she stood about here in the yard waiting for Thomas to bring up the wagon. She had a food hamper looped over her arm, warm breezes bathing her face, birdsong lacing through the elms, while her own three, but a year younger, skipped about her singing "Mulberry Bush." She'd felt such a deep fondness for her family then—even for him.

Her spirits suddenly lifted. She changed her mind and went.

Now Susanna Walcott, who'd been so excited yesterday learning that her aunt would be returning to church, felt only frustration in this moment. Because earlier, when she was first snapping the reins to take her father's two powerful draft beasts out their gate, a carriage came rumbling up and nearly collided. All of them were tumbled. Her mother banged an elbow on the backboard and slightly tore a sleeve, which on such a warm day would need to be hidden underneath a shawl. Then worse—her mother changed her mind about letting her drive at all, ordering one of her brothers to do it!

She refused to relinquish the reins, insisting that it had to be her sitting beside her Aunt Ann. But not until she burst into hard tears did her mother relent. Though not for her daughter's appeasement.

The truth was Goody Walcott had remembered how snappish Ann was around her boys, and also knew that Susanna would likely simper the daylong. She hadn't the patience for either nonsense, or they would be late to church and arrive a spectacle. So she permitted her daughter to drive, but ordered Susanna not to speak. Which was, for one like Susanna, a true misfortune, because with her favorite person in the world sitting beside her, she could engage in no conversation, despite all she had to gab.

Mercy sat in the back-bed amid her charges and their handful of young cousins.

Those three girls, though, seemed unsure in their mother's proximity of how to behave, so they only twiddled their thumbs in silence, watching their cousins play, till she encouraged them to join in—which at the moment meant bouncing on straw-filled sitting sacks.

When a large clump of straw landed on Goody Walcott's cap and then some of the rick fell into her lap, she shouted for her children to settle. When they didn't, she looked behind to properly scold them, and viewed her sons' white church shirts green-stained, and her daughters' aprons and caps crimped and also stained. She thought how at church today she'd be judged as poor a mother as her sister-in-law.

Ann's servant was supposed to be keeping order in the back, a task Susanna normally performed. But instead was gazing away, oblivious to that ruckus, neglectful even of Ann's three. Yet however much she wished to excoriate that person, she couldn't risk cracking her in-law's fragile shell with criticism, even of a servant. So she held in her tongue, like Susanna, and said not a word to Ann.

Mercy was more than distracted, because the wagon had just rolled past the hillside pasture, which led down to the grassy bower. Heart-soreness filled her remembering Joseph Putnam's hard-presses, rough handling, and other demands. *Hated, yet desired still. Unwary. Unwise.* Why hadn't she taken Bridget's warning to heart? But instead, written a note to give to his farmer friend at church to bring to him, explaining her master's Boston business. It sat inside her pocket right now, sealed in wax, with her master's stolen imprint upon it.

The Afflicted Girls

38

THE THEME FOR TODAY'S SERMON WAS *"HOW TO pull down good men's proud conceits."* For hours last night, Reverend Parris had sat composing clever phrases and practicing his inflections for this first warning to the faithful in rutting season:

> "There are no paragons of virtue here. All are
> guilty . . . of heart whoredom, heart sodomy,
> heart blasphemy, heart drunkenness, heart
> buggery . . . heart idolatry —"

Because Covenanters all—even the most virtuous—strayed too easily from goodness in temperate weather. *You must be a Paul to their Philippians. Teach them to temper temptation.*

> "Turn your face away from temptation
> praying to be blessed in every manner of
> carnal temperance —"

The Lord knows you hold no conceit in it.

Upstairs, Abigail awoke breathless from the stifling heat in their chamber. Then realized that Betty, whose chore it had been, had left embers burning. A frowning yawn, a stretch, and she bolted out from bed to drench those smolders. Then she flung open the window and stuck out her face, expecting to breathe in morning coolness. But warmth and fragrance bathed her instead. While yonder, east to west, stretched the clearest bluest sky filled with white woolly tufts sailing in her direction. All of it gave her the sensation that something marvelous was imminent.

Then it was as usual—her cousin astir and yammering whilst sitting on the chamber pot. Afterward, washing her face at the bowl as Aunt Ugly stomped in. Who proceeded to choose a Sunday dress for her cousin, although first she picked up that embroidery hoop from the floor—or wherever she found it—but surprisingly today didn't complain of poor stitching, only used it for a fan. And now her aunt addressed her, but not with her usual dourness: "Your uncle says he is pleased with you, Abigail. He calls you an apt pupil. For that, I am giving you permission to recreate. If you like, to go on a picnic with your friends . . . although conscientiousness should be its own reward."

Abigail grinned. *Glorious day, she says I am to be alone in you!* She didn't thank her aunt remembering how only two weeks prior, she had begged for permission for a picnic but Aunt Ugly had cruelly refused, and then lectured her repeatedly regarding idleness. She had arranged for a picnic anyway. And now this was God showing He approved.

"A picnic, mama?" squealed Betty with a suds-covered face.

Her mother grimly replied, "Oh no, not you. You're too young to traipse with older girls."

"But I'm apt as Abby! I learnt my hornbook!" Abigail would have exposed the lie, but the praying mantis had already wrung her hands of it.

"Lord knows I do not like saying this, issuing as you have from parents who are not in the least sluggish. But you're a lazy child, Betty, with a slothful mind, whose father is not pleased with her." And now, to stem her child's flood of tears, before it drowned her Sabbath Day, Mrs. Parris reluctantly offered, "To encourage you to do better, I will allow you a picnic, too . . . in the dooryard pasture."

"I don't want one there! I want Abigail's!" the child retorted, curling her fingers round the hoop in her mother's fanning hand. Yanking it free. Flinging it across the room.

For talking back, for being ungrateful, for ruining a nearly completed linen cuff when the hoop landed in the piss-pot, Betty Parris got a slap on her hand, and a threat of her father's ruler, and a promise that after service she would be locked inside her room until supper.

Abigail inwardly grinned. Seeing her cousin crushed to dust was a reward in itself.

≈✦≈

Her Uncle Parris' sermon had not been pleasing to her ears and the final hymn took forever to conclude, but when Abigail was able to flee the church house, she sprinted home to fetch her picnic basket, which earlier she'd secretly packed and hidden from prying eyes underneath her uncle's desk. Hugging that hamper to her heart now, a dark cloth hiding its contents, she curtsied as her aunt, and cousin and the slave walked in.

Waving her out, Mrs. Parris looked into a bowl and picked out the least wormy crab apple to nibble on her walk to Goody Osborne's. She hadn't eaten breakfast, so disturbed was she by her daughter's rebellion; and then at church, she'd begun worrying that the corruption of envy had arisen in her child at all. She reminded Tituba how discipline was a watch-guard against sin, and that Betty was to sit inside her room without amusements.

Hearing that, Betty maddened. Because she had begged so hard to be forgiven during silent prayer and saw now that God hadn't forgiven anything! And because of it, that usually gentle child took hold of the propped door which her cousin had just so happily skipped through, and jealously slammed it—but unfortunately, slammed it in someone's face, grazing the tip of that visitor's finger, a person whose anguished wail rattled her, her mother, and even Tituba. Hurrying to pull the door open, Mrs. Parris beheld an alarming sight: Ann Putnam weeping, swooning back against the wall and holding up a bleeding finger. (But although the injury was from now, the weeping had come with her: for she had left the service early, when the closing hymn began, to go over to the burial ground and visit her babe's resting-place unobserved; where she wept bitterly for him and also mourned at the graves of each of her lost infants. Her two youngest living ones were with her now, having just been collected from her in-law on the green.)

Mrs. Parris brought Ann Putnam inside, along with those niggling children, ordering Tituba to fetch up a healing balm from the cellar. Betty was barked to her room. At once, those two tykes protested the absence of the playmate their mother promised. Mrs. Parris shushed them: "My daughter is being punished. You will have to play on your own." She had forgotten how she'd invited Ann Putnam to tea, which meant that now she would have to forego her Sunday visit to Goody Osborne, and likewise forfeit that woman's needed tithe. *Not so. Mightn't she send John Indian to collect it?* Well, not to ask directly, but to deliver her regrets with a promise of a longer visit on Lecture Day. And couldn't she also send a note with him extolling Reverend Parris' sermon point of how *'right tithing connotes a godly man,'* and trust God to make Ruth understand? But today was Sunday when their manslave was already hired to the Deacon for full day labors. Which meant that she would have to send Tituba on her errand . . . or to the inn to labor in John's stead, while he went on her errand. *Which means I shall have to cook the Sunday dinner without help, since niece is on a picnic.* Her brow furrowed. *And with this wounded creature visiting, the meal will be late for a certainty. Samuel will not be pleased.* So she was vexed, very vexed, leading this unexpected caller with two cranky offspring into the parlor.

The Afflicted Girls

Ann Putnam did not listen to Mrs. Parris' blather or offer one utterance back, because these were Thomas' friends, not hers, Godly by their own accounts and by hers, tedious ear-graters. Nonetheless, she sat politely while the parsonness chewed her ear, and her children cloyed her hands. *Why had the servant reminded her? Why had her in-law compelled her to come? Why did everyone mind her business?* Her head was throbbing—*or was it her finger?* Attending church had been such a blunder. She'd not found any solace. She wished only for her bed now, her one place of safety where she could sink into forgetfulness and not be expected to think. She closed her eyes. She had to.

At that, Mrs. Parris led those youngsters back down the hallway to the kitchen, where on the threshold she warned them sternly: "If either of you wanders farther than the woodlot, both of you shall be punished." They ran off giggling, while she stared about her kitchen. Not one potato had been cut nor had the fish been gutted or boned. Hadn't she told Tituba to do both before departing? She picked up a knife to do it herself. While her daughter, in the room above, set down her sewing shears. Because earlier, after seeing Tituba saunter away from the house, Betty turned into Ugly Betty: grabbing the shears from the sewing basket and snipping off the collar of Abigail's new half-made dress. Then afterward, knowing she'd be punished for it, crying for a good half hour. Till only moments ago, when feeling just as vengeful, she snipped off the cuffs as well, since she'd be punished for the dress anyway. And now she stared out through her window, glaring irefully down at those selfish Putnam girls sporting on *her* woodpile, hoping they'd trip and hurt themselves.

But the slave, when she looked back up at that window, knew exactly what was inside the parsonage house festering, taking root wherever it could like a creeper—an unwholesome mean thing which Abigail had brought with her. It was wallowing right now in that little girl she loved.

39

SUSANNA WALCOTT, LUCY PUTNAM, MERCY Lewis and the farm boy John Doritch traipsed behind Abigail up that same narrow footpath she and the slave had trod, but which by day wasn't sinister, only lush with filtered sun, lacy ferns, and green glazed mosses. No heathen shadows. Mercy noticed none of that serenity, being far too anxious about this walk. Yet, she also felt relieved that her crime had been thwarted; for Joseph Putnam's friend hadn't been at church, so her rashly written note remained undelivered. Numerous times by now, she'd felt inside her pocket to reassure herself her foolhardiness born of weakness hadn't fallen out and been lost. She checked again.

John Doritch, behind her, wondered if she'd slowed for him; hoping it was so, he rushed to reach her the sooner and bumped her hard, causing her foot to catch under a creeper root. Her hand flew out to a tree to break her fall, and the note she'd been clutching sailed to the ground. John lurched to pick it up, saw the wax seal and wondered what it was. Held it up to minced sunlight, but couldn't read its contents.

Mercy seized it and crumpled it back inside her pocket and now she hurried to catch up with the others, even more anxious now because of what the farm boy just saw.

But all that John Doritch really saw was the rejection of his flirtation. Still, he was enjoying his first jaunt ever to the woods with females and had that girl-itch in his groin now. So he stopped and scratched and rubbed, and happed to notice a cardinal settling on a branch. He considered how all girls prized red feathers and thought maybe that would earn him a kiss. He reached down to grab some pebbles for his sling, and saw—to his horror—that growing all around him was *Mother Die*. White wild carrot. He quickly scraped his shoe bottoms till he was sure none of the plant was stuck there, because if he brought *any* home, even a speck or a flake, his mother would surely die. He heard his name being called. So, instead, he jogged up that woodland path forgetting red feathers and kisses, *Mother Die* and itches.

Abigail had settled her companions in a shady spot near a broad-shouldered oak, which was also home to a family of noisy wrens. A fresh clover daisy-dotted blanket grew underneath it. "Here is a soft bed for us to sit upon," she announced with a rare, contented brightness of spirit. Then decreed: "This is our 'Haunted Chamber.'"

As John plunked down beside her his stomach growled fairly loud, because at home right now he'd be sitting down for his grandest meal of the week. Propping up on an elbow, he picked a sprig of clover to chew, while he stared at Abigail's bottom—for she was bending over to spread her sitting cloth. He shifted his gaze to her basket when she sat. "What have you brought me to eat?" She pulled off the cloth and took out an egg and a drinking glass. Was she offering him a boiled egg? If she was, he didn't want it. He'd eaten two at breakfast and was hankering for something tasty. He reached across her lap and stuck his hand inside her basket. Abigail *tsked* him with a daisy, "No, boy! First come our games."

"Is the egg newly-laid?"

"Laid this morning. Is that *new* enough?"

"I don't know, Abby. I only know what—" Mercy stopped herself from speaking Bridget Bishop's name.

Was written in the Sorcerer's Book! Say it, Breaker of the Ninth Commandment! "And I know what I know," sang Abigail. Of course, both cousins were watching Mercy curiously now, as she cracked open the egg and poured between the shell-halves till the white and yolk were separate and only the white was put into the glass.

"First try is mine!" Susanna cried, rudely snatching the glass before Abigail could take it, because she knew all about this game, other maids she knew had played it. Though never had she. And now she gazed into that secret substance. Crystal gazed. Then fretted. "Jelly in a beaker is all that I see."

"Because you didn't recite the charm, rude-body," Abigail sniffed. "Of course you'd see nothing, however hard you tried."

"What charm?" Susanna inquired, more meekly.

Abigail considered her contrition . . . but first she crystal gazed herself . . . then afterward told Susanna: "Looking glass, looking glass, show me the man I'm to marry."

So Susanna took the glass again, and spoke the charm; and when still no pictures came, she called the game a fake.

Abigail snickered. "You cannot scry, because your Walcott mind is too common . . . although an auguring cake might fix it." She pulled her basket into her lap and pulled off its cloth cover and took out two red-hued patty-cakes and broke them into fours. The largest piece of the larger she gave to the boy, and kept the other half herself, while the other two pieces went to Susanna and Lucy, with none to Mercy Lewis, who was not to participate in her fortunetelling games.

John Doritch was so hungry he gobbled his in one grand chomp, and thought it such terrible cooking that he would never want the minister's niece for a wife, and would also warn his brothers.

The Afflicted Girls

Susanna's expression curdled. "Ugh! Ugh! I've never tasted anything so foul!" And then surreptitiously, she slipped that piece into her pocket and only pretended to be chewing.

Lucy nibbled her cake bravely, and although its taste was truly terrible, she swallowed in small bites, all the while wondering what *scrying* was.

Mercy, curious by habit, had retrieved a crumb from the grass and touched it to her tongue. Its taste was extremely bitter, like a malefic. Concerned, she looked toward Lucy, but the girl seemed well, even happy. So this cake, with its taste reminiscent of something feared, was likely harmless, or Abigail would not have partaken. For Abigail *had* eaten some. So she began reflecting how common plants oftentimes appear alike, being related in genus, yet possess different properties. How seeds from one can sustain the most fragile bird, while their twin is a viperous poison. Long ago, she'd learned this fact from philosopher John Ray's book, *Methodus Plantarum Nova:* how the wisdom and power of God could be understood only by studying His creation—the natural world. So she'd studied it, beginning then. And studied it, still.

Susanna was badgering for another turn now that she'd *eaten* auguring cake. She immediately avowed a scryed vision: "I see my husband . . . not clearly though," because she wouldn't admit to seeing only jelly. She handed the glass to Abigail. "Would you like to see him?"

"I already have seen you both," informed Abigail. "You are plumper than you are now."

"Plump, and married?"

"Exceedingly, although your husband is even fatter. He resembles a well-fed hog. A shopkeeper by appearance, for he stands underneath a dry goods signage."

"I don't care if he's fat, as long as he's rich. If he's a shopkeeper, he must be . . . is he?"

Abigail crystal-gazed again. "I suppose, for he wears a monocle and a mercantile suit, but which ill suits his piggish folds. But as you are porcine yourself then, Susanna, you hardly notice!" And now she snorted piggish at that friend.

Susanna only realized the joke when John Doritch heehawed, and even Lucy caught the giggles. She knit her brows into a frown. She didn't like being made fun of, but wouldn't dare insult a minister's niece. But an indentured servant could be insulted without *any* grief. So she whisked her eyes to Mercy: "At least, I'm going to have a husband!"

"You are fortunate in that," answered Mercy, summoning patience.

"Fortunate without a fortune, you mean!"

"Quiet, Greedy-guts!" rebuked Abigail. "You have twice as much as the rest of us and yet are never satisfied! Oink again and I'll give you a kick instead of a fortune!"

Susanna, red-faced, was too upset to reply. Having just been publicly humiliated by a person she'd deemed likeable, who now turned commoner in her eyes than her aunt's penniless servant. *While she was the daughter of a third-generation freeman, with one grandfather a man of wealth before he died, and his father before him, a landed founder!* Her status merited respect!

The afternoon was passing quickly and there were other games to learn.

Abigail pulled her basket into her lap again, and considered first the sieve and shears, but then decided on her uncle's skeleton key and Book of Psalms—because possessions of his might foretell something wondrous. But then she changed her mind again, thinking how *his* should be saved until last. "We'll conjure next with sieve and shears. Then with the Psalter and key." She handed those four items to Mercy.

The Afflicted Girls

Lucy, seated between them, timidly asked: "Could I try the looking glass?"

Abigail shrugged, "I suppose so. But only if you gaze deeper than your cousin did." And actually, she was curious to see if this girl had inherited any weird traits from her strange mother.

Now while Lucy Putnam thought seeing pictures in a glass was miraculous, she was yet unsure if it was God's or the Devil's doing. But because it was Mercy Lewis teaching them, she trusted it came from God. Also she remembered how olden prophets were oft times taken up to Heaven by holy visions. So she stared especially hard into the jelly thinking about Him, ignoring that her head was hurting, and lungs were seizing up and clamping down. (For by now, Abigail's "auguring cake" was hammering at her fragile constitution.)

"Do you see anything, cousin, anything at all?" Susanna prodded. "If not, you've proved the minister's niece a liar." Abigail threw a pebble and hit her shoulder. Susanna tossed back a twig. Soon it was clumps of clover, haughty glares, stuck-out tongues, and mumbled insults.

Staring, coughing, trying to catch her breath—for the child could barely control her debility now, or fast blinking eyes—Lucy Putnam had her vision: "My husband . . . dressed in a shimmering robe, walking with his friends on the high road—but behind them, oh—are they wings? Oh my! 'Tisn't my husband! But our Lord and His Angels that I see!"

"Blasphemer!" screamed Abigail, rising to her knees to yank away the glass and pour out its sinful jelly: "No one dare look upon the face of God, or His Heavenly Host, until they die! Only then, if they've served Him on earth! Like my uncle has! Have you ever served God at all, Lucy Putnam?"

Lucy shook her head sadly. "But I-I want to . . . serve our Lord."

215

Someone's hand was rubbing her back and a soothing voice assured her. "But you do, you already do serve Him, Lucy. Each day in your innocence and thoughtfulness."

It was Mercy, strong and protective. But Abigail's voice against her ear spoke louder: "Ferreting out the damned is what innocents do! Have you ever once ferreted the damned, Lucy Putnam?"

"Don't listen to the minister's niece, cousin," Susanna warned. "She only means to scare you. Let her hunt hellish creatures if she likes. We don't have to do it."

Abigail cupped the confused child's ear and told her this fact: "They steal our souls while we sleep, Lucy Putnam, and deliver them to Satan."

"W-who does?" shuddered Lucy.

"The Devil and his demons. The witches who serve them." Abigail pointed toward amassing clouds in a dark eastern sky. "Look there, Lucy Putnam! At God's sign that what I say is true!"

When Lucy looked, a black roiling terrible sky was, indeed, stampeding toward her.

Abigail clasped her hand to her heart and looked up: "I ferret to serve God. For the sake of all who live purely and serve God faithfully, I denounce Tituba as a witch. At night she fornicates with Satan in the woods! I've seen her! God strike me dead if I'm lying." Turning to Susanna, "Who else is a witch? You've lived here longest and would know best. Name one and her power will lessen."

Susanna hesitated. She did know someone like that, and so what if she cried out on her, since she already hated her to Hell? Her cousin, though, didn't know this. But now she would. "Our step-grandmother Mary Veren Putnam is a witch. She fornicated with the Devil, then with our grandfather, bewitched him and stole our inheritance."

The Afflicted Girls

"Pockmarked beggar Sarah Good is another witch," Abigail informed. "Aunt Parris says she's a harlot who fornicated with the devil and gave birth to demon children. And that she never attends church, or recites The Lord's Prayer, because her tongue would burn if she ever tried to say it."

"Beggary buggery!" the dimwit exclaimed. John Doritch had grown wistful. "I wish I knew a witch."

"But you do, boy, you do," Abigail hinted. "One was sitting next to you in church."

"W-witches go to church?" he shuddered.

She nodded, "But only to mock true Christians," because she hadn't yet learned the parishioners by name, although she recognized most faces. One face her uncle particularly disdained was all stained and wrinkled with a hairy chin, a bony nose, and a goosey neck on a crooked frame.

Susanna pondered. *What witch did Abigail mean? Who was John sitting next to?* But he wasn't sitting—he'd been standing during church, leaning against the middle window. *By the Nurse clan's bench! At the end of which sat the old scold herself, who always corrected her, corrected everyone except her own!* "Goody Nurse!" she gasped, having just realized why it was so. "When she was a child, her mother was nearly caught and was put on trial for witchery—"

"And black blood is inherited," advised Abigail.

Susanna nodded, though the reason was fathoms worse. She couldn't look at her cousin now, but told it nevertheless: "The reason no Nurse child has ever died. While so many of my aunt's have." *No, she daren't. But she must! No, she daren't! But she must!* She looked at her cousin: "She is a mid-witch, Lucy!"

Lucy Putnam shivered at this terrible revelation, picturing Goody Nurse coddling her baby brother, letting him suck on her wrinkled knuckle right after he was born.

"Goody Rich Osborne!" Susanna quickly declared another witch to turn her mind, and her cousin's, from that horror.

"Everyone knows she fornicates with her Irish servant. He's so handsome he *must* have bewitched him! She's twice his age!"

Lucy stood up into a head pierced with thorns, wobbled a few steps saying she was going home. But the oak tree kept spinning round her, spur'galling wrath off, not wrens. Hands caught her before she fell.

But Abigail forced them apart, clutching Mercy. "Not you. You have to stay to teach us other games." But she pushed Lucy away. "You go home, Lucy Putnam, home to your mad mother at Putnam Farm. And don't ever return here. The 'Haunted Chamber' isn't for children."

Mercy scolded her: "Fie on this game of spreading malice. Those people may have faults, which may have begrudged grievances, but none of them are witches. It is a sin to say that they are."

"My uncle said today that demons live among us. Are you calling him a liar?"

"He didn't say that as fact, Abigail, only pedagogically. You misunderstood, you misinterpret his meaning—"

Abigail bristled. *He is my uncle to interpret.* "You wish to shield them from discovery!" She turned to the others. "Mercy only denies it to deceive you. She was herself once servant to a conjurer."

"To your shame, Abigail. That is a lie."

"Your lie not mine. Uttered often enough in your sleep at the almshouse, while I lay beside you listening."

Mercy turned ashen-faced.

John piped in, "What did he conjure?"

Susanna prodded, "What was his name? Speak it and his power will lessen."

Mercy declared adamantly: "There never was a conjurer. And there are no witches. The only deceiver here is Abigail. I've known her long and well. It's attention she craves." But then she regretted her words as soon as she said them . . . for Abigail was spitting back: "Better to crave attention than what comes from spilling milk out on a grave!"

Mercy took it as a threat, because if her secret were to be blurted now, she knew Susanna would run direct to Putnam Farm and tell her master and mistress. And in this maelstrom of wrongs wasn't she equally guilty? Hadn't she agreed to teach them unwholesome games? Hadn't she set them on this path? She offered a truce: "I take back my unworthy words, Abigail. Won't you take back yours?"

"Take them back? When my Glorious Day of Rest has turned *ugly* because of you!" No one would meet her gaze now. Susanna Walcott and John Doritch were deliberately ignoring her, because she'd just been shamed outright by someone older, called a liar and a deceiver . . . when it was she who'd spoken truthfully!

But it wasn't for *that* reason John Doritch turned away. Though he liked girls, even Abigail, he had no interest in girls' games to begin with, much less in their whining bouts. The only thing interest to him at the moment was sitting inside Susanna Walcott's basket. He had just reached across her lap and pulled out a mince pie, which was so full of suet, he was sure he'd never tasted a better one—and three other pies were beckoning.

Then of a sudden it came! None of them had noticed the swooping black clouds rush in and gobble up nearby treetops until the tempest burst full upon them: with shards of lightning, deafening thunder, and deluging rain.

Mercy dragged Lucy, confounded and sick, back up that muddy pathway with Susanna slogging close behind. John had considered running for home, till he saw the minister's niece begin dancing in the drumming rainfall, outstretching her arms and swiveling her hips (in that same erotic performance she'd seen Tituba do). So he watched bug-eyed instead, as Abigail's dress grew so sopped her nipples showed through. Then her girl-breasts burgeoned into womanly Bridget-sized breasts. Then it was four teats growing out from her-no, roots . . . or was it clover? Entwining his legs from his ankles to his bully sacs till he couldn't budge an inch. And now randy hands of a tickling woodland spirit undid his britches and made sport with his penis.

"There's another game I know," sighed Abigail, "more to a boy's liking." She stuffed another witch-cake into his maw, pushed him back onto the clover and climbed astride, raising his clumsy hands to her unclad breasts, and wantonly guided his fondled length up inside her.

And in that *splend-furious* engorgement of sense and spirit that next coursed through him, John Doritch was sure he'd gone to Heaven, just like Lucy Putnam.

The Afflicted Girls

40

THE STORM WAS STILL RAGING AT DUSK WHEN A soggy desperate threesome came racing across Putnam farmyard to the house, and on the kitchen threshold Susanna collided with her aunt who was lugging out a pot to empty. Ann cursed her niece as water sloshed over them both.

The roof had been leaking for hours—first in sputters, then dribbles, thrumming drips, and now rivulets. The old house's armor had finally buckled under this relentless pounding. Shingles, blown free, were halfway down to Boston. Even those proud, protective wineglass elms lost limbs. While Ann Putnam's own limbs fought storm and exhaustion—carrying down numberless buckets, cauldrons, pots, skillets, bowls, tankards and beakers to empty, with only two crying frightened youngsters to assist her—and that, despite her injured finger and lack of strength.

Yes, she had rallied to her house's aid. But knew that in her recent illness she would have just let the rain pour in, would have lain on her bed, head sunk into her pillow, eyes watching the ceiling drip to distraction. But now with her sanity restored, she saw the storm's purpose clearly: it was designed to ruin her few remaining possessions of value, meant for her daughters' dowries. So she battled it back for their sakes.

"Where were you? Your mother couldn't find you anywhere!" she screamed at her niece.

Susanna weakly reminded, "In the woods, on a picnic with the minister's—

"—But not on the green where you were meant to be sitting!"

Susanna, who would never want to upset her favorite aunt, nevertheless defended: "Well, the parsonness gave us permission. We only lost our way when it started to rain." She explained how the footpath disappeared in the torrent, and that the green, when they finally reached it, was also flooded. "By then, the minister's niece wasn't with us, so we couldn't shelter at the parsonage. We ran to the inn, where Mrs. Ingersoll lent us shawls and heated up cider, while we warmed and dried by the fire. The inn was busy, so we had to wait there. Deacon Ingersoll brought us home just now. But his carriage top was leaking."

All this while Lucy had been slumped against Mercy. Now she moaned. Her mother reached for her forehead. "She's afire. My girl's afire!" But before yanking her away, she barked at her niece: "Up to my room, Susanna. Put on a dry gown of mine, then come back down and take soup. If a pot or pail sits full upstairs, bring it down to empty. You're lucky your uncle isn't here to stripe you, though I'm in a mind to do it myself." She spat at her servant: "I blame you for this. Only you. Now help me carry my daughter upstairs."

Wrapped in the thickest quilt, lying in her mother's bed, it was the first time since infancy Lucy Putnam had been cradled in those arms, but sadly she didn't know it, suffering such a dangerously high fever and delirium.

While next door, Susanna Walcott also suffered—suffered pins in her feet, from dangling off the end of Lucy's too-short cot. For nearly three sleepless hours she'd suffered, wishing she were at home. Then later, when she finally slept, a dinging annoyance awoke her. On horribly numb feet, she hobbled over and opened the shutters. The night sky was clear. It was only the soaked inner eaves that were still dripping.

Lit by moonlight, her two cousins appeared like ringlet cherubs. But pretty as they were in slumber—for both were cast in her Aunt Ann's image—they were disagreeable girls she was glad were not her sisters. She didn't even like them as cousins. She stared down at the flooded yard, considering family resemblances in general. How her mother was long-boned and plain-faced like Uncle Thomas, but that she, by a slightly better fate, more resembled her father's comelier, though plumper kin. Which summoned that looking-glass memory of her fat future husband, and Abigail Williams' derision. Frowning, she picked up the source of that annoying ding and carried down that pail, water sleepily sloshing out.

She returned later with her bare feet and borrowed gown covered with mud and straw, and sat cross-legged on Lucy's cot, pulling out from that same pail a glass and two freshly laid eggs, still warm. And yes, she'd crawled through a filthy wet chicken coop to collect them! She prepared her looking glass much the same way Mercy had done. But before gazing, she crumbled the rest of Abigail's auguring cake into a bowl of yolk and cold soup, and ate that horrid mush in big gulps. Resolved, that if the minister's niece and her cousin could scry and have visions . . . so could she.

41

BETTY PARRIS AWOKE IN THE DARK IN A SHIVER with a cry. She'd been dreaming she was on Abigail's picnic, and it wasn't a good dream: in it Abigail was wearing her ruined dress. She guiltily reached out for her bedmate with her usual poke and pinch. Her envy hadn't lessened. Seeing Abigail so jubilant returning home, despite being rain-soaked and late, very late, coming in long after the Sunday supper had turned cold on the plate, which earned her cousin a harsh rebuke, and only made her that much more jealous. Yet, she was desperate to hear about their woodland frolic. So she poked again.

Abigail clung hard to sleep, but after Betty's fifth poke, she rolled to her side, filthy locks covering her face, and scowled: "Leave me be, Betty Parris. I don't tell secrets to tattlers."

"But I won't tell," the child begged. "I promise, cousin. And tomorrow I'll do your chores."

Abigail reconsidered. Underneath this mattress was the perfect hiding place for auguring cakes, and stuck in between the tight-strung ropes of their bedstead was what Betty was demanding. Her hand slinked down at the side like a cat's paw. "We ate cakes."

"I had none for supper."

"Then my little mouse must be hungry for a cake." When Betty nodded, Abigail opened her hand. "I would give you this cake, cousin, despite that you are forbidden them. But then you'd tell Tituba, and I'll be the one punished."

Betty shook her head, "I won't tell, Abby. I swear."

"Of course you say that now, Betty, but the flesh is weak. So you must take a sacred vow for a sacred taste. You must swear: 'God strike me dead if I ever tell Tituba,' or anyone for that matter. And, you must say it with conviction or He will. God will strike you dead and cast you into Hell's oven of lost souls, where He'll bake you for the Devil to eat, and demons and witches will eat your crumbs."

So now Betty hesitated. Because she'd never before taken a vow, no less a *sacred* one, and this was such a *fearsome* one. But the Lord had closed His heart to her today—first at home then at church—and then also refused her apology, which was sincere. So now for the sake of that cruel dismissal and denial of forgiveness and a picnic she was excluded from, she exchanged God's Holy Name for a smidgen of curiosity born of envy.

Abigail kissed her cousin's pasty cheek, "At times, you can be the perfect playmate, cousin." She handed Betty the cake.

The child took a bite, instantly spat it out. "'Tisn't a sweetcake!"

"Of course, 'tisn't!" mocked Abigail. "'Tis a *sacred* cake bringing revelations and wonder! The *bitter fruit* of which all the Prophets ate!"

It was on Lecture Day two weeks past, after her uncle had borrowed one of Ingersoll's carts to take Aunt Ugly with him out to the Putnams; and then Tituba and Betty left on a walk to pick berries, and did not invite her company either; and John Indian had already gone up to his afternoon labors at the inn, that Abigail found herself gloriously alone at the parsonage.

She'd sat at her uncle's writing desk admiring his miniature portrait and reading the most recent inked pages of his diary, of course she also leafed through his current tithing ledger, which read lean. His lock-box remained locked, so she was still lacking in knowledge of its contents. Hungry, she came into the kitchen and pried out the slaves' fresh hidden secret loaf—she'd discovered its hiding place—but by her second dry bite, she realized that being unobserved she might filch anything from the stores. She knew where her aunt hid special tithed items. So she went downstairs to the damp cellar and fetched up a tub of curd and a jar of jam. She lathered her two slices and savored every bite. Then realized that being alone today, she might take that prickly pod, which had fallen from Tituba's basket, to bake more auguring cakes for future use. Only two were left of Tituba's that she'd raked out from the ash. She had no doubt as to one ingredient. And when else would she ever dare to bake them?

So she retrieved that pod from her coffer, cracked it open—not with her teeth of course, but with the mallet—scraped out the seeds and ground them in the mortar with soaked rye and rancid grease. From the garden, she had dug up a beetroot to give the sticky mixture the right red color. And she added what was left of her crab apple jelly to sweeten.

Raking out her auguring cakes from the ashes later, they looked much the same as Tituba's, and tasted equally horrid, despite sweet beet and jelly. But *her* cakes brought visions quicker; and then the vilest headache she'd ever suffered, with the foggiest vision in her memory and the sharpest-cramped gut ever felt. She ran numerous times outside to the privy till she had emptied from both ends. And she barely could climb the stairs again to collapse on her spinning bed. (Because something vital had been overlooked, the most crucial part of the recipe—for whenever Tituba baked her Jimson cakes, when she felt called to visions, she'd boil the pods first, and then also soak thse blanched seeds in vinegar brine for days more to purge them of their poisons.)

But Abigail had no way of knowing this.

The Afflicted Girls

Outside, noisy rivers fell as Abigail struck the flint and lit the
stubby taper, and quietly taught her nine year old cousin Betty
Parris the proper way to eat an auguring cake: small bites
swallowed quickly, eyes closed with nose pinched. She took a few
small bites of another cake to demonstrate; which the child copied
and was praised for. And now she tipped that burning stub and let
drops of hot wax cover her cousin's thumbnail.

"Ouch!" cried Betty. But she was ordered to keep silent, lest
a mother or father catch them. All because Abigail had cleverly
understood: *Why get soaked for the sake of a new laid egg? There is no
need for true fortunetelling. This dunce will not know the difference.* "I
have made your thumbnail a looking glass, Betty. Stare hard at it,
and you'll soon see the man you're going to marry."

The stub was stuck back onto its stick. Then Abigail tucked
back into bed to either fall into dreams or be dazzled behind her
eyes even more awake. As her cousin, sitting cross-legged on the
bed-top beside her, gazed down at her thumbnail in expectation.

Finally, in the candle's sputters and flickers the child's
pupils began to dilate, and when her eyes stopped blinking, Betty
Parris had her vision: A young man was smiling up at her from
her thumb! *Was he her future husband?* "Oh, I see him, Abby! I do!"
Grinning large, amazed at this handsome suitor. But then, her
young man turned wrinkled and old. Shriveled and decayed and
was being worm-eaten. *Hadn't her father warned her? Why hadn't she
listened? Fortunetelling was vanity. Or was it profanity?* She couldn't
remember which. He turned into an ugly horned toad sitting upon
her thumb. *No! A horned-Devil with bulging eyes,* still smiling up at
her, but evilly now! His black tongue darted out, forked its way
around her. Was pulling her down into Hell's oven! "The Serpent!
The Serpent!"

Abigail awoke to view her cousin falling from the bed in a
jerking fit, and then twist and thrash about the floor eyes rolled

back, mouth snapping open and shut, with white froth foaming out from it. Malevolence filled the room. *What had Betty summoned?* Her eyes filled with terror and she screamed.

Both adults froze in the doorway seeing a demonic creature—once their little girl—with no eyes to speak of anymore, only whites in her sockets—writhing back-arched on the floor.

Abigail ran to her uncle while Mrs. Parris let loose a blood-curdling scream of her own, which rushed down the chimney flue, rattling the slaves awake. John Indian guessed the master had died. But Tituba said "no," that it was something *unwelcome*. They pulled on gowns and rushed upstairs to see.

At once, Tituba scooped up the stricken child and laid Betty on the bed-top. She tried to force that small, contorting body to straighten and was surprised to find she that she lacked the strength for it. John was too terrified to come in. But when she told him to hurry and put a hand on the child's sternum and with his other hand pin down those fiercely kicking legs, he obeyed. She rushed then to seize a stick from the tinderbox to use for prying open Betty's clenched maw. She'd just had it—when that maddened creature snapped her jaw shut on the willow nearly biting off two of her helping fingers.

"Take my mule! My mule! Summon Dr. Griggs!" shouted Reverend Parris to his manslave, trying not to look as a river of green bile poured out from his child's mouth.

Overcome by an urge to regurgitate, he turned toward the wall to steady himself. His wife had already fainted into a chair. His half-crazed niece was huddled, whimpering against his feet. He forgot to look toward God.

The Afflicted Girls

It is shown that, on Account of the Sins of Witches, the Innocent are often Bewitched, yea Sometimes even for their Own Sins.

The Malleus Maleficarum (ed. 1620)

42

R. GRIGGS WAS MUDDLED IN HIS DREAM. HE found himself standing at the edge of a ledge of a bluff of grand views, a highland reminiscent of his Scottish birthplace. However, this wasn't Scotland, but the place upon which his current house was built at the flat end of a twisting elevated cartway in the hilly eastern region of Salem Village, near Beverly Village. He now could see both settlements in the distance in a mist. But after another snore, he was back again in Scotland, inside that chilly stone dwelling of his childhood, but which tonight housed only his long-dead Salem Village spouse. Not that he missed her particularly.

A widower for more than a decade, he never lacked companionship, because ailing local goodwives, even more so widows, and even a few hale ones called him often enough to bedchambers for his ministrations. And his young Hubbard niece came thrice weekly to keep his house.

Frenzied door pounding summoned him back from his sojourns, and in a fluster of fading sights he bolted down the stairs, half-expecting to see his wife's jealous ghost standing upon his threshold. But it was the parsonage slave from Salem Village delivering a master's message—but a message so garbled that it was impossible to tell who was sick from it. He sent that half-person out to hitch up his carriage, while he quickly dressed and gathered up remedies and instruments. As soon as they had reached the bottom of his rain-slicked driveway, he left the mule-rider behind, lashing his carriage horse to run.

Twenty minutes later, he arrived inside that parsonage sickroom. On first sight of the minister's youngster in her throes he called it a case of *epilepsy*. But then he doubted that diagnosis, when the minister kept insisting that it had been more than two hours since his child's fit began. He knew an epileptic torque would have ceased by now. So instead, he contemplated a brain lesion, much more serious of a malady, though not aloud, of course, or he'd alarm the child's mother. It was a terminal prediction—and the woman was already standing apoplectic by the window, peering out into the rainy night, so distraught that she hadn't even turned to greet him:

Because Mrs. Parris was convinced now that her daughter's affliction was God's retribution for her being an unfit mother. Just this morning hadn't she hardened her heart to Betty on purpose? When all that innocent lamb did was ask to be included on a picnic? *What child of nine wouldn't ask the same?* She'd remembered how she had meanly withheld favor from one, while giving it to the other one in front of her. To the one she utterly disliked. And by that one cruel deliberate gesture, had herself undermined Betty's gentle nature, which in turn spooled out God's wrath toward her through her daughter.

And what about that strange dream she'd had this night of a lame goodwife guiding a plow downhill? *Odd to be dreaming of Ruth Osborne* she had thought (before she awoke to screams) *who didn't get her Sunday visit.* While she was not the least bit superstitious, she understood as well as anyone dwelling in a farming village how a downhill plow in a dream portended Death! But did it mean Ruth Osborne would die? *Or would Betty? Would God take her only child to the grave for a single day's lapse? Yet, who was she to question Him? And why couldn't she shed any tears?* She'd been trying to, for more than two hours she'd been trying to cry. Yet, no tears came. It was another harsh rebuke from Him.

Because God knew how miffed she'd been earlier hearing Betty moan and groan from her delirium only for Tituba, never for her: *"I's here, swee' pet. I's right here,"* the slave kept murmuring into her child's unhearing ear. And all she could feel was envy.

So it was really she, not Betty, who was in thrall to that deadly *Sixth Sin*.

Abigail grinned, because her uncle had finally walked up to her and stood almost touching; because for most of this night he'd only paced the room worrying about her cousin. Sometimes holding the mouse's hand while he prayed on his knees beside the bed. Twice, he had put his buttery lips onto Betty's oozing cheek. And especially *that* caused distress—to see his tenderness being directed elsewhere. Not the yellow stain on his lips.

So while he kept praying for a miracle for Betty, she prayed for her cousin to sink further.

The child herself confirms it! Dr. Griggs had realized the truth: that this malady was neither a brain lesion nor an epileptic episode nor anything else physical, or typical. Because no Christian child would ever clap her ears and scream out hellishly and flail her limbs in fierce protest when a minister—in this case, her own father—prayed to God for her restoration. *Only a child possessed!*

He hurried over now, and touched Reverend Parris' tense shoulder and gestured for this father to follow him to a corner so the goodwife wouldn't hear when he explained: "I say this circumspectly to you, Reverend Parris. Your daughter suffers no physical affliction. The Evil Hand is upon her. The Devil has visited your house."

Reverend Parris reeled from that slap: "Impossible! This is a Christian house! My daughter suffers epilepsy, or some other such malady. Look to your own books, doctor. Please! Not to mine."

Abigail knew about books. She remembered one now with a drawing of the Devil's Hand, which sat on the third shelf in her uncle's glorious library. Extending her hands out to her sides: "Whish! Whish!" she flew past them, flapping her wings having just now transmogrified into an angel. And now she would fly through that opened window where the tall insect stood. Because hovering right outside was Lord Jesus, beckoning with opened Arms. She outstretched hers and soared and her sad life might have ended then, had not Mrs. Parris startled, clutched at her Abigail's gown, and struggled to hold on till the men had rushed over.

Breaking free of hands, Abigail flew now to the hearth now to smear her face with soot, till hers was blacker than John Indian's. She pointed toward the bed: "The Black Man stands next to Tituba! The Devil's Hand holds Betty's!" She back-pedaled, warding off her invisible attacker — that demon trying to suck out the Goodness Christ had just bestowed. Her face twisted and she moaned: "Oh, I won't sign! It isn't God's Book, but the Devil's!" because she knew about books. And now she melted like a candle.

Reverend Parris rushed over. He lifted her into his arms. "Who is it that torments you, Abigail? Who is it that you see?"

Her eyes fluttered open. She saw *him!* "Uncle Parris—" Then her eyes rolled up and she suffered a jerking fit just like Betty's.

John Indian hid the rest of this weird night in the cellar, crouching and shivering behind a tall shelf, and only emerged, reluctantly and suspiciously, after six cock-a-doodle-doos. He began his morning labors, and saw Dr. Griggs' carriage depart. Then he heard his master cursing loudly behind him. Turned and saw his wife being dragged along by her braid. He hid. And now the master seized a riding crop from a hook and shoved Tituba inside the barn, followed her in and kicked the door shut behind them.

John hurried to put his eye to a crack in the wood.

"Devil worshipper! You bewitched my children! Brought the Devil into my house." The master accused.

"D'int, master. 'Tain't true."

Reverend Parris yanked up her chin.

"Of course, you did it! Who else could have done it?"

"'Tweren't me, master! Swears, I swears to God!"

Reverend Parris cursed her for blaspheming. And then began whipping.

Grabbing his gravedigger shovel, John held it aloft outside the barn door, ready to strike down the master when he exited and crush the jelly from his bones. Of course, he kept trying hard not to listen to his wife's piteous wails, but he couldn't stifle that sound. And when the shovel's staff broke in his hand, he grabbed up the pitchfork and pointed it, instead. But soon abandoned it, too. Cast it like a mighty African spear into the woods. He pressed his defeated face against the clapboard, knowing there was no way to save her. Because Tituba could survive another beating, but neither of them would survive a master's murder. In Barbados once, a runaway slave they knew well was torn limb from limb by search dogs for breaking the hand glass of a mistress. They'd been made to watch that hunt by the master.

"Confess or you'll burn in Hell a sinner!" Reverend Parris lashed.

"I confesses," Tituba cried.

"You admit you brought this Evil into my house?"

She sobbed, "Din't mean to, mast'r, you knows I loves Betty."

Whipping her a final time, "Do not speak that innocent name ever again!"

When Reverend Parris stormed past him, John Indian rushed inside to scoop up his broken wife. He lifted off her blood-soaked shift, flinched seeing so many welts and stripes. Tried mopping them, but Tituba moaned that she couldn't bear to be touched, even by him. So he held her gentle till her shivering set in. "Evil things happenin' . . . juz' like you seen comin'. You an' me, woman, we gotta run."

"Ain't nowheres t'go. Anywhere we goes, they gonna catch us an' kill us."

"Don' matt'r. We juz gotta run."

"Ain't no *we*, John. Juz be me. I's gonna beg to the master. Tell'm I wants to come to God n' I does what he sez."

He didn't say no, because always Tituba knew better. But this time, for the first time, John Indian wondered.

The Afflicted Girls

43

REVEREND PARRIS ASCENDED THE STAIRCASE, and entered the bedchamber with his hair disheveled and spatters of blood speckling his nightshirt. But Mrs. Parris ignored that, asking only: "Our ordeal has ended. Hasn't it, Samuel?" She reached for her husband's hand. He nodded, knowing he dare not mention the slave's confession; because his helpmeet, while wise in most things, knew nothing at all about the *unholy*, and he had to protect her at all costs, and even more now these children.

"Do not leave me again so soon," she chided when he turned to go. She saw him frown, short-tempered.

"I go only as far as my library, Elizabeth. What help can I give you here? When I am not a mother, but a father. You must find your own peace in the protection of daylight."

She felt chastised, yet persisted: "I do not deny you your needs, husband. Please do not deny me mine. Do not tarry for long then, as I sit in fear even of daylight now. I am not in my usual strength." Wincing, she turned away. And *now*, her tears came.

Reverend Parris took her face into his hands. He pecked her trembling, needle-thin lips. And gazed past her at those two innocents side-by-side in the bed, who were barely breathing in a heavy slumber they now shared, from a draught of laudanum the doctor had administered. They were like two already dead.

His heart pounded suddenly, realizing how this might only be a weird fever brought north on a sailing ship. For he'd just remembered how there'd been two foreign sailors at his service last Sunday, and that his niece had been mingling quite near them. And how many countless times in Barbados had he viewed robust persons lying prone and agape in their own bodily wastes in sickbeds, struck down by some nameless tropical blight? Hadn't it happened to his own father that first year in Barbados, and years before, in his misty boyhood, to his mother in Old England? Hadn't *she* succumbed to a mysterious ailment never named? How he wished he could remember her better.

Whereas, Griggs was no authority, only a poorly educated Scot, who was longer-toothed in superstition than education. While Tituba was a crafty Indian who frequently lied—of course, he knew it. No, this mystery wasn't solved, nor their ordeal likely ended. But he couldn't tell that to his wife.

Downstairs, he lit his reading candle and instantly smelt a sweet scent pervading. *Honeysuckle?* He looked round his study puzzling at the absence of flower. Then realized that the fragrance was coming from the burning wax itself. He couldn't help but smile that his clever niece, their household chandler, had devised this method to surprise him. He gazed up past the rafters through the ceiling planks vowing to protect her always. For Abigail Williams, blood of his line if not of his blood, was as precious to him now as was his own natural daughter. And her life, too, was hanging on a thread.

He reached up to his top shelf and withdrew a particular volume: A Discourse of the Damned Art of Witchcraft by William Perkins. He tucked it under his arm, and took down a second book: The Displaying of Supposed Witchcraft by John Webster. A pamphlet, which had been folded up inside its pages, fell to the floor. He picked it up, noticing it had been authored by Increase

The Afflicted Girls

Mather, his august mentor at Harvard, and its title "Present State of New-English Affairs" made him think: *if only he were here to advise me in this present state of affairs.*

He recalled how one time, at that institution, Increase Mather had confided to a group of novices, himself included, a dark personal secret: how during his own student years in Dublin at Trinity College, on the very night he learned of his mother's death in fact, he tore a page out from his Bible—specifically, the one succeeding the frontispiece and lacking sacred text—and scribed upon it all of his sins. That he then burnt that list in his fireplace while praying to God to be purged of those weaknesses. Confessing to them who were listening so rapt, how he'd been a neglectful son, at times a lecher; but that when flames consumed his paper, the Spirit of Peace entered into him and he experienced his first true Conversion.

Was that not image-magic? Reverend Parris answered: "Yes, for a certainty it was, albeit in God's service, not Satan's." For he, like both Reverends Mather, had delved into metaphysical subjects, and he, like them, owned a superb collection of such works. Although he was more a novice and a dabbler, whereas they taught openly in North Church, against common convention, how the invisible world was as real as this one and could spill at any moment into ours . . . and now it had, into his!

He searched his shelves for Cotton Mather's popular treatise: Memorable Providences Relating to Witchcraft and Possession for it contained case studies of beguiled children. He now carried these three selections to his desk, where curiously (perhaps, supernaturally) as he was setting them down, Cotton Mather's book fell open to a page, which confirmed his suspicion:

> *Go tell Mankind that there <u>are</u> Devils and Witches; that, though those night birds least appear where the Daylight of the Gospel comes, yet New England has had examples of their existence and operation. Not only in the wigwams of*

> *Indians, where pagan powwows raise masters in the shapes*
> *of bears and snakes and fire, but also the Houses of*
> *Christianity, where our God has had His constant Worship,*
> *have undergone the Annoyance of Evil Spirits. Go tell the*
> *world this . . . and also what those Monsters love to do—*

He leafed through its succeeding pages searching for a reference, now vaguely recalled, and found it near to the end:

> *Witchcraft is spiritual. But the effects of it are dreadfully*
> *physical and thus punishable by law.*

Dreadfully physical and thus <u>punishable</u> <u>by</u> <u>law</u>! Yes, here it was—his answer—succinctly stated by a gifted young divine, ten years his junior, who stood at a pulpit of spiritual wisdom, which he had not yet attained.

And now came his usual pinch of envy toward that prolific young minister, understanding how he would need to write humbly to Cotton Mather for advice.

Fortunately, though, he was too weary in mind and heart and body to do so now. Besides, Mrs. Parris was calling.

The Afflicted Girls

Among the wonders done by enchanters are: the procuring of strange passions and torments in men's bodies and other creatures, with the curing of the same.

A Discourse of the Damned Art of Witchcraft
William Perkins, 1608 (Eminent Theologian)

44

ANN PUTNAM AGAIN MOPPED HER CHILD'S fevered brow (using Lucy's discarded dress) and then gave her daughter a sudden sharp embrace to stave off the Grim Reaper—all the while knowing that she lacked the strength to make a poultice or plaster, no less defeat that persistent dark angel; all because she had banished her serving wench to sleep in the barn after striping her. Sitting up alone here through the night, she wept as much for her own affliction of sleeplessness and exhaustion as for her stricken motherhood.

As daybreak came, she wearily peeled out from her rocker to go summon her niece to sit as her daughter's watcher. But when she opened the children's door, instead she viewed Susanna writhing deliriously on the cot, moaning as fevered as was her daughter, but also stark naked and red-skinned as a devil. Her tykes were sitting up in their bed, giggling and goggling at their cousin's indecencies. She quickly gathered up their garments and rushed them from the room, downstairs and up to the barn and screamed into the loft for the wench to come down. She ordered Mercy: "Deliver them to Sister Walcott. Say only that our daughters fell ill in the storm, but that I am taking care of both. I will not have her coming here! Do you understand? I will not allow it!" Not because she didn't need her in-law's help—but because the contagion was scarlet fever. She knew this because her niece displayed that angry rash. Her poor devoted niece, who was relied upon in that family like a backbone, and on the morrow might be dead. Like her eldest would be. And perhaps now even herself who'd shared the sickroom and a few times stretched out beside Lucy on the bed.

"Mistress Putnam, is there a doctor I might fetch?" asked Mercy, rousing the woman from sleep because by late afternoon, both her patients had worsened, despite repeated attempts to quell their fevers. She was worried.

Ann winced, "Don't you think I would have sent for him if I could? And who will pay the man? An absent husband without money?"

Mercy opened her hand. Two coins were cupped in her palm. "Use these." She felt responsible. Because before the rain, before Abigail gave them cakes, before she ever taught them games, when she still had choices, she had pulled the evil door open. She had entered the graveyard.

Ann took the coins and wrote out a note to send with them. "In the hilly east lives a Scotsman named Griggs. He calls himself a doctor. You can ask directions at the inn. But should anyone there inquire your business tell them it isn't theirs."

❧✦❧

It was dark when Mercy delivered the man. And because the narrow staircase was now alit with funerary candles, she grew fearful that one of the girls was dead. So when they entered the first sickroom and she saw Lucy in the bed, she felt relief, but then didn't, because her young friend had clearly worsened. The doctor nodded to her mistress and then walked up to the bed.

The Afflicted Girls

Opening his bag, Dr. Griggs was thinking how lucky for Goodwife Putnam he'd been summoned to the parsonage last night, or he'd be in Boston at this moment, for that had been his plan. And this serving wench was lucky or her mistress would have punished her when he wasn't found or brought. And he was also lucky— perhaps, the luckiest of them here.

Because after leaving the parsonage as he was driving along the meetinghouse road, he changed his mind and decided to hire a room at Ingersoll's instead. There he slept some hours and woke up refreshed. Then, instead of traveling to Boston, he ate a satisfying meal and went for a walk to the village glassmaker's shop to examine flagons for his apothecary. He made no purchases because there was better, cheaper glass to be found in Boston. And following that, by luck, as he was readying his carriage planning to visit his favorite local widow, this prettiest maid he'd ever beheld accosted him in the inn yard.

"But I am Griggs. I am the person you seek," he advised her after hearing her request and taking her pittance. He asked and learned how she had walked the distance from Putnam Farm. So he offered her a seat in his carriage. As they were driving here, sitting close, he began to match her attributes to those of his Hubbard niece who tidied his house and scrubbed him in his tub. As devoted as he was to that girl, he'd much prefer to have this one do it—whose long slender fingers were, no doubt, more adept at milking than were his niece's clumsy coarse ones, which were often also unclean. *Why not purchase her indenture from Putnam?* He did a mental calculation and settled on a modest sum and then halved it, so he could raise it when Putnam balked. How much *really* did one need to offer a debtor for a wench?

His mind returned to his task. How this child was suffering the same affliction as the two at the parsonage. But not wanting to raise the alarm that witchcraft was at work in this house, too, which would mean the scourge was spreading, he asked only to view the niece, and was escorted to that other chamber by the goodwife followed by the wench.

Upon viewing Susanna Walcott writhing sensually on the bed, a grunt of surprise escaped him. Though no longer naked, it made little difference: for she had her knees bent up and spread apart and wore only a flimsy muslin gown, which was clinging in fevered dampness to her sweaty skin. Suffering *the Devil's internal heat.*

"Suffers what?" Ann had heard him grunt.

He stroked his chin. "An infected pustule, or perhaps a cyst. To know for certain, I will need to examine her . . . in that unseen place. With your permission."

Ann Putnam nodded her consent.

Mercy considered that malady. A woman she had known some years ago, an almshouse mother of four, had died of a burst cyst after suffering greatly. She'd attended in the final hours, and cared for those orphans afterward till they were taken to another workhouse. Susanna's illness did show similarities, but it wasn't the same. She knew that.

Her mistress also was doubtful. "It isn't scarlet fever? But she looks the boiled lobster."

"No, not the scarlet fever. It's that your niece is ginger-haired," the doctor explained. "A sanguine type always flushes with fever." He put in his magnifying monocle and knelt beside the bed. Pushed up his patient's gown, and asked for the lantern to be brought which Mercy did. Parting those struggling thighs, soft plump ones he noted, he now used a curlicue on Susanna's pubis to calibrate his focus. He parted her labia and observed inside her, also probed a bit with his finger, while his patient moaned and writhed. He sniffed that finger afterward, slightly smiling, "No cyst nor even an infection. Your niece is healthy inside" *and intact.*

"But something has sickened her!"

"Spoiled victuals? What did she last eat?"

The Afflicted Girls

"The same as I did, and my other two . . . but that was after she got drenched." Turning to Mercy, "Did she eat in the woods? Did Lucy?"

The doctor's ears perked up. "They visited a wood? Well, Goody Putnam, fevers can arise from insect, snake and toad bites, and many a red rash is suffered after barely touching an unfriendly woodland plant. Her skin will provide us a clue."

He pushed Susanna's gown up over her breasts, and then cupped those two beauties in his palms. He pinched her nipples, and traced her aureoles round. "Her mammary is uncommonly swollen, abnormally tender." (Now this diagnosis Ann could understand—for her own breasts were chronically sore, so much so she could barely suckle a newborn, and never a teether. Couldn't bear, really, to have them touched.) "But no wheals and no bites, though there might yet be invisible biters."

He went to his knees again and combed the ginger-colored pubic mound, looking for tiny culprits, while Mercy was instructed to search Susanna's locks. When no marks or mites were found, he rolled Susanna onto her belly to better view her buttocks—also red, robust and hot to the touch. He drooled only a little, before advising Ann to turn her back, explaining how his next procedure was unfit for a goodwife's eyes.

So she walked over to the window and worriedly gazed out; as the doctor inserted that same probing forefinger up into his patient's anus.

Against this extraordinary intrusion, Susanna went berserk, but he held her firm against himself delving deep and wiggling, till he felt a tremor and release. Then he withdrew the finger and went to wash his hands at the bowl with the very strong lye soap he carried with him for this purpose. He announced his diagnosis with a satisfied grin: "The source of the fit is found, Goody Putnam. It is nothing a strong anthelmintic will not cure. Your niece suffers worms."

Before departing, Dr. Griggs bled both girls with the same leeches, which had sucked at the parsonage earlier. He administered the same sleeping draughts. And gave Ann Putnam a bottle of pills for her agitation, knowing that against witchcraft his remedies would be useless; for witchcraft was at work here, of this he had no doubt— the girl's unhealthy appetites betrayed it.

"Rest assured, Goody Putnam, both girls will recover. But as your daughter has greater need for your watchfulness, go in to her now. Let your servant sit with your niece. I will show myself out." He ushered Ann to the door and closed it behind her, telling Mercy how the room needed to keep free of drafts. He summoned her now for a final instruction. But when she came, he grabbed her around her waist and pressed his open mouth onto hers, and thrust his horny tongue down her gullet.

She tasted his sour spittle, felt him undoing his belt and rubbing; he was dragging her toward the cot. She wildly flailed for the standing torch and tilted it, setting afire his sleeve.

And now he ran to douse the flames in the washing bowl. And then he washed his hands of her—although Mercy was already standing ready with that *firearm* to defend again. But he avoided her as he scrambled toward the door. Leaving in his wake, her disbelief, and disgust, that this doctor, this lecher, this offal dog had violated her friend in front of her, had ruined a maid for life, had molested Susanna, raped her, without the mistress or her even knowing, and that she had been the cause of it, the cause—the procurer.

Fetching the doctor had been her idea, no one else's.

Out in the yard, Dr. Griggs rolled up his sleeve and frowned at his scorched forearm—the beginnings of a blistering burn. He climbed up into his carriage, unnerved, *but safe again,* he told himself, *from two ungodly vixens. One possessed by a succubus and barely of an age for it. With the other a lure to the Serpent's lair!* He lashed his horse harder than his wont, but after a short gallop, he turned from the road and parked behind a high hedgerow, in a dark place well hidden. He glanced uneasily in the four directions to assure himself he was secure from observation.

Then he loosened his belt and reached down inside his breeches to give his throbbing member the attention it still demanded, despite the danger to his soul.

One would blow up a feather in the air; another would dart straws at it with much fury; another, stark naked, would sit up in a corner like a monkey, grinning and making mows at them.

> <u>The History and Present State of Virginia</u>
> Robert Beverly (1705) *(Description of British soldiers in 1676 after eating a salad containing Jamestown weed.)*

PART SIX

45

BEN NURSE, RUSHING DOWN THE WIDE CENTER stable walkway, upset a young colt being first-time shod, bellowing out a rumor he'd just heard at the mill. The animal whinnied and reared with a horseshoe dangling, knocking Joseph's cheek a bruising blow. Expert hands calmed it, got the task done. Then Joseph cursed his friend. His cheek hurt. He could feel it swelling, and rubbed it.

"But what if their claim is true?" Ben worried, picking up an iron shoe from the pile, and rubbing *it* for good luck. "Not that I'm of that mind."

"Why not? You need to think more stupidly between your ears. "

"Oh, you think that I fear for myself? When it's tykes being struck down by the twos? What if the Evil Hand reaches to Orchard Farm, what of our youngsters there? How would I defend them?"

The Afflicted Girls

Joseph put a steadying hand on this other skittish colt's shoulder, advising his boyhood friend: "Such an evil could never befall Orchard Farm. From your fruits to saplings to seeds to woolly forelocks—he gave Ben's a good hard yank equal in pain to the lump on his cheek—you Nurses are too good."

Whereas Mary Veren Putnam stated bluntly upon hearing that same rumor from her son: "Well, why shouldn't witches invade our village and afflict our enemies?"

"But you don't believe in witches," Joseph reminded.

She pursed her painted lips, "Well, in this instance, I shall. In fact, I shall pray that it is true."

He studied her. *Had everyone in this village turned pillow-brained overnight?* With Ben Nurse, he didn't doubt it. But his mother hid some devious purpose saying it, something to her advantage. But which he had no time to discover since his most valuable brood mare, the Arabian, had laid down too early to foal, and was in distress. He'd only returned to the house to give his mother that news and to advise her to take supper without him.

And that is what ruffled her most. "Can't your servant see to the beast?"

"It needs its master's presence."

"Well I require you, also, Joseph. Unless you prefer that creature's company to mine?"

He didn't answer.

"Nonetheless, you cannot leave yet. There are pressing matters I need to discuss with you."

"Just not as pressing or needful as mine."

And later, Mary was so peeved at the lack of a dining companion that she passed Ben Nurse's rumor indiscreetly to her lady's maid, whose collar immediately flew up. As soon as her mistress had finished dressing and dismissed her, she raced down by the back stair to the kitchen to tell Cook, her mother, the frightening news. Cook pushed her out the door, ordering her to fly on the wind to the stable, to tell her brothers to go hurry and nail up horseshoes in their carriage-house. "Over every door, window frame, hearth and bedstead! Hurry, daughter! Run!"

That young woman did her best to outrun the Devil, but he tripped her along the way and she scraped her chin badly when she fell. She daubed it with a perfumed doily she'd once pilfered from the mistress' laundry. Used it again to smother the smell when she entered that longhouse stable and rushed past the rows of snorting beasts. One rammed its gate and gave her the Evil Eye. *Where, oh where were her brothers?* She heard a piercing wail, like a dying banshee's cry, rattling the stable wall. She ran terrified to the rear.

Out of doors again, she calmed her thumping heart, and heard men's shouts. She nervously threaded in their direction around sacks of fodder and bales of stacked green hay toward the foaling shed. Near to it, she almost tripped over a dead, unborn creature lying abandoned in the dirt. Sill enclosed in its fleshy, bloody membrane. The gruesome sight sickened her and she retched.

She saw her brothers inside the shed kneeling and holding down a prone, bellowing beast. The young master was shouting frenzied directions, and his apron was stained red, bloodier than her father's ever was on butchering day. She knew that both he and his horse were doomed. She backed away in search of her father now. To tell him how that fertile farm, their great hope and future, was now lost. How this place was evilly cursed. *Too late here for horseshoes.*

The Afflicted Girls

46

DESCRIPTIONS OF THE AFFLICTED GIRLS IGNITED every gossipmonger's tongue, which each wagged the rumor along—although, always with a different notion as to why these particular four had been struck. But no tongue as yet had made mention of an afflicted boy. For John Doritch, even though that farmer's son was equally stricken, wasn't known to them—likely, because his parents had been too poor to hire a doctor.

John's strangeness began last Sabbath night at his family's supper table, when he knocked over his father's chair while padding about on all fours. He snarled and snapped at his brothers as they tried to catch him; how they all laughed at him . . . till he bit their mother on her hand. And then raised his leg to pee against the table leg, and fouled his Sunday suit.

His brothers dragged him outside to the barn, stripped him naked, dunked him in the trough and then wound a rope around his ankle while he barked and snarled in confusion. They threaded that rope through knotholes in the barn wall and tossed a horse blanket over him, and then took turns kicking him black and blue for biting their mother. That poor cur curled up and slept outside the barn on Sunday night, and still was doing that, just as maddened, four days later.

But now John the Dog cowered whenever any of them came near him. He even shied away from his mother when she brought him out his food. Canine instinct made him chase away any crow or blackbird, that dared swoop down to peck at his food. And he growled at every night-crawling varmint coming to view his leftovers.

Despite Goody Doritch's protests, Farmer Doritch insisted that "tied-up" was only way to keep John safe, explaining to his wife how this middle son was a runner too fast for him to chase down with his gout, especially if the boy took to roaming. So with reluctance, she accepted John's fate, but could not comprehend what had befallen him.

Nevertheless, twice daily, she brought John out his food, using her garden hoe to push the bowl closer, because he still bared his teeth at her. Although today he seemed in friendlier spirits, so she braved stepping nearer. Slowly stretching out her arm to set his food down beside him. That's when John licked her hand. How she wanted to pet that matted red mop and then pull it to her breast, but she was too afraid to attempt it. She decided to summon her husband home and have him watching. But then, a peddler wheeled his barrow to her gate and told her a terrible rumor.

She affixed her bonnet, glancing only once at John the Dog, before clambering up the farm lane to the road and hurrying in the opposite direction.

"My boy's bewitched!" cried Goody Doritch. "And only you can save him, Goody Bishop!"

Bridget, who was crouched in her vegetable patch weeding, looked up and saw that excited goodwife trample her sprouting lettuce. And now Goody Doritch hopped backward squashing her sprouting beets and chives, as well. Quickly Bridget stretched out her torso to save the squash and young tomato vines from annihilation. And now she stood up to complain. But sobered at the sight of her visitor's anguish. And what were vegetables compared to that? She wiped off her dirty hands and without further thought of her garden, inquired: "How now, Goody Doritch? What is it you're telling me?"

"My boy's been struck down by evil, turned into a red devil's dog. Never walks on his feet, only on fours. Howls at the moon, laps at the trough—"

"Feverish is he?"

"Oh, he won't let me touch him, so I don't really know. But he's more than flushed with fever. Bright red he is, and even could I ask he'd only bark or growl in answer. But today he licked my fingers, and I took it as a sign. Till I heard how other youngsters in the village are the same-wise stricken. So I came hither to you."

Bridget had heard the rumor. "When did his fit begin?"

The farm wife counted on fingers. "Five days gone. Began last Sunday while we were sitting for our Sabbath supper. I set down a meat pie, and he jumped up on the table and put his snout in it, gobbled it up like a starving pup. We all laughed, thinking him funning—for our John sometimes does that. But when I reached in to save some for my others, mad as a wolf he bit me." She showed Bridget her injury: tooth-marks punctured her palm. "Then he did worse . . . will my boy die?"

Bridget put a consoling arm around the woman's shivering shoulder. "Becalm yourself, Goody Doritch. If your John's not dead after five days, he won't be dead on the sixth. I'll give you a gut purgative—green willow to ash and mix into his food. The madness will pass out eventually."

As they walked to the house, Bridget considered a wild creeper, which when grazing animals ate with their natural forage, caused them to run amok in circles, bray in frenzies, and attack keepers—even docile sheep. But were those animals *red-skinned* under their coat? That she didn't know, for no farmer had ever skinned one and told her. But whatever had caused this boy's fit, and those others, while his life wouldn't be forfeit, his sanity might be — for John's wits, to begin with, were slim. And plants of any malefic ilk can undo weak minds permanently. But he wouldn't die, no. For even when those beasts toppled over and the meat was cooked and ingested, no death came to the eater or the passing on of madness. But really, to reckon rightly, she'd need to see the boy for herself.

"Wait here, Goody Doritch . . . I am coming."

❧✦☙

Thomas Putnam, while returning home from Boston on the High Road, drove his wagon past two local women striding in the same direction on the outskirts. He didn't stop to offer the walkers a ride. Nor did his in-laws tip their hats. But all of them turned to stare — not at the farmwife, only at the scarlet harlot, Bridget Bishop. And now about her, they shared some lurid gossip. So in giddy spirits they pulled into the inn yard and parked to go in and share a congratulatory drink before parting ways.

But Nathaniel Ingersoll, spying them through a window, came rushing out to the yard to inform his nephew Walcott, and also Thomas Putnam, how their daughters were gravely stricken, ordering them: "Home now to your wives! With urgency!" He didn't mention details, although his rooms had been awash with rumors all week. And now he watched those two worried fathers depart, thinking how one of them — not his nephew — was the unluckiest man he knew. Trask walked past and climbed the steps intending to have his toast, if only with Ingersoll. He sat down at their regular table, and couldn't help but flap about their "victory."

"What was the war?" asked the innkeeper nonchalantly.

"Thieving back a family's thieved inhe—" he gave a sheepish grin, having remembered how he and his in-laws had agreed in Boston to keep their business private, since the outcome wasn't carved in stone. "Well, I won't say what exactly, Nathaniel, but know that most of it was by my doing." He laid down a coin, which the innkeeper took. And now Nathaniel Ingersoll fetched up a bottle of strong whisky, not the ale Trask had ordered, to empty this beanbag of his beans.

Goody Walcott had not seen her daughter for nearly a week because her brother's wife wouldn't allow it. She'd suffered torments worrying. But when Ann willfully and cruelly held Susanna in thrall, refusing to relinquish her, even after her three eldest boys went out to Putnam Farm in the wagon to fetch their sister, she grew furious.

Now viewing Thomas' wagon pulling into the yard with her husband sitting beside him, she praised God they'd come home. But then, from that same second storey window, this mother saw a body lying prone in the back, wrapped in a coverlet. Her heart fell through the floor; *was her daughter dead?*

She stumbled downstairs, rushed out and over to the wagon. But the girl moved. She heard her moan. She gave a prayer of thanks as she caught her husband's sober eye, and then her brother's. But she knew that she dare not mention Ann to Thomas, since he, while a good brother to her, couldn't stomach criticism— not even from a sister as loving as she. So she would have to bide her time till their daughters had recovered and he next complained to her of Ann. But at least now he could take his two youngest home with him.

They'd been nothing but trouble for her, constantly whining, fighting with each other and with her children, telling deliberate made-up stories about a beloved sister. Intolerable imps they were, cut from their mother's cloth. Thomas was hardly in them. "Your two," she said, wishing to hand them up, for her husband was already in the back-bed lifting Susanna. And her nieces were straining to go to their father, as hard as she was to her daughter.

Thomas shook his head; "You need to keep them longer, sister." And before she could protest, he had lashed his horse and turned the wagon, and rolled out.

Her husband half-ran across the yard with Susanna in his arms, with herself keeping up, and behind her that mayhem of tykes chasing. Reaching the threshold, she put a halting hand up and instructed: "Children, you're to stay in the yard. None of you is to enter this house till I allow it." She quickly followed her spouse upstairs, and walked into their daughters' chamber just as he was setting Susanna on the bed. When suddenly, that girl clasped her father round his neck and kissed him wantonly on the mouth, as a Salome might, but a daughter never!

Horrified, Goodman Walcott threw her down to the mat. While his wife slammed shut the door and hurriedly latched the shutters, as if sparrows on branches might see that great sin. But God could, she knew, as she stared agape at her husband, not knowing what she felt. "Unclean spirits possess her" was all the poor man could say. And now both of them went to their knees to pray away this corruption.

Susanna was oblivious to her parents' spiritual mutterings, and was equally unaware of her own familial bedstead; but feeling softness of a horsehair mat, as compared to her cousins' hard straw clumps, she grated her hips more smoothly now as her phantom lover, with the pleasuring hands, again lay himself atop her.

One by one those banished Walcotts tiptoed up to the door and took turns pressing their eyeballs to the keyhole . . . to discover how their Putnam cousins were not such fibbers like they thought.

The Afflicted Girls

47

VILLAGE PARIAH SARAH GOOD, HAVING HEARD the same rumors as everybody else, trekked out to Putnam Farm hoping to catch a glimpse of the devil-born youngsters—useful information to barter for better fare from housewives; because this morning no door had opened to her and Dorcas. Not even at the parsonage.

She kept a wary eye out as they walked this particular western road. For that new junior constable also resided on it. And while that person hadn't yet put her into stocks for *thievery*, being a newcomer in these parts he wouldn't know she was no thief, only a widowed former neighbor of greedy-gut villagers, who'd *thieved* her few possessions of value.

A rider appeared down the road. She pulled Dorcas aside toward a tree, but then noticed a ramshackle shed. So they scurried uphill to that better hiding place. And because it was near to dusk, told her: "We rest in here till the moos come in. Then we go across the road to milk you a bucket." She knew her daughter was hungry because her own stomach gnawed, and her legs were swollen double their size, and her blistered feet were festering inside these man-sized shoes. But before anything, she went to put her eye between two slats. *Bugbear! Rats-bane!* She nearly laughed out loud, spying John Willard on his horse. *Well, well, said you!* So her powers hadn't failed her. And now she stretched out on the dirt mightily pleased, patting her thigh for her daughter to join her.

The next thing Sarah Good knew it was morning. Strong shafts punched through the skimpy slats, with one hot sunray settling on her cheek. She opened her eyes. She was alone. So she got up and yelled out from the doorway, "Dorcas Good! You snippet! Come to mama!" If that farmer heard her and came up, she'd spit in his eye.

Loud honks had awoken Dorcas around dawn, and when she scampered outside she discovered a flock of wild geese had landed. She waddled off after them, honking at the end of their line, in search of goose eggs to bring to her mother. Those birds found a stream, where they fished and bathed and preened. But laid no eggs. When they flew off, the brook was lined with feathers, which she gathered. She also picked pussy willows that tickled her skin. And ate water onions; she was hungry. But then her tummy hurt. So she crouched to play with a frog while she burped. And it croaked back like they were old babbling friends.

She was playing with her new pet, when her mother stomped down and pinched her arm and pulled her up and slapped her bottom: "You're not to wander away from me!" She bawled as she was being dragged back up that slope across the road to a gate, while her mother complained they'd lost their best chances. Of course, she felt sad. She wanted her mother to be happy.

Sarah Good called out gruffly: "You there, give us food! Be neighborly!"

Mercy, sitting on the stump, looked up from her sieving and saw a scraggly woman with a child entering the gate. They were walking toward her briskly. And when they came up, the woman picked up her pail of cleaned grain and handed it to her. "Gimme some o' this."

Mercy glanced up toward the house. No one that she could see was watching from any window. "Hold out your apron, mistress, quickly."

Sarah Good did, and received her bit of rye; she tied the apron into a bundle and let it rest upon her bulge. "I promised my tyke milk. And these seeds won't feed a fledgling. I eat for two, besides. And there's three of us here that's needful."

"My mistress saw me carry in the pails. She knows how much milk she has."

"Say you spilt some."

Mercy shook her head.

Sarah Good frowned, "Eggs, then."

Mercy hesitated. Their hens were not good layers. But this child was starving—her distended belly displayed it. She thought how she might give her portion—one egg. "They have little ones here, too, mistress, with not much to spare. But if you wait by the gate, I'll bring something."

Sarah Good grunted, then shuffled away with her daughter. But as soon as Mercy had disappeared around the house, she dragged Dorcas in the same direction.

About an hour after Dorcas Good went waddling after geese, two naughty Putnam tykes were delivered home by their Uncle Walcott; and at this moment were frolicking outside the chicken coop, playing with newly hatched chicks.

Spying them, Sarah Good snickered, "Golly gum! Golly gee! Here are the very sprites the witches made sick!"

The sisters looked up and saw a pock-marred face leering down at them. They cried out and Mercy came rushing from the coop. She caught the younger one sticking out her tongue at the beggar, while the older one informed rudely: "We don't give to beggars." She pulled them aside, explaining in a hush, "We never refuse to feed a hungry person. Charity is not only our Christian way. It is a necessity. For one day it might be our own self in need at someone else's gate."

She had planned to give her one egg to the beggar, though that was hardly charity. Until a moment ago, she had thought to give two—her morrow's portion as well. But now she decided to give the beggar four eggs—these children's portions, because her charges needed a lesson in kindness. She crawled back inside the coop.

And now *both* sisters thrust out their tongues at the beggar, and made sour faces at her little girl.

Sarah Good sneered, "Wouldn'a be so proud were I you. Since it's your ma, *not* hers, births the babes of Beelzebub." She cleared her throat twice and spat out a wad of phlegm, aiming at their bibs. Shrieking, covered in muck, they ran back to the house to tell their mother how Mercy had taken a beggar's side.

"Hop-hop little frogs," cackled Sarah, gloating when they stumbled, each one pulling the other down.

While Dorcas stared sadly after those children, wondering why—even in her pretty parsonage dress—no child liked her. Why no one ever wanted to be her friend.

The Afflicted Girls

48

THOMAS HAD LEFT HIS FIELD LABORS EARLY AS the sun began to set in rare florid color. Arriving home, after scrubbing off at the well pump at the height of that display, he viewed his serving wench bringing in the milk cows from pasture, with his two youngest pulling tethers. Cowbells, child-song, birdsong enhanced the bucolic idyll. And because of it, he felt inclined to go inside and be cordial to his wife.

Ann had returned to some housewifery, but they hadn't spoken much . . . despite his progress in Boston. Each time he'd hint at legalities, she'd turn him a cold ear because of Lucy. But now that the girl was improving, his wife's disposition might too. So he came into the kitchen and invited Ann to stand with him in the doorway, and planned to put his arm around her shoulder while they stared at God's Glory together. But she ignored him. So he took in that beauty alone. And now afterward, with his spirits still painted, he sat down on the settle and asked how her day had fared.

"Fare? It is fare that I lack! Meat for my pot! Flesh for these plates! Food for three growing tykes!

"I was only trying to converse with you, Ann."

"Converse instead, Thomas, how not once in weeks has our suffering girl had meat!"

"She's recovering well enough, isn't she?" he grumbled.

"She isn't! She malingers!"

"Stop your mewling!"

"Not till you slaughter me a beast!" Saying that, she banged the lid on the pot of the bubbling meatless stew, which he saw as a sign of what was coming next. He got up. "All right, all right. I'll go kill you a chicken."

"No, chicken! No fowl! Something four-legged! Full of blood and marrow and muscle!"

"A chicken is what you'll get, Ann, or nothing!"

"Only a miser denies his sick child!"

"Only a nag-hag complains of it!"

She fumed, and lest she curse him—because her curses stuck—he yielded. "A hare then." He reached for his gun.

"No hare! No hen! But the bloodiest creature we own! And I'm not meaning mutton!"

He curled hatred through the gun's lock. But then slammed down that musket and took up his butchering cleaver instead.

Outside, he yelled for the serving wench, the real cause for his wife's hysterics and his daughter's *malingering*. Before that person came to this house, Ann never held kitchen opinions. He ordered his tykes down to their mother and tossed a rope to the wench. "Bring a calf to the slaughtering shed. Whatever one thrives least." He'd let Ann have her way in the kitchen. He'd have his later in the bed.

Ten times, twenty times, he'd showed the stupid wench how to hold a pail steady underneath a jugular that was cut, while he forced up the calf's throat to drain it. And it was a fighter, which meant it thrived! At market, it would've brought him more than damn spurting blood!

Mercy was trying to collect that lifeblood, but the animal kept shaking its head, and now it knocked the vessel from her hands. What little she'd collected soaked into the dirt. The creature had broken free of her master and now it cowered in a corner.

The Afflicted Girls

Agonized bellows filled the shed as her master grabbed it and caved it to its knees, while she rushed over with the bucket.

The calf looked up at her as it gave its final bloodless whimper. She was sure that it saw how her soul was screaming with it.

⋘❦⋙

In the first part of her dream, Mercy heard a calf's agonizing bellows. Now it was vicious snarls and yelps. She woke, and rushed from her settle thinking the dog pack, that lately had been ravaging neighborhoods, was attacking their mongrel. She spied the ax wedged in the splitting post. Could she kill a creature though?

Knowing she couldn't, she grabbed the rake instead, and rounded the house with caution, and saw *him*, Joseph Putnam, pressed back against the clapboard, fending off her master's mean dog with kicks. She ran back inside the kitchen to fish out a marrowbone from the stewpot. And now, with a low whistle to the creature, she displayed her offering before tossing it down the yard. It sprinted away, as Joseph hastened toward her, took her arm and drew her away from the house. She glanced uneasily at an upstairs chamber window and he misunderstood. "My brother is in Boston. Do you fear his mad wife, as well?"

She shook her head. *He has been home since yesterday* but she didn't tell Joseph Putnam that, because then he would not wrap his possessive arms around her and give her that first sweet kiss she had wanted. Tongues met now and bodies pressed, and her eyes closed to windows, and to Putnams and their threats.

Entering the ink-black barn, she put a hand on the small of his back to better guide him toward the hayloft ladder. Up in the loft, they gathered straw for a bed. Both were quick to undress and embrace in a truly shared fever. She wished she could see Joseph

Putnam's eyes, but at the same time was glad that she couldn't. Or he'd have seen the bruises covering half of her body—after her master slaughtered the calf, he'd fisticuffed her. She banished that intruding thought because Joseph Putnam was inside her now, not brutally like before but tenderly like the husband she sought, beyond bruised skin or any skin . . . and she was inside him, too. Spiritually. Exhaustion overtook their passions, and now sleep did as well. They fell asleep still joined. And although he hadn't said he loved her, for Mercy it was a fact.

He slumbered deeply, but she, only a little. Because she'd forgotten to look up at the position of the stars when they were crossing the yard. She didn't know the hour of night. She kept waking and listening for birdsong, while each time urged by her lonely soul to drink her lover into another fever, even though love's certainty was gone. But she didn't. Only thought her confusing thoughts. Then later, when the lead cow lowed and she woke into daylight, she extricated and quickly pulled on her gown, and kneeled beside him and brushed his sleeping lips.

"Leave me," he muttered, thinking it was his mother teasing him awake. He rolled away to his side. Mercy said it was morning and that he had to wake and go. His eyes groggily parted. He saw a face, but it took him longer to recall whose. When he did, he yawned. "I was dreaming I bought your contract from Thomas. What's your yearly price? Ten pounds?"

She didn't answer.

"Even at thirty, you'd be cheap."

"Cheap chattel? Is that what I am?"

"Not cheap," he smiled. Nevertheless, he wasn't the one who made her what she was. He tried to pull her down. His body wanted her.

She stepped away, and said soberly: "But in your dream, did I work my fingers to blister by day and lie down with you by night in haylofts and bowers, while you rode your purchased bones?" She didn't wait for his answer; she could read it in his face. She went to the ladder and climbed down. Her body was bruised, but her heart now hurt her worse.

Joseph shook his head, thinking how his affairs with brash young women always ended badly. They were too much like his mother; and he wasn't the sort to be commanded by a milkmaid commanded by cows. He reached for his breeches, which then uncovered his ruined boots. He frowned. He'd paid a small fortune in London to a courtier's cobbler—a high price for one night's sport.

Mercy was waiting stiffly by the door. When he came, he offered her his opinion: "It's not me who considers you a workhorse. Only yourself who views the world through blinders. By buying your contract I could buy your freedom, arranged without my brother knowing. You might have gone your own way then if you chose, though I'd prefer you came to me. To be a servant in my household, yes, of course. But only in other people's eyes, not in mine."

She looked into Joseph's eyes, and saw him clearly—encrusted with shadows.

"With my choice," she answered, "I will choose to be a wife."

Quills covered him, quills and disbelief. She was twisting his generosity, he said. She argued that she loved him. He insisted it wasn't love, only a physical craving between them. *Of course, he craved her . . . what man wouldn't?* Though what man *hadn't* was really his question. She was proficient. Although he could also see that she loved him in her soul. But the position of wife was taken, or sold, or lost in a bad gamble, but never could have been hers at any cost. She aspired too high above her place. So even if he did buy her contract, she'd serve only trouble in his mother's household. He would have to let Thomas keep her. *Thomas . . . oh yes, Thomas.* He'd nearly forgotten his purpose in coming. "Why did my brother go to Boston? Do you know?" Mercy shook her head.

She was hurrying down the yard, back to the house to quickly pull on her workday clothes and fetch her pails. The rooster was already crowing, prancing atop the coop. But it was only a tad past the noisy time she normally arose. So she felt a small measure of safety. But then as she approached the door, it opened on its own and her master stood facing her on his morning jaunt to the privy.

Her shocked expression, randy scent, the straw in her hair, told Thomas something was amiss. He seized her by the arm and dragged her down to the gate, out onto the lane, and saw a rider in the distance. He knew who it was from the horse's high gait. "You've been spying on me! Spreading your legs for my enemy!"

Mercy denied it.

Knowing she lied, he slapped her across the road up to the shed. Where he picked up a stick outside, but inside used only his fists, because broken bones on a serving wench would be scorned.

In the midst of his vigorous pounding, the Devil caused Thomas' member to rise. So he got down and grabbed Mercy by her hipbones and fitted her onto his hard prick, and with his length inside her now, and with her no longer resisting, he held her iron-clasped and had her. Hungrily sucked the nipples previously denied him. How deep could he go? Deep as he wanted, pierce and ram through every orifice. She was his betrayer.

"God Almighty," he shuddered entering his throes. He'd never felt such lust before, not even in his marriage bed or in any city brothel. Rod engorged, ready to express, he pulled out and got up on his haunches, breathlessly ordering: "Spout in the mouth, drink a frothy brew, swallow my tasty manhood!" He'd always wanted to say that to a harlot. He took her face and forced it down, and shot his juices into her mouth. The more she gagged, the more he pleasured.

He pushed her off but then covered her with himself. She was his bed to sleep in, his pretty wench to copulate and rub on. He rolled her over to view her flesh, which was his flesh. Enough bruises on the skin to remind her, though luckily not on the normally visible parts. He wondered how long it would take his rod to recover its strength so he could humiliate her some more. But he knew his family would be rising soon. So he told her she was a worthless whore, who deserved what she got. He cleaned himself off with her garment, thinking how his brother had actually done him a favor. He put a foot on her mound and wedged his grimy toes inside: "From today, you open this only to me."

Her eyes were tight shut, so he couldn't view her submission, but guessed it was complete. Her nipples were well-sucked purple. With them, he couldn't stop. So he got down on his knees and took a final long suck. If she'd resisted, he'd have hardened, despite being spent. She provoked it in him, this young unseemly wench, and would do it again. He got up: "Was fair exchange for what you did to me. Do it again I'll kill you. Bury you and say you ran off. I'm within my rights as a freeman."

He was passing underneath his grandfather's wineglass elms when those sentinels stared down with more than their usual disapproval. He heard rustlings and looked up. But saw no birds in the limbs or squirrels or any leaves astir. But then he saw what they saw: how he'd just gone down the road to Hell and was possessed there by a demon!

He reeled around to see if any fiendish thing was trailing, but viewed only the shed across on the hill with the wench still inside it. He suddenly knew. *Tool of the Devil drew me in from the start. Laid down a trap for my soul. Delilah!* It was he who'd been sucked! Sucked dry! Sucked of goodness! By a Hell-born succubus vixen! He had just fucked the Devil's flesh!

He carried that sin into the house. Upstairs when he went to call his own to morning worship. He was unsure of his position now—before, he was always husband and father, priest and prophet, who each morning had to turn his family's minds toward God. He knew today could be no different.

His wife wasn't in their bed. Nor was she in the children's chamber. He looked down at his three girls asleep—two wrapped together in a clutch, with the eldest wheezing on her cot. He'd let her rest, he decided, picking up only the youngest two and carrying them out, one on each hip. Those two jostled youngsters woke up not understanding where they were—for never did their father carry them. They rubbed their eyes. Then the littlest one sweetly murmured "Papa"—his name spoken by innocent lips. He felt cleaner of a sudden, and vowed to value them more, as he set them down outside the parlor and then led them inside.

Ann was sitting in her chair turned round, staring out through the front parlor window . . . at what? He wondered how long she'd been sitting there and what, if anything, she'd seen. Unsettled, he took his place at the head of the table and opened the Family Bible to *Corinthians*. He preached and read—with no attention to words, and with his wife as yet unreadable—praying for the jade not to show her face this morning, for his sin would be scribed upon it. He concluded his morning service with the singing of the 51st Psalm:

> "Cast me not away from they presence,
> And take not Thy Holy Spirit from me—"

Too late, Thomas thought to himself.

Upstairs, Lucy awakened to the sweet sound of that hymn-song. She yawned off remnants of her gossamer dream, and saw that she was alone. Stretching upward, she breathed and smiled.

And realized, how she'd just breathed deep for the first time since ever. Thanks to God. *Sweet Lord Jesus, let me visit again to Heaven.* For it was of Him, and of that Place she'd been dreaming, and that's why her breath flowed, because all breath flowed from there. Sweet music was wafting up the chimney flue, joining with her gratefulness rising to the sky. She Psalm-sang, too, asking for God to come and lift her:

> "Cleanse me of my sin with hyssop
> That I may be purified—"

'Visions will come easier if you each eat an auguring cake.' Abigail's words rang clear. Was it in Answer to her prayer? *No,* it was a distraction—because she was not praying properly like a good Christian child on bended knee beside her cot . . . but lazily.

So she went to her knees, and clasped her hands. But now she spied a cloth stuffed underneath her cot—that dress she'd worn on the picnic, left in a heap by someone's neglect . . . but remaining undiscovered till now by *God's doing*! So excited was she to find that magical token that her hand trembled while turning out its pocket to receive her bitter *hyssop*:

> "Wash me and I shall be whiter than snow—"

Uneaten pieces of Abigail's red auguring cake sat upon her palm.

> "Let me hear sounds of joy and gladness—"

Joy and gladness! Hyssop whiter than snow! She ate her blessed *hyssop*, not caring about its taste (or *red* color) as she stretched up her arms again and breathed waiting to be lifted. Soon her newly restored body began to twist and jerk.

> "The bones You have crushed shall rejoice.
> Turn away Your face from my sins,
> And blot out all my guilt--"

And it was Lucy Putnam that was blotted out now and crushed.

❧✦❧

Bridget Bishop had promised her no man would ever again use her ill again. *But men would always use her. It was her shape in His Grand Design. God had wrought her for this affliction. She was a Lot's daughter till the End.*

Mercy pulled on her befouled gown onto her befouled body, and stumbled out from that shed of blood and semen in search of cleansing water.

The Afflicted Girls

49

G OD'S PUNISHMENT FOR HIS SIN THIS MORNING? Galloping his horse down the Topsfield Road, Thomas Putnam agonized over his daughter's new affliction. His wife insisted he summon Dr. Griggs when their eldest fell into a new thrashing fit, and herself into new hysterics. Although it would have been wiser to take the girl in his wagon to seek out a better physician in Beverly or Salem Town, and he said as much.

But Ann refused that common sense, refused to relinquish Lucy at all. So he carried her into their room and strapped her down to four sturdy bedposts with rope, because Ann couldn't control her; Ann barely could watch. Nevertheless, the woman kept prodding him: "Where's my wench, Thomas? Why wasn't she at worship? Did you give her a task? What task? Send her up before you go. Lucy needs her. I need her. Where is she, Thomas? Tell me!"

He said he didn't know. *And she had better keep quiet about it or I'll string her up on tenterhooks.* Well, at least, he hadn't lied.

He deposited his other two at the kitchen table, throwing down their hornbooks and slates, ordering them to practice writing letters till their mother came down or the servant returned. But those little ones were not interested in lessons before breakfast. So they ate last night's marrow stew and then wandered out in search of Mercy, deciding that if they didn't find her, they would play. Their father couldn't fault them for that, could he?

269

They skipped down to the wishing well and spooled out the bucket till it splashed at the bottom. They gave each other rides in the wheelbarrow—round and round the tree stump and then up to the coop. They crawled inside and scared out every chicken, and also found two eggs nearly hatched. They cracked one open on a mother hen's feathers, to see what a fowl might do. Then scraped out that half-born chick, which struggled not to die. When it did, they buried it deep inside the hay pile. Then bounced a while on the straw.

The barn door was ajar so they went inside. They puzzled seeing the milk cows tied up in stalls. Hadn't Mercy taken them to pasture? Should they? After eating so much salty stew and then forgetting to drink at the well, they were thirsty. So they drank milk from those udders till their mouths and bellies lost interest. And now they began squirting each other in a wasteful game, until the elder one spied a fishing pole leaning back against the wall.

"Let's fish," she said.

"Pretend fish?" wondered her sister. The other shook her head, and took the rod and the box in hand.

"Can't," the little one protested running after her, "not allowed beyond the fence." But then, like she always did, she hurried to catch up, following her middle sister lugging that fisherman's box and long fishing pole up the road to the *landgrubber's* wood where a river tributary flowed, before trickling into their pasture carrying only tadpoles, flies, and sand.

Mercy did not return to Putnam Farm out of fear or submission. But she came stealthily, in full resolve, to retrieve her few books and diaries from her traveling trunk. Because she would not leave behind those possessions: her written years of inscribed memory of her family — or even Lucy Putnam's shared small treasures, which would leave behind hurt feelings.

Upstairs, Ann sensed a presence and stopped rocking and listened. She hadn't seen her tykes yet today. Nor had the servant appeared. She supposed they'd all gone off somewhere together. Curious, she came downstairs, to the kitchen, where she saw her servant's empty coffer sitting open in the middle of the floor. Something her tykes might have done. She called out their names from the kitchen doorway and then from the front doorway, and now also from the edge of her sitting porch, which gave the best vantage toward the road.

She glimpsed the serving wench in the distance striding beyond the neighbor's farm. She raced down to the lane, yelling and waving with both arms. "Come back! Help me! Lucy's dying!"

Mercy clutched her satchel and walked faster. *Flee . . . pretend you do not hear her.* But kindness made her turn and call out, "Lucy is recovering, mistress! Now you must do the same!" She hurried on knowing how that woman would never heal, and then quickened her pace more.

Ann was utterly winded when she caught up with Mercy far down the next lane by cutting across that neighbor's hay field. She slapped her hard on the cheek. "Didn't you hear what I told you? My girl's dying! You don't believe me?"

Mercy clutched her satchel tighter.

"What have you got there? What have you stolen of mine?" Ann yanked it away, and the bundle fell and spilled.

Mercy crouched to gather her items, but the mistress kicked them aside, save one she put her foot on — Anne Bradstreet's volume of poems she presumed belonged to her sister-in-law. "Thief!" Ann snarled. "Get back to the house! Or I'll put the constable on you!

Lucy's fit led into another fit, a stranger one. In which her eyes fixed open, unseeing and unblinking, limbs lay motionless and stiffened under the tethers that bound them akimbo to the bed and cut deep. In one frozen clenched hand were red crumbs from a turned-out pocket.

Mercy felt for a pulse. Her sensitive fingertips barely could detect a wisp. Lucy's hand was cold as ice and so rigid she couldn't bend it backward at the wrist and barely forward. But she managed to open it and find the crumbs. *Coldness, stiffness, eyes dead but alive.* Knowledge of the antidote had never been revealed to her. But she knew that the black minister knew one, and of anyone here, Bridget Bishop might. Without caution, she told her mistress.

"Fly to the witch then!" cried Ann.

So Mercy took to the road again: a second chance to save herself and flee. Gathering up her journals, she wrapped them safely inside her winter cloak and hid that bundle underneath a neighbor's hedge.

It was four miles' walk to Bridget's. But she half-ran, while praying for a long and happy life for Lucy Putnam. Because that good-hearted child deserved a chance to live and grow, not fall from the precipice like she once did, when the black minister fed her too much poison and she died. He claimed it was a coma when he brought her back with another of his brews. But she was never certain, for she was no magician. Nor was Bridget Bishop.

If Lucy Putnam died today, she'd be dead.

⁓✢⁓

Two slow moving wide-base wagons and then a herd of unmoving sheep forced Thomas to take a crow's shortcut across a landgrubbers' fields; which were rich-soiled and productive and un-assailed by vermin, unlike his. Clean-smelling, healthy sprouting rye filled his nostrils. He crossed an old timber woodlot, which had belonged to the same founding family till poverty forced them to sell. He fought envy all the way. Then he entered that marshy uninhabitable wasteland—that no man's land no one wanted, even him—said to hide quicksand pits. If he died in one today, he deserved it. But he emerged alive and well from that swamp. A local carter directed him to the doctor's dwelling. There, a doltish maid answered the door, curtly replied that she didn't know her uncle's *wherewithals*, and abruptly shut it in his face.

With the mid-day sun so strong in a cloudless sky, Thomas wished he'd worn his hat. He gulped water at the doctor's pump then trudged out onto the spur to gaze down at the landscape, pondering his choices: in two places dwelled physicians superior to Griggs but who commanded higher fees, which he couldn't pay anyway. Griggs at least took IOUs, but for useless pills and plasters. An hour had passed since he'd departed. Two more it would be if he rode on to Beverly, and more than three, possibly four, if he went to Salem Town to search a physician willing to come. But if he went home through Salem Village at least he could bring the minister home to Ann. He had to bring someone. If he arrived empty-handed, he'd face that harpy's wrath.

Then by God's Grace, or pity, there was Dr. Griggs standing out in the parsonage yard consulting with Sam Parris. He dismounted by the gate. Were they ignoring him on purpose? For even after he'd walked over and nodded, they continued their private discussion. But now both stood conspicuously silent as he described his child's new ailment. Soon as he finished, they exchanged a weird glance between them. As if they knew its cause. He bowed his head and begged.

❦

His daughter was stiff as a cadaver, arms stuck rigid at her sides, eyes frozen open. "She's dead!" Thomas cried, punching the doorframe of the bedchamber.

But Dr. Griggs was reminded at once of Betty Parris. Unbeknownst to this father, the minister's daughter was lying in an identical stupor right now at the parsonage house. The far-reaching curse had struck two youngsters miles apart.

"Sir, step aside," he nudged gently, brushing past Thomas. He went inside and opened his case, and withdrew a small hand mirror to set underneath the girl's nostrils. He'd done the same at the parsonage, when the minister doubted his daughter yet lived. With one difference: in this house, the devil's victim was covered with a hell-born swill, not stool or urine or bile like Betty Parris, but true *brimstone, Devil's excrement,* in some profane mockery of Christ.

Of course, Thomas had noticed the filth, but he knew better what it was and how it got there.

After sending her servant away, Ann had begun spoon-feeding Lucy last night's blood stew for its healing power. But the child's frozen mouth could not be pried open. By now, the bedclothes, floor, both their gowns, faces and even unkempt locks were caked with mush, while that sooty cauldron now sat empty in Ann's lap. "Come here, wife. Give the doctor your chair," Thomas urged, utterly embarrassed, but mostly enraged seeing all that good meat wasted.

Ann didn't respond, but kept rocking up and back, with her arms hugging her pot. Her spouse was invisible to her now, as was the doctor. All she could see was a dead daughter on a bed—the firstborn of her blessless black belly.

The Afflicted Girls

50

H ER HAND WAS NUDGING THE LAZY CAT FROM her money-counting table, something she'd done countless times. But this time the creature hissed, and sank claws and teeth into her flesh drawing blood. Bridget swatted it. "Lowly creatures should know better than to turn on their masters," she looked up at Mercy, "like yours has turned on you."

"I-I fell . . . from the hayloft ladder."

"Aye. But not into hay." Nevertheless, she had no use for prying off lids, gleaning chaff from unwilling kernels or wanting to know beyond what a person willingly gave. She said nothing more about it, only slipped off her ribbon necklace. "I am giving you this . . . to sweeten your hayloft dreams and bring them to bear. Lord knows your life needs sweetening." She placed that carved amulet inside Mercy's hand, and the closed hers around it. "'Twas this pendant brought my first true love to me. And twenty years later, Goodman Bishop, my next husband." She didn't mention him who was with her now. He'd come on his own.

Mercy set down the gift. "I am not here for myself but for the child I rear, Lucy Putnam, who has bravely borne affliction all of her twelve years. But today her suffering turned the most evil corner—"

Bridget's visage hardened. She slapped the tabletop. "And whose game was it? Who baked that poison into a cake and gave it to that child? I went and viewed the Doritch boy. Brought him back from his fit. But even then he wouldn't name names. Yet someone is accountable. Was it you, Mercy Lewis? Did you play a deadlier game than the harmless ones I taught you?"

Mercy shook her head.

"Who then?"

Mercy told herself to keep silent. But it was Lucy's life, not hers, dangling from a thread . . . like Bridget's amulet was from this riband; she stared at the metal-bound carved crystal, wondering how much of her story, and which parts, she could safely tell.

"Take off that muzzle! Look me in the eye! Tell me all that you know about it! Have you forgotten your pledge to keep that child safe?"

"But she couldn't have known the—(*harm of it?*)" she looked away. Despite that Abigail was no friend, only a tormentor who had never cared for anyone. For that's how life's cruelties had shaped her. And yet because of the charm, Bridget's love charm, which Abigail dangled over her in the minister's face, that in the end had brought only deep sorrow, violent abuse, and no love, despite this woman's assurances, she couldn't betray her. Nor would Bridget's amulet bring her any comforts . . . she set it down on the tabletop. *Abigail may have twisted my path, but it was a path you urged me to follow, Bridget, which I then led my companions down. Aren't we all three equally guilty?*

But Bridget had already surmised the baker's identity. Because the conjuring games had been taught for one person's amusement. And yet, there was something not being told besides a name. "Whether your friend knew the harm of it or not, today she will learn it with consequence. I am going to tell her uncle."

"Please no. You cannot tell him."

"You'd sacrifice a child to protect that person . . . oh yes, now I see your loyalties."

The Afflicted Girls

Mercy shook her head. *How selfish she was really* forgetting Lucy in Abigail's cause. "Can you save Lucy Putnam, Bridget?" There was nothing more precious to her than Lucy.

Bridget frowned. "Tell me something useful and we'll see."

Mercy described the symptoms observed today in the child, and the ones endured by herself long years ago, which were not visible to the eye but which the child was also likely suffering.

Bridget collected an assortment of roots and seeds, and leaf powders from her stores and brought them to the table. She explained each uncommon use, while Mercy's own knowledge expanded with these new correspondences.

"Dandelion revived a strapping tree. Can it save a dying sapling? That I cannot say. There is a threshold where life decides. Green willow is to burn to ash to pull poison from her gut. And the juice is for her blood. Root of peony is to sew inside her pillow to ease her fears and bring on healing sleep. But you will have to urge your young friend to return from her lifeless stupor, and pray that she hears you, for she stands near her end. Sometimes it is our choice." She eyed her visitor warily. "Treatments these are, not antidotes . . . there is none that I know of for Devil's Trumpet, except the body's own healing power in time. I told the same to Goody Doritch. But there is an old charm that can offer a mother hope. To be used by you in private, when no one else is listening."

As soon as her visitor departed, Bridget gave orders to a hireling. Then donned her gaudiest fringed shawl and headed west on the High Road, taking the village turn-off, however long she had avoided Salem Village, however many years had passed since she'd last set foot in that place.

Much as she expected, tongues began wagging, eyes shifted sidewise, crooked fingers pointed the moment she walked through the village gate. Overheated from such brisk striding in a hot afternoon sun, she stopped and without thinking lifted her floss of unbound hair and dabbed at her neck and sweaty breastbone with her shawl. She also buttressed her cleavage, but deliberately, tightening the laces on her crimson vest, which had loosened while she walked. And now she walked on.

She overheard a spoken insult, followed by snickers. She turned sidewise to glance at her detractor—one of the Trask clan she supposed—standing in a gaggle of like-minded crones. Behind them was the meetinghouse. On her last visit here, it was newly built. Now it looked a ruin . . . another sign of the lack of care in this place. She approached it as a crow flew from a treetop and landed on its roof. Those cavilers quickly scattered from its walkway of trampled grass. She peered inside through a fractured pane and saw the minister standing. Lucky sight, she thought, because she hadn't wanted to knock at the parsonage door and alert the girl or encounter another self-righteous goodwife.

She took stock of this man she had never before seen: straight-backed, tall and fair, thinning hair, but more comely and better proportioned than had been described to her by her lover. *So men are equally ungenerous.* She smiled, and then frowned considering how wrongly she'd pictured the sheath, though not what resided within it.

Reverend Parris was facing forward, toward his pulpit, wringing his hands. *Was he praying?* She couldn't tell, but she knew for a certainty that *his* God wasn't hers.

With his daughter and niece suffering Hellish afflictions, Reverend Parris spent portions of every day here alone, supplicating God, always with his meetinghouse door bolted from within ensuring his privacy. Knowing that were he needed urgently at home—should one of his children spin downward, or worse—he'd be summoned promptly by four knocks. So his heart leapt out of its cage hearing that heavy oaken church door behind him open, which was locked, and footsteps approach. He spun around and saw her — that person who had supernaturally entered his sanctuary . . . or had he forgotten the latch?

Of course, he'd heard much about the local sluttern, Bridget Bishop, who marked herself by a profligate vest of red. But never before had he seen her. And here she was now, breaching the very purity of his church. So he tensed as she drew nearer. But then his thought suddenly veered to the fact that he should cloak her as a Mary Magdalene, a sinner coming to a person of piety to mend her ways, to repent to Christ through him. Yes! It was the reason she'd come! He was about to bring about a harlot's conversion!

Bridget stated who she was. He answered that he knew. Then she began to vilify his niece. He deflected forcefully: "But you are the cunning woman and Sabbath-breaker! Not my niece who is afflicted herself!"

"Believe what you will, Reverend Parris. But I have here the proof." Unfolding a small cloth square kerchief, she showed him several pieces of a red cake — crumbled remnants retrieved from both Goody Doritch and Mercy Lewis.

He thrust her hand away, knocking her crumbs to the floor. "A devilish concoction made by yourself, no doubt!"

Bridget staved him in the eye. "By your own niece, in fact! A poison she baked into cakes inside your own parsonage kitchen! Won't you see the truth of what's happened? When your own child lies ill from a cousin's mischief and might die from it?"

How dare she speak of Betty . . . or accuse his niece. "Thy evil eye and evil word cannot sully sanctified walls." He put up a hand to ward from Bridget's glare, and felt an uncanny strength pour into him. He commanded her: "Go to your knees! Confess your sins, Goody Bishop. Beg God for forgiveness."

"What for? He already knows my goodness as well as He knows yours."

So now he sent against her as much shaking-wrath as Aaron's staff once did in Egypt, pointing an arm and finger:

"Begone then! Mocker of Christ! Witch of Endor! Witch Bishop of Salem!"

For the briefest moment, Bridget was stunned. Then she shook her head and hurriedly left.

Reverend Parris glimpsed her wavy locks angling down her feminine back, and her wanton gait. Of a sudden, he couldn't breathe. He prostrated, landing atop her *red crumbs*! Sweeping them aside, gasping, he began praying. But like Samson his strength was utterly drained, and along with it his clarity.

But in time mental vigor restored and a revelation came: *Bridget Bishop was the witch who'd sent afflictions into the village! She'd confessed as much just now. For the guilty always blame the innocents for their crimes.* And by being named by the witch directly, Abigail became more than a niece to him now, or even a victim. She was a martyr of Christ, a living Saint, who held inside her poor afflicted bones the chaste power to destroy Evil.

She was to be his Holy Sword!

The Afflicted Girls

51

N OT WANTING TO BE SEEN, MERCY STEPPED INTO the tree shade, but stood more inside her own shadow of envy. It was her rival coming down the road—that silk clad peahen maid Joseph Putnam's arm had so easily draped around at Bishop's Ordinary. As the carriage rolled up, that pretty young person caught her eye, and smiled down in common friendliness. She saw no rival now, only a kind creature who smiled easily at everyone. Who, unlike herself, wasn't proud, wasn't vain in fortune or face—someone worthy.

She imagined *him* appearing next, escorting his *betrothed*: "Are you spying on me, too?" he would ask with that snide disdain he'd now shown her. She'd attempt equal coldness: "Is this road also your purchased property? If not, ask those two waving and calling out to you. Since they are the only ones spying."

Of course, that carriage would have stopped by now and its two occupants, mother and pretty daughter, would be waving back at him, calling out for him to come; while he and she stood arguing another point to no conclusion. He would stare down the road at the Porters, considering them. But then would wave them on, choosing her instead. He would offer her a ride to Putnam Farm, and would try to woo her along the way inside some hidden bower. *Would she allow it?* Would he force her if she didn't?

She recalled that first time riding with Joseph Putnam, how she'd felt her life's first surge and believed a safe harbor lay before her, which he had warned against, and was proved right. Their next encounter was at Bishop's Ordinary, where he sat with his amiable maid, and jealousy sealed her fate. Better to forget his cruelty in the bower. Their fourth joining was last night, and was tender until it wasn't. But it dawned on a terrible day. So now if he appeared at all, it would be their fifth paths' crossing. And despite her right impulses but wrong turns, crushed hope, and his deceptions, in this unhappy hollow she felt in his absence, she would chose again to ignore why she shouldn't go with him, why she couldn't trust him really, and would stretch up her hand to take his, expecting all. But only because they hadn't, as yet—either of them—reached their journey's end.

Clutching Bridget's satchel, Mercy Lewis walked on.

❧✦❧

Tonight, an unexpected visitor sat beside Lucy Putnam's sickbed. But Reverend Parris had not come here to Putnam Farm solely to beseech God to restore the child to health, or to deliver her parents from worry, though both were his deep-felt intentions (but which also could be served from afar). He had ridden out on his mule because after his encounter with the witch harlot in meetinghouse earlier today, he felt compelled to compare afflictions. And yes, he now discovered that Lucy Putnam's bloodless hand was identical to Betty's and that her stupor was not unlike Abigail's, who even after his endless endearments and tender strokes remained oblivious to his presence. He viewed this stricken child as an ally of his two. For it meant that his daughter and niece had not been singled out by the Devil for afflictions, as Dr. Griggs had alleged.

He'd come, also, to harvest information, having learned long ago that to prosecute any crime the wronged party must gather pertinent evidence: look under every rock, peer through every crack, consider every condition—as till now he hadn't the spiritual understanding or power to shield an innocent from a spectral assault—because for that he needed Abigail—but he could, at least, ready their case before God.

He offered up another prayer, glancing over at his good friend, Thomas Putnam, whose eyes were tight-shut and who was likely not listening. He studied the unkempt wife as well, who was rocking in her chair and whose eyes—ever since he had known them—had been clouded over with bitters, turned away from the world. He considered his own goodwife's despondency—so different. And when the door creaked a little, when someone arrived outside, he didn't look up, but continued praying.

Thomas, though, thought his youngsters had strayed up from the parlor where he'd earlier put them to bed and meaning to stop them, looked, because this was a sickroom full of contagion, which they must not enter. But it was his jade standing in the hall. Before he could think what to do, Ann had rushed out.

He hadn't thought much about the wench. *Was that even today?* He barely caught a glimpse of her face just now, and couldn't guess what awful untruth she was telling his wife from that. But he imagined it, and would have followed them down, but that would have left the minister with his daughter alone, unforgivable for a parent on a deathwatch to do. So despite wife and wench together downstairs, and because of it too, he closed his eyes, and prayed.

"What have you brought me?" Ann demanded.

Mercy handed her mistress the satchel, which was poured out onto the tabletop, with each pouch's contents spilled. "Useless! I've lost her! Only a few breaths are left in her! Dry as a bone, blind as a bat, hot as an oven-and-Oh God, I cannot think!"

But was any time left? Mercy worried. *Do this one thing,* Bridget had instructed, and until this moment she had planned to do it secretly: *Bake three cakes, from separate roots mixed with the child's water, one each for the healing of body, mind, and spirit. Feed them to a dog or a pig, soothsaying* — she asked permission to fetch the child's chamber pot. But her mistress rushed up to get it herself, while she began grinding roots.

Later, standing on the threshold when she whistled for the dog, it came running and was ravenous and gobbled their cakes in three bites. No one had fed it yet today. Her mistress spoke the charm.

Reverend Parris had heard that whistle, but got up to answer a different summons. To call a derelict mother back up to her sick daughter's bedside. Ann Putnam perturbed him. Coming into the kitchen, seeing strange grasses and roots spread out in neat piles on the tabletop, he wondered what salty nonsense Ann Putnam had been parsing. He heard muffled voices outside the door. Walking closer, he overheard the witch-harlot's name spoken — *Bridget Bishop* — but in praise, not blame. He lunged through the doorway.

Ann Putnam, in her current state of agitation, might have bitten off his upraised finger had it pointed in her direction. But without censuring her, he suddenly he withdrew it, and left them, and went hastily back upstairs. Because a paradox of Biblical proportion had just occurred to him: *If a person is cured of witchcraft through witchcraft, is God in that healing, too?*

Ann pushed past him on the stair rushing into the chamber first, to clutch her *cured* child to her bosom.

While downstairs, Mercy urged her feet to run. Because this had been her plan all this day, and now here was the darkest night to flee into. To offer Lucy Putnam hope was the final task. And it was easier to abandon Joseph Putnam now too, who didn't love her, and never would. But she felt too weary to trudge thirty miles to Salem Town now, and then decide east or south. *If I took the master's horse, if only to begin?* She only tiptoed upstairs for a final glance in at Lucy from behind the door's crack. She saw no change in her young friend. But her master saw her, and glared, and ordered her inside the room.

It was noisy with all of them shouting. The minister goading with his oily tongue: "I am your Good Shepherd, Lucy. God is with you now. He wants you to name the witch who afflicted you. Speak that person's name aloud to God." While her master woofed: "Answer the minister's question, daughter!" While her mistress exclaimed, repeatedly: "My girl's awaking! She's awakening now!" But Lucy wasn't. And might not.

She'd only delayed out of a need to know that her young friend would survive . . . and now she did know. Lucy's right pinky *moved* a fraction, and then a foot. Soon both fists had unfurled into kneading fingers. All those same sleepy urges she had felt so long ago, when sensation first returned to her own paralyzed limbs.

Lucy Putnam's eyelids groggily parted. A hazy face met hers—the sharp, pointy face of a demon. *Where was Lord Jesus? Wasn't she in Heaven?* Her head throbbed, pitchfork prongs pierced her ears: "Who afflicted you?" "Answer the minister's questions!" "Leave her be or you'll throw my girl down again!"

The demon was arcing over her. Pinching her up by her shoulders. "Think, child, think! Some witch has done this to you! Speak aloud that person's name to God!"

A blessed angel of golden luster stood in powerful guard. But it wasn't a glorious angel. It was Mercy Lewis, alit by a candle torch, standing at the foot of her cot. She was in her own room, inside her own bed. And it wasn't a serpent bending over her, but Reverend Parris breathing angry fire.

Sluggish memories in drizzling slivers: *her sisters banging drums, taking her turn at the shovelboard, Bridget Bishop's jugs, Abigail's Haunted Chamber, wrens, lightning, hot cider, sweet-cakes . . . other cakes.*

And now a waterfall of emotion: *the egg looking glass, her vision of Heaven, Susanna's mid-witch, her baby brother alive then dead.* A dry gravely voice said something. *Was it hers?*

Reverend Parris bent low and put his ear to Lucy Putnam's parched lips: "Who, child? Who did you just say?"

The Afflicted Girls

52

REVEREND PARRIS, THOMAS PUTNAM, AND THE Junior Constable, John Willard, walked up to the door of a white-washed cottage, stomping less on its even-placed stepping-stones than on delicate flowerbeds at either side. Reverend Parris gave the door a heavy blow with his walking stick. But it was John Willard who instructed the manservant who opened it: "Tell your mistress a constable is come."

The fellow shook his head, informing them in an Irish brogue: "Cinnot, sur, she be sleepin' . . . ye'll hafta coom back."

Reverend Parris blistered. "Who are you to disobey a constable? I am her minister. We are authorities here, and also your superiors. Or would you wish to sit the stockade?"

The servant scratched his chin saying he was foreign born, only five months come here, and was unsure of the local custom. He brought them inside, across a knick-knack filled parlor on bright braided carpets set end-to-end, and then up a narrow staircase and down an even narrower hallway to a garret door at the end. Reverend Parris ordered him to open it. When the man obeyed, he looked in over his shoulder. But the room was too dark to see, though he heard an occupant's snores. So at least the fellow hadn't lied to them. "Let in sun and wake her," he instructed.

The Irishman went and unhinged the shutters, opened the casements, and morning light flooded the chamber, along with air, which was needed, for the room was stuffy and stale. Now they could see her.

Goody Osborne was heavily asleep, but dressed not in a modest dowager's gown and cap, rather in a bright doxy yellow shift with no cap covering her unfurled hair. Also, she was lying inside a gaudy Jacobean four-poster with lace curtains falling from a canopy of green, more suited to lust than envy. And now, as that hired fellow gave her a slight nudge and then bent down to whisper his news, she reached up and took his brawny Irish hand and tried to brush her vein-laced cheek with it. But he hopped backward, noting their scorning eyes.

Reverend Parris whispered, "Clearly her familiar," and Thomas Putnam nodded.

Now, cataracts in Ruth Osborne's eyes prevented her from viewing objects sharply. But she was generally able to distinguish large items by their shapes. So she knew she had visitors and that they were three men stomping toward her, which made her pull up her coverlet to her chin. "What nonsense is this, Timothy? Why have you brought these men into my chamber!"

John Willard held out a parchment. She squinted but didn't take it, so he put it into her hands. "That is for you to read and understand, Goodwife Osborne."

She brushed him away with it and then dropped it to the bed-top. "Are you and your friends making fun of me, Timothy?"

"Your servant knows nothing of our purpose. I am Junior Constable John Willard of Salem Village come to arrest you. The warrant explains the charge. My companions are your complainant and his witness."

She prickled. "Well, obviously, as I cannot see I cannot read. But whatever it says I've done and whosoever it says I've done to, know you've come to the wrong house. Since I've done nothing but be sick in this house for nigh to six months."

The Afflicted Girls

Reverend Parris stepped forward. "You've been doing more than that, Ruth."

A hint of Caribbean accent informed her at once who this was. Someone she'd missed sorely, whose presence she'd craved often in these months of infirmity. Her face brightened. "Why, it's my minister, Reverend Parris. He'll settle the mistake. He'll tell you I'm a church member of good repute counted an Elect of the Covenant." She reached out, "Come closer to me, Reverend Parris. Timothy, bring my prophet a chair."

The servant carried over the visitor's chair. But Reverend Parris didn't sit in it. Instead, he stood stiffly beside the bed, frowning down at her. "Half a year you've avoided church, Ruth. Finally, I know the reason."

"You already knew the reason! Since your goodwife visits me every week and brings you back my generous regards! I've been sick, sir!"

"And from your sickbed you sent curses into our midst! Laid waste to four innocent children!"

Ruth struggled to sit up. "Why, that isn't true. What utter nonsense. Who is it that accuses me? Goody Bibber? Well, you should all know how that gossipmonger's been flapping my name for years. So if you ask me, better than anyone Reverend Parris, you know the verity of my faith. You know I love God. Well, know that I love all youngsters, too."

Thomas Putnam stepped forward. "What we know is you love men in your bed younger than the stepsons you disinherited. You're a hag-harlot, Goody Osborne. That's what we know."

And now Reverend Parris quoted a passage from a 14th Century treatise: *"The bawd-witch is one who in her old age, when she cannot otherwise afflict men's hearts with love, becomes a diablesse, worse than the Devil himself."*

Ruth exploded, "How dare you insult me! Get out from my chamber all of you! I'll give no more pearls to swine! From this day, my tithes go to Salem Town Church, whose minister preaches a Godly-wit better than you ever did, Reverend Parris!"

That slap hurt, ire raised up in him so strong, he would have struck her, despite his profession.

But John Willard had stepped forward in the meantime, and picked up the arrest warrant and put it back into her hands. "Your accuser isn't Goody Bibber, Goody Osborne, but a child of twelve years, Lucy Putnam, this man's daughter. She claims it was you who cursed her nearly to death."

Ruth was stupefied. "And how could I do that? Stuck as I am in this bed? With legs that no longer work?"

The minister answered, "By witchcraft, how else? From her own innocent lips, I heard that child name you."

Willard instructed the manservant, "Wrap your mistress in her bed-cloth and carry her down to my cart. Later, collect what else she might need and bring it to the jailhouse, knowing a cell has no hearth." *Or heart.* He was trying to be kind.

As her manservant lifted her, Ruth laid her dizzied cheek upon his sturdy shoulder seeking solace. He callously flinched her off. She sputtered, disbelieving: "But-I don't even know the girl-I never met her-please, no. Timothy, where are you taking me?"

❧ ✦ ❧

A handful of goodmen were summoned to an upstairs chamber at Ingersoll's Inn to stand as witnesses while the Chief Constable of Salem Town interrogated Ruth Osborne's servant. That official had only one question for the man: "Is your mistress a witch?"

The Irishman clutched his cap, answering: "Dinna know if she be one o' not, sur." And with that, the interrogation concluded.

Reverend Parris rushed over annoyed. "But has she ever asked you to sign a Black Book? Or told your fortune? Or fashioned a poppet and stuck it with pins?"

The Afflicted Girls

The servant shook his head, "Ne'er seen 'er do none o' tha'. B'sides 'er fingers is cricked so 'tis me does the sewin'."

"But she *is* a Sabbath-breaker, and a sinner. So you must have seen something in her conduct, or on her person . . . besides her long nose, hairy chin and crooked fingers?"

The Irishman swallowed hard, having just realized that sure as a black crow flies on the Devil's business, those telltale witch-marks were indeed features of his mistress.

Reverend Parris turned to the Chief Constable. "This man refuses to answer, because he is her familiar. He is bound by the Devil to protect her from detection at all costs."

"Oh no, sur. I aren't no family to me mistress. I jus' does what she says, an' she pays me fur 't."

Reverend Parris whirled around. "Pays you for her devilries and obscenities?"

That fellow, a pious Papist when alone and unobserved, crossed himself unwisely in front of Puritans. "No, sur. Jus' fer me servin' labors."

Reverend Parris suggested to the constable, "Which is to say that he shares her bed in nakedness and slakes her unwholesome appetites." Turning back to the Irishman, "Do you claim never to have tasted her bawdy flesh?"

The Irishman bowed his head, ashamed. "I cinnot deny't. God kens t' to be true. Would'na been neether, but fur the money. 'Tis her orderin'."

Reverend Parris raised his hand. "Then I order you now, sir, with a warning to your Roman soul in peril, to name every witch-sign you've ever seen on her person!"

The manservant shrugged, not sure of the minister's meaning. "Well, um, she got a weird nip in 'er private patch . . . if tha's wha' ye be askin'?"

Reverend Parris nodded, and the interrogation now rightly concluded.

291

❧✦❧

Reverend Parris, this same night, was jarred from his slumber by a blast of frigid air. As his heavy-lidded eyes opened, he viewed Bridget Bishop climbing in over his windowsill. But in his next squint, she was standing beside his bed, unlacing her red paragon bodice. Also lifting her petticoat to display an even more enticing attribute: a pudendum, dripping with milk. He commanded his body to resist her, and it did. Till she had teased off his clutched coverlet and eased up his nightshirt above his waist and had set her cherry lips upon that disobedient organ, which had swelled now to unnatural length. She climbed astride and was a perfect fit.

He resisted, clutching her wondrous breasts, while she taunted him in his own Island accent: "Will you not confess your sins to God, Goody Bishop?" Answering in her own: "Would you have me stop *this* nocturnal feast for *that* Holy Bugbear?" He moaned his current truth, "I would, indeed, Bridget Bishop . . . but not until — I'm — uh, I'm — "

"Undone," she advised with a feline purr, sinking down onto his consummation.

A forgotten presence now rolled to her side, bumping him with her bony hip: Mrs. Parris. Bridget Bishop vanished.

Reverend Parris awoke soaked in sweat, still filled with tremors, and as swollen in his loins as he'd ever been in his youth. His affliction of impotence cured, he fumbled for his wife's modest breast through her night cloth to signal interest. But she shifted to her edge of the bed feigning slumber. And then continued to ignore the sounds of his single-handed battle with Satan, till the sloppy deed was done. Then both of them slept, but neither well.

He'd been supernaturally assaulted — that Reverend Parris knew. But someone had given the witch-harlot's spectre entry.

The Afflicted Girls

After finishing his breakfast, in sober decision Reverend Parris marched Tituba away from the parsonage up along the byway leading past the militia camp, double stockade and whipping post. To the constabulary lane, but past that place, too, stopping only at the feldspar-granite jailhouse at its end, studded all about with grim iron spikes. Inside, he handed her to a jailer, and slapped her when she begged to stay free.

He then went to lodge his complaint at the constabulary. But now John Willard informed him that despite Tituba's being "his property and no person," she could not be legally jailed without an official arrest warrant being issued in her name—for the sake of the Village Book and county record—and that this would require a properly written accusation. And because the man was both an enemy and a stickler, he hurried home to write out a list of her crimes, recounted from the beginning of their intertwined lives. And while John Indian was equally suspect, he would have to ignore, for today, his manslave's transgressions, lest he be the one tending mule and pigsty, woodlot and privy, and losing all that extra coinage John Indian brought him from Ingersoll.

His *surprise first charge against the Devil* inspired utter elation that morning, but by afternoon had stirred up only doubt. Yes, he'd shed himself of an obvious witch. But when that notice was tacked onto the constabulary door and folk began to whisper, he realized that by having branded his household slave as corrupted, he'd marked his parsonage as a place to be avoided. Support would siphon even more, when benches already sat increasingly empty at his lectures and sermons. By four o'clock, he was ready to withdraw the accusation and bring his female slave home.

But then his niece recovered—according to his wife, Abigail was sitting up in the bed cured, asking for him to come to her. *So he had steered the right course after all!* He chided himself for doubting it, realizing that all he need do was to bandy about *this news:* how a Divine Healing had occurred first at the parsonage house . . . in the wake of a witch's arrest! He felt so inspired, in fact, he barely heard when Mrs. Parris next advised him: "But to the same degree your niece has improved, your daughter has worsened."

And sometimes even the longest-lived tenderness between kindred souls sours quicker than milk does in a pail left out in the summer sun; particularly, when a certain shadow comes between them. But by the morrow, Mrs. Parris had a slew of reasons for her curdling: With Tituba in jail she had no household slave to assist her. While Abigail, clearly and miraculously recovered, refused to offer a hand with any chore, even to sit inside a room and watch-guard a very ill cousin. And now today, three days after that miracle, her husband criticized *her*: "This household lacks timeliness and cleanliness, Elizabeth. You must try to do better. I expect it."

She irritably retorted, "And I expected your niece to have resumed her chores by now, and could have managed with that. But you deem her too fragile. Well, I judge her hardy and a burden on our backs. I insist you refrain from molly-coddling her, Samuel."

"I forbid *you* to address your husband like that. Or to speak badly of his relation."

"Provide me with an indenture then. Any girl from the parish will do. If you did not hoard your pennies, husband, I might go out and hire one."

His face reddened. "Yes, you are poor in your cash-box, Elizabeth. And you blame me for it? Knowing my salary goes unpaid for six months? Have I not been working hard for this family, nevertheless?"

She bowed her head. That *was* true, and she'd forgotten. An apology was due him. She looked up, repentant. But he was so full of ire, he further castigated: "In fact, wife, not only must you make do without a servant, you must make do and serve better this penny-pincher God has bound you to, who is less a niece-coddler than a disappointed husband!" And those were the last words they'd spoken . . . yesterday.

All during today's lecture on *stalwartness*, Reverend Parris stared much at his wife's empty seat. Returning home a while ago, he deliberately avoided the kitchen where she labored. Hiding out in his study, he opened his empty ledger and wept. Because all this day he'd been remembering how many hardships his helpmeet had suffered in her life after marrying him.

When his father-in-law was struck dumb (and she nursed that man unselfishly). When he'd lost his own employment, both his ministry and reputation (and she bolstered him with hope). When he sold off her well-loved possessions (and she never once complained). When they were evicted from their Boston house (and she lovingly packed his things). When Death visited her first painful childbed (and, because of her *stalwartness*, left empty-handed). And even that next year, after losing their firstborn son, she nonetheless promised to bear him others. How during all of her travails, it was she who'd uplifted him. In fact, she'd propped him until a week ago, despite her only child's collapse. *So why was she wavering now?*

His neglect. The failures were his. His eyes filled with sincere regret. He heard a tap at the door, and thinking she'd come, he leapt up to open it. But it was his niece curtseying on the threshold. "Beg pardon, Uncle Parris. May I enter?"

One sight of that healed angel reminded Reverend Parris of that higher ground beyond the marital plain. He would confess his pride to his wife later, he decided. "My door is always open to you, Abigail, even when it's closed." He resumed budgeting sums and deciding priorities, and also thought how on the morrow this girl would be returned to her household labors for his wife's sake, but that he'd wait until supper to tell them.

In frustrated spirits after another ugly encounter with her aunt, Abigail had run here to her uncle seeking solace. But all she received was his disinterest. So she stood by the unlit fireplace staring down at her family andirons, which no longer sparkled but were again coated with soot—neglected, the same as she was. But even before her illness, following that evening they had placed them by this grate, had he ever once again commented about her gift, or mentioned her sweetened candles, or declared how well she starched and ironed his collars? She frowned at his lack of attention. *Would he have cared if I had died?*

She looked up at him scribbling away. And now from a different sort of spite from what she served to her aunt, to win his attention back, she stated soberly, inwardly snickering: "Uncle, I am fearful."

He answered without looking up: "Of all in this parish, you have less to fear than anyone, I assure you."

"Oh, I do not fear for myself, Uncle Parris, or even for my poor cousin upstairs . . . because we are both protected by God, and yourself. But my traveling companion has no one's protection. Mercy Lewis. That girl you rented to Putnam Farm . . . who suffers an even worse affliction than Betty."

He looked up, mildly interested. "I saw her at last Sunday's service looking hale, if not happy."

"So she makes herself appear."

He frowned. "I have no time for riddles, Abigail. I am not dismissing you. Only asking that you speak plainly."

"Well . . . when in your lecture today you said that we are all under Satan's assault, I knew this for a fact. Because my friend once lived under a conjurer's roof . . . a fact she keeps hid for obvious reasons."

The Afflicted Girls

This intrigued him. He laid down his quill.

She continued: "It was prior to our acquaintanceship at the almshouse and of that time I know naught. But as bedmates I often saw her suffer his midnight assaults. One time our candlestick tipped without reason and set our coverlet ablaze. It was I who doused it, while she cowered and confessed how she'd seen his face in its vapors. He meant to murther us that night, Uncle Parris! Murther us both . . . until I thwarted him!"

This chilled him to the bone. His spine straightened. "And the fiend's name? Do you know it?"

Abigail shook her head, "If ever she spoke a name aloud, I cannot now recall it. But she may have made mention to her counselor Bridget Bishop. Those two are peas in a pod."

Reverend Parris flushed, and abruptly dismissed her.

SUZY WITTEN

Every poor and peevish old creature cannot but fall under suspicion. Every accident (more than ordinary), every disease, whereof they neither understand the cause, nor are acquainted with the symptoms, must be suspected for witchcraft.

Select Cases of Conscience Touching Witches
and Witchcrafts; John Gaule (1646)

53

J OHN WILLARD ASKED, "IS IT POSSIBLE THE CHILD dissembles?"

"When my Walcott niece who was afflicted says the same?" Thomas Putnam grew insulted. While his companion, Reverend Parris, merely warned: "Witch's victims do not prevaricate while crying out about afflictions to their fathers. Issue the warrant, sir, or your own twins might suffer the same fate."

Willard knew he would need to comply (though not because of the minister's threat). But he took pleasure knowing one of these two was as good as fired, with the other doing less mischief because of it. His cohort Israel Porter had confided to him the other day how the parsonage deed had now been stamped for conveyance to their faction and bore a judge's signature. One minister would soon be gone. Another would be hired. Their children had been stricken, *yes*. He would allow them that with sympathy. But children fall ill in every season and some even die from it.

Nonetheless, he wrote out the warrant, because he, and even Porter's judicial relation, John Hathorne (the source of that news) were under the thumb of Chief Justice William Stoughton of Boston Town, who was a staunch believer in witches and curses and who had just issued mandates to all county and village

The Afflicted Girls

officials advising them that spectral accusations were legal accusations — a mandate he was compelled to obey.

The next day, John Willard tacked a "Notice of Arrest" onto the constabulary door: *Sarah Good was apprehended last night while sleeping in the glassmaker's barn.* He predicted to his deputy that the glassmaker would soon appear at their door claiming how his kiln had cracked down the middle while the "witch" slept under his roof, or that his children awoke with hellish blisters and burns, or boils or rickets. But even being a newcomer in these parts, he'd seen how that man worked his kilns and kin to the bone. And thought it was more likely that the homeless beggar was the better parent. Nevertheless, he also wrote in counts of "vagrancy" and "theft." But only of those was that surly widow likely guilty.

Two self-appointed apprehenders found her. They wrestled her to the ground and carried her tied up to the jailhouse; and ever since last night, she'd been locked to an iron ring kicking and screaming, pointing at Goody Osborne, sprawled on that narrow bench underneath the tiny high cell window: "But that's her! You already got the right Sarah! She afflicted the tykes! Not me!"

That's what she told him, too, after she spit in his eye. And when he left, and when that iron-barred cell door clanged shut, she turned again to glare at her fellow prisoners — Goody Rich Osborne and the parsonage slave — thinking how only one of them, the Indian, had ever helped her and Dorcas, whose ears she'd wanted to box last night for ignoring her calls, which was right before they seized her. *Her stray had learned a lesson all right!*

༄

Abigail had just completed her most dismal chore yet: scrubbing two weeks' worth of dirt from grimy floorboards with a useless brush of boar's hair. Then sopping up harsh lye suds with filthy rags. Thinking how a labor this hateful was a chore only slaves were born to do. As she emptied her final bucket, she thought how Aunt Ugly was again her uncle's favorite and that she was in thrall to an insect, again. She angrily kicked that pail across the yard to the clothesline where garments and linens, boiled and hung up by her earlier, were not quite dry. She jostled the line, causing two of her aunt's aprons and also a dress to fall. She glared at the upstairs window now, knowing how her lazy aunt was inside that easy room fiddling over *poor* Betty; or reading to herself from Scripture; or taking an afternoon nap. Well she, too, deserved a nap!

There! Over there! In her uncle's warm sunny pasture! But first, she'd steal down to the damp-cellar and collect as many rare tidbits as she liked for a meal equal in value to four hours scullery!

And now, as she climbed atop her bucket reaching up to the topmost shelf for the flask of medicinal spirits, which her aunt kept hidden behind a box, the pail tipped just as she had grabbed the bottle, and she fell backward. But luckily, she landed on the slaves' straw mat—or rather, no one's straw mat now—because ever since Tituba's arrest, John Indian was banished to the barn. Feral stench filled her nostrils. But after one long swig and two more slurps, she hardly noticed. Lying down on it, closing her eyes, she tried to imagine how that ill-matched couple entwined themselves in *delicto*. Because John Indian was bulky and big with long legs, and likely had a big dong, while Tituba was squat like a melon. Twisting into weird positions, she suddenly felt something hard underneath her. She sat up and parted the straw. She pulled Tituba's gathering basket into her lap.

It was filled with pods, roots, leaves, berries and seeds . . . and more red cakes! She ate one now, washing it down with the rest of that flask of spirits. But at the bottom of this basket, best of all, was a heathenish necklace made of colorful shells and whittled beads, and the most brilliant feathers which the slave had surely brought here all the way from Barbados, for no bird in this land ever sported such dazzling plumage! She put that fabulous, savage thing around her neck and at once desired to dance in it.

But the damp-cellar was too cramped for sport. And besides, her knees were sore from hours at bent labor. And her head was woozy from the drink. And while a nap in the warm sunshine in her uncle's pasture appealed so much more than one on this foul straw, she stretched herself out on this stench of slaves, because her head had begun to spin, and the dreams and visions were already coming.

❦

Six local goodwives, all of mature age and sober mind, were summoned to be a jury for the physical examination of Goody Osborne. While the Lord was the searcher of the witch's heart, only women of a certain age were permitted to be searchers of her body—never men. Two removed her self-soiled garments exposing her naked flesh.

After weeks inside a cold unforgiving stone cell the invalid was succumbing. Though aware of their presence, she was confused by it, and shivered and flinched each time a callused finger probed her clefts or mounds—because the *witch's tit* was normally found near the breast or vagina, being parts of the female body where the Devil derived his greatest erotic pleasure. Or so Reverend Parris had informed them this morning to their chagrin.

Goody Bibber cried out, "I have found it! The witch's tit!"

"That is a wart," dismissed Mrs. Ingersoll with certainty, for she suffered warts and knew. Nonetheless, she'd have disagreed with Goody Bibber anyway, being the mother of a damaged daughter, who required much fending from that hurtful woman's disparagements.

Of the six here, only one—Rebecca Nurse—hadn't been handpicked by the minister but by her own nosy self, being the most experienced in women's physical complaints she had insisted to her husband's constable friend. She stepped forward now to view the suspect bump, and then vociferously agreed with Mrs. Ingersoll: "That is a wart, Goody Bibber."

The gossipmonger would not be dissuaded. "It is a *witch's wart* then, which is as good as a tit!"

"It is a common wart! The same that anyone suffers!"

"How would you know, Goody Nurse? Have you ever seen a witch's tit?"

"Certainly not, Goody Bibber! And neither have you!"

Another grey-haired matron walked up to view the bump for herself, concluding: "Whether it be wart or tit, it's not big enough for the Devil, or even an imp, to suck on."

Goody Bibber reached inside her apron pocket for the pincushion she'd brought for this purpose. She pulled out her longest darning needle. "I shall prick the witch's tit. If blood, bile or water comes we have proof the Devil can suck sustenance." With that, she pierced the wart straight through and the protuberance bled.

Ruth Osborne screamed out, and then mercifully she fainted. No one tried to revive her—not kind Mrs. Ingersoll or knowledgeable Rebecca Nurse. Nor would either of them, or any other, offer this invalid solace ever again, or any further defense.

They were frightened of her now, especially the Doubting Thomas Mrs. Ingersoll. Her warts never bled.

The Afflicted Girls

54

ABIGAIL HAD BEEN ORDERED TO STAND AT THE foot of the bedstead until her aunt had tucked Betty in. Now that insect said to her: "I have decided to sleep beside my daughter tonight. You, niece, will take your rest on the parlor settle, and you will do that from now on. A mother's closeness is what my daughter needs to recover. But being motherless yourself, you would not understand this. No go latch the shutter, affix your bed-cap, and remember to remember us in your prayer."

She has put me out from my bed, and will soon take away the rest! Abigail left those shutters undone, and stormed out from the room without her cap or a curtsey. Downstairs, she tore her aunt's cloak from the kitchen peg and ran out of doors with that garment flaring. For she would rather sleep in her uncle's weedy pasture like a stray, than on that insect's furnishing, would rather stare up into God's starry firmament, than a ceiling, above which her uncle slept alone. She lay down and now drew that ugly cloth around her, and cried herself to sleep.

In a late chilly hour, she awoke damp and sore. Pebbles were clustered underneath her. Hordes of crickets and ugly spade-foot toads were bellowing out in full screaming song. She tried various positions, but none gave much comfort. So she sat and brushed the gravel to the side. Then a sound caught her ear. She looked up. Soon a vehicle rolled in unchallenged through the village gate. It didn't park in the inn yard like she expected, but drove right up to the graveyard fence, not thirty yards beyond her, where it parked. The watchman's lantern was nowhere to be seen. *We are poorly guarded in this village. Uncle Parris should be told.* A man emerged and entered that sullied place, strode with haste and purpose past its gravestones.

Had Aunt Ugly's whim tonight been higher ordained? Was here another midnight mystery to solve? She shivered, thinking how this might be Mercy's conjurer come, summoned hither by her own disclosures. But curiosity overruled that fear.

She crept alongside the fence till she beheld the man. She frowned. Now she had not thought about Joseph Putnam since the day of her arrival. But she did recall now how rude he'd been to her uncle while lusting after Mercy. He was rich she could obviously see, certainly richer than his clodhopper farmer friend. For he was wearing a fancy brocade suit, trimmed round in bric-a-brac thick with gold thread. He was even finer garb than was her uncle in his miniature portrait—a fact, which piqued her sharply.

Raiment suited to a fop. Not to a man of stature.

Although Joseph's mother, not knowing that fact, had purchased it for a pretty penny in Boston Town from Lizzie Porter's dressmaker after noticing it hanging in his shop. And then tonight, earlier, she'd badgered him into wearing it to a betrothal supper in his honor in Salem Town.

He had only put it on in ridicule of her. But she had tricked him, again. Because after calling for their carriage, she burrowed into bed instead, complaining of "turbulence in her temples." He guessed it was more that their host, Porter's judicial relation, had ruled against her in her recent ironworks case.

So in this uncomfortable embarrassing harness—that would later tonight be tossed onto a midden-heap—he'd endured three boring hours at that judge's unhurried table, before he and Porter and a few other men were removed to the library to smoke and drink. He tore off the coat, unbuttoned the waistcoat, rolled up his sleeves, and then downed enough of that judge's confiscated rum to drown out the memory of his mother, and the rest of them. Until that empty-headed girl wandered into the room and sat on her father's knee across from him, and reminded him of another parent: when Israel gave her a fatherly kiss and deliberately kept her cradled on his lap.

The sight of them struck him hard. Because not once since he'd returned from Cambridge had he visited his father's grave—his own devoted father, who had loved him just as much, gave sensible advice always, needed now in so many corners, but which was usually refused, with him taking only his mother's side . . . and only her kisses. His eyes began to smart thinking on the life to be lived without him.

His eyes were closed when Abigail snuck up unnoticed to his side, and crouched behind a nearby stone to observe this mourner more closely. His buttons were gold, not brass like she'd thought, with tiny sculpted horse-heads upon them—on a full moonlit night their red eyes would be sparkling—but even tonight she could tell they weren't rubies, only lapidary garnets, since rubies were worn only by kings. She loved this coat! No, she hated it, and him for wearing it, with her uncle growing poorer daily and forcing her—his own niece—into scullery! She needn't show this person any respect. He wasn't her uncle's parishioner. He paid them no tithes. He only hoarded his gold . . . or wore it! She threw a pebble at his back and then hid behind her stone while he puzzled.

When he turned again (after her third throw), only then did she pop up and startle him. She forced warmth into her voice: "Oh sir, I did not wish to frighten or disturb you . . . only to see if you were finished . . . to warn you. When I saw it was *you*, I ran hither to tell you how my traveling companion visits this selfsame grave, though not to pay her respects like you. But for a sinister purpose."

He recognized her now. "What purpose?"

With a visible shudder, Abigail advised, "Oh, I could not imagine. Nor would I dare. For Mercy Lewis is a strange and secretive creature, who comes here often in the wee-most hours . . . and mostly sits. But once from my window yonder"—she pointed at the parsonage and he looked—"I saw her digging in this spot, though not in respect for the dead. For no flower has ever sprouted from what she buried."

With a disrespectful kick to his father's mound, she sprayed his fancy trousers with dirt. Then she sprinted off, climbing back over the fence to hurry home across her uncle's pasture, suppressing her glee until she couldn't anymore, stopping now and tittering with delight, half-bent over with giggles. And when she reached the parsonage yard, she was thinking how the gravy had thickened by itself in the pot!

Rushing inside, she went not to her aunt's parlor settle, but to her uncle's library chair—her second best bed—and rested her head dreamily upon his desktop, with her fingertips grazing his ivory portrait. She fell asleep like that, ruing how his husband-bed could not be hers until Aunt Ugly also slept in a grave.

❧❀❧

For once, Ann Putnam slumbered dreamlessly . . . until a cacophony of unearthly voices woke her. She bolted upright in her bed and heard their high-pitched whining voices: *Ma-ma--ma-ma--ma-ma!* Then she saw them: those bug-eyed infants with ghostly bodies loose-wrapped in their burial shrouds, climbing up onto her bed, reaching out to her, trying to embrace her—their living mother. She tried to scream, but found no voice to do it. Nor could she escape their pincer fingers, or move a muscle in this netherworld. But somehow she managed to bodily tumble herself off the bed, and writhe about the floor, while those eternally hungry infants descended upon her to suckle.

The Afflicted Girls

❦

John Indian went again to sit his nightly vigil underneath Tituba's jail-cell window, where he softly hummed, sang, and whispered his news, knowing his wife could hear him through any walls, even these of spiked stone—though never once yet did she hum or whisper back like she used to.

He knew he wasn't clever, or given to visions like she was. And thinking of a way to save her was the hardest work he had ever done. But ever since the master put her inside this devil's box, every minute of every day he'd think till his head hurt, but always lacking a plan at the end. And then, in the after-midnight shadows with his ear pressed up against the cold stone, he'd listen for her to tell him. And when she didn't, he'd think some more, and listen harder.

PART SEVEN

55

THE SKY WAS OVERCAST AND GLOOMY. Weathervanes were spinning. Rain had been threatening for hours. A mangy trainband of fifes and drummers wended up and down the village byways. Essex County's militia was marching in rare regimental drills.

Because a Holy War, declared by Reverend Parris in church a fortnight ago, was beginning today, and scores of folk had already gathered to fight this first battle against Satan. Not only Salem villagers, curiosity seekers from Topsfield, Andover, Wenham, Lynn, Beverly, Salem Town, even from Boston and towns bordering Connecticut. Because it had been more than a decade since a witch had been discovered in Massachusetts, and now here in Essex County alone, in Salem Village, there were three.

Of course, last night there'd been much pushing and elbowing to get into Ingersoll's Inn, for it was here that the witch examination was to be held. Fistfights started again this morning to gain entry just for standing spots. While others shut out, who didn't feel like fighting, amassed and loudly complained. By now, all but two of Ingersoll's expensive beveled bottom-floor windows had been broken, and that village Head Selectman wasn't pleased.

The Afflicted Girls

A short while ago, the two judges had arrived—one from Salem Town, the other one from Boston. But no one would let them pass when they angled forward arm in arm toward the inn. Like everyone trying to move up, they were rudely shoved, bumped and elbowed. Chief Justice William Stoughton, just now, was pushed so hard he lost his balance and fell backward onto a clod of trampled manure. His fellow judge John Hathorne helped him to stand, but didn't brush him off or tell him.

Nathaniel Ingersoll had been keeping a steady eye out. He now fought his way into the yard to get them. But by the time he'd managed to get to that flattened horse-pie, the judges had removed. He asked someone to hoist him. He spied them standing in the stable-yard readying a carriage, and hurried to stop them.

And now, William Stoughton advised him brusquely how the proceeding was postponed to a later date in Salem Town.

Of course he had to protest, not only for the sake of the business he would lose and all those extra stores he'd purchased, which all would rot—he wasn't about to tithe them. And what about his broken panes? Bedeviled glass, he said (did he mean *beveled?*) was expensive to replace. Not least of all because the Devil would claim the first victory!

So he suggested: "Since you've come this far to our village, why not move the examination to our meetinghouse? It was built to hold three hundred, though that number has never yet sat in it."

Stoughton glanced toward the rundown structure . . . just as a first raindrop hit his cheek. He now looked in the direction he'd be heading—south—and saw black storm clouds and a bolt of lightning. He'd be driving through that tempest, possibly getting stuck in mud. So he instructed: "Go inform your minister to prepare his church house. Tell the constable to bring the prisoner there upon my signal. Lastly, and with haste, sir, find your militia captain and bring that person to me. The fool who does nothing to stifle this bedlam, instead parades!"

When Ingersoll hurried off, Stoughton looked at his companion. "I suppose I should have expected such from uneducated farmers."

Hathorne didn't answer. He knew that militia captain, who had been a brave leader in battle. He also had blood ties to this village, to persons of importance here, but who would not be in attendance since they kept themselves apart from local controversies, as he would himself knowing the rancor of this place.

≈✦≈

Reverend Parris' early morning family circle was lately held beside his daughter's sickbed, not in the parlor like before.

"Help us, Lord, as we begin this fiercest battle of our lives. Knowing Satan has raised an army against us, enlisting a fearful knot of malicious creatures to afflict our—"

But today his child, even in her insensibility, could not bear to hear such scarifying railing. From her deep unknown oblivion, Betty began to wail: "Tituba! Tituba!" Calling out for the one sure comfort her sleeping soul remembered. And each time her mother sought her hand, somehow she knew, and always flicked it off.

"Why won't she let me touch her, Samuel? Why does our daughter cry out for that witch, instead of me?"

He knew, of course, but wouldn't dare tell her, because that would frighten her too much, as it did him. A letter he'd received from Cotton Mather had confirmed it:

If any are scandalized that Salem Village, a place of as serious piety as any I have heard of under Heaven, should be troubled so much with witches, I think 'tis no wonder. For where will the Devil show the most malice, but where he is hated, and hateth most?

The Afflicted Girls

"She is biting me! Make her stop, Uncle!" His niece was fending an invisible attack. Reverend Parris seized Abigail's arm. "Who is biting you?"

Mrs. Parris pulled him away. "Husband, please—"

But Abigail tugged harder: "The demon child, Dorcas Good. Don't you see her running about the room, biting and scratching Betty and me? She says it's in payment for what Aunt did to her mother!"

Mrs. Parris turned ashen. *She'd admonished a spiritual laggard, yes . . . because that was her duty as parsonness. How could she have known that Sarah Good was also a witch?*

Reverend Parris pushed up Abigail's sleeve and beheld tooth-marks on her skin. He yanked the quilt off Betty. Bloody scratches lined the length of his daughter's legs. That imp witch had attacked his children in front of him in the midst of his reaching to God! Righteous anger boiled up. But he realized that he had to wield his God-given wrath through his God-given sword. He summoned Abigail to him. The time had come to tell her. He took her hands, pulled them to his heart and looked into her frightened eyes, pouring her own purpose into her: "You see evil where others cannot. It means God has chosen you, Abigail, to weed the demons out. Is it not said: 'A child shall lead them?' So a child shall. You, niece, shall lead us to victory in Zion today. And I, for one, shall follow." He opened his arms to her.

No, no, no! Cried Mrs. Parris wordlessly, when his niece threw herself into them.

❧

This same morning, hours before first light, Thomas Putnam walked up to the neighborhood bathing shed, built a bonfire and boiled rocks to heat water for a hickory tub soak. Returning home, he ordered Ann to bathe, telling her his daughters were also to be cleansed, that he wanted the stench of witchcraft gone from them. For once, she agreed.

Finally it was Lucy's turn in that stale water who although it was heated, shivered while Mercy sponged her. Because she knew where they were going.

"And when they ask you today, you must explain it was all a dream," instructed Mercy.

"But it wasn't. It happened. Mama said so."

"Because it was her dream, as well. But you are sensible again, Lucy, and need to remind yourself right now that to accuse a person falsely is itself the work of the Devil. You are too kind a soul for that. You would never hurt a person deliberately, or condemn a neighbor falsely because of a feverish dream . . . however real it may have seemed . . . knowing you could be wrong."

Lucy pondered and agreed, but then her eyes shifted sideways. "That man in the corner says I should not listen to you, Mercy."

Mercy spun around . . . there was no one standing in the corner. She ran outside and scanned the landscape. No one was visible in any direction. *The child's mind is not yet right.* But why then was the fire cold white ash, when only moments ago it was blazing? It wasn't five minutes since she'd last stoked it with logs to generate warmth for drying Lucy's hair.

≈✦≈

"Get up, we're late. And don't wear that filthy stable apron to the spectacle," directed Ben Nurse, giving the straw a third strong kick. But Joseph, who was sprawled asleep on two bales of hay set end to end inside the stable door, didn't rouse; and when his friend didn't rouse, Ben badgered and kicked again: "Don't you want to see that Mammon-spouting preacher and your prick of a brother cook in their sauces when their lies are exposed?"

"A sauce served to half-wits, you among them?" One of Joseph's eyes opened.

"Better than having a clever neck like yours wrung out by vengeful hands," shrugged Ben, offering him a hand up.

Joseph declined, saying he wasn't going, adding soberly how he'd just been dreaming of his dead father—well, of his father's ghost sleeping in its grave near that foul event, being rudely awakened—like he had just been—and forced to listen to the lies of scoundrels, which alive he'd never have allowed in a village he governed, near a church he'd built for succor . . . and how that was Thomas' revenge.

Ben Nurse, in all seriousness now, said he understood.

The mid-day chime woke Joseph again, or perhaps the current downpour did. Not wishing to be trapped at his mother's table, despite the rain he decided to ride to Bishop's Ordinary, which wasn't far, and take a meal there. He went to the tack room and hung up his apron and waistcoat. He thought about changing his shirt, which also smelled, but didn't have a clean one hanging. So he changed only the waistcoat. He brushed straw from his britches and used a clean currycomb on his hair. He would have changed his manure covered boots but his expensive London ones were filthy too, and ruined.

He reached up for the nearest saddle, and noticed something caught in a stirrup and untangled it—cloth, torn petticoat linen, *her petticoat*. That day they rode home from the hunt was the last time he'd used this saddle. But even then, unbeknownst, that grackle-girl was already on her hunt and would soon haunt his father's grave, as if disturbing the dead could change anything in the living. He shivered. *His poor twice abused father—no, thrice.* First, thrust into unkempt weeds next to

Thomas' mother by the son who hated him, yet insisted and got his way. Because he, himself, wasn't present on the deathwatch, being in England, and his mother hadn't opposed it. *Why?* Why didn't she refuse? Instead allow his father to be abandoned to that tainted place? When that good man should have been allowed to rest here in his own protected soil near to those he loved. Not exposed in his ghost, and made vulnerable to every sinister purpose, with his bones used for curses and his ears assaulted by crimes.

The Afflicted Girls

56

TWICE AS MANY FOLK WERE NOT ABLE TO FIND seats as were, but Ruth Osborne's manservant was escorted to the front of the meetinghouse by a sheriff, who sat him down on the Ingersoll family's first row bench not knowing who they were since he hailed from a different hamlet, brusquely ordering Nathaniel Ingersoll to make room for one more.

The Irishman sat in dread, as much of them around him as of that sheriff, the other constables, the judges, and of course mostly *her*. He'd been summoned as a witness against her, and was being watched, or else he'd have run away despite his market wench. He averted his eyes when his mistress was carried in, carried right past him on a chair, and set down only a few feet in front. He shrank opposite to all others, who all jumped up to view her. He recognized no one, save a handful of market faces. He looked but did not see his wench. He'd never been a worshipper at this church, and before five minutes ago had never been inside it. He drove his mistress to services and lectures, but waited outside.

When Goody Osborne was advised she'd be required to stand during her questioning, Junior Constable John Willard, who had carried her in on that chair along with his deputy, informed the judge she was an invalid who would fall down if forced to stand, that she had little strength in her body, with none left at all in her legs. He proposed they let her use her chair turned round for support; which Judge Stoughton agreed to, and the *Oyes* were called.

Ruth could not recognize faces with her clouded vision. But when she heard Judge Stoughton's booming cheerless voice, she knew that here was a haughty high-hat, whom God would have to guide her to dodge. And then, as Reverend Parris led the opening prayer, despite his previous insults her hopes raised a little. She closed her eyes and begged God to change her minister's heart—to have him stand as a witness for her innocency, both him and his wife. Deep down he must know she was faithful. His wife couldn't doubt it; who had for three years been her closest friend. And she had no other friends in this village except for Mrs. Parris. No relations either, save two adult stepsons who hated her and would bury her tomorrow if they could.

There were four accusers she learned now—not just the one she already knew of—who were seated together on a bench to the left of the magistrates' table. She could discern their forms, though not their faces . . . except in her mind's eye. She wondered which was Thomas Putnam's daughter, her chief accuser. Their names were announced and one by one they stood: "Abigail Williams, Lucy Putnam, Susanna Walcott, John Doritch." Familiar surnames all. Likely she knew their parents. Though these youngsters weren't what their families supposed. These were no ordinary children, but the Devil's spawn, born and bred for heinous mischief. She was thankful for one thing only. That she'd been brought again into the Lord's house after such a long time. How many heartfelt prayers had, for years and years, soared from her heart through this roof? The Savior would remember. So she fought off fits of faintness, weakness, doubt, and fear in respect for Him, and to keep herself aware for her own sake.

Someone today was not dressed in her Sunday best, but in her aunt's *very best Sunday, Monday, Tuesday, Wednesday, Thursday,*

The Afflicted Girls

Friday and Saturday best, put on this morn without permission — an expensive, embroidered rust-colored, fashionable nub-silk dress that Mrs. Parris had long owned but never once wore; it had been a parting gift from her wealthy Boston sister and she treasured it.

Mrs. Parris only discovered the crime when Abigail came down to breakfast table wearing it. Of course, she was ready to punish her outright for the theft, but all too quickly her husband walked in and undermined her authority, saying he was delighted at his niece's appearance, likely believing she was its cause.

One *victim* was conspicuously absent — her own poor child Betty, who was far too ill to comprehend day from night, no less good from evil. With reluctance, she had to leave her in the crude care of John Indian today. What else could she do? When her husband insisted that her long acquaintanceship with this accused witch was so well known in the parish that her absence would fan suspicion? So as the minutes passed, her worried thoughts distracted her, and she barely paid attention to the questioning.

"Did the Devil force you to afflict children?" Chief Justice Stoughton had asked the accused, pointing his gavel in the victims' direction.

"No sir, h-he did not," Ruth stammered, squinting sidewise at her accusers.

"So it was by your own *free will* that you assaulted them?" Judge Stoughton leaned over, mumbling to Reverend Parris, who sat at the end of his table as scribe and court recorder. (He had said: "Write down her confession.")

Ruth winced, "I have not hurt anyone, sir. I scorn it . . . I am a gospel woman."

"A gospel witch she means," advised Abigail, standing up.

Ruth protested, "Don't listen to her. They, there, are all cruel children, who only pretend to be afflicted! When it is I who is afflicted by them!"

Hearing that, Goody Doritch, knowing more than most here, took off her wooden clog and flung it the length of the hall, striking Goody Osborne neatly on the back of her head (her being an expert horseshoe pitcher).

Ruth staggered, but didn't fall, because the junior constable had caught her in time. But when her hand went up, cupping the back of her head, blood from the gash wet her trembling fingers, and again she nearly fainted.

Abigail had clasped her own head, groaning even louder than was the widow. Susanna Walcott and John Doritch soon suffered that same injury. And although Lucy Putnam, who was sitting at Susanna's side, had reached up to her head, it was only because Mercy Lewis had combed and braided her locks in such a pretty style, she didn't want Witch Osborne to muss it.

So now each time Goody Osborne bit her lips, the afflicted children bit theirs, save Lucy, who by now had begun to cough from the draft. Although the storm had passed, the wind was still blowing through fractured and missing panes behind her.

And when the widow squinted and wrung her hands, and finally said she'd had enough, Abigail claimed she'd been pinched. Ruth turned in her direction. "But I did nothing to you just then, nothing, nothing, not now, not ever, child. However your pinching happens, I do not know it. Can you not see how I am ill and pinched myself? You cannot imagine the pain I suffer."

Abigail looked at the judges as she called to her uncle. "Uncle Parris, she blames God, while she gives us the Evil Eye."

But Junior Constable Willard contradicted her, informing the magistrates how his prisoner was half-blind, blurry-eyed at best, and could not see well enough to give anyone an Evil Eye, nor even to read her own arrest warrant.

Abigail glared at him now, too.

Frightened of the Evil Eye, and chilled, Lucy Putnam suffered a wheezing fit and soon was fighting for breath. Susanna embraced her stricken cousin, and also began to cough; Abigail and John Doritch did, too. The coughs in the room grew into a chorus. Even Mrs. Parris felt a bothersome throat tickle.

Chief Justice Stoughton stood up, ordering John Willard to turn the prisoner's face away. "I will not have her staring or sending out curses."

Dr. Griggs, sitting in the second row, nodded, leaned up and tapped Nathaniel Ingersoll's shoulder, whispering: "She has no need for images to practice her witch magic. Her body can serve that purpose: biting the children, by biting her own lips. Pinching them with a fist-clench."

Ingersoll, clearing his throat, agreed it was probably so. While that frightened Irishman, next to him, was remembering all the bites she'd given him.

"Look! The witches of Essex County are assembling in our pasture!" cried Abigail. She turned to Goody Osborne. "Don't you hear their drum beat? They're calling you to dance with them! Crying, 'Dance, lame witch, dance!'"

Now, that blow to Goody Osborne from the wooden clog likely caused a concussion; ever since it had happened, her mind had been pounding inside her skull like an angry judge's hammer. Yet, she fought to hold on to the chair, and her hearing, and her sanity, and her dignity till now. But *this* abomination utterly collapsed her.

John Willard lifted her from the floor and set her slumped frame onto the chair. He used his hat to fan her back to her senses.

But stopped, when a timid voice from the witness bench sounded the next alarm. Everyone gasped, because it was Lucy Putnam, the chief accuser, pointing at the nearest window: "A man in a black minister's coat is in the pasture. Dreadful. Dreadful. Are ministers witches, too?"

Farmer Doritch, when he looked out, saw nothing in 'Parris' Pasture' except its tree. But he hurled his pitchfork anyway, because he, like other men here, had come armed against Satan at Reverend Parris' urging.

"He's been struck!" cried Goody Bibber from atop her middle room bench. "His minister's coat is torn!"

"But he isn't dead! Only changed his shape into a cat's!" corrected Abigail.

"A black cat!" confirmed Ann Putnam, steadying herself on her husband's shoulder, as Thomas craned to look. "There now, running into the parsonage yard!"

Reverend Parris stopped his fiercest scribbling and stood up. But all he saw were obstructing heads; for by now, half the assembly clustered over by the windows. He climbed atop his chair, in like manner to the magistrates on theirs, but saw nothing still except his weedy pasture. *Did earthly scales cover only his eyes?* He set both feet atop the magistrate's table and color drained from his face. A black feline creature was slinking amid the stalks of his dooryard garden. *Oh Lord,* he prayed, *do not let that fiend come so near to my house! So near to my senseless daughter!*

Chief Justice Stoughton banged his gavel. "Order! Order! Return the prisoner to the jailhouse! This examination is adjourned!"

He, too, had seen the cat.

The Afflicted Girls

57

THE LARGEST ASSEMBLY IN SALEM VILLAGE SINCE its founding had not yet fully dispersed. While many folk had hurried over to Ingersoll's Inn to claim tables, eat, drink and debate. And others had proceeded home. More than a few remained outside the meetinghouse, loitering in small gossiping groups. One of them was Mercy—not gossiping, only listening, and waiting of course; but only because she'd been ordered by her master to bring Lucy up to the inn at the conclusion of the magistrates' interviews. She overheard many opinions, all of which were wrong, none of which she could clarify. Finally, Lucy came out with the others, and she waved.

At the same time, a few maids braved to approach Abigail, and were invited by her to join in the walk to Ingersoll's—despite that these were only silly gigglers she somewhat knew from church. No boys were waiting like she'd hoped, even though their workdays had been cancelled. Had they gone instead to Bishop's Ordinary preferring that woman's smiles to hers? Was there any doubt?

She frowned and yanked off her cap, setting free her locks, frowning more when she turned and caught Susanna and John Doritch flirting; never mind that she had told them to walk together. And then, as they were all approaching Ingersoll's steps, someone grabbed her arm from behind, stopping her; and her companions didn't care and skipped inside

"Whether or not you choose to listen, I will tell you what you've done." Who else, but Mercy Lewis? She knew it before she looked. Herself, she sniffed disinterested: "I have never wanted your opinions, Mercy, yet you always gab them in spite."

"Oh, it is you who is the spiteful one, Abigail. False in all you say and do, wickedly dissembling, and causing your friends to do the same. Even Lucy, who nearly died from your trick."

"When I haven't seen that whiner for weeks? If anyone has given Lucy Putnam opinions, it is her mad mother who is full of them . . . or Witch Osborne, who plants bewitchments."

"Blame me, then. Tell your uncle I baked the cakes. I would falsely admit it for your sake. I am a faithful friend."

Abigail sneered. "Of course you'd now want to claim that which bestows power, because you no longer have any. You are not above me anymore, Mercy. My status here is higher than yours."

"Heed my warning, Abigail. I know more than you think. I know how the web you're weaving will ensnare you in the end."

"*You* threaten *me* with snares and webs? What conceit! When you're the one who frequents graveyards and casts netting spells."

Mercy chilled, for that was a fact. And it suddenly made her see that from Abigail's vantage, she was the tainted one. Yet she must urge her old friend to a better course. If she didn't, who would? That minister-uncle? Who hoped the world would fear him? "I've been the way you've chosen . . . it will be hard coming back."

Abigail answered wildly, indignantly: "But I haven't chosen! I was *myself* chosen! By God! I am *His* 'Visible Saint! Called to this noble task *by Him!*"

The Afflicted Girls

But *Him* was really Reverend Parris, and uncoiling that serpent's hold on her friend would be nearly impossible now. For even today, he'd sat and scribed at the judges' table, deceiving even those powerful men. "Though you believe this in your heart, Abby, and it is also your uncle's surest belief, it will lead you, and him, to nowhere but grief. Do you really wish to cause him lamentations beyond the bearing? For you will." *No,* she must urge more kindly. "You have only to bury your old bitterness and turn the other cheek. That poor sick woman never caused you harm. She is not to blame for what happened to your loved ones."

"You'd let her strike *me* down instead?" screamed Abigail, ending the conversation. And now she ran inside Ingersoll's Inn to join her friends. The past was only the past, after all. The New Day was just beginning.

Everyone inside wished to make her acquaintance, although none of them were boys, only ill-breathed wrinkled old gabbers. So Abigail was grateful when Mrs. Ingersoll brought her into the kitchen and fed her.

She'd just escaped through the rear door, rushing home across the green, but halting as soon as she spied the doctor's carriage parked outside the parsonage gate. She hated that old lecher. She saw her uncle exit the house, carrying her limp-limbed cousin. Aunt Ugly followed behind him. She was carrying a quilt. Her heart began to pound. Arms outstretched, she ran to them to weep alongside her aunt. And when her uncle leaned in to plant a good-bye kiss on Betty, she swooped in and put her lips on her cousin's other cheek, and their eyes met and fastened. But he must have felt a misgiving, for he broke from her gaze. So now she cried real tears for herself.

The doctor received that lump of flesh while eyeing hers, or rather, a certain bulging part of it. She pretended she didn't notice.

And when her aunt passed up the quilt to the doctor, she quickly took her uncle's hand.

And though Reverend Parris had intended to embrace his wife at this moment the carriage pulled away, he reached for her instead.

Better than any boy Abigail thought.

Till Aunt Ugly yanked him away, and ushered him back to the house.

Reverend Parris had arranged for Dr. Griggs to deliver his afflicted daughter down to Boston, to put her into the care of his wife's wealthy older sister, who'd volunteered a home. With no augur for her recovery here, at least in Boston surgeons could attend her. The doctor, of course, had asked for a small fee.

He had previously, weeks ago, dispatched two letters. One was to Cotton Mather, requesting that minister visit Salem Village and observe his stricken daughter first-hand. Although that man wrote back expressing interest, he also claimed he was too busy. The second letter was to his wife's sister begging a shelter for their ill daughter. But now because Betty would be residing on a nearby Boston street, where Cotton Mather could more conveniently visit and observe her, he wrote another letter to that minister yesterday, which Dr. Griggs offered to deliver.

Because it was a well-known fact that in addition to being a *Glorifier*—an alchemist of the soul—Cotton Mather was also a chemist, a trained physician of the body corporeal. So of any person on this earth in such dangerous times as these, that was a man who might possess the requisite knowledge and Goodness to free his daughter from her Hellish shackles. Since he, himself, had tried, and couldn't.

The Afflicted Girls

58

COTTON MATHER'S FATHER, INCREASE, SHORT weeks ago, set sail for Old England on Commonwealth business as Governor Phips' newly appointed Ambassador to the Royal Court. Prior to his departure, he passed his mantle of preeminence permanently to his son. Charging Cotton with the care of this largest ministry in Boston, North Church, expressing confidence that his son could lead it equally well, even while authoring his books and essays and conducting medical experiments, not to mention tending to his own young needful flock—not six years married and still in his twenties, Cotton had already sired a handful of offspring, with his eldest boy, Creasy, that grandfather's namesake, rebellious of authority and needing frequent caning.

In the wee hours of every third night, North Church's new pastor found time for correspondence. He'd read the village minister's latest letter, and tonight would be writing back. William Stoughton, his good friend and parishioner, had shared additional details. He'd viewed the bedeviled child twice, and planned to visit her again on the morrow. Admittedly, he was intrigued. And now he remembered a relevant instruction in the <u>Gospel of Matthew</u> and decided to include it with the letter:

> And when the devil was cast out, the dumb spake.
> And the multitudes marveled saying 'It was never so

seen in Israel.' But the Pharisees said, 'He casteth out devils through the prince of the devils.

Those priests of the Jews had understood abomination, and very soon so would this village minister, he thought, as he picked up his sharpest quill.

Reverend Parris had brought Cotton Mather's letter to the parlor to read aloud to his niece—because at supper tonight, that angel had asked two questions of him that he had asked to Cotton Mather. How like him she was in mind. Although he was not too surprised by it, since the same blood coursed through her as through him, though not as thickly, of course, since she was only a *Williams,* and not a *Parris,* descending from his slightly inferior maternal line. And when he shared that minister's theological opinion, how:

> *It is certain that the Devil has sometimes represented the shapes of persons not only innocent but very virtuous. But I believe that the just God then provides a way for the speedy vindication of the person thus abused.*

It inspired a vigorous discussion between them, of the sort he'd once enjoyed with his wife. Of course, then, he mentioned that his opinion differed.

On Goody Osborne's examination day, Israel Porter, in cheerless spirits, spied a cat taunting a fledgling, which had fallen from a nest—a tiny creature that had been condemned by fault of its own fragile nature. It was the somberness of this day that made him go to its aid, to force the feline aside with his crop, and retrieve the bird and put it into his hat. He led his horse the rest of the way up to the hitching post, while that stalker meowed and scratched at his boot. He kicked it aside, but gently. For it was also a creature alive. "Were this a blackbird or a crow, I'd let you eat it, cat. But a meadow lark has a song worth saving."

He entered the premise at the rear, and viewed Bridget Bishop ankle-deep in apple rinds. Her half-smile greeted his. It had taken her hours, she confessed, to pare only this many apples, her mind being so disrupted. He nodded, understanding. She laid down her knife and took the shivering bird from his hands; it calmed immediately in hers. She ministered to its wing. Then filled a basket with kindling straw for it and put in apple seeds, and a rind for holding water.

Israel offered to hunt for a worm.

She shook her head. 'Let us not harm any earthly creature on this foul day."

He sobered, remembering the reason he'd felt moved to preserve that small insignificant life. He hung the basket from a high ceiling hook, because Bridget's cat was still circling. Which reminded him, once more, of that other relentless stalking. "So what do you think, Bridget? Are their youngsters sickened by curses?"

"Oh, the Devil is always about, Israel . . . but more likely it's tricksters. For what child isn't brazen in that way?"

"My child," he answered without thinking, and saw her wince; but not for the reason he was thinking. He sighed and took her hand. "Well, if that's all it is, we can put a quick end to this madness."

She shook her head. But couldn't tell him the fact. Because if she said all that she knew, she'd draw him into the maelstrom. "We cannot stop this tide, Israel. Too much hatred exists in that village. The more the lie is believed, the fiercer will be its wake.

Sturdy vessels will overturn . . . good lives will go under. If I could think of a way to stop it, I would. I am so deeply troubled."

He drew her close. "Let's both of us put our troubled minds into calmer waters then." He led Bridget up the back stair to her chamber, and locked the door behind him, and easily embraced her, his passionate lover of many a year.

The Afflicted Girls

59

THOMAS PUTNAM RE-READ THEN SEALED WITH wax a document prepared the night before by him and an in-law, with two Wilkins neighbors signing as witnesses.

And now in irritation, he called out for the wench, thinking how this was an errand for a trusted son, not a trustless wench. But he had no sons, only useless daughters, a pitted wife, and this jinx. He couldn't deliver it himself, because he had other matters more urgent. Last night, a pack of wolves, or dogs, had breached his sheepfold and further *dwindled* his flock.

"Deliver this to the constabulary," he frowned at Mercy. "No dawdling."

Farmers and shepherds, who before would always wave to her, today scornfully turned their backs. But Mercy guessed that their animus was aimed more at her master than at her. They knew him, of course, but not how desperate he'd become since his recent setback in Boston. And if not for the wax seal, she might have read his new petition. Not that she was personally curious—but Joseph Putnam would be should their paths cross again—if Fate, or her charm, or Bridget's jasper amulet decreed another chance encounter; of course, she wouldn't offer it, but he would seize it from her hands anyway, and read it, and jeopardize her again.

At the creek, she stopped to drink, and in her hidden spot where it was tranquil and foliage was thick, she rested on her favorite rock slab, soaking her feet in the coolness of that pool, studying the patterns of afternoon sun glinting off her toe ripples. Till her focus shifted and she glimpsed her reflection, and saw what she carried, and understood that this was no petition concerning an inheritance, but a witchcraft complaint against another innocent person. No wonder the yeomen hated her for carrying it; she hated herself for it, too.

I'll kill you, bury you and say you run off! Her master, himself, had planted the seed. She would flee instead, she decided, and leave the document on this stone, or throw it into the water to drown it. Were it to be found downstream, by then she'd be miles to freedom, hundreds of miles by public coach. She could barter Bridget's jasper amulet in payment; it had value. *Too late! Too late!* A rider was turning from a side road up ahead, and now cantered in her direction. Her venture utterly collapsed.

She ran back to retrieve the parchment, knowing that her unhappy life would continue as it was, but that today somebody else's would be ruined. It wasn't Joseph Putnam, but a yeoman from the neighborhood, who frowned down at her as he rode past. She quickened her pace. *No dawdling.*

"Aye, she's one of them. Blood be on her soul," spat a villager into her footprint, while the woman's husband muttered, "Jezebel." Shop doors bolted, nervous hands latched shutters, and even when she passed the militia camp backs were turned. All of this was only imagined, though. But now, as she reached the village constabulary and went in, all of it was real. She told the constable sitting there: "Mr. Putnam sends this."

"Which Putnam?" John Willard asked, though he knew.

"Thomas, sir." She curtsied.

He took the scroll, pointed it toward the bench against the wall. "Sit there, while I read it."

She shook her head. "Cannot, sir. Master said I mustn't dawdle." She recognized this man who lived near to Putnam Farm and daily rode past their gate, often looked in, but never once had acted friendly. And she knew her master despised him.

"Stand then till I dismiss you," he ordered, considering her. "You're acquainted with the afflicted children, aren't you?"

"My master's daughter is one of them."

"And Walcott's?"

"Yes, a cousin. "

"Do you know any others? "

"The minister's niece was my companion before I came to this place."

"So you are in the thick of it and yet haven't succumbed. Why is that do you think?" He tapped the scroll against his hand.

Mercy answered that she didn't know.

"But you do know they've been sick. So explain their illnesses to me in your own words, knowing I wish to hear only truth."

I am being asked by this man to stand up to Evil. If I don't, who will? But, if I do —

"Your belief? "

She might play the country wench. "Oh yes, they were very sick, sir."

"And if I paid you to explain how they came to be so sick?" He opened his purse, clearly very full with currency, and took out a silver crown and laid it on the table—many months' pay, coach fare for a hundred miles.

But it wasn't for the money that Mercy answered now, or to foist blame on Abigail, and never on Lucy though she was still so angry with the child. She answered truthfully, because things might be set right if she did. This man was a constable who possessed more authority than her master or the minister. "It began as a game, sir."

"For sport? Their bringing out of witches was for sport?"

Her cheeks flushed. "No, sir, for husbands . . . a fortune-telling game for husbands."

"And instead, you brought the Devil to your beds. Bodies twisted into impossible postures, demonic bites and scratches, comas, asphyxiations? Before you explain that inexplicable part, know that perjury is a crime as *punishable* as is witchcraft." His expression had darkened. He held out a blank piece of parchment in a cold, unfriendly manner. "You are now to write your confession on this and sign it, knowing you'll be called to testify to the magistrates."

She crossed her arms, retreating. "But I lied, sir, lied—I know nothing of it really—only goodwives' gossip, same as anybody." She turned the doltish maid. "Your reward was what I wanted. Beg pardon, for my greed. Master waits at the inn. Mustn't dawdle." She ran out.

John Willard broke the document's seal and read it:

> *Unspeakable crimes committed by her spectral form,*
> *including murders of numerous infants*—who?

Crushing it inside his hand he ran to the door to summon the wench back, but didn't see her. She'd disappeared. And she wouldn't be at the inn, he knew, nor would her master. Those were lies. The wily wench had tricked him. He should have twisted harder—because servants knew their master's secrets. And this one knew those, and more. Returning inside, he took that same blank sheet, and with a trembling pen wrote out his resignation as Salem Village's junior constable. Because this was an accusation so terrible, that never in his life, not even to save it, would he ever serve the Summons on.

❧✦❧

The Afflicted Girls

Bridget wrote another sum into her ledger and then mentally tabulated her next stack of coins. For this was month's end, her usual time for tallying receipts. And she'd been very busy all this month, though she would have wished it otherwise. Footsteps made her muddle her count.

She looked up annoyed, expecting it was her worker coming down to the cellar to fetch more stores. But it was Mercy Lewis rushing to her table.

"So what if you ran? I'd have done the same. Who doesn't fear a constable?" shrugged Bridget.

"But I wanted not to lie to him," Mercy anguished, sitting down. "And before that at the creek, I lied to myself. Why does my resolve always fail me when it's tested?"

"The question should rather be . . . what would *he* have done with your truth? If I saw Willard's palm, I perhaps could tell you." Bridget held up her hand to the lantern light, pointing to certain lines and creases. "Here are my own taints and weaknesses . . . my follies . . . lies . . . a grievous death of which I will not speak, but which I caused . . . every personal failing, innocent or otherwise is written here. But there are some, like your friend the minister's niece, and your master and your mistress, who will cut *false* lines into their palms and then get others with weak minds to believe their lies and further them. So in my thinking, it was better *not* to have told the constable. Thus, your resolve failed you once, and saved you once." She sighed, "You see, in my resolve, I actually told one person. But all *he* did was defend his niece and blame me."

Mercy said nothing but now a new fear overruled her other fear. For this meant that Abigail would likely know now that Bridget knew. And only one person could have told her.

60

BEN NURSE IN MUDDY LEATHER LEGGINGS WORN over high jackboots blasted like a musket ball across the clean, polished wet kitchen floor of his grandparents' saltbox, depositing his oversized footprints before either aunt could stop him. He slogged into the parlor next, muddying a braided carpet as well, while his cousins and sisters, who were quilting and knitting and darning at the table, pointed their needles at him and scolded. Clambering up the staircase two steps at a time, he came up to the door of the gable room and stopped. Quickly, he shed his muddy boots and wiped his forehead sweat on his sleeve, and his filthy hands on his pants (from digging a well with a brother-in-law). Because this room he respected. He knocked. And when he heard no answer, in bare feet — which were hardly any cleaner — he entered.

Rebecca Nurse, who slept inside, had been taxed beyond her endurance keeping her old bones awake and aware while birthing a granddaughter's firstborns: wrong-sitting twins — one up, one down — who came too early and did not emerge in tandem, but a day and a half apart . . . an unlucky sign to an old midwife. Fearing loss of the mother, one babe, or all three, she soldiered on.

That stubborn boy was finally spit out this morning, and was bigger than the wee lass born already. As soon as he breathed steady and took to the nursemaid's nipple, after watching him suckle, this great-grandmother came home to sleep.

She had retired not two hours ago, shutting her bloodshot eyes mulling one thought only: how her granddaughter had knocked loudly at Death's door and that it had opened more than a crack. And how in all her long years as a midwife not one of her brood had ever flown to Heaven early nor had a newborn ever failed to thrive. She wasn't sure yet about these two. Something wasn't right. So she knocked on her own wood bedpost, thinking how one ought not to take such a rare boon from God for granted. Though also realized that she had for years not only taken it for granted, but openly bragged about her luck outside her family circle. And then, she fell into dreamlessness.

Ben bent over his granny and lightly shook her shoulder and also called her name. Her tongue darted out to moisten dry lips, but she didn't rouse. He nudged more times with increasing fervor but gently, till one of her sagging eyes eventually squinted open. He blurted his news.

"Say what?" she asked drowsily, through a thick blanket of unfinished sleep, unable to relinquish her inner bed.

He told her again and saw her wince. But then she asked wrongly: "Which babe is dead?"

"Neither, Granny, none. It's worse!" He sat at the edge of her featherbed and clutched her knob-knuckled hand in his dirty one, and sobbed. She held him, her favorite grandson, asking: was it his sister? For that's who'd just given birth.

"Granny, it's you! You! You're cried out as a witch!"

"Which what? Say again into my other ear." She turned it toward him.

"Ann Putnam accuses you of witchcraft! Not just of witchcraft! Of murder, too!"

Rebecca's hundred wrinkles flattened, her shocked mouth dropped open. "Witchcraft . . . murder? But I don't understand."

"That lunatic claims her dead babes came out from their graves in winding sheets, saying it was you who had done them to death! She accused you of their murders!" He grimaced. "I'll go wring *her* neck myself with a winding sheet!"

She said tut-tut: "Don't speak such nonsense, Ben. Pity her instead." Though she herself didn't pity Ann Putnam at all, but was incensed that this selfish person she'd so many times served without getting hardly a pittance or a thank you, could turn so false and mean.

"But why accuse you? One of God's true Saints!"

Underneath the coverlet she was trembling. But she kept her face calm for his sake. "Well, I don't know, Ben. I really couldn't say. I was her midwife many times over . . . 'tis true. But, her babes were all born rosy. It was afterward they malingered and turned blue, when I wasn't there to save them—"she stopped, her mouth closed. The words had tasted bitter.

Could *she* save any life? Was she any babe's savior? Hadn't she counted herself one today when that bonny boy was born alive and took to the nipple? How many other times had she set herself in God's Place, or before Him? "Many, many, far too many!" And in this instant, Rebecca realized the *why* of Ann Putnam's lie. It was a hard slap down from *Him*. *And how many other un-repented sins were left inside her needing excise? Could she even count them?*

≪╋≫

Mercy forced worry from her mind, because today she had promised to teach the Putnam girls the game called *cat's cradle*. But also, she told them they would first need to finish dividing and sorting beans and writing answers on their slates.

While they worked, she searched for her knitting basket, which they'd hidden. She found it but then discovered how those mischief-makers had also hidden her spools and yarns. She decided on a trick. Lately, she'd been shearing sheep up in the fold, and wheeling the wool down to bundle and store it in the barn. She would quickly spin new strands of yarn for the game. She went up to the barn, where the spinning wheel sat.

Two lengths were looped and she was spinning a third, when something suddenly fell down from a rafter striking her arm. She looked up and saw Joseph Putnam in the loft. Her heart rushed up to him. But he had jumped down, stomping over to crush the object he'd thrown at her. Her mandrake.

"God help the next poor devil you force into your bed," he spat.

Her retort came quick: "And all poor maids forced into yours." She retrieved her charm, defending badly: "What I did was done for love of you. Your own mother has done far worse for money. I put my heart's hope inside your father's grave. Dig deeper and see what *she* has buried there."

She was sobbing into her hands when those little girls found her. Mourning not a true love gone awry, but her own heartless cruelty: that picture she'd just conjured which would poison his mind forever — of a murdered parent.

SUZY WITTEN

We whose names are hereunto subscribed, being desired by Goodman Nurse to declare what we know concerning his wife's conversations in times past, do hereby testify, to all it may concern, that we have known Rebecca Nurse well, and according to our observation of her life and conversation, never had any cause or grounds to suspect her of any such thing as she is now accused.

"Affidavit of 39 Persons In Support of Rebecca Nurse" (incl. Israel Porter, Joseph Putnam, Mary Veren Putnam) June 1692

PART EIGHT

61

REBECCA NURSE CLUTCHED HER GOOD BOOK TO her heart while the jailer unlocked her ankle cuff. Staring at her feet that were free again, she considered how whatever lay in their path today, her hands held all the strength that she needed. But then he made her leave her Bible on the sheepskin her kin had brought her for a bed, saying all books—in particular this Book—were banned from proceedings by the magistrates, lest some witch or warlock read it backwards and curse their accusers, witnesses, or a judge.

God's Word . . . image magic? Rebecca reeled with disbelief, because even hinting at such a thing was blasphemy. She chided that those judges should better fear God's Judgment, as should he.

Meanwhile big-bellied beggar Sarah Good, eight months pregnant, swooped down and snatched up that Good Book and dangled it by its cover in front of the midwife's nose. Not to keep or to read, but to barter: "You *Stingies* have plenty in your coffers! Want your Book? Cost you two pound."

Little Dorcas, jailed now too, was sucking her thumb, watching that wrinkled granny try to wrestle back the black book from her mother (from her *new* mother's lap). For Tituba now kept this abandoned tyke close to her, like once she had Betty Parris, countering another mother's indifference and child's unhappiness with songs, soft cossets, and kisses.

Also present, was the ailing pilgrim, Goody Osborne, who saw none of this hen-fight that the guard, guffawing, allowed. Because by now she'd drifted too far upstream: after her head injury her legs had miraculously healed and on them, she crossed the Slough of Despond and traipsed the entire By-path Meadow, and today was finally stepping onto lighter Sacred Ground in the Eternal Sunshine. Heading up that flowery white-pebbly path leading to a whitewashed cottage gate in the pearly distance.

≈✛≈

Three generations of angry Nurse men led by their patriarch lumbered down the center aisle to claim their usual seven rows. All folk seated thereon were made to move by that brawny bunch. They'd come absent of spouses, sisters, mothers today, for the Nurse womenfolk remained at home to watch-guard the children. Francis was worried for them all, but mostly for his wife.

Ben, while worried for his granny, nonetheless couldn't keep one eye from settling on the Porter maid's back, for that girl sat only two rows in front. He thought about his friend's reluctance to wed her and decided that were Elizabeth Porter to be spurned, like the rest of Joseph's maids, he'd offer to be her swain. He looked around the crowded meetinghouse, this makeshift courtroom, counting supporters' heads. All their faction was present, except Joseph (but at least his friend signed Granny's petition, and his friend's rich mother did, as well). Israel Porter, at least, was present. And had promised to be staunch in his support, which forecasted a good outcome, his wife being related to one judge.

They booed when the chief accuser, the witch herself Ann Putnam, was walked down the aisle by her husband followed by their tykes, and granny's betrayer—a person now fiercely hated by him, however prettily she smiled. Because according to John Willard the accusation had been delivered to him by her hand. He counted supporters' heads again, and worried. Far at the back, Joseph Putnam pulled his stable cap low on his forehead, and turned away before Ben Nurse could eye him. He stood by a window waiting for the prison cart to arrive. And when it did, he offered a man on the rearmost bench a six-pence for his seat.

The jail carter helped Rebecca Nurse down.

Shaky in her legs after having been two weeks sitting on a sheepskin, she leaned heavily on his arm walking up that trampled grass. She was surprised. Her church had a fresh-painted exterior, new hewn clapboard, sweet smelling shingles, with no sign of fractured windowpanes anymore or unhinged casings. Seeing God's house shine so bright on such a frightful morn betokened to her now how a thing so broken and ruined can be mended. She felt more hopeful. Until that brash new constable and his deputy, who were waiting outside the door to bring her in, grabbed her arms and then half-dragged her down the center aisle like seized prey. Nevertheless, she kept herself as erect as her hooked frame would allow.

The room was crowded. She ignored all staring faces. Her heart sank spying her loved ones clotted on the family benches. How she wished Francis wouldn't stare at her so hard with such fear-filled eyes. It frightened her. But then her heart failed completely, seeing the empty seat beside him—her seat—with his hand set firmly upon it. Not allowing anyone to sit in her place. She forced her eyes away, and now caught sight of Goody Putnam, her accuser, that liar, not to mention fraud, who was standing by an angled bench at the front. And right behind her, upon it, sat the accusing children, those same four who had outfoxed Goody Osborne. There was also, today, a second angled bench where sat an assortment of goodwives wearing sour masks.

"Ann Putnam's supporters," the new junior constable remarked to his deputy. She snapped at him like a turtle, "And where is my supporting bench?" Though she knew.

Chief Justice Stoughton glanced down at his written list, but still asked the same first question of Goody Nurse that he had of Goody Osborne. Though she was the only one to answer him: "Say again, judge?" cupping her ear. "Louder . . . I could not quite hear you."

He thought her a crafty old tool. So, he shouted into the assembly, asking if anyone had an ear-horn, lest this accused witch use that clever excuse again to avoid all other questions. And when one was passed up, he saw how she clearly disdained it, which he took as a sign of her guilt.

The truth was Rebecca couldn't admit she was nearly deaf, not even to her fifty-years' spouse. She hated implements of any sort that signaled age or infirmity, especially these clumsy ear-horns one could barely hold with two hands. And being forced to use such a dirty one (despite that her own ear wasn't much cleaner) rankled her no end. But she did hear the judge's voice clear as a crow's when he said:

"Why did you murder Ann Putnam's infants?"

She stated vehemently, "I murdered no one, sir! When those babes died, I pitied them with all my heart and went to God for them . . . and I mourn them still!"

"Then why do they claim to their mother that you did?"

"Because they lie in their graves as little liars!"

"You'd do well, Goody Nurse," Judge Stoughton warned, "to admit your guilt before accusing infants newborn, who are in natures as innocent as God made them."

"Dead babes that never walked a day in their lives till they walked five miles to her? Oh, the wool inside your head, sir! Believe instead—and let God be my witness—that never have I hurt any *real* child . . . not even in a dream! But many have I helped, including hers!" She turned to the populace, "If you believe otherwise, neighbors, then all of you are ninnies!"

She wasn't contrite. Not one bit, thought Judge Stoughton. "How quick you are, Goody Nurse, to call down our Lord to testify, when you know He will not appear, not even by a witch's conjuration." Nervous titters laced the room. But Judge Stoughton wasn't laughing. "Do you have any familiarity with the Devil, Goody Nurse?"

"No, sir, only with God." She stood her ground.

"But the Devil has familiarity with Him . . . so your reply is cleverly concocted."

"I answered plainly, sir, not cleverly." Her ruffled brow was now covered with sweat.

"Then with plainness answer this question, Goody Nurse. Can the Devil appear in any shape? Or only in his own?"

It was a difficult concept. One Rebecca had never pondered. But she took it to heart, for it was pertinent for a Calvinist to consider. "I suppose, judge, that the Devil can appear in any shape. After all, he is a spirit."

"Indeed, he is, Goody Nurse. So he might appear in your shape if he wanted."

She was about to nod 'yes' when she suddenly saw the trick. "Oh no, sir, no. He has *never* appeared in mine."

Judge Stoughton summoned Ann Putnam up to the witness bar, which today was the minister's oak pulpit turned round. She took an oath, and stated: "I awoke in a chamber dark as tar, which then filled with an infernal light when *she* appeared in it—"

"Who appeared, Goody Putnam? Be specific."

Pointing at Rebecca: "Her! Goody Nurse! Wearing a blood-soaked shift, also carrying a black-bound book with red names written inside it. She showed me every page, and vehemently urged me to sign it, as well. When I refused, she threatened to tear my soul out from my body saying God had no power to save me."

All who heard this were aghast, including Judge Stoughton.

But Rebecca looked up and thanked God. Because imagine if she'd been clutching her black-bound Bible just now, instead of this crusty ear-horn? The beggar had saved her. That woman would get compensation for her trick. But not any two-pound note, because her family worked hard for its money, and for a derelict like Sarah Good, two shillings would suffice.

"Was your husband present?" asked the other judge, Judge Hathorne.

Ann Putnam nodded, relating that her husband was indeed in the room.

"Then he must have heard her threatening you."

Thoughtlessly, she nearly said aye. Then suspected a trick, and advised: "Well, he didn't, sir, for good reason. Though I called out to him and strenuously tried to wake him, he was under a heavy spell."

Judge Hathorne considered this testimony. "Yes, I see Goody Putnam." And yet he also saw the hole in it. He turned and instructed Reverend Parris: "Record that there were no witnesses."

Ann screamed, "But *I* was the witness! I, and I cried 'Goody Nurse, be gone! Aren't you ashamed of yourself?'"

"But ponder this, Goody Putnam. Mightn't that have been only the Devil in her shape? Not Rebecca Nurse herself. Did not Judge Stoughton, a theological scholar of the first order, just explain to us how this very thing could happen?"

"Oh no, sir, no, it was definitely Goody Nurse. Of that, I am certain."

And now two other victims, namely Abigail Williams and John Doritch, prompted by that accuser's niece—and with her, in chorus with a handful of fitful goodwives and two other recently stricken maids—arose from the angled benches, claiming Goody Nurse was their afflicter.

Rebecca shouted back at them through her ear horn turned round, which made her shrill voice bellow: "Neighbors, children, it just is not so! No shape of mine has ever gone out anywhere!"

Judge Hathorne made a final attempt, since this grandmother wasn't helping herself. "You may believe that, Rebecca Nurse . . . but mightn't you have had a spiritual lapse, when the Devil assumed your form?"

Rebecca fibbed, "Oh no, sir, no. I am entirely clear of that intrusion."

Ann Putnam suddenly rushed up to the prisoner within inches of Rebecca's face, though no one can be sure whose shape she really saw. It could easily have been the usurper's, Mary Veren's—when she screamed venomously: "Blare-eyed witch! Blaspheming devil's whore! Murderer of my future!"

That wash of seething wrath made Rebecca reel backward. But it was Ann Putnam who now collapsed.

Thomas ran to his wife, while everyone jumped to their feet or onto benches, having heard of bestial fits, but never before having witnessed one. Including both magistrates, who stared down with appalled faces at their thrashing witness, while Reverend Parris scribbled down every curse Satan poured through Ann Putnam's blaspheming mouth.

And strangely, in the midst of this cacophony, Rebecca Nurse grew wistful. She lowered the ear-horn, recalling how her own mother had once suffered this same humiliation: brought up on a false charge of witchery, but which ended in a verdict of *innocency.* And how, in that aftermath, at the age of eleven she had vowed herself to a life of piety and good works. *But why was she drifting toward that loved one fifty years dead?*

She winced back at her husband for reassurance, but Francis was standing liver-faced with an angry upraised fist, shouting curses after Thomas Putnam, as that man carried out his loony collapsed wife. And she viewed not the virile, handsome husband he'd always been, but a feeble, stooped-shouldered murky old man. A stranger.

She knew now that she was lost.

62

A CLEVER IDEA TODAY FREED ABIGAIL FROM HER chores, and also from her lessons. Or she'd succumb to sudden fits where the Devil would seize her tongue, aiming evil aspersions at her aunt . . . but only when they were two alone together. So after this day, Mrs. Parris urged her husband to keep his niece with him promising no more complaints; the girl did so unnerve her.

But Reverend Parris had no use for a young companion, being far too busy with the ever-increasing demands of his burgeoning ministry, pending lawsuits, and neglected collections on delinquent accounts. Yet, being cut from a similar cloth as his niece, he devised an equally clever solution: to send Abigail out to sickrooms in his stead, and in particular to persons whose relations owed him money. Instructing his niece that before she prayed for any sick person, she should ask for the amount owed to the minister—because as their Spiritual Pilot, he could not legally charge a farthing for prayers or fasts. But his niece who was Higher-called could ask any amount for any reason. And yet, since it would be perilous for a maid of her tender years to wander the roads alone with the Devil running rampant, and since he couldn't spare John Indian for that purpose, he allowed her an escort, a male companion: the red-haired farm boy named John Doritch.

On those evenings, while sitting together in the parsonage parlor, Abigail was always asked for a report, which Reverend

The Afflicted Girls

Parris recorded in his diary. Tonight she described to him how she'd seen two demons today—one standing at the sick person's head and another at her feet—and that both had "mocked her." She wondered, should she mock them back?

Reverend Parris pondered that question, suggesting that the next time she saw a fiend besetting a victim, she should lay her hands upon the sick person, exhorting the fiend to leave, using the same banishing words Christ's disciples had once used.

As Abigail began doing this, her reputation spread so far and wide so quickly that Reverend Parris had to tack public notices to both his meetinghouse and parsonage doors to stop a steady stream of infirm folk and relations of infirm folk from knocking at them:

> *Any who find themselves sick and sore, but are not yet*
> *bedridden, let them gather at Ingersoll's Inn on*
> *Thursdays after lecture to be ministered to by my niece.*

When Abigail herself succumbed, he took his notices down and granted her request: to traipse the countryside freely, wherever God might lead her to heal, as long as the boy went with her.

Today a gaggle of four girls accompanied her, her boy and Susanna Walcott out to Endicott Farm, including an Endicott daughter. But after walking two miles under a hot baking sun, as they were nearing Bishop's Ordinary, she declared a need for refreshment and went tramping to that tavern. All her companions followed, save the worried daughter, who waited out of doors.

Drunken chatter silenced the moment Abigail entered the shovelboard room. She was nervously handed the shovel. But before she could aim it a firm hand yanked her shoulder.

"Come with me," ordered Bridget, forcing Abigail back to her kitchen, where she gave her this caution: "You're undoing your soul, Abigail Williams. Digging a grave around it, though you are not yet lying inside it."

Abigail sniffed, "I lie in God's bed, unlike you Goody Bishop." And now she cried out loudly, turning toward that open doorway: "Help me, John! Help! Witch Bishop has caught me in her paws!"

John Doritch came running to assist, but turned sheepish in front of Bridget, who gave him a mild cuff on his shoulder and then tussled his hair before she pushed him out. While Abigail rubbed her own pinched shoulder, frowning how he was *her boy* to cuff . . . not Bridget Bishop's!

Despite having seen *fiends*, Abigail called them spoilsports and said they would not be invited again, as she banished three teary-eyed companions from future ventures, after there hadn't been a healing at Endicott Farm. Now she told Susanna and John to walk her to "The Haunted Chamber." While John had to go, Susanna declined, until Abigail had tempted her with more sinister facts gleaned from her uncle's volumes: "Demons can be male or female, and can shift their sex at will."

Susanna called it silly, but then mulled that aberration while tramping into the woods after Abigail, because there were legions more witches to discover. "In Ipswich, Topsfield, Beverly, too." said that leader of the *finders*.

"If I see their broomsticks," promised John, taking out his slingshot, aiming at a blackbird on wing, "I'll shoot them down."

"Look up to the sky on the next new moon, boy. It's the night they hold their conventicle in my uncle's pasture. Twice now, I've seen them."

"If you saw them, you know who they are," Susanna reasoned.

"Well, I saw the witches cavort. But I didn't see their faces. Because both new moons were misty, likely by their doing."

"What do *cavorting* witches do?" John wondered.

The Afflicted Girls

"Ask Mercy Lewis. She was participant in both heats. The Queen of the coven has befriended her. A person who hates me," Abigail rubbed her shoulder, "though not you."

John scratched his red mop.

"Bridget Bishop," Susanna whispered.

"Mercy's black minister is their Witch King," Abigail continued, "and he sports with them all, while Bridget sports with naked village men of her choosing. Constable Willard for one."

Susanna was suspicious. "You said you saw no faces."

"If I did, the words were put onto my tongue."

Reaching the Haunted Chamber, the farm boy sprawled out in the shade for a nap. At once, Abigail straddled and kissed him, not caring at all that Susanna was staring and frowning.

"I am going home, yes I am going," Susanna warned her fondling friends.

"But wouldn't you rather be tangled up in this kissing heap? Abigail offered.

Susanna hesitated. "No. 'Tisn't right, 'tisn't clean." She saw a whisper pass between them and then a lanky arm sprang out and grabbed her foot. Both friends pulled her down, and pinned her underneath them, and began smothering her with tickles and kisses, till she was laughing louder than they were. But then a hand crept up underneath her petticoat and found her *nonnyno* and began kneading. Her eyes closed. And now she, too, *cavorted*.

By the time one was panting and the other one humping, Abigail lost interest in the game. She was bored with John Doritch anyway, who had no manly skills beyond what she'd taught. Clumsy, always coming to spurts too quick, it was far more interesting watching another friend's first screwing.

SUZY WITTEN

Here are but 2 parties in the World, the Lamb & his Followers, & the Dragon & his Followers: & these are contrary one to the other. Here are no Newters. Every one is on one side or the other.

Rev. Samuel Parris (1692)

63

SARAH GOOD DIDN'T NOTICE HER DAUGHTER'S absence, but wouldn't have cared anyway now. Something had snapped. The daylong all she did was pace the cell dragging her iron chain, muttering invectives mostly at her oversized belly, but sometimes at the torn-up Holy Bible she kicked about. Occasionally, she kicked Goody Osborne.

Days ago, that invalid had slid down from the bench to the straw-covered dirt, moaning. Though mostly now she was unconscious. And it was the old midwife, Goody Nurse, who sat upon that bench now reading aloud from the Bible—although it wasn't her own Book she held, but the large worn yellowed one which had been abandoned when the widow fell. And she read aloud only those passages she deemed essential to others' ears.

Proud peahen sniffed Reverend Parris, staring in through that iron barred cell door.

He covered his nose when it was unlocked for him, for the enclosure stank feral with the scent of unwashed, anxiety-ridden aging female bodies. And from an overfull chamber pot filled with feces and urine, a stench no covering straw could stanch.

He strode past Tituba without a sidewise blink. But, really, the slave was glad for it, because she worried for the child, who'd been pulled from her arms by the jailers. Had her master tried to grab her she'd have resisted him, too, for the sake of leaving that tyke with this clump of faces, even for a sight of John.

Rebecca Nurse noticed him walking up. She extended her hand.

Reverend Parris withheld his. Which was no different from her husband withholding tithes—for he'd not seen a penny in goods or coin from any member of the miserly Nurse bunch in half a year. Though never did they miss any of his sermons or lectures.

"The Lord has sent you to me, Reverend Parris. He has heard my humble prayer," she announced loudly.

Before Reverend Parris could denounce her for a fraud, the beggar swung in between them like a globe on a post, cackling: "That's not who she asked! She asked the Old Boy! I heard her!"

He shoved Goody Good aside, addressing only Goody Nurse: "I've come not to console you, Rebecca, but to urge you to confess your witchcraft to God."

"But I know nothing about any witchcraft! Would you want me to belie myself to God?" Insulted now, she swatted at a horsefly buzzing by her ear, one of a plague of them in this room. Reverend Parris felt a sudden barb in his. *Image magic. She stabs me with her image magic.* He backed away, while she continued tongue-lashing him: "Were I even to speak such a falsehood, then who will answer to God for my lie on Judgment Day? Will you, Reverend Parris? And do not fib, for God is listening."

He raised his hand. "I see you are yet too proud to confess your sin. Know it is you alone who condemns your self to Hell's eternal torment. I had hoped to save your soul before your *excommunication*. On Sabbath Day hence, you're to be abandoned to the Devil." His message delivered, he retreated with haste. At the door, he shouted for a jailer to unlock it.

A moment later he was gone.

And now that great-grandmother fell forever from her bench of certainty. Her piety was rejected. Her Rock of Faith cast into a bottomless pit. The True Church was expelling her.

Reverend Parris heard a high-pitched squeal. The door wasn't locked and when he opened it, he viewed the beggar imp, Dorcas Good, the one who'd attacked his children in front of him, bound neck to heels on a tabletop. He went in. She was simpering, blood trickling from her nose. She was terrified . . . deservedly. Although he approved of their method of repeated pinches and buffeting slaps, he did not see them succeeding:

"Your mother made you a witch, didn't she?" "Has she familiars? Demons that do her bidding?" "Have you a familiar, Dorcas Good?"

He waved the jailers aside, asking in a more pleasing, though oily tone: "But we already know that she does. So it is better if you tell us about it. You recognize me, don't you? You've seen me before, haven't you? Aren't I the minister who has a daughter? Well, these men are also fathers. They did not mean to hurt you, or frighten you, and will not do so again while I stand beside as your friend."

He told the jailers to remove her bindings. "Is that better now?" he asked leaning in, because he, too, had questions. "Have you ever seen your mother with a cat?" (Dorcas didn't answer, because now that she could suck her thumb she did.) "Perhaps it was a black cat? Or a black bird . . . or yellow birds?" Her blank eyes darted from his face.

He took out his pocket kerchief and instructed her to press it against her nose. "What about you, Dorcas? Have *you* an animal familiar, some little creature that does your bidding, a woodland playmate, perhaps? If you tell me what it is, these fathers will take you back to your mother." Dorcas looked up unsure: "Green wriggle snake? Frog?" Reverend Parris nodded.

The Afflicted Girls

Glad should I have been, if I had never known the Name of this Man; or never had this occasion to mention so much as the first Letters of his Name. But the Government requiring some Account of his Trial to be inserted in this Book, it becomes me with all Obedience to submit unto the Order.

> "The Trial of Rev. George Burroughs of Wells, Maine, formerly of Salem Village, August, 1692" Excerpt from <u>Wonders of the Invisible World</u>; Cotton Mather (1693)

64

THE CHIEF CONSTABLE IN SALEM TOWN ALSO oversaw constabularies inside his Essex County jurisdiction. Occasionally, he visited. Arriving in Salem Village today, he sent the new-appointed junior constable to summon the old one back. After Willard was brought, he sent that fellow on a longer errand — to Rowley to arrange for his arrival.

It was on his recommendation that Willard had been hired originally. They were friends. And now the Chief Constable handed him the newest stack of complaints filed by various local parties. "Your replacement seems more eager to collect fees for each writ served and warrant issued than to serve your citizens justice. Were it up to me, John, I'd lock up them that's bewitched before all in this place are named witches and wizards."

Willard said he'd have done it had he understood the grim fact. He took them over to the bench by the door, and sat and began reading. And not much later, when some persons entered, he didn't look up from his commission.

"This wench has a complaint to lodge," Thomas Putnam announced, but then paused when he saw it was the Chief Constable of Salem Town sitting at the desk and not the newly appointed member of their faction. Reverend Parris, who had entered behind him, didn't care and told him to continue. So now Thomas slapped the serving wench forward, mentioning how there had once been a minister at the village church—

"Un-ordained, thus not actually a minister but a preacher," Reverend Parris corrected.

"Who fled in the middle of one night owing money to my father, unpaid to this date, which occurred not long after he murdered his wife at the parsonage," Thomas divulged.

The Chief Constable wondered, "So is your complaint for mayhem, theft, or murder?" He shot Willard a glance that lacked amusement.

Which made Reverend Parris look behind him, and when he spied an enemy listening to their business, he pinched Thomas' arm, whispering that they should not yet state a word of it. But Thomas was already blabbering: "Though a murder did occur, which I know for a fact, because that woman's ghost appeared to my goodwife crying out for vengeance, saying how he'd choked her and also stabbed her to death, sealing her wounds with wax to prevent her blood leaking—"

"But that's not this wench's complaint," interjected the minister, stating the point clearly: "This girl knew that imposter minister in another place. So it is hardly a coincidence that she resides now in the house of Thomas Putnam, where the murdered woman's ghost appeared and where evil afflictions arose, after arising also in mine where that fiend had once dwelled. Because from the first day this man served in Salem Village, the Devil found a roost here." He fumbled through his papers and handed one to the Chief Constable. "I have copied this precisely from the Village Book of Record, confirming the dates of his employment." He handed him a second paper. "And this is a copy of that wife's certificate of death."

The Afflicted Girls

The Chief Constable reviewed both documents. "One states no cause, only that she died and was buried. Neither one says it was murder . . . and money isn't mentioned." He set both documents down.

Thomas argued, "Because the agreement wasn't written! Till his dying day my father, who hired him, only ever used a handshake!"

Reverend Parris grimaced.

All this while, John Willard had been glancing between the two buffoons, trying to decide which one deserved to be pilloried first. He eyed the girl, also, wondering her part in it. Of course, he remembered her.

Reverend Parris handed the Chief Constable a third page he deemed *enlightening.* "A letter to me from an almshouse proctor in Maine, explaining how this girl once served in that false minister's house. I was the person who arranged for her to serve in Thomas Putnam's. But you will understand it better, when you hear the rest. Remembering how it was in our own two households that children were first afflicted." He nodded to Thomas, who swatted Mercy on her back.

Who did she fear more? She glanced between her master and the minister, praying God would make this consequence fall on them. A name was spoken, which slithered up from her depths, bringing with it all the bitterness of her ruin: "Concerning my former master, Reverend George Burroughs of Maine—" she didn't recount all of her sordid tale, just enough to convince them true evil had occurred.

☙❦☙

Reverend George Burroughs of Wells, Maine, formerly of Salem Village, for days now had been sitting in chains on the passenger's seat of a traveling coach locked between two sheriffs, looking out through the isinglass windows on either side, wondering where he was being taken; for no one had yet told him. But this morn, he began recognizing local landscapes and guessed it was regarding very old unpaid debts. For in few places was money more valued than in Salem Village.

After the coach parked in the inn yard, and after he stepped ably down despite his wrist and ankle cuffs, he finger-combed his hair, which was jet-black and without a strand of gray in it, and then smiled showing nary a wrinkle and perfect teeth.

These northern sheriffs had guessed he was in his middle thirties, like they were. Which Reverend Burroughs didn't disclaim although he was well past fifty. His skin was clear and taut as a blushing maid's, because he used potions. And underneath his black minister's coat was a body cast of sinew.

"I would prefer to stand," Reverend Burroughs stated after being ushered into a dingy-lit upstairs chamber where shutters were drawn and several men were standing. "Or would you prefer I sit?"

"I'll ask the questions . . . and y-yes, you are to stand." Chief Justice Stoughton of Boston had armed himself for this interview through fasting and prayer, but grew nervous, nonetheless, in this initial encounter knowing the history of that godless stare. "What God do you serve, Mister Burroughs?"

"The same God that man serves," Burroughs answered, noting Reverend Parris' minister's garb.

"Your accuser claims otherwise, sir," the Chief Constable of Salem Town advised, as he stepped up into the torchlight.

"My accuser? And who is that, sir, may I ask?"

"Your former servant," blurted Reverend Parris. "A girl called 'Mercy Lewis.'"

The Afflicted Girls

Chief Justice Stoughton frowned. *Stupid man.* He hadn't wanted the accuser's name divulged, lest something supernatural assault her prior to her testimony.

Reverend Burroughs seemed genuinely surprised. He said he hadn't thought of that orphan in years. "I took her in for a time in Christian charity. But as I remember, she was a severely troubled child, who listened in at doorjambs, and often returned goodwill with spite."

Reverend Parris grew emboldened. "Worse had been said of you, sir!"

"And not of you, sir?" mocked Burroughs.

Reverend Parris flustered, "No sir, not of me."

65

ALTHOUGH HER UNCLE HAD TWICE DESCRIBED his unsettling encounter with the black minister at the inn, Abigail felt unsatisfied. Because he'd ignored more questions than answered.

So now in a wee hour, she tiptoed into his library to consult his books about the matter. Tilting her head sidewise reading spine titles, but smartly tonight not her candlestick, so tomorrow no wax spatters would be left on the floor as evidence:

> _The Alchemist;_ by Ben Jonson (1610)
>
> _Daemonologie;_ by King James I (1597)
>
> _Saducismus Triumphatus;_ by Joseph Glanvil (1677)
>
> _A Treatise Proving Spirits, Witches and Supernatural Operations;_ by Meric Casaubon (1672)
>
> _Melampronoea: A Discourse of the Polity and Kingdom of Darkness;_ by Henry Hallywell (1681)
>
> _Wonderfull Discoverie of Witches in the Countie of Lancaster;_ by Thomas Potts (1613)
>
> _The Displaying of Supposed Witchcraft;_ by John Webster (1677)
>
> _A Discourse on the Damned Art of Witchcraft;_ by William Perkins (1608)
>
> _A Perfect Discovery of Witches;_ by Thomas Ady (1661)

The Afflicted Girls

Daimonomageia. A Treatise of Sicknesses and
Diseases from Witchcraft and Supernatural
Causes; by William Drage (1665)

This last was the book she chose, because its author had a name suited to a black minister. She took it to the desk and sat and opened it to the frontispiece: *To learn the rules of demonology whereby innocents are afflicted.*

Outside now, John Indian was heading off to his midnight vigil underneath the jailhouse window. He noticed a light flickering in the master's study and walked over and peered in. He saw her, the *nastee girl, one put trouble on Tituba.* Also saw that heavy book she was reading. *Good as a shovel crack 'er coconut. Mast'r find 'er dead morrow morn, he think some witch done it.*

Abigail sensed malice. Whirling around, she saw no one behind her. She grew nervous. *Was the black minister on the prowl? This house had once been his. He knew its every nook and cranny and even murthered his wife in one.* She rushed from the room without straightening her uncle's desktop, or picking up his Jerusalem Bible from the floor where she'd set it, or returning that heavy William Drage book to the third shelf, or even grabbing up her candlestick, which by now had dripped a hill of wax onto her uncle's ledger.

In her shuddering rush to safety, she stubbed her big toe on a step so hard the toenail would blacken tomorrow. But she swallowed that cry till she had reached her bedchamber. She quickly pulled the coffer to the door as a wedge, and put the tinderbox atop it and stuffed tinder inside the keyhole (her aunt kept the keys, so she couldn't lock him out).

Disappearing underneath her coverlet, she keenly listened for gliding steps or ghostly whispers. She also thought about what would happen on the morrow when her uncle found his things so amiss. *Well, mightn't she say an imp had done it?* But her candlestick was the telltale! *Well, couldn't an imp have filched it while she slept? Or better . . . the black minister himself?*

When next Abigail awoke in the dark she was in a high state of confusion. Then suddenly a flash of divine insight came, and she knew it was rag dolls she must make on the morrow; perhaps, because it was the chapter she'd been reading.

The next morn, after her aunt had traipsed off with Mrs. Ingersoll to visit merchants, she searched the rag and mending piles for old cloths of her aunt's. Upstairs, she fetched the scissors and slit the underside of her mattress picking out tufts of horsehair.

Later when she laid her two dolls upon the bed-top, though sewn hastily and lopsided, she was excited. From Betty's pincushion she took out a pin; then stopped, for she'd just remembered something else, nearly forgotten, that was wrapped in an apron and stuffed inside her winter bonnet at the bottom of her chest. She retrieved Tituba's voodoo necklace and put it around her neck, and now took all the headless pins, and stuck her two puppets—one rusty dull, the other faded blue—reciting a charm she'd learned from William Drage's book, picturing the two persons she utmost hated—Aunt Ugly and Bridget Bishop:

> *Each pin stuck into this head,*
> *Into hers go till she is dead.*
> *Each pin stuck into this heart*
> *Into hers go till she depart.*

She had diligently searched the rag pile for something belonging to her aunt, but found no discarded cloth. The insect was no spendthrift. Knowing that she dare not use an item currently worn, she settled on one that was her own and red-stained. And for her second doll, the ugly doll, she cut up that dull blue dress abandoned by Betty—the Sunday twill she'd once admired—that was near enough in hue to *gray.*

The Afflicted Girls

"Mother! Father! I am bewitched!" cried Elizabeth Porter sitting up in bed, tearing at her head, as both parents in their nightclothes came running into her chamber. Struggling to rise to go to them, her legs collapsed underneath her. The floor had opened up. Hell was sucking her down its foul spout. Jetsam rammed and bruised her.

But that was likely her father swooping her up into his arms and carrying her back to her bed, while Lizzie Porter felt her girl's forehead. "A high fever," she whispered worriedly to her husband. *Far too high,* she told herself.

By now, Dr. Griggs was used to being awakened after midnight—though little could be done for the witchcraft victims, except to pray for God's intervention, and protection. That same advice was given to the prominent freeman who'd pounded at his door demanding service. He advised him: "A Black Death which seeps under Christian doors as easily as under Pharaoh's, cannot be stemmed by me."

But when that man opened his purse and offered to pay any price, although Dr. Griggs preferred his bed and knew his medicines would be useless, still he packed his bag with ointments, tonics, tinctures, potions, plasters, metals, leeches, every pill he'd manufactured and instrument he possessed, and dressed quickly, and went. Because this was wealthy Israel Porter, whose afflicted child was quite pretty, possibly ripe for the plucking, if not by the Devil, by him.

66

THE LARGEST LOOM MERCY HAD EVER THREADED was strung now with the multi-colored yarns dyed and wheel-spun by her three diligent apprentices, part of their education in the art of the spinster and weaver.

She'd first taught the children using handmade tacked twig squares and tufts of fleece they'd found stuck on thorn-bushes. When that collection of woven squares grew into handfuls, she began teaching them how to bleach and stew wool in small vats, into diverse colors harvested by themselves from the dooryard garden or wild nature: middle green out of coltsfoot, darker green from motherwort, pink from dandelion, red from beet, varying yellows from Dyers broom, goldenrod and marigold, orange from an onion, blue from hollyhock, purple and brown from different heathers, and black from the root of yellow-dock, the only plant that produced that color.

The loom itself dwarfed the barn's biggest cow, being nine feet tall, five feet across, and wide enough to weave a seamless blanket for a married couple. When it first appeared in an unused corner of the barn, she and Lucy were puzzled. Especially Lucy, who had never before seen such an apparatus, and couldn't know that it was in fact her mother's own property, which one day would be her livelihood. She guessed, as did Mercy, that her father had borrowed or bartered for it so that she and her sisters could develop earning skills. But today, she discovered that weaving was a labor more taxing than milking.

Now while this loom might belong to her family's matrilineal heritage, not once in married life had her formerly privileged mother Ann Putnam ever used it; insisting, instead, that all cloth be purchased mercantile. And it had been for years. But now Thomas couldn't afford purveyed yardage. So his wife and children were made to make do with whatever ill-fitting hand-me-downs his one sister, who had offspring, offered.

Years ago, he'd taken this loom apart for its wood, intending to use it in building the extra wing. When that room was left unfinished, the pieces were stored in a shed. Left to crack, warp, splinter and grow wormy. But recently, when he observed his servant teaching his tykes their warps and woofs on a small nailed square, he remembered that old loom and decided to rebuild it. He hauled what pieces he could find up to the barn and reassembled them like a puzzle, not to perfection, but workable enough. That night he went up to his sheepfold and sheared a yearling and left a pile of fleece. Because woolens, even badly wove, could earn him more shillings than a raw bundle would.

So, in part, Lucy Putnam had guessed rightly.

❧❀❧

"It's getting dark," complained Lucy as the sunlight began to fade. Even then, her sisters refused to depart the high pasture, wanting to play more with the newborn lambs. They'd come up here three hours ago to gather tufts and berries and were surprised to find those babies born, and already standing up. It was a pleasant afternoon spent. She was content until her siblings wouldn't obey her command to come home. So she picked up their baskets, and warned them they'd get lost in the dark or punished.

Her friend wasn't at the hearth when she came in, although a stew was bubbling on the fender. Was Mercy in the parlor or upstairs? She looked but didn't find her. So she came back to the kitchen and lifted the lid off the pot. It was a fish stew cooking— her own least favorite supper to be sure. Which meant that Mercy had gone fishing without her, while she went berry picking with her sisters. She frowned. She'd much rather have fished with Mercy than eaten cobbler with them.

Thoughts of fishing with Mercy summoned thoughts of a magical fish. So she fetched the family Bible from the parlor and sat, searching through the pages for the new favorite, the "Book of Tobias." When she couldn't find it, she told the fable aloud to herself, in between nibbling blackberries and thimbleberries. At the part where the offal was put inside the bridal bed to vanquish the demon, in the midst of that great victory, the kitchen door burst open startling her, and her hand accidentally knocked her basket to the floor. And now her bad uncle, Joseph Putnam, worse than any demon, stomped those precious berries and grabbed her arm and yanked her up from the bench, ordering her: "Get me your mother."

Neighs and barks awoke Mercy, who was taking rest under an elm. At once, she hurried up the yard to see who'd arrived before that person went inside, and called out and bothered the mistress. Most likely it was a Walcott son, bringing something from his mother. Instead, she saw Joseph Putnam's horse by the trough, nipping at their mongrel. And knowing that he would never come here in daylight for her, except to betray her, she rushed into the kitchen. "Do you mean to give me away to them?" He outstretched his hand. "Stand away from me, limb of the Devil."

"I beg you not to, Joseph."

"If my betrothed dies," he promised, "I'll tear your black heart out from your body and feed it to that jackal dog."

The Afflicted Girls

She retreated to a corner, not to cry. Enough tears had been shed already for this selfish man who hated her.

By now, footsteps were flying down the stairs. Ann Putnam's eyes goggled seeing her enemy inside her kitchen. Pushing her daughter aside, she grabbed the first thing within reach—an iron skillet. Brandishing it, she stormed the usurper. "Be gone from my house! Satan's son!"

Joseph easily wrested away the pan and threw it down gouging a floorboard. He grabbed his in-law's arm, forcing her face up close to his: "If you or any of your household dare hurt any in mine—or those bound for it, Ann Putnam—you'll pay for it with this house." Too stunned to retort, she followed him out and now screamed out her warning to him: "You're next! Devil's bastard! Next!" But his horse was already jumping the gate.

Returning in a fury and seeing her servant's tortured mien, she suddenly guessed what was behind it. She retrieved the skillet, and held it over Mercy, and swung down in such distemper that she would have killed her outright, had not Lucy yanked her backward by her skirt. So now Ann threatened her daughter instead. Before Mercy could get to her feet to protect the child, Lucy was struck and fell hard, and was about to be hit deadly, if her mother had not noticed that open, accusing Bible staring out at her from the tabletop.

Her face drained in horror. She ran out from *His Sight*, a murderous mother!

67

BRIDGET BISHOP PROTESTED WHEN THE NEW junior constable and his deputy searched her cellar (even though she'd bit her tongue earlier while they were ransacking her upstairs quarters) . . . because these stores were sacred.

Armed with chisel, hammer, ax and awl, that official fool was breaking open every tar-sealed keg and cask, cutting open her apple sacks and grain sacks, a precious sugar sack, and a salt sack—she winced at both bad omens: the loss of sweetness, and of luck from spilling salt. He upended loose floorboards, and pried out suspect wallboards, and repeatedly kicked her cat.

He searched her chimneys, too. Doused the flames in the kitchen hearth and thrust the broom handle up into the shaft, moving it around, but bringing down only soot into her cook-pots. He did the same in her main hall fireplace. But in the shovelboard room, out from that cold chimney where no fire had lately been lit, he pulled two poppets—one sooty red, the other sooty blue. Headless pins were stuck in them.

"Those are not mine," she insisted.

But her denials and then face waxing pale convinced him that they were. He crowed to his deputy, "Vermin nest in chimneys . . . inventions like these do not. Unless some fey witch has put them there for a reason."

The Afflicted Girls

And then he accidentally stuck his finger on a pin in one and waxed even paler than Bridget.

⚜

John Willard's farmhouse had been combed through, and he was at this moment of Bridget's apprehension, sitting accused of wizardry and confined in a Boston jail cell amid thieves and thugs, and two confused men from his own village.

Nonetheless, he counted himself lucky. His wife had been spared. Because when the new junior constable came to arrest them, upon seeing his face, perhaps recalling his connection to Salem Town's Chief Constable a blind eye was turned to his wife and twin sons. And in that one stolen moment, he had urged his wife to flee. Today he learned that she was safe when his friend, the Chief Constable, paid an unofficial visit and informed him she'd escaped to Connecticut to her mother, who was his own second cousin. He also explained that it was Thomas Putnam who had filed the complaint, along with an affidavit claiming how in less than a year as junior constable he had brought about the unnatural deaths of numerous individuals in order to steal their properties, said the Chief Constable.

"An odious, ridiculous lie," Willard insisted. Because everyone knew how part of a constable's lawful employment was to take possession of a deceased's lock-box, particularly when that person's cash, deeds, titles and legal instruments might be locked up inside it. But only to safeguard, of course, until a certificate of death could be issued, a funeral arranged, relations notified, and the will read to them. It had been his official duty to protect estates. He only had done his duty, he insisted.

The Chief Constable said he didn't doubt it. But that Putnam was claiming how before a body was even a day cold, that he, Willard, would have foisted an offer to purchase that abode and abandoned land lot, and farmland, and sometimes even the household chattels, which either a grieving or impoverished relation was likely to accept.

Well, that part was true, Willard admitted. Nevertheless, he always assessed a fair value, and sometimes paid the full price. He said he believed firmly that Putnam's accusation was the result of one particular property he'd obtained in that way—the farm tract and farmhouse on the sunnier, fertile side of Thomas Putnam's hill.

The Chief Constable agreed that was likely.

But the truth, although connected, was really Ann Putnam's even firmer belief that this neighboring farmstead to theirs had been purchased by a *fiend* hoping to aid the Devil in carving out an unnatural kingdom. It was she, not her husband, who first cried out upon John Willard, although Thomas, not she, had signed and lodged the complaint.

Because in her blighted mind, this young wealthy landgrubbing neighbor was as choice a substitute for Joseph Putnam as the old midwife had been for the usurping mother-in-law, Mary Veren. Both men were in their twenties, carried themselves with pompous airs, wore clothes cut from expensive cloth, ate rich meats three times daily (while her tykes ate mostly gruel), owned more land and livestock than they ought to in God's Kingdom, and suffered no money problems—but rather, made others suffer them.

The Afflicted Girls

PART NINE

68

A FIFTY YEAR OLD OAK OF COMMUNITY WAS SPLIT down the middle and the vilest, most sulfurous sap was spilling out catching all in its glue, even prominent freemen. One faction was gathered tonight at Putnam Estate by Mary Veren Putnam's invitation, her attempt to further a son politically. Without asking, she had joined the discussion in the parlor, at times offering comments, but mostly prompting Joseph's.

And when she retired, finally, these men revived their sagging spirits, admitting to each other more openly now, how they minced their words in public fearing invisible watchers. Then they worked.

Francis Nurse fell into a rage when his proposal was flatly rejected, after Israel Porter advised how an appeal on Rebecca's behalf would be fruitless and ill-timed — his reason being that the new Massachusetts Charter was nipping long-held civil liberties forcing the populace back under the royal wing, and that noisy protests were rising up all over New England with calls for tar-and-feathering Phips. Thus, how that new governor was occupied with saving himself, and no one else. Porter reminded his faction: "Let us be mindful of our purpose tonight: how on the morrow, we begin our search for a new minister, one who'll restore sanity to this village. We'll soon be rid of the canker."

Francis Nurse said he no longer cared. And then spoke not another word.

When the meeting disbanded, Israel followed him out. He stopped him from mounting his horse, explaining what he couldn't say in public or inside that particular house: "What fuels Rebecca's nightmare, Francis, is that you were a witness to Putnam's will. They've seen your name written at the bottom."

"But it was you who made me sign it!"

"That's why I grieve for what's happened to her. I suffer as much for Rebecca as I do for my own daughter. Believe me, friend, you have my sympathy."

"What? Your sympathy that just refused to save her?"

Israel answered nothing. But he gave the angry codger a foot up. And then watched as Francis jogged his nag to the gate. It was wrong for the man to blame him. No one could have foreseen this, if even Bridget couldn't, who for years had read his tea leaves advising him on every business venture, including Putnam's will. He called for his carriage. But soon realized he'd forgotten his hat, and returned to the house to retrieve it.

Going against Francis Nurse had upset him. For that was a good man, though not an important one. Yet, what did that matter, when someone's wife was being crushed under so great and terrible a weight? He wondered if he'd fight as hard if his own wife Lizzie were taken? He couldn't quite picture it, but would admit that he didn't love her in that same strong obstinate way Francis did Rebecca. How if Lizzie were taken for a witch, he wouldn't miss her nettling silliness, frills, or pricey gewgaws, and definitely not her fatty rinds. But, of course, he would fight to free her, same as Francis. For in motherhood, she was unparalleled, and his daughter would succumb without her. And while it would sadden him to lose his wife, losing his daughter would undo him. So he *could* understand how Francis Nurse felt.

(Yet, Ann Putnam never would have accused Lizzie Porter, and not because of her family ties to a magistrate—but because they had never had a connection. And neither would Thomas Putnam accuse him. Though he, like Francis Nurse, had witnessed Putnam's will—was not just its witness, as a matter of fact, but was its actual drafter. Because should he, or his wife be accused, unlikely as that was, he could argue how his own child was afflicted as sorely as was Thomas Putnam's. And Dr. Griggs, with his greedy open palm, would testify to it, or any other truth he paid for.)

He spied his hat on a small table near the parlor doorway. As he walked up, he noticed Joseph Putnam sitting inside in an armchair. So he went in and sat in the opposite chair, and picked up the tobacco caddy and suggested they smoke a pipe. Not unlike a father to an in-law son. He commented about the tobacco's unusual taste, and was informed it was a blend of three sugar-cured strains of African origin purchased in Old England as a gift for Joseph's father. He lamented that good man's passing, but heard no comment back; and now was unable to catch the boy's eye again, or get any response to anything he said. So he finished his pipe in silence.

He then asked for a glass of the liqueur Joseph was drinking, and was told it was an inebriant popular in London salons, which he knew meant *brothels*. Joseph poured him a glass.

He detected the ingredient *wormwood* for heightening pleasure. He was a worldly man, so he drank slowly, while observing his future son through a diffusing veil, picturing his daughter in such unhappy arms, wondering if anything would ever improve the boy's moroseness.

And they sat like that in silence a long while.

When the candle stood an inch shorter, Joseph looked up abruptly and smiled, "Let us drink to your daughter's health, that I may marry her the sooner."

"May your words herald it," slurred Israel, pleased. He knew the breadth of the Putnam estate. Knew he had no need to attach a rich dowry to his only daughter; this boy had no use for it. Yet, he discussed in piecemeal, once again, what she would bring to the marriage, unwilling to consider any other outcome.

While Joseph drank more absinthe, shuttering his ears to that inventory, because this man's insipid moth, however long she flitted, however large her fortune, however blank her face, would bring him nothing but nothing. But because for his sake she'd been afflicted, for hers now, so was he.

∾❦∿

Rebecca Nurse's excommunication came and went without fanfare, was barely noticed in her parish with so many new faces present. A quarter of these current brethren lived in other places, but as they'd all done commerce with Salem villagers and had their names and professions known, they lived in fear of being named as witches or wizards, too. So they had abandoned their own churches and now flocked here with their kin on Sundays.

"Doomsday is imminent," bellowed Reverend Parris taking for today's inspiration Wigglesworth's fine book: <u>Day of Doom</u>. Gloomy subjects had always intrigued him, sparking those latent flicks of madness his maternal bloodline carried, which in today's simmering weather—which was so apt for the excommunication of a witch—further fanned his fervor.

> "The blessed in Heaven look down with joy
> upon the torments of the damned. Because there
> is never to be any mercy on those God destines
> for damnation—"

The Afflicted Girls

He dabbed his sweat-dotted forehead as he perused the attentive roomful. *Were any here damned?* He caught sight of one who was, but who didn't matter—John Indian.

That parsonage slave stood where he usually did in summer, as ordered to by his master: at the rear, propping open the wide meetinghouse doors, standing there as sentry. He was clutching his wide-brimmed Sunday straw hat that Tituba had made him, not listening to the master's babble, thinking only his own spirit thoughts.

"Every sin deserves God's wrath and curse, both
in this life, and that which is to come—"

Abigail was wilting, sitting beside the *praying mantis* trying to ignore her aunt's profusion of stinky sweat.

"If ever there were witches, men and women in
covenant with the Devil, here then there are
multitudes . . . which itself is a sign that
Doomsday is imminent—"

She forced her mind back to *him*. But then her nose once more succumbed. So down to the floor she went, not exactly in a faint or fit, rather in sensual trance-like slithering, and viperously bit that offending ankle, though not too hard. This time, the insect didn't even flinch. (For Mrs. Parris had grown accustomed to these sudden attacks from Abigail. Which usually startled but never injured.)

But loud gasps arose suddenly from other corners of the room when a crow flew in through the doorway and alit on an overhead beam, began cawing, and then splat on a goodman's head and into a goodwife's lap. For although small birds often flew round the meetinghouse in summer months, never once till now had a crow ever dared to enter.

John Doritch guffawed at the plight of that muddled couple as he filled his slingshot with handfuls of rye-seed, and then showered a swathe of wide-brimmed hats and laps. Goodwives screamed, raising arms to defend from that hellish downpour protecting youngsters. Whereas, the children laughed when that angry bird flapped and swooped—after it, too, felt that sting.

But like his wife, Reverend Parris ignored even *that* devil's mischief and preached continuously throughout. For he was also, now, used to it.

Lucy Putnam recognized the crow. It was the one that always sat on the meetinghouse roof, eying village doings. She didn't mind it at all. But after it was chased and flew out, something truly awful occurred: her mother stood up and shouted that a "perfidious witch" had infiltrated her household.

At once, her father grabbed Mercy from between her sisters and began dragging her friend up the aisle. *Perfidious?*

Shades of a slaughtered calf and a sacrificial lamb prompted Mercy to struggle and twist to get away from him. Thomas lost his grip on her, too. And now she propelled herself forward to the pulpit, shoving the minister aside and shouting out what she needed to tell them . . . before she couldn't anymore: "This man is a false minister! He preaches a dark Gospel not of our Lord! This church is Hellish! It turns children fiendish! It crucifies innocents! Turn away from him, good people! You must!"

Reverend Parris dug his long fingernails into her cheek and drew down the length of it. (For it was common knowledge that scratching a witch's face and drawing blood from it broke her power.) But to everyone's horror, most of all his, she did the same to him, and then punched him so hard in the heart with her milking fist, he crumpled to one knee. She looked down at him.

"You are a weak, pathetic, soulless man. I pity you at best, for the ignorant must be pitied. But God, if He is God, will hold you accountable . . . on your *Day of Doom*, Reverend Parris." And now Mercy's eyes closed to what she knew was coming next.

And this was the moment John Indian got his *Answer*. He backed out from the meetinghouse, closing those double doors behind him, and ran home to the parsonage straight to his master's room of books. He grabbed a devil-dog andiron and smashed the wooden lock-box into pieces. He stuffed his pockets full and a sow's-ear pouch with notes and silver coin, and a few of Spanish gold. And then, with that useful andiron still clutched, he decided to go get his wife and hammer her jailers dead. But Tituba's clear voice filled his ears:

> *Save yerself. I wants ya to, John. Ya know I seen this comin'. Take you an inn horse. Go where ya wants. No arguin' 'bout it if ya loves yer Tituba. I be followin'.*

No one observed him when he galloped that fine looking saddled beast out from Ingersoll's stable into the woods. Nor would they have known who he was, dressed as he was in the innkeeper's city suit and traveling cloak and high hat, and riding boots, and also wearing his master's soft white silk mourning gloves he'd always coveted. He took his master's walking stick, too. Because he was the one who'd carved it.

The position of sun and smell of sea steered him rightly through forest to Salem Town Bay. But he bypassed that place, after Tituba whispered again. He followed the coastline southward till he reached Boston Town harbor. The horse ran swift. He arrived before eventide.

He left that animal tied to a quayside post; but first unhitched its fancy-pants saddle to keep, giving a lad a coin to fetch it hay and water. Shambling off, humming to fight his fright, he saw a ship readying its sails. Having sailed once on the high sea, frightening though it was, he knew that staying was the greater danger. And he'd learned enough in his menial life of observation to go barter with its captain for a berth—he didn't know to where, and didn't need to: *Go where ya wants . . . I be followin'.* But he had the good sense, all on his *clever* own, to use only his slaver father's tongue.

Every rogue who saw or overheard this *Blackamore* giant on the quayside—putting forth his queries in French and opening a stuffed sow's-ear purse in plain sight of pickpockets—guessed he was a fearsome freebooter. And didn't approach.

The ship's captain, however, decided that his well-dressed black-skinned white-gloved gentleman passenger, holding an expensive saddle, and a walking stick, was not so much a North African pirate, like his crew all supposed, but a *harlequinades* actor from the London Drury Lane or the Paris *Funambules*; as he'd once conveyed a troupe of such actors and dwarfs (a French Blackamore pygmy among them) from European ports to port.

He grew convinced of it later, when at high seas heading to England, he heard his passenger sing.

≈✦≈

Nathaniel Ingersoll's patron did not learn of his loss until he was standing outside in the inn yard waiting for his horse to be brought. (Which luckily for Ingersoll, occurred right after he'd been paid for three days lodging and board.) When he gave the man a hem-haw and blamed the theft on witch-mischief, they nearly came to blows. Instead, the man huffed off to fetch a constable.

Across the green about this time, Reverend Parris with his Cain's brand on his cheek greeted no parishioners on his church threshold, and thus received no tithes. Embarrassed, he locked himself inside the empty meetinghouse, waiting until the green had emptied also. Then with his hat held covering his cheek, he sprinted home across his pasture, and did not expect that standing inside his gate would be Nathaniel Ingersoll in an equal state of agitation. And because this was his benefactor, he had to listen and advise:

The Afflicted Girls

"Say to your patron, Nathaniel, 'Am I my brother's keeper? Do I control the vicissitudes of fortune?'"

Ingersoll scoffed, "Well, I, too, have vicissitudes, Sam, which are long overdue. But if you promise to pay me back the money you owe before my patron sues me, I promise I won't sue you."

Reverend Parris flustered. And now he was forcibly made to agree to pay Ingersoll a fifth of what was owed now—though barely could he manage that—with the rest to follow in smaller monthly sums. They went inside to conclude the unfriendly commerce. And that's how Reverend Parris discovered—to his horror—that he, too, had been robbed! Every shilling, note, crown, doubloon ever secretly hoarded was gone! Only pence remained! And to add insult to the injury, the innkeeper, even after viewing the room in a shambles and seeing his minister's moneybox splintered, still insisted he receive his payments in the manner just agreed. Or, Ingersoll mumbled as an afterthought, he *could* take the chattel of John Indian for six months . . . in lieu of money.

And that was how Reverend Parris discovered that John Indian was missing, too!

69

REBECCA NURSE SQUINTED IN LATE AFTERNOON shadows, reading aloud in the overcrowded women's cell in a kind gesture toward Goody Osborne. Because it was her duty to remind a dying tenant of God's Covenant about the coming Resurrection and Redemption, despite that she, herself, wasn't counted such anymore.

Having attended innumerable deathwatches in her life, she did the same now that she always did. Though she did wonder why no doctor had been to see Ruth, because the woman might have lived had her festering head wound been treated with a common physick. How many times had she told the jailers that?

Her mouth had turned dry from reading. She tried moistening her sore cracked lips, thinking once more about that sad neglect. Then she began clucking censoriously about callousness in a Christian, that particular *Christian* on her tongue being a doctor named Griggs. (Who unbeknownst had been summoned here, but refused to come. Unwilling as he was now to wrestle the Devil for any life . . . even that of a wealthy widow he'd once or twice bedded.) Of course, all the goodwives here agreed, but without saying so.

All, that is, except the harrier, Sarah Good, who was half-heartedly suckling a wailing newborn on an emaciated breast, muttering curses in between the midwife's clucking and the rich-wife's rasping, and everyone else's moans and groans. Two nights ago, she'd left that unwanted heap of new flesh lying on the straw. The Indian got her to nurse it by bartering to confess her own self as the curse-monger. She muttered "aye" to it. Why not? She wasn't its cause.

But did these condescending white caps give a hoot? They all thought her guilty when she wasn't, condemned her because of her pox and poverty, shunned and out-cast her, even though she was once one of them—was a good wife to a good man, who miserably died after one of their husbands ran him over with a wagon. She never was paid her due recompense, was paid only scorn. Her tyke Dorcas was that husband's issue. This one was a rapist's grunt.

So when she heard how their spouses had been carted to jails as wizards in even heavier chains than hers, she heard music and danced; also each time another piddling wail or moan rose up from that old wives' corner. (Because by now over one hundred fifty persons from all over Essex County sat confined in jail cells, closets, sheriffs' houses and constabularies in villages and townships all the way down to Boston. Locked up in heavy chains newly forged by every blacksmith and tinker the way south to Connecticut—because only bindings of iron could thwart a witch's spectre from going out and harming victims. Ropes were ineffectual.) *Costing a pretty penny, too,* she thought. Pennies never spared for her. *Well, they'll all soon see how metal rubs the skin raw.*

All, that is, except that witless 'other Sarah' who now stopped her rasping finally with her goner eyes fixing on nothing.

Sarah Good set down the babe and went and gave "Rich Osborne" a kick, wondering who'd get her money.

Bridget Bishop shooed her away, and felt for a pulse in the invalid's flabby neck. But the soul had already fled. And though Bridget hadn't known this woman personally or heard much concerning her deeds in life, she closed those sagging eyelids and kissed that mottled brow, and kneeled a moment in respectful silence and prayed; and only then rattled the dead woman's ankle chain, yelling for the jailers.

Strangely, watching that spectacle, Rebecca Nurse felt hopeful. Despite that Bridget Bishop was such a harlot, and Ruth Osborne had never been a friend, and barely could be counted an acquaintance and had a bad reputation to boot—nevertheless, she'd been one of the Chosen Covenant and was reuniting with the Lord right now in Heaven, and could convey a heartfelt plea from her! How this was all a mistake!

But then, just as suddenly, her countenance dimmed, realizing how the dead woman probably couldn't because of her excommunication from that *Covenant*—though unjustly and through no fault of her own—and so her Heavenly life was still uncertain. She was also trying to ignore the harlot's preachy fanfare about how death by disease was part and parcel of life but that death through persecution should be counted "a murder." She agreed, of course, but would never let Bridget Bishop know it.

All this while Tituba had been staring at the dead woman's flimsy spirit standing in crippled confusion between the worlds. She told it to hurry up and walk, or fly if it wanted; but it only limped away, dragging its leaden legs toward the door, which wasn't any barrier, and neither were these stone walls, though *it* still thought so, and stood waiting for the cell door to open.

Eventually that door opened and two jailers dragged in a new prisoner past the ghost.

Tituba knew who'd scratched this person's face—because he'd done it often enough to her. Though she was surprised to see that bright star so darkened, who once had sat at their table dipping her stale bread into cider, thinking deeper thoughts than most.

The Afflicted Girls

A jailer rolled the corpse. "Queer timing it is. Saves us a shilling." His nervous partner agreed. And now together they lifted that unholy burden onto his shoulder to carry out like a sack of potatoes, not bones. Both of them forgot the chain, till it snapped him to a halt. So now that shackle was quickly undone and clamped onto Mercy Lewis' ankle.

Rebecca Nurse sighed, "Doesn't God hear our hearts anymore?"

Sarah Good spat, "Shut up, sawsbox! Shut up, bawd witch!"

Bridget turned away from her shock at seeing Mercy to stem a different kind of wound: "Be respectful, Sarah Good. An innocent woman has just gone to her Maker because of a lie."

"Her, innocent?" cackled the beggar.

A lie? Though they'd hardly locked eyes, Mercy knew what she had to do. Her hand went up to that dangling touchstone and she pulled it from her neck. Then tossed it at Bridget, its giver, because *it* wasn't innocent, and because: "A lie belongs to its Maker. A lie, to its liar."

Bridget retrieved her necklace from the straw. This was a precious relic, no trifle. She tied the amulet around her own neck, wanting to say something—but not quarrelsome, because quarreling with Mercy Lewis was never easy. And although admitting her role might anger some here, she felt a need to defend herself. "Your hand told me life had cheated you, and that you were meant for a better one. But we embarked on this course together. Also, you came to me, not the reverse. Even so, my charm had no love in it, and the love you conjured had no charm in it. I might have tricked you to make you think so. I will not deny that. But what came from it came naturally . . . from you, from him . . . but not from my charm. That charm was never real. This one, however, was." She fingered her precious amulet and turned away in hurt, despite her opposite feeling.

Mercy answered soberly, "It was as real as what will come from it, Bridget. Yes, you did your best to trick me, to play God with my life, and with his . . . and still think it was for my benefit. But in the end, like Lucifer, you tricked only yourself. For after all my travails and unbearable shame suffered most of my life, it is only you who has murdered me . . . and murdered all these good women, and yourself."

Those goodwives clotted at the back of the cell feverishly began exchanging whispers.

Goody Nurse was all ears now, too, and turned her good ear back from those goodwives, as Mercy turned apologetic eyes toward them all: "A gallows is being built for us on Danvers Hill. We're going to be hanged."

Bridget was stunned. She had thought, at worst, the pillory. Before, it was *always* the pillory, and a fine. She reached to a post to steady herself, as blame and accusations from sharp tongues struck, because the finger had been pointed. But these were all envious wives of men who desired her, so she ignored them.

But in the days to come, doubt plowed through her till it reached her barren core. Much of the time she sat with that bitter backbone pressed against the stone, eyes dry as mulch, unaccepting of how she'd perched herself on a haughty lap, judging them insignificant and beneath her—unless, of course, they sought her advice then she'd care about them somewhat. But always absent of grief for their miseries. *Why?* Had she never cared about any girl's lovesickness . . . only *hers*? Nor was a real friend to any woman . . . not even to those she might have liked?

These goodwives scorned her rightly, huddling in their petty pack, shedding tears aplenty for each other like neighbors, and sisters, while she shed none, because she couldn't. Because the only lap it could have been was Lucifer's . . . and the only one to blame for what was coming to them all here was herself.

The Afflicted Girls

70

THE SEQUENCE WAS THE SAME FOR ALL PERSONS arrested: first came the swearing out of a complaint for acts of witchcraft, wizardry or idolatry; then an arrest; the gathering of evidence and taking of depositions; leading to a public examination conducted by magistrates, with both the accused and bewitched persons present; after which came an indictment; and lastly, the jury trial.

At any point during this process, to force out a confession, the "witch" or "wizard" might be tortured: for instance, locked inside a standing closet for nearly a week without food or drink.

"Starve me," Bridget urged weakly on the fifth day of her ordeal. "And when I die from thirst and hunger in this box, it will prove I was never a witch and that you murdered an innocent person. God will exact a high price for your treason. Because a witch, no less the Witch Queen you claim I am, would have flown her confinement or conjured up a feast, inviting you to share it."

Her circuitous, blasphemous logic convinced them of her guilt. This was no ordinary female. Certainly none of their mothers, and especially their wives, was ever so clever.

Today, Bridget's trial convened in the General Court of *Oyer and Terminer* in Salem Town.

For good reason had Chief Justice Stoughton summoned the entire Essex County militia to guard the courthouse. Because this was the *Witch Queen*, not a mere minion, who could waft curses up into clouds and rain down enough brimstone to poison an entire village. He had citizens to protect.

When the doors to the courthouse opened, people rushed in to find seats, including twenty-two young men of the Nurse clan, who had ignored their militia summonses, not out of fondness for Bridget Bishop. Well, Ben Nurse was fond of her, particularly fond of her love for the bawdy song. But like his brothers and cousins, father and uncles and grandfather, he'd come only because Granny Rebecca's trial was convening here next week.

His grandfather's petition to the governor, with so many prominent signatures upon it, including Israel Porter's in the end, offered no hope now. Because that highest official—the only one who could pardon his granny—was already weeks absent from Boston on a military campaign.

But even had that governor been sitting at his desk on the day that they delivered it, their appeal would have failed—failed, not for lack of supporting evidence, logic, proof of timely tax payments or the goodness of Goody Nurse herself. Failed, rather, because thirty years prior, when Willie Phips was an eleven years old ships-boy, he was proselytized into the True Faith by Increase Mather, who'd been a passenger on one ocean crossing, and who put him under his coat a few times and made him set high ambitions.

That same "Willie Phips" now occupied the high-most seat in Commonwealth politics, as well as the front-most pew at North Church, where both his Mather ministers, Increase and Cotton, had advised him *not* to interfere in *any* witchcraft proceeding, explaining how these were spiritual matters—not mere civil ones—which were best left to God to ultimately decide.

He, himself, had anchored his brigantine last night in an unmarked northern inlet and given orders to a hundred soldiers to prepare for battle on the morrow. He sat up hours more in his cabin with lieutenants plotting an offense against the French encroachers and their bloodletting savages. Not realizing that the greater threat to his King and colony was looming in his own seat of power: to the Common Good from bloodthirsty Salem villagers. Thus, as that northern battle was being fought and won, the one in the south was just beginning. But at least prior to sailing, he'd appointed a third magistrate to the judges' panel—Jonathan Corwin of Salem Town—who, while not as versed in Commonwealth law as the other two, was at least a man like himself who frowned on superstition. Because Phips knew he had to insure fair verdicts lest the citizens' current discontent foment into outright rebellion. So three judges would decide all pending witchcraft cases. And if that didn't work, next time, five.

⁓❧⁊

Chief Justice Stoughton had asked his minister, Cotton Mather, to attend the Salem Town trial of Bridget Bishop.

Yesterday, when they were driving up from Boston in his carriage, they discussed the children's afflictions. That evening they took lodgings at his favorite Salem Town inn and shared a supper, during which Cotton Mather mentioned a treatise he was planning to write should Bridget Bishop be convicted: "'Wonders of the Invisible World.'" "Horrors not 'Wonders,'" he quipped, thinking *of course she'll be convicted*. But later, when drifting into sleep, he did worry which magistrate, himself or Corwin, the waffler John Hathorne would agree with by the end, for that would determine whether Cotton Mather wrote his book. But at least he'd pulled the long straw, which meant that he'd be the one summarizing her crimes to the jury, and in that employ he could be persuasive. So it was more than likely the pendulum would swing to *justice* and the minister would write his book, and the Witch Queen would swing like a pendulum.

385

Folk were lined up at one side, hoping to present years' worth of grievances against Bridget Bishop; most of them she didn't know.

But the one currently taking his turn at the witness stand was Goodman Trask of Salem Village, and his was gruesome testimony. He told how his second wife went out of her right senses for a full month's time and at the end cut her own windpipe with a dull pair of sewing scissors; and he'd brought those very scissors to lodge as evidence, took them out from a satchel now and pointed them at Bridget Bishop, naming her the murderer of Christian Woodbury Trask of Salem Village, then only age twenty-nine, and a near saint, insisting it wasn't a *suicide* at all but a spell his young wife was under, cast by Bridget Bishop after a feud. Removing his specs, he dabbed his moist eye mournfully: "Opposed to youths playing shovelboard at all hours on the Sabbath. She attempted to curtail it."

"By setting fire to my public house and nearly burning it down! With lodgers and patrons present!" cried Bridget, incensed.

"That was never proved!"

But, all here of a certain age from Salem Village who recalled that event remembered how Goody Trask had openly boasted in her circles that she'd set fire to Goody Bishop's shovelboard room. Though now they speculated this, too, might have been witchery. Because if Bridget Bishop could bewitch faithful husbands to lust, and drive wives to insane jealousies, and ruin good crops with sudden floods, and turn cows' udders sour before the milking, and drive a pig so loopy as to refuse its slop, and make chickens more senseless than they naturally were, and smother youngsters in their beds with spectral hands and invisible pillows, couldn't she put false utterances onto a pious young goodwife's tongue?

The Afflicted Girls

Another witness to the tragedy confirmed how there were "three deadly manglings: on Goody Trask's windpipe, gullet and jugular, which a dull pair of sewing scissors could not possibly have rendered . . . except by supernatural hand."

Corwin, the new magistrate, queried, "Were you the coroner?"

"No, sir. The doctor he told. That man has since died," Dr. Griggs advised.

Meanwhile, Goodman Trask had walked up to the judges' table to hand Chief Justice Stoughton the Salem Village Book of Record for the year 1686, urging him to tear out the page upon which was written:

> Christian, wife of William Trask of Salem Village, being violently assaulted by the temptations of Satan, cut her own throat with a short pair of sisers to the astonishment and grief of all, especially her most near relations.

Judge Stoughton understood why. Suicide was a *self-murder* resulting not from fate or accident, but from a person's free will; and for that, both laws, of God and man, dictated an unchristian burial.

All here who were present, at some point in youth, including him, had to memorize the Shorter Catechism:

> Q. *What is forbidden in the sixth commandment?*
> A. *The sixth commandment forbiddeth the taking away of our own life, or the life of our neighbor unjustly, and whatsoever tendeth thereunto.*
>
> Q. *What doth every sin deserve?*
> A. *Every sin deserves God's wrath and curse, both in this life, and that one which is to come.*

It was her own 'suicide' that required Goodwife Christian Woodbury Trask be ignominiously buried under a cartload of quarry stones in a common gutter-ditch off the High Road, with no Catechism in her chasm, or anything to mark her life.

71

O N THE SECOND DAY OF BRIDGET'S TRIAL, THE evidence of her sundry sorceries piled higher than an autumn haystack. One man told how she'd come to his house to argue a debt after which his middle son fell sick. "No, he didn't die—he lives yet, into manhood. But only because God saved him."

"Ask him if he ever paid me my money!" prodded Bridget.

Everyone laughed, but not her.

But the most damning accusation came from her next-door neighbor, who claimed to have witnessed a second brutal murder. She took painful offense, because it was her own husband, Edwin Bishop, that he named the victim.

"When I tried to warn him," shared Goodman Louder, "she spectrally tried to choke me . . . changed my hens into imps with monkeys' bodies, claws and human faces and heaved them over my fence to attack me. Luckily, I knew enough to throw salt!" (All here, knowing him, took *him* with a full sack of salt.)

Bridget took him far worse. "My Edwin died a natural death like his father before him. His heart might have failed him, but his wife never did. I loved my husband well."

"She loved only his money!" cried Louder, louder. "He had years to go till he married her! Rode him into an early grave, while the Devil rode her!"

The Afflicted Girls

"They'll see who loved his money more, if I tell them what I know about you, Goodman Louder! How you cheated your loyal friend to gain an interest in his sawmill! And then tried to do the same with his tavern! But defending my life is more urgent than telling what I know about you!"

Reverend Parris, court notary, didn't write down her retorts because Goodman Louder was his tithing parishioner (however tight-fisted he was). But he did write down that man's insults of her: "Flirt-gill!" "Lewdster!" "Giglet!" "Witch-bitch!" The rest he couldn't record.

≈✦≈

Abigail judged her uncle weary. He kept shaking out his hand and then writing less and less. She was weary, too . . . of the endless yammering about Bridget Bishop.

So she began counting how many times her uncle nodded to himself during testimonies: *eighty-seven.* Also how many times he smiled at her: *barely nineteen,* and not even once in this past half hour! His eyes had even twice closed and she thought he'd fallen asleep—while she was yet to be called! She wasn't pleased. So she looked elsewhere now, because that handsome *young* Boston minister seated in the front row was alert in both mind and pen.

From the first *Oye,* Cotton Mather had been taking copious notes, hoping mostly to witness a supernatural event. None had occurred. And now a church chime was announcing the workday's end. And since there was hardly a modicum of fading light left in this room suitable for reading scribbles, he closed his notebook, nodded to William Stoughton, who understood his meaning: that no torches were to be lit. Rather, an adjournment called.

Of anyone here, Abigail was *most glad* for the delay. Reaching inside her pocket, fingering its content, she followed her tramping aunt out, thinking how pure souls had as much right to view the invisible world as the wicked.

Of course she glanced sidewise at that visiting minister her uncle so highly esteemed as a person of rare gifts, throwing back her shoulders, breathing in to lift her bodice, and tilting up her chin. Unfortunately, he had looked away just then . . . although he certainly would not on the morrow!

For she would embroider her tale just for him . . . and he would write down her every word and marvel. Despite that she'd thrown away her wrong-made cakes onto the midden-heap to let coons and weasels and crows come and eat, because vile creatures deserved to die. She was grateful for this one precious half-cake still sitting in her pocket, her last remaining cake of Tituba's. How she wished there'd been more to find . . . because after tomorrow, without *that rare gift*, her door into wonder would close.

❧

At commencement on the third day, Reverend Parris, court recorder, a figure hardly noticed until such moments, stood up and read aloud from the lengthy list of allegations presented on prior days, which he'd sat up last night summarizing at the Chief Justice's request:

> " —Disturbed the peace of Salem Village; afflicted
> innocent children with Belial's fits; sowed discord
> inside families; bewitched her own good husband to
> death, and also one pious goodwife; nurses a
> succubus imp on her belly nipple, it lives
> underneath her skirts; practices image magic using
> idolomancy —"

He picked up the two confiscated poppets and held them aloft, worrying less about their taint, than his own unimportance, while Abigail worried that Aunt Ugly would surely recognize the cloth.

But in fact, the insect was only distracted by the next sorcery listed:

> " — Immobilizes goodmen in their own beds despite
> the warding presence of their wives, who cannot
> even cry out against her indecencies."

Reverend Parris saw a number of abashed faces, and more than one inside the jury-box, as he felt a flush come into his own.

Finally her name was called!

Abigail sailed up and set her hand upon the Good Book (which her uncle held) swearing to speak the truth (while gazing into his proud eyes). And then she looked visage to visage at the jurymen, memorizing each of their expressions for a future accounting. She knew their names, although not in the current sitting order — she'd memorized a list left out on her uncle's desk: *Fisk, Fisk, Batcheler, Fisk Jr., Dane, Evelith, Perly Sr., Peabody, Perkins, Sayer, Eliot, and Herrick Sr.* She'd wondered then if any were bachelors. Now she didn't care, since not a handsome face sat among them. She also looked about the room to make certain all were attentive. Especially that Boston minister Cotton Mather, who was scribbling in his book and thus failed to see her smile. Disappointed, she began with a pout:

> "I saw Bridget Bishop administer the sacrament
> on the Witches' Sabbath. Midnight of the last new
> moon, I was awakened by the sound of a great
> horn blowing — "

By now the courtroom had dissolved into the supernal light and in her mind's eye she beheld her uncle's pasture, but greener and vaster and brighter than it ever was. Brim full with cowslips, a frothy brook, pretty blue and white violets, fragrant lilies, and of course no screeching crickets, biting bugs or grunting frogs, only golden billowy butterflies — *no, NO! 'Twas midnight when the witches consorted!* She blinked and now saw a hint of a slivered moon, her ally, dangling not above the crabapple tree, but a tree abundantly adorned with crisp red succulent apples, bigger and rounder than were Eve's.

> "I ran to my window and saw from all directions the damned mounted on their broomsticks. A great whirlwind had arisen. Then those three-score witches swirled down and landed in my uncle's pasture like a flock of cackling caw-birds. They grounded their sticks and, one by one, renounced their Baptisms. The witches took out red bread and cake from their pockets, while the wizards built a great bonfire. Then all shed their clothes and danced naked around it. Bridget Bishop walked amongst them giving them blood to drink: *'Consecrated wine of newborn babes! Drink in its power!'*"

There arose another whirlwind now (comprised of horrified gasps, titters, outraged whispers) followed by thunder (Judge Stoughton banged his gavel). When she again heard *witches*, she continued:

> "I came outside and hid behind our tree. Though the ground was set aflame and the grass was burning to cinder I stood and watched and wasn't burnt. I saw as Reverend Burroughs was crowned King, and Bridget Bishop his Queen, and he told them: *'Once the Church is overthrown, all will be well! We'll have maypoles! Christmas! Cockfights! Cockatrice! All Hellish pleasures!'* The witches cheered. Then all of them began fornicating in the four-footed way of beasts . . . with witches' rumps held out to warlocks' pricks, which were now grown longer than a man's arm wrist to elbow—"

The Afflicted Girls

"Stop! Tell no more!" Reverend Parris cried from his table. *These were abominations no child should ever see! No less speak of!*

Lurching to his feet to go to her, his cuff caught the lid of his inkwell tipping the bowl. Wet sinister blackness spilled out onto his trial ledger, shaping into a smirk, swallowing up his inscribed words. *Sorcery!* He swiftly blotted, shuddering, preserving what text he could.

For three days, Lucy Putnam along with the others who'd suffered maladies, curses and afflictions sent out by *Witch Bishop* had been made to sit on the witness bench. But she had not yet been called to testify, and was grateful for it, like she was for this recess, because she did fear the trollop. She truly did.

She climbed atop the bench, glimpsed her parents in a stream of exiting folk with her father carrying her sisters. And soon, she was pushing her own timid way through that mass of impassable bodies and excited voices—searching for plumage and a glint of brassy buttons.

The Chief Constable of Salem Town felt a tug at his sleeve and heard a small voice say: "It isn't what she said. But it is too terrible to tell." He looked down and saw one of the afflicted girls.

From the day of their picnic in the Haunted Chamber, Lucy Putnam had been confused and ill. But not only from lung fever caught in the storm or her accidental poisoning afterward. And by now, she'd recovered from both.

There was a worse abiding affliction inside her soul deeper, which grew unbearable in Mercy Lewis' absence.

> *Yes, she had always feared unholy demons and witches, servants of the Black Man who was God's foremost enemy Satan, the bogeyman and the banshee, hobgoblins and her mother's ghosts, Mercy's black minister, and their own pointy-faced minister Reverend Parris, whose mean niece Abigail Williams*

she somewhat feared, like she did her own parents.
Though never did she fear her sisters, cousins, aunts
(even when stern) or her uncles. But most of all, she
didn't fear Mercy Lewis . . . who would soon be put
on trial just like Bridget Bishop, for being only pretty
and wise and kind.

The Chief Constable lifted that anxious, coughing child and carried Lucy Putnam into a private chamber.

❧❦❧

The jury foreman's face drained of color as he was handing the verdict to Judge Stoughton, who read it stoically to himself and then passed it to his fellow judges, ordering Reverend Parris to record it. And now that chief judge rose to his feet behind the judges' table, and didn't look directly at Bridget Bishop. Because he didn't want to be cursed by her, when he said:

"Bridget Bishop, you have been judged guilty of witchery and are condemned to hang by your neck until dead. If you repent, God may grant you forgiveness. Thus, I advise you to confess for your own sake." It was his duty to explain that which he hoped she wouldn't do. Hell's fiery oven was a more befitting end to her.

Bridget answered nothing at all. Throughout her trial, she'd ignored his reptilian eyes, as well as the eyes of desperation constantly impinging at the back of her neck. Not once had she turned round to look at Israel Porter . . . until now. And now when she did, the coward looked away. Of course, she knew that he would—that he'd be lily-livered when it counted, that his iron backbone and manly rod, so highly boasted, would shrivel into straw at fire's first sight. She didn't look at him again, not even when the guards forced her past him and he reached out and tried to touch her. That was finished.

394

The Afflicted Girls

A jeering crowd waited at the bottom of the steps to jab and poke her clearly. But then someone stuck out a foot and she tumbled headlong forward. Two sheriffs caught her before her head hit the stone. Saving her neck for the gallows. She saw the irony, of course, as she glanced back to see who hated her so much. It was no one she knew, just a stranger. But in that instant of looking back, from inside the courthouse arose a deafening crash, which everyone here heard and feared.

A worm-riddled, rotted ceiling beam had come loose, likely from having a bunch of rowdy youths sitting upon it for three days. The nails had separated. And when it fell, it missed Abigail and her friends by inches, and crushed the witness bench they'd all just arisen from.

And although Bridget never learned what had happened, she was blamed for it in her trial's record.

❧ ✦ ☙

Like other women who refused to confess, Mercy was subjected to a physical examination: brought into the jail's examining room, undressed by jurywomen elders, tied prone atop a table with her legs outstretched, gagged with a rag stuffed into her mouth, groped while they searched for witch's marks.

A kind face, peering down, said it would hurt less if she eased, so she tried. Till a knobby, callused finger with an overly long nail probed her incorrectly, probably meant to hurt her, and a voice cackled: "The Old Boy has planted his seed in this one."

She had known it, though not exactly. Yes, she had known she was with child the day Joseph Putnam came to Putnam Farm to revile her. But she couldn't tell him then, because the father might be either brother. It was a Putnam's seed was all that she knew—so her mistress had beaten her for a lesser betrayal. That was the night she decided to kill it. She stole up to the neighbor's

395

stream to pick deadly nightshade. She drank near a kettle full, and soon suffered violent cramps. When her body purged and fevered, she was sure the pollywog had flushed.

But it hadn't. And however this babe was conceived, in love or hate, passion or rape, it had been spared for some purpose, God was giving it life, a life only His to take—a life which had just saved hers. No woman with child would be sent the gallows.

The jurywomen had not encountered this situation before. All other prisoners were long past their moons, while the beggar had been emptied of her Devil's spawn before they got her. "We should kill it now. Before it knows the taste of flesh." "But what if it already has its human shape?" When no one knew the answer, one of them fetched a broom. It was that same cruel crone. And Mercy knew what she meant to do—probe her with filthy bristles to pry loose the fetus and get it to expel. The babe would die after all, and so would she—of infection before they hanged her. For midwives who used this method would always soak their reeds in rye whisky first. And even then, half the mothers died.

For most of her life, she had longed for death to come. And even yesterday, would have welcomed it. But this brand-new heart beating inside her, strumming whoever's name it bore, wanted life. It was screaming that to her—for her to survive for its sake.

Mrs. Ingersoll shook her head and wagged her finger: "Put down that broom, Goody Bibber. 'Tis a horror to be sure . . . but one for the minister, not us goodwives, to decide."

The Afflicted Girls

PART TEN

72

THE UNRAVELING BEGAN PRIOR TO BRIDGET'S trial and before Mercy Lewis' arrest. When Ann Putnam was called up to be a witness at Rebecca Nurse's examination and stated bluntly to the judges, after swearing a sacred oath on the Bible to speak the truth: "Goody Nurse bewitched my infant to death as ordered to by Satan."

Lucy Putnam knew that her mother was lying.

Because months ago, on a terrible, blizzard-y night, she'd been jolted awake by the howling wind, pelting hail, rattling panes and both sisters' snores. But despite all that clamor, she also heard a lullaby being sung—likely because in *her* house no one ever sang lullabies. So she got up from her bed to investigate.

Hush my dear, lie still and slumber,
Holy angels guard thy bed--

She pressed her ear to her parents' chamber door and heard her mother singing tenderly to her newborn brother. She kneeled on that dark landing, shivering in her flannel, peering in through the keyhole, and viewed them in candlelight. How she wished now that she had knocked, or if her father had not been stranded out by the storm. The storm grew ever more violent, but it no longer frightened her, even though sleet was slamming clapboards, flapping roof shingles, and the chimney howled like wolves— because something frightened her more.

Heavenly blessings without number,
Gently falling upon thy head.

She saw her mother lift that wee slumbering swaddling out from his cradle and hold him too close to the burning candle. Then sneer when he started awake. She puzzled when her mother laid him down next on the wintry wood floor, and rudely roll the swaddles off him till he lay naked and crying . . . and then her mother pressed her hands upon his unhappy face.

She could hear his muffled whimpering, saw his tiny fists and feet flailing, but was frozen, like he was, in her place. And when no more cry came out from him, she saw his tiny soul fly up in a wisp to Heaven. (But that might have been only tallow-smoke sucked up by a ceiling draft.)

All these months, all this time, she carried that dark sinful secret, that dreadful unbearable knowing 'twas her own mother who did her baby brother to death, who'd sent his soul to Jesus. *Not Rebecca Nurse.* And though it strangulated and sickened her, she had never revealed it anyone, not even to Mercy Lewis.

But now with that friend in such jeopardy, Lucy Putnam told her terrible secret to the Chief Constable of Salem Town.

Yes, it *was* a horror beyond reason. But in Ann Putnam's disturbed, disordered mind, this murderous act upon her infant, which she repeated with every newborn son, whenever the Devil sent one, was justified. It meant her daughters would *never* have brothers to betray them, or steal their inheritances on their wedding days, or turn their husbands against them.

❧❦❧

The Afflicted Girls

Dr. Griggs deliberately decided not to tell the Porters that their daughter's lung infection would shorten her life, or that young Elizabeth was afflicted with a virulent strain of pleurisy, which would prove fatal eventually, having done her bellows permanent damage. He preferred to let them think it was witchcraft, since that was feasible and equally likely. Did it matter, really, if one girl wasn't bewitched, when so many were? They would get a year or two more, maybe three, in her company before some future infection did her in. For the duration, he could sell them his remedies and consultations, and visit that sweet maid of whom he'd grown so fond.

Lizzie Porter was a mother superior in all regards, devoting herself ceaselessly to her daughter's healing, knowing how other children had sickened and survived. More than five times daily, she'd apply hot pulps to her child's heaving chest, painting that cave-in with warmed molasses, sometimes in the doctor's presence. Through every pill and poultice, sponge bath and hour of bed-rest, she would guard her, never losing faith.

When some days ago, a hint of natural color began to return to her daughter's pasty cheeks and Dr. Griggs declared the contagion contained, she begged her husband for permission to open the sickroom to others, hoping to revive their girl's fallen spirit. When Israel agreed, she sent word to her dear friend Mary Veren Putnam, asking for both her and her son to come.

Mary came only to evaluate the girl's true condition, because she was no longer averse to breaking off the engagement; in these last two trying months, she'd discovered other suitable matches for Joseph—creatures also wealthy and pretty, but with stronger constitutions. Joseph came because he was forced. And when their mothers exited the sickroom he supposed to talk of the nuptials, he was hardly relieved. The girl was still asleep, and although he hadn't prayed for Elizabeth Porter's demise it wouldn't have been unwelcome. Yet, she'd survived. Somehow she'd lived. Which made him picture his future bedchamber like this one: reeking of sickness, with a wasted occupant inside his bed. Disgusted, he dragged his chair over to the window to look out and breathe in air. Perhaps, that sound is what woke her.

She weakly smiled. He attempted to smile back. Also inquired about her health. She didn't have the strength to say how poorly she felt, only raised her head a little then sank back into her pillow. He hoped her eyes would close, and when he suggested it, she obeyed.

When her mother returned, without his, he took his leave. While descending, he heard overheated voices coming from behind a downstairs door, and wondered if his mother was quarreling with Israel Porter about the dowry. He knocked. When no one answered, he opened the door to summon her, and saw a red-faced man standing confused, lambasting an empty room. Israel turned and said to him: "If only she'd pled her belly, like that serving wench of your brother's."

His face drained paler than was hers upstairs. Did he really think he'd crushed Mercy Lewis by crushing her mandrake? Couldn't he have guessed she'd find another way to ensnare him? And now, she had. She had. Inside her now, not from any conjuration, born only of his own wastrel *charm*, grew a child inside her belly. Her black blood had mixed with his.

The Afflicted Girls

73

I T WAS LONG-NOSED GOODY BIBBER, WHO FIRST insinuated that Thomas Putnam was the fornicator who had spawned a demon-child upon his witch-servant. In that one neighborly blink, the comment sparked from hearth to hearth, and tonight arrived here.

Returning home from his hard day's field labor, Thomas was met by a bombardment of crockery, and no supper. Picking up shards, Ann threw them, too. A broken glass beaker was used to swipe her faithless husband's cheek. "Fornicator! Blight on my virginity!" Unmasked, Thomas fell to his knees and confessed his lust—although not every purple detail he'd previously muttered to God. And while God may have long ago forgiven him, Ann clamped her ears to it, not wanting to hear how he took their servant only once while under her libidinous spell. Shouting instead that she was done with him, kicking him out, cursing *his* children. Then sobbing at her table vowing vengeance.

After that, she went up to her bed and stayed inside it for days, leaving those confused sisters to fend for their own sustenance.

Meanwhile, their father alternated between bouts of fury, shame, rye, ale and guilty blackouts in Sister Trask's second room or any empty stable stall at Ingersoll's. Mostly he was left alone, while they gossiped. But today before first light, his in-law Trask came and dragged him out from his last night's bed of dung, dunked his face in the trough, and pushed him up the lane to his own well's pump, got him washed and dressed in some clean under-britches, breeches, a shirt and a vest, and brought him inside to his wife's table, where ham and eggs were waiting on trenchers for him and Thomas. But only because of the day it was.

❧✦☙

Bridget awoke breathless from a dream. When her eyes adjusted, she saw those goodwives clustered together in their usual knot of sleep, with even the surly beggar resting her head tonight on someone's thigh, and being allowed. Goody Nurse was curled up on her sewn-together sheepskins, but abutting other bodies. And the slave was coiled round the children.

Only she and Mercy Lewis kept themselves apart, always at opposite ends of the cell. She stared at that girl who slumbered, and her heart quickened with hope. *Tonight I dreamt of a bottomless pit with a bridge of gossamer spanning . . . that I felt in my heart was not for me. I watched as you safely crossed it . . . and heard the laughter of children. There will be a way for you, Mercy Lewis.*

Keenly aware in both waking and dreaming, Tituba heard all things whispered and most things thought. And while she felt a certain kinship with this owlish woman, she kept that knowledge to herself. They walked separate paths. She pulled the slumbering Dorcas closer, and brushed her lips on infant Good's cheek, tucking that wee boy better into her elbow's crook against her heartbeat, and returned to her own dream, clutching them tighter. These two walked with her.

Bridget sat up the rest of this night with her arms folded cross her knees, staring often at the other women — all wives and mothers —

402

thinking about their children's unhappiness soon to come. Remembering herself as a mother long ago.

Mercy Lewis had been the reminder from the start; a girl so near in likeness to her own beloved daughter who'd died of the smallpox, fathered by her first love, who also died from it. The eyes of all three were that selfsame deep dark blue, which resided in no one but them. Her bright-faced child, had she lived, would have been about the age of Mercy Lewis, exceedingly as clever, and also a great beauty. *Would she see her in Heaven on the morrow? If so, would it be as a child of five . . . or in her nearly grown semblance? Which husband would she choose? Both had loved her with complete passion.*

She'd choose neither of them, she knew. Her life as a wife and lover was finished. But if she could see her child in any form, she would leave this world in joy, not regret. Even forgive God, that eternally punishing father, His injustice.

She glanced once more at Mercy Lewis, as she'd done repeatedly this night, wondering should she wake her now and tell her of the will filed with the General Court in Boston two months ago, bestowing on her all of her worldly possessions and properties. As eager as she was to disclose that fact, it could wait until morning. A mother of an unborn needed rest.

(Although Bridget had seen the gossamer bridge made of light, and this girl's future, and the spirit smiles of her lost loved ones, one thing she never saw was how local village officials would seize her assets upon her execution, and the greedy cheaters who'd condemned her, including Goodman Louder, would get all: her tavern, orchard, chattels, livestock, lock-box, modest sawmill—and at bargain prices. Because that new junior constable, who'd been pricked once by a poppet in her house, would see to it as part of his constabulary duty.)

The *Witch Queen* was rudely roused, as was Rebecca Nurse, and also the beggar. The three were herded out to a waiting cart. Guards seized the old midwife first and rudely lifted her in and then crammed the harlot next to her. But Sarah Good, fighting not to be lifted, also cursed so loudly she woke up nearby roosters.

A few early risers held torches. All of them Rebecca Nurse knew. She'd been inside their houses. But they averted their eyes when she sought their recognition. Instead, they gossiped with each other about the *wizards* who'd been delivered up yesterday from Boston, who would be coming out next.

And now that *Witch King* emerged from the jailhouse, looking much like Bridget had pictured. She felt spiritually chilled viewing her young friend's ruination, this black minister from hell, knowing what the flesh contained. He was draped in heavy chains. *Fittingly*, she thought. For she and the others now were bound only with rope, their chains having been taken by the jailers for someone else's imprisonment.

Reverend Burroughs was shoved past her to the rear of the cart. He barely had brushed against her but must have felt her utter contempt, because after he was padlocked, he turned back and met her burning eyes — but he was the one who looked away first.

And now John Willard was brought out, escorted by two jailers, both his friends, who nervously balked when he begged them to get a message to his wife.

That other beggar, Sarah Good, didn't mind seeing this junior constable brought low. For more than a year now, he'd made her life a misery, chasing her and her tyke out from barns and sheds, and even woodlots, as if he had that right. And his rich young wife was flint-skinned as any. How many times had she knocked at that never-opened door?

The Afflicted Girls

The five prisoners were secured to the cart-rails, and now the driver prodded his ox team down the jail lane and back alleys to the village gate. A militia wagon followed with men-at-arms.

The world sat in somber silence and murky morning mist. Numerous wagons were already rolling down the High Road. And folk were also tramping on foot—people who owned no carts, indentures mostly—all traveling to Gallows Hill.

But then the cart turned south not north, and veered off in a second wrong direction. They rolled across a covered bridge. Not because this aged carter was confused in the dark, or bewitched by his burden, but because oft-times he'd hauled goods for the Nurses and was always paid fair. He took this detour upon himself; he was not bribed.

Night turned to dawn soon and the mist dissipated. And a familiar scent made Rebecca Nurse's tight-shuttered eyes unwedge. She viewed a familiar funnel of bounty spread out before her. Gold ripening corn, rye and flax, pearled barley that Francis and her boys had planted . . . cavorting lambs and kids, calves and foals, otherwise resting flocks, and mooing herds. She lamented how her own little *lambkins* would nevermore have new yearly coats, capes, hats, scarves, mittens, waistcoats, britches, dresses, bodices, petticoats, sleeves, collars, and aprons knit, spun, crocheted, laced and sewn by her.

The orchards, she could not quite see for the distance and the moistness of her eyes, but in her mind's eye they were dotted with the crispest apples and sweetest cherries to be found anywhere in the Commonwealth. Thinking of them, her parched mouth watered for a gulp of *cherry-bounce* . . . the bounce she nevermore would taste. She sighed. Her daughters and granddaughters would have to carry on, making bounces and pies and sweetmeats using her recipes . . . or inventing their own.

Her lilacs were in full bloom on this summer morn and were filling the world with fragrance. But she could not look past them to the houses atop the hill, which contained all of her joy. This was unbearable. She begged to be taken no farther. That well-meaning carter turned round his oxen and cart, and the militia wagon followed. Bridget put a comforting arm around the old midwife's bony shoulder and held Rebecca in her collapse.

Rebecca Nurse wept while squeezing her neighbor's hand, but it was a hollow gesture without affection. She had also turned away her mottled cheek, because Bridget Bishop was a profane and ungodly person, and she disdained being touched by a harlot—even now. She felt another hard slap from God, and her spirit smarted, and she cried harder. And then she understood the why of His displeasure . . . and confessed with humility on this road to perdition: "Your act was kind . . . like that of a daughter, Goody Bishop . . . kinder than mine."

Bridget humbly told her: "I was one, Goody Nurse, a lifetime ago. But you are mother to us now."

Rebecca pulled Bridget into her lap, atop that precious ill-treated Bible she'd only just this morning reclaimed, and comforted Bridget like a mother would.

And Bridget Bishop, that daughter of someone long dead, mother of someone long dead, wife of two men long dead, on her way to the gallows, was finally able to weep.

This, too, was God's doing.

That overdue prison cart wended up the spiraling ascent of Danvers Hill toward the rocky flat top where the populace was already assembled; it being the most barren and big enough place in these outer village boundaries to set a gallows and collect a crowd.

Half of those waiting had been wagering, taking bets that the jail cart would never arrive, that it had escaped instead to the netherworld.

The Afflicted Girls

A couple of latecomers got an eyeful, when a rear cartwheel went off a sharp edge and nearly tipped all the witches to the turve. It took five strong-armed militiamen to haul it back onto the cart-way. (*The Devil pushed it off*, those stragglers would later claim, describing how they saw him do it. And that tale would live on longer than they would.)

That carter, unnerved, kept his straining oxen to the middle. But as unwholesome as this hill was, from this glorious height now, the condemned could see all the way down to Salem Town Bay — its placid green waters and white-sailed ships. And, in the other direction, to the vast northern vistas of rolling hills, brimming with summer goldenrod and blue aster.

And now that goodman halted his cart briefly, so that he, too, could view this great beauty.

74

THE JAIL WARDEN LOCKED THE OUTSIDE DOOR and glanced around cautiously before heading off to the privy. But when exiting that closet, because of the relief he felt, he forgot to be vigilant, and was struck at the back of his head and knocked unconscious.

Inside that pike-clad structure, two other jailers sat on stools playing their first game of tiddlywinks of the day. They heard the door unlatch, and thinking it was the warden didn't look up, but kept on snapping their coins into a cup, which currently held six hay-pence. Neither noticed the cesspit shovel either before it swung in from the side, knocking them both senseless.

One lay flat on his face. The other was only stunned and saw stars in which was a hooded attacker readying his weapon for a finishing blow. But with such clobbered vision it was a scythe, and not a shovel. He howled that the *Grim Reaper* had come for him, and had enough wits to dash on wobbly hands and knees to the doorway and pull up by the doorjamb and desert his post. Because his old grandmother warned him yester night how that Unholy Spirit would be stalking the village today. She made him promise to be wary.

Keys in hand, the intruder unlocked the jail's inner sanctum, and began unlocking doors. The first two were standing closets, both empty. The next, a fettering-room held implements of torture and had been recently used, for it stank of urine and feces. This last door was to a true cell; it had a barred window and through it he saw eleven women. They all gasped when he entered, judging him their executioner because of his hood.

He unlocked Tituba's ankle cuff first; she sat closest to the door. He frowned under his mask seeing a young child also in chains, winced at the wee infant in ties also. He hadn't known children had been taken for witches. He tried patting the little girl's head, but she shied away, clinging to the Indian. (Actually, these three escaped today's gallows by Reverend Parris' doing: Some weeks ago, he had written down confessions for Tituba and Dorcas Good and made them each put their thumbprints. He wanted the little beggar to indict her mother, and believed that his slave would be returned to him promptly after a confession was lodged, since she was his property anyway. Then he learned how the court had set a bail on Tituba inordinately high, which occurred right after John Indian stole his money. So whoever paid that fine now would get her. For the second time, he'd been robbed.)

The man handed Tituba a coin pouch, with a watchword: "Go north to Quebec. Your kind knows freedom there. But leave these children on a Christian threshold first. It is my order."

Tituba grunted no agreement when she lifted Dorcas onto her hip and laid the newborn on her opposite shoulder, and ran out carrying them both. She knew how in summer woodlands there was always plenty to eat. And special plants that could make milk flow from even barren breasts.

Nine other women, who all had trials pending, were released now from their fears and fates; but God only knew to where and for how long. But not yet her who'd pled her belly.

Mercy's deadened mind raced to recall her prior plan for reaching freedom. Yet the man didn't approach. Only stood fixed, staring at her through his mask, rather, *through* her. Even though she was the only one left in the cell. *Because he knew she was guilty, unlike the others. He condemned her. That was clear.* "Sir, please help me, not for myself, but for the sake of the innocent child growing inside me." When she said that, he kicked the sheepskin aside, came over and crouched, brashly grabbed her ankle cuff. But then he fumbled the jailer's key. It dropped into the straw. As he reached for it, she recognized his hand. And however much she ached to reach out and touch that hand, and look into Joseph Putnam's clouded eyes again, she didn't. But kept hers lowered. That he'd come across a room was enough.

The Afflicted Girls

75

CHIEF JUSTICE STOUGHTON BUTTONED HIS NEW summer coat up to his ruffled collar. He then ascended the steps to the scaffold to instruct the black-hooded hangman waiting about certain things, and now that person again examined levers, hinges, pulleys, beams, and rope-knots. While he glanced down the line of his militia-guarded prisoners, wondering which of them, if any, would confess.

Sarah Good, the beggar, didn't when he asked her that final question: "Will you confess to save your soul?"

"Spill my blood a drop, mean mister, God'll give you gallons more of it to drink!" She was about to spit in his eye when she noticed a pipe poking out from his pocket. So instead asked him *her* question, more agreeably: would he let her smoke a few puffs on his pipe? He recoiled, for she stank. But he had only to ask the question once, as the law required. But now some interfering fool in the crowd below them tossed up a lit pipe that bounced off his coat and tipped embers onto his expensive sleeve.

It was a villager who'd once put Sarah Good into the pillory, thinking that she'd robbed him of his victual stores. Turned out it was his son who'd done the crime. But never did that man admit his mistake or cancel his complaint or her punishment, because he didn't want his boy publicly shamed.

Judge Stoughton brushed off his coat, kicked the pipe aside, and walked on, his first appeal concluded. The executioner picked up the pipe now and stuffed it into Sarah Good's maw. But she spit it out again, cursing loudly that on her last day on earth she deserved better than a well-gummed corncob "from a liar!" She had always known the truth of it. She was not born of stupid stock.

John Willard aimed his fury at this judge. "I was fraudulently convicted, which you know, Stoughton, having done the interviews."

Judge Stoughton was dismissive. "The evidence proved otherwise. Nonetheless, if you confess to wizardry, John Willard, you'll save your soul."

"One-sided evidence! Those with the means to disprove it were not allowed to speak in my defense. Why did you begrudge me? Why were my witnesses barred? You've wronged a loyal citizen, Stoughton. And a Christian."

The judge's demeanor stiffened. "You were judged, not begrudged, and not by me, but by God and your peers. I refuse to argue the law with you, any law. But if you confess to your crimes today then you won't live on in Hell."

"Go to Hell yourself, sir."

"How dare you insult me?"

"How dare you murder me? Do you think there won't be a price to pay? With my final breath I swear there will be. That far worse will be waiting for you in that place."

With a haughty *harrumph*, Judge Stoughton, twice cursed now (and not liking it) moved on to Bridget Bishop.

"Queen of the witches!" the populace was shouting.

Whore of Babylon, he was thinking. So he kept at a safe distance for fear of contamination. When the uproar drowned his voice, he was forced to move closer to ask his question. Bridget Bishop showed no sign of contrition, or interest. So after proffering it twice, he moved on . . . down the scaffold, relieved that this particular appeal had concluded well.

Now Rebecca Nurse's age and pious reputation gave Judge Stoughton pause for two reasons: First, a rumor had reached his ears only this week that her chief accuser, Ann Putnam, had recanted; or something to that effect. He had yet to confer with Salem Town's Chief Constable to learn the actual detail.

Second, this sharp-tongued biddy had been found innocent on her first jury-count—but only after a mere hour's deliberation. Of course, he had to send the jurymen back with instructions that were she actually guilty and found innocent a second time, that her crimes would be paid for by someone in God's Court, most likely by her acquitters. She was handily convicted on their second count, as he knew she would be, although not unanimously, not even then. So there remained doubt concerning her. "Do you confess to witchcraft, Goody Nurse?" he screamed, recalling her deafness.

She shook her head vehemently, "No, sir, I do not. I will never confess to a lie! Lying is God's betrayal!"

A rotten egg was thrown up at him. It splattered on his silver buckled shoe. He angrily looked down to that crowd, vowing to find that rabble-rouser and mete him a fitting punishment. He wiped egg from his shoe as folk guffawed. He ignored them, shouting again into his prisoner's ear: "By not confessing, you betray God all the same. Stubbornly throwing down to the Devil your own rotten egg of a life that should have been held by you sacred."

She answered sternly now, thumping her Bible to her heart, craning her neck, "Your tongue wags nonsense, sir: 'Thou shall not bear false witness' is a *sacred* commandment! There is a Higher Judge than are you Judge Stoughton, a higher Judgment than yours. He is the Judge I'll have judge me."

Contentious hen, he thought. Of course he'd been correct overruling his fellow judges when they dissented following her verdict . . . whereas he'd only felt elation that another witch stood convicted. He supposed that if he'd erred with Goody Nurse, it was there—in his overjoyed emotion, *which might have been more circumspect*. But even then, his good friend Cotton Mather had confirmed: 'Witchcraft is the most nefarious high treason against our Majesty on High.' Admitting privately later, over supper: 'Had I been one of her jurymen, William, I could not have acquitted her.'

No, he'd been correct in his original assessment. Nonetheless, he would proffer, once more, that merciful option in view of her popularity. He wasn't stonehearted: "Confess to your spectral crimes, Goody Nurse, if only to save your eternal life."

Rebecca stretched her goosey neck sideways and honked, "Look to your own crimes, mister, not to mine. Be not a Pilate, Judge Stoughton. Mine is innocent blood that you spill . . . unlike theirs."

He couldn't believe his ears. He retorted: "Do you set yourself up as *their* judge ruling from *false* piety's high bench? Fie on you, Goody Nurse! Let God show mercy to you, and to these others. Otherwise, God has no need to exist!" With that, he walked away from her.

Her shoulders collapsed, her knees went weak. Only her sin of pride stood with her.

From the moment that wayward prison cart rolled in and parked, until now, George Burroughs, minister from Maine, had been devoutly bellowing *The Lord's Prayer*.

Hearing sincerity in his voice, seeing his sacred suit, but mostly not knowing who he was, a few onlookers began calling out to the soldiers to show the minister mercy. And by now, many were.

The Afflicted Girls

Alarmed, Reverend Parris, in his poorer minister's suit, ran up to bottom of the scaffold to educate the populace, pointing up at Burroughs: "Citizens! Brethren! Beware! The Devil is never *more* himself than when he puts on holy guise! This man is no ordained minister, but a tool of Satan, who once lived in my own parsonage house and planted bewitchments there! A plot to destroy God's Church by poisoning its children! My children! Your children! Doubt this and the Devil wins!"

Hearing that, Judge Stoughton thought twice about the need to offer redemption to a black minister. So he announced the conclusion of appeals. And a drum roll sounded.

The executioner pulled his own favorite pipe from Sarah Good's mouth, and tossed it away forever, and set the burlap over her head, looping the thick hemp noose around it. She blasphemed and struggled fiercely; but grew quiet when he tightened it. He released a lever, which dropped her. She was hoisted up to a beam by three soldiers, and now dangled dead.

All eyes stared upward, so hardly anyone noticed when a young goodwife of means climbed that ladder-stair and stormed cross the scaffold, pushing the hangman out of her way.

It had been more than a month since Goody Willard fled to Connecticut—but only to put her toddlers into her mother's safekeeping. She returned here in secret two weeks ago, prior to her husband's trial, going house-to-house in disguise, asking and then begging his friends to save him. All claimed they'd tried, though they hadn't. Acting on her heart's impulse now, without aforethought, to save her husband from bearing this evil on his own, as she flew past she pulled off the executioner's hood, revealing that person's face, well known to both her and John, and to many others. And as that shame-faced man scrambled to retrieve it, she madly embraced her beloved, who kissed her full on the mouth re-knit in their souls, till the militiamen dragged her away. She called back to him, "I curse this accursed place and all who dwell in it, John! May the same be done to them as do it to--" Judge Stoughton slapped her face with such an outrage his hand smarted. He ordered her arrested. All of which poor John Willard witnessed, right before the burlap blinded him, and noosed and gagging, he died.

Israel Porter was absent today, and would ever more be inconsolable. Bridget had understood this. It was why she'd offered him her farewell at the courthouse. She hadn't thought of him since, nor looked for him today. Her eyes were fixed only on Abigail Williams, who today would be cinching her own unfortunate fate—for all deeds, good or ill, sprang back upon themselves like bear-traps on careless trappers. She perceived that girl's sad future, although she took no satisfaction in it. For despite all that she was and everything she'd done in the shadows, not only in the light, Bridget was not vindictive:

> *You will advance through your loveless years, selling favors to men in alleys and docksides, and will die from a gutter pestilence before reaching the age of thirty.*

Her second sight was so keen in this final moment that if she'd chosen to stare at Reverend Parris as well, she would have seen his future:

> *How no church would ever hire him again. How he would nevermore call souls forth to righteousness or get any graces himself. But would spend his remaining years picking out a lowly living as a petty glove peddler, a widower, an imbecile's father—a penniless, luckless man.*

The hood and noose were slipped over, with the knot tightening on her precious amulet. Bridget smiled as she was choked, remembering who had given her that stone, giving thanks for her life, for all its glories and wrenching sorrows, uttering her daughter's beloved name *'Christian'* in that soothing sigh called *death*.

"Judas Stoughton!" was catcalled repeatedly when the hangman reached Rebecca Nurse, pausing that already reluctant man in his duty. Judge Stoughton rushed up to the front again, this time screaming down that all troublemakers would be arrested. Nonetheless, they kept ringing their bells, waving fists and canes, and throwing more eggs at him. While the executioner, behind him, was confessing into Rebecca's good ear, lips up against it, how he was suffering doubt about her.

She told him to touch her Good Book. "Be at peace, son. It is not you who does this to me, but him."

Nonetheless, he appealed to Judge Stoughton for mercy: "Can't we let her live out her remaining days? They're few enough in number to be sure. For the good, she's sometimes done."

The judge considered. "Yes, why not. And since the noose is already tied, we'll simply hang you in her place to appease them."

The hangman set the burlap over Goody Nurse's head, adjusted his noose, and lamented: "You brought eight of mine safe into this world, Goody Nurse, now here am I sending you out from it."

Rebecca didn't hear him. Her ears were deaf. Her eyes blind now, too. And her Bible was pressed so hard against her heart, she felt Salvation pass down into her toes as she was hoisted.

And now that Good Book fell to the dirt and a boy of her clan came running to retrieve it. He took it to his great-grandfather Francis, who for the remainder of his days, would never agai͏̄ open it, or believe any word in it

Reverend Burroughs did not go quietly into the day. He cursed God, and butted both hangman and judge as he flung himself forward in a great wiry leap, soaring free of his iron shackles.

Luckily, Judge Stoughton, a large man, had grabbed that felon's coattail, and he held on till his militiamen could rush over. But it took four of them, a blacksmith among them, to hold down that ferocious boar and get him hoisted.

❧

Five lifeless bodies hung from the gallows beam, as now a wind rose up increasing their swinging motions—a bitter wind of *Moriah* Reverend Parris told himself—an ancient sign from God of a sacrifice accepted. Spying Thomas Putnam, he bounded over excitedly to share his insight with his friend. "Isn't it a great thing, seeing those five firebrands from Hell hanging?"

Ben Nurse, standing just behind, overheard that comment. In sobs, he lunged for the minister, knocking Reverend Parris to the ground, where he pounded and pummeled him with distraught iron-knuckled farmer fists flying till a pearly tooth also went flying, a patrician nose was possibly broken, definitely was bleeding, a well-formed lip had swelled, and an eye had begun to blacken.

Abigail screamed for the lout to stop. She kicked Ben Nurse repeatedly, while her aunt only stared agape. But it was Ben Nurse's own family members who pulled that bull off her uncle and hurried him to a horse, leaving her Uncle Parris prone and lying in the dirt, whimpering and bloodied, pathetically begging for aid.

No one stepped forward to give it, not his friends Thomas Putnam or Nathaniel Ingersoll, who both stood watching and then retreated with all the rest.

The Afflicted Girls

❧✦☙

The sun sat low in the west. But Danvers Hill already sat in dusk. And now the five stiffened bodies were lowered and dragged to the fissures for disposal—no Christian burials for them.

But before Reverend Burroughs was discarded, his corpse was stripped and his minister's suit was burned.

Those soldiers who undressed him were amazed to view his piddling worm. They guffawed about its size, long after they'd tossed that mighty blusterer down into the same shallow shale shaft, which held the beggar and the constable. Then those three broken-necks were covered up with dirt. While the other two, cast down earlier into a deeper narrower crevice, were caught wedged between stones about twenty feet down.

On the first night's watch, the weather turned weird. Not with a strange dry wind again but a howling wet storm that assaulted the premonitory hard. A bolt of lighting struck the scaffold direct, causing it to smolder, with two frightened guards sheltering underneath. They abandoned their post.

At dawn, it was scavengers and vultures coming for breakfast: Reverend Burroughs' eyeballs, cleft chin, sinister lips, and Sarah Good's warty toes, the menu. While John Willard, blanketed by those other two torsos, remained largely unpicked.

On the second watch-keep, not knowing the place was abandoned eleven young Nurse cousins quietly rode up the hill armed with ropes, pick-axes, shovels, knives, and their fathers' muskets ready to do battle had they met any foes. They used lanterns to search in the crags. With Ben, deemed the most agile and strongest among them, tied at the end of a rope and lowered into fissures till he found the wedged broken body of his Granny. He sobbed harder than he'd ever done, cupping her in his arms. They all did.

They took their matriarch home to bury in the family plot, with purple blossoms blanketing her mound and generations of loved ones wailing.

He'd retrieved Bridget Bishop's body, too, and they let him bring it back to Orchard Farm, where they buried her apart, but also under lilacs.

The Afflicted Girls

76

BOSTON'S DOCKS WERE BUSTLING WITH NOISY rhythms at dusky eventide. Shouts, neighs, clops, clangs, beeping horns and screaming whistles filled the ears of two tired horsemen, as they rode through this maze, weaving around flatbed trucks, trolleys, beasts stacked with merchant goods waiting to be lodged or loaded. Cargo blocked one passageway and they were pointed toward an alley. Where now they passed sailors in various states of whoring drunkenness. Two faded women propositioned them, too, tugging at their leggings and walking alongside. One boldly grabbed a boot and caressed it lewdly warning how she wouldn't let go till the gentleman gave her a coin.

Mercy, in that high boot and gentlemen's coat, turned to Joseph anxiously.

She'll soon be one of them, he thought as he threw those trollops their coin to be rid of them. Those worn-out women scooped up their pittance and sauntered away pleased with their luck, ready to bother the next high-hats to bumble into their thieves alley.

And now, urchins swarmed in their path. Joseph used his crop to fend them back, yet they pursued for the length of the alley — a persistence born of hunger.

Mercy wished she had some pennies to throw, remembering herself as a child begging on harbor streets. Half a shilling would feed these five for days. She'd have asked for another coin, but a ship's whistle was sounding in the distance, and Joseph said they had to hurry.

At the end of the pier was a slip where a mid-size schooner, *The Arcadia*, was berthed. Here they dismounted and Joseph undid his saddlebag and took out a leather wallet, but then stared at it so long and with such displeasure, that when he held it out to her, Mercy hesitated to take it.

So he thrust it into her hand informing it contained bank notes and traveling papers. "Your passage is paid. This is for your settlement. The captain, a New York Quaker, has promised to help you. But do not think that I wish you well."

"Thank you for my life, Joseph, and—" she wanted to say *for your kindness*. But the words wouldn't form.

He broke her silence sharply: "Understand this, if nothing else. I reject your bastard and will have nothing ever to do with it. In fact, I'd rather it wasn't born. Even that it will not survive. But I will not pray for either as I am not an uncivilized man." He meant for his words to sting her, and they did. He had said them to be free of her. Despite the answer she still owed him: "I've paid enough for you to tell me now: Was I bewitched?"

Until his cruel words about her child, Mercy believed that by his bringing her to safety at his own peril meant he planned to flee with her, or would find a way to join her. It was the future she had dreamed once, and her final self-deception . . . because now she understood. *Joseph Putnam had never been her true love, or her destiny, or even an end to loneliness. He'd only been the means to it.*

The whistle blared loudly. They covered their ears.

She gave her answer to his question, but not the half-truth he was seeking. She hoped he would use it to further break their bond. "Not you, never you. It was I who was bewitched. By a man I met on a roadway by chance, who undid me with lust and empty promises. I might have carved a root as a charm, but only to unlock an empty heart, and fill a chest of cold stone with endless treasure."

She winced. Today her stalwart mentor had been slain. She grieved for Bridget Bishop now, the final chapter in this terrible story. *Believe whatever you choose, Joseph Putnam: That I have sinned against you. Bewitched you. That a terrible, dark creature I must be . . . for I leave evil behind me wherever I go. I know what I am. No docile deer to be preyed upon by men like you. But a creature, which even direly wounded, can survive the cruelest winter.*

A sailor on deck was calling down through a bullhorn that the anchor was being raised. Joseph mounted, grabbed the other horse's reins. Mercy hurried up the plank. He didn't look back at her. But she pressed against the rail, searching the crowded vistas, till she thought she saw him—a rudderless man leading a rider-less horse through a flurry of lantern light.

On a cobblestone lane, two miles inland from the sea, Joseph Putnam got his answer. His eyes began to smart. But not from the acrid smoke rising from scores of surrounding pot-fires on these backwater streets—but from his *unspoken* words, negating his other words, and all of her next words . . . nevermore to be heard.

The *Arcadia* pushed out, rowed by her crew beyond the shelter of the bay. Her white sails unfurled and brisk wind gusts filled them. She was being steered to outrun an incoming storm. Rolling, listing, dancing through the wild whitecaps.

A ships-boy, a younker, tied off the high sail-knots then shimmied down the center mast. He guessed their young gentleman passenger was in mourning, standing so stiff at the stern-rail, staring back at the harbor beacons, sea-spray mixing with tears. He remembered his own dear mother and sister, who'd succumbed to the pox when last he was at sea. He said a heartfelt

Quaker prayer for the living, then for both their lost loved ones, and returned to his labors sadder.

On Boston's Beacon Hill sat a prominent dwelling near to the summit, but not the brightest amid so many impressive homes on these winding wealthy lamp-lit streets. Though tonight it beamed above the harbor fog, as if it were the only mansion awake and aware in John Bunyan's Heavenly City.

And when that Governor's house was also enveloped by mist, Mercy Lewis went below to her cabin to sleep.

The Afflicted Girls

PART ELEVEN

77

G OVERNOR PHIPS HAD BEEN DELIVERED HIS nearly three months' worth of missives, and the one he was reading now was a letter that had been sent to him—his secretary explained—by Salem Town's Chief Constable and marked "A Matter Most Urgent."

Also since he'd returned from campaign, he cursorily began reading the voluminous handwritten record of the Salem Village witchcraft trials, still ongoing, which William Stoughton, his Chief Justice in the proceedings, had provided. Because among his governing duties was to send periodic reports on Commonwealth doings to King William. And all during his military expedition—it was early October now—that duty had been shirked. Unfortunately, one of the King's advisors had now noticed the lapse. There'd already been an inquiry. Lest he lose his governing post, he read the daylong into the night. But at least he could report he'd been victorious in the north.

His wife was also sitting in this room on a brocaded davenport, while she stitched a child-size shirt. She looked up puzzled when he cried out dismayed: "Justice has miscarried. Gravely, gravely, I fear." Lady Phips set down her sewing. "How so, husband?"

He read the letter aloud to her:

> *A child of twelve, Lucy Putnam, one of the afflicted girls, and a chief accuser of several persons hanged, has privately told me the fact. I wish to convey the same dreadful truth to you, Governor Phips, that never was there witchcraft in Salem Village, but only spectral invention masking murderous intention and revenge —*

He looked up, incensed. "How could experienced judges decree death penalties based on lies? What will King William think of my governance? I know James would turn over in his grave. Do you know, wife, do you know, you are accused yourself now of being the Devil's consort? I suppose I am that Devil!" He handed her the letter.

Her face drained of color as she read how certain girls in Salem Village were claiming to have suffered spectral assaults sent out by her, and that a complaint with her name affixed had been lodged in that constabulary. "What will happen to me, William?"

"Nothing! Not to you, wife, not to anyone anymore! I'm putting an end to this madness!"

He grabbed his quill and nearly broke its point writing out his decree, which he sealed with wax and impressed with the royal signet. He hollered for his secretary, directing the man: "Deliver this to the Salem Town Court of *Oye Terminer*. I have just dissolved it. Any persons yet restrained in jails, constabularies or even houses are released and are pardoned. No further trials for witchcraft will be held anywhere in this land. Should additional accusers cry out, tell them: They're the ones who'll hang!"

The secretary was thoughtful. "What of the twenty already hanged? Are they also pardoned?"

A good question . . . Governor Phips turned to his wife to seek her counsel, but she was weeping into her sewing cloth. Shaking his head, he answered: "I can extend the King's mercy only to the living, pitiably no farther. God will have to do that Himself."

❧✦❧

Chief Justice Stoughton's blood boiled upon learning of the governor's order. Afterward, he decided to write down his own thoughts on the matter; so the truth of it, at least, would be known by his posterity:

> *We were right at the verge of clearing this land of witches, when the governor obstructed our course of Justice.*

78

I N BOSTON'S NORTH CHURCH IN FROSTY MID-November, Reverend Increase Mather, fifty-three years of age, officiated at a marriage blessing and advised the marrying couple:

> "Adam and Eve were husband and wife as naturally as they were man and woman. A wife is a necessary good, a man's helpmeet in all things, and a medicine against uncleanness."

To the groom, specifically:

> "A husband must love his wife as his second self. Must provide for her needs, and in turn, receives full use of her body."

To the bride, an admonition:

> "A wife is her husband's property for all time, made for his comfort and convenience. She is to submit to him, the same as she does unto the Lord. Her husband is her priest and prophet. And her most pressing duty is to receive her husband's seed and nurture his progeny."

To them both:

> "God created woman from man for man—"

He detected a tinge of color eke out finally onto the girl's sunken cheek. Till now, Elizabeth Porter's face had been pasted only with pale worry. He'd been comparing her to that rosy housemaid he'd had recently after one of his sons discarded her. That girl wasn't half as fair or innocent as was this one, but they were of a similar age — sixteen — the best time, in his mind, for an unspoiled maid to first ride the cock God sent to shape her.

He now pictured himself as her groom, thrusting through her virgin's veil, emptying his seed-sacs into her womb. It was an image he always conjured during nuptials of young lovers, but was not an expression of his own bodily lust — rather, was intended to impress the surrounding ethers with God's sacred entrust — in him — to prepare the young couple's conjugal bed for the planting of a fertile future. Since only an army of angels can defeat an army of devils.

And these two were both sorely wounded, and nearly defeated, before the musket even raised — one in body, the other in soul. And without his *spectral* benediction, their battle was likely lost.

He recalled how when he and his wife were newly wed, they were both possessed of sturdy constitutions and a lusty appetite; nevertheless, of their ten offspring only four had survived to adulthood.

"Elizabeth Porter. Do you accept the duties of a wife?"

That girl, still in the wake of illness, stood with her vacant eyes lowered, in a bridal dress so many months in the making hanging loose about her, staring down at its hem, or at her feet.

"Elizabeth," he repeated, a little louder, and now he took her hand and joined it to the bridegroom's. "Do you accept the duties of a wife?"

She nodded.

"Joseph Putnam. Do you accept the duties of a husband? Understanding that husbands are superior to their wives, just as parents are to their children and masters are to their servants? But that all are subordinate to God?"

Joseph answered joylessly.

Reverend Increase Mather now wound the satin ribbon around their loose clasped hands and tied the wedding knot, affirming: "That which God has joined together, let no man put asunder."

The wedding feast was held that night in splendid fashion on the same harbor hillside where the governor dwelt, in a great house that was owned by a wealthy Boston merchant, who had found himself in debt to the bride's father—for although Mary Veren Putnam had long planned to hold this event at Putnam Estate, after Cook and her family fled some months ago, she decided to let Lizzie Porter arrange it; because Salem Village was not a place for happy occasions anymore. But this grand house, thirty miles removed, with its hundred twinkling candles, European dances, musicians, and superb imported table-fare was all that she had imagined.

"Here's to Joseph Putnam's health!"

"To his prestige, here and abroad!"

"To his deflowering that wilt before all her petals drop!"

"Bag o' bones, you mean."

"The one the Grim Reaper slings."

These jesting Boston youths, all friends, boisterously drank another round. They didn't know the wedding couple personally; they'd only been invited because their parents sported important surnames.

Elizabeth Porter Putnam overheard every cruel remark, and each of them cut her sorely. But she reminded herself that she was a married woman now, who needn't suffer the opinions of any man except her husband—even her father didn't count.

Too weak to dance the *hornpipe*, she sat slunk inside an oversized chair, watching the guests learn the popular steps. Her French heels tapped a little, but only when her mother jigged past. She whispered her new name: *Elizabeth Putnam*. But it sounded hollow and untrue. She looked about the hall, and was relieved when she didn't see him. Joseph Putnam. She dreaded being his wife. She tried to imagine them sleeping in a single bed, but longed more for her own bed with her mother lying beside her. Her husband didn't love her, or even like her; and this marriage was more for his mother, who also didn't like her.

But although it might appear that way, it was in fact Israel Porter, her own father, who first designed this union sixteen years ago, planned for this marriage of fortunes, when this bride was in her swaddles and the groom was barely out of them.

It was in jest that Israel Porter once wrote this stipulation into a business contract with Putnam those many years ago. Last autumn however, not in jest, he delivered that old paper into Mary Veren Putnam's hand, who was so distraught at the time and not too clear thinking with her husband on his painful deathbed, that she was easily persuaded to add this clause to the will that Porter was helping her husband's feeble hand draft, believing it was her his final wish to please her knowing of her long acquaintanceship with the girl's mother.

To her mind, the match was reasonable enough. Especially with her son now standing at manhood's cusp and possessed of a sexual nature she couldn't control, and of an equine obsession she equally abhorred, as well as that lifelong moroseness that kept boring itself deeper; and now with her widow, it was only wise to give him a wife . . . for his taming and training, or visa versa.

Because, whether or not this girl survived for long, her dowry, nevertheless, would. And using herself as an example of a second wife, she'd let Joseph choose the next mate himself and, hopefully, she'd be the one to make her son happy.

But it was solely her own decision to disinherit her spouse's first three children. Who had always despised and diminished her, and by it had made their own empty beds now. She'd only ever wanted to be their friend, especially during her lonely beginnings at Putnam Farm with a husband three times her age. She even had considered taking Thomas for a lover then, till he turned his haughty back to her. But had he been that, then Joseph might not have been a hated half-brother, but his own secret son; and she'd have been more generous.

Or, had she known all that would befall as the result of her meddling, she might have decided to give her *stepson* his due anyway, and been kinder to his unkind sisters; though she and Joseph would have been a whit poorer. But it was too late now to turn back *that* unwound clock. Though so much would have changed, when it sprang forward again:

Thomas Putnam would have inherited the fair portion due a firstborn son, removing the stigma of poverty, as well as that son's rage born of a father's contempt. Jangling his rightful wealth in his pockets, he could have bought his way up all rungs of the village committee ladder (much like Israel Porter had done) and reaching the top and taking the helm after his father, his first order of business would have been to prohibit land sales to outsiders. Salem Village would have remained in the sure control of its founding stock. He'd have tithed to his church generously, and gotten others of his faction to do the same, ensuring security for Minister Parris, and status and stability for his own Putnam heirs, including his sons — because he'd have had the money to sue Ann for divorcement for "physical cruelty" and then would have married a fertile fawning wife.

Ann Putnam, even rich, might have continued murdering her male offspring and robbing any husband of sons. But no one would have learned of her crimes, unless Lucy Putnam had told them. And most likely that shy frail girl would never have uprooted the family secret, but would have taken this festering sore to her grave. For if they had been rich, there never would have been the need for the minister's charity of a household servant named Mercy Lewis, who taught her truth telling.

It's hard to say if Abigail Williams would have been different: a badly-wove basket never serves a use. But she'd have had less influence on her uncle were he prosperous . . . and none on her peers.

Because Susanna Walcott, sporting inherited pearly hairpins and the most envied dowry in the county, would hardly have paid attention to an ungainly orphan from the north amid so many attentive suitors, especially not a girl who might try to be a rival — although Abigail would have noticed her and sought her company.

For certain, Tituba and John Indian would be together now, not pining for each other half a world apart.

And while Bridget Bishop might have met Mercy Lewis, and Mercy, Joseph Putnam, and a fatherless babe might have come of it, with that mother a nobody and a servant in some other household, with no wiles to plant or conspiracies to conduct, hers would have remained an unwritten history, with her babe inheriting only the same unfortunate fate of all bastard offspring of rich masters and pretty sculleries.

And for everyone else in Essex County — and even the whole of the Massachusetts Commonwealth — it would be generations more, three centuries at least, before Satan again blew trances into innocent New Englander youth through "Devil's Trumpet."

Or maybe never — if Israel Porter had not opened that first door the Devil walked through.

After so much slipping, sliding and promenading around this glossy high-polished floor, Judge Hathorne went to deposit his overheated dance partner at the side. Lizzie re-joined her friend Mary Vern Putnam, while fanning herself like a hummingbird.

"Isn't it wonderful, how our lines are now joined? Jus*ss*t like we always wanted?"

     Mary was vexed. "Ye*sss*, of cour-*sss*, Lizzie, but where *is* my son?"

In cold shadows and crosswinds on a balcony at the mansion's rear, Joseph had spent most of this night adrift, pondering his missteps, and one fatal step not yet taken, while staring down at the black churning waters of the sea.

The Afflicted Girls

The parent asked:
> *What doth every sin deserve?*

The child answered:
> *Every sin deserves God's wrath and curse, both in this life and that which is to come.*

The Puritans Shorter Catechism

ЄPITAPH

I N 1696,
Mrs. Parris died of a stomach ulcer and was buried in the Village of Stowe. Reverend Parris, bereft, composed an epitaph for her gravestone:

> *The best wife,*
> *Choicest mother,*
> *Neighbor and friend.*

He considered her a saint; and himself, a doomed, long-suffering martyr of Christ. He was no longer a husband or father—because after his wife entered Heaven, their daughter Betty declined and soon met her own comatose end. He wasn't a minister either anymore—and because of it, his ungrateful niece, Abigail Williams, ran off to seek her fortune elsewhere as soon as he lost his, refusing to housekeep for an itinerant peddler. She stole back her sooty andirons and sold them to the blacksmith in Stowe, and also thieved her uncle's three rare-most valuable books, since his new lock box held naught. He never again encountered her.

Mary Veren Putnam died in 1695, after breaking her hipbone in a tumble down her staircase. All of her possessions within doors and without were left to her only son, Joseph

Putnam, a widower now, whose young wife's death preceded his mother's by two years.

As soon as the usurper died, Thomas Putnam, along with his sisters, sued once more to regain their inheritance, claiming their stepmother was mentally incapacitated when she wrote out her will. Dr. Griggs, who'd attended, testified that, indeed, Mary Veren Putnam was lacking in sound mind and was mostly unconsciousness or staring into space at the end. But Joseph, with his higher status and three full coffers, prevailed.

Thomas' middle years brought him more difficulty. He was forced to sell off his farmland piece by piece, and eventually lost his house. He died intestate at the age of forty-eight, leaving behind a sizeable debt and a scandal in his wake: his homicidal spouse Ann Putnam, who had preceded him into the grave, was never prosecuted for her crimes of infanticide. Nonetheless, she had been judged insane, and was widely shunned.

His three daughters, too tainted now to marry, were sent off into indenture. And when their first five-year bonds were paid, with their parents both dead, and their relations with relations now strained, those sisters indentured themselves for another five years as three tied together, though not here. They permanently left for parts unknown and their Walcott cousins lost touch with them. But before they left, Lucy, now twenty-one, gave a public apology during Sunday service at Salem Village Church, after being encouraged by its new popular minister. And although she begged sincerely for her neighbors' forgiveness, admitting her sins, she was never sure it was given.

Thus was Thomas Putnam's branch severed from the family tree, and that old oak stump in the yard initialed by three generations of Putnam males, uprooted and sawed into firewood by Putnam Farm's current owner, a landgrubber from Surrey, who burned that wormy timber in his first autumn bonfire during a feast to which all of his western neighbors were invited. Because not only was this man's first harvest bountiful, but he profitably raised Essex County's most succulent swine, which daily sniffed at the roots of twelve disapproving wineglass elms.

Susanna Walcott had married a farmer's son—not John Doritch, but someone equally witless and poor—after having been left with child by a wayfaring rogue, or someone else. She didn't love her husband, or any of the numerous offspring inherited from the previous wife, and sometimes couldn't tolerate her own. But having to care for so many so soon after marrying turned her into a young scold. By the age of thirty-seven, she gave up her ghost, likely from exhaustion.

At the height of the witch craze, Reverend Cotton Mather delivered a blistering sermon regarding the Apocalypse. He proclaimed that the Day of Judgment was at hand and identified four men: Governor Phips, Chief Justice Stoughton, his father Increase, and himself (Reverend Parris, of course, felt snubbed) as the four symbolic *Horsemen* handpicked by God to lead this Final Battle. After the culling was halted by one of these chosen Horsemen, even then he remained obsessed, propounding witchcraft accusations from his North Church pulpit each Sunday till he was deemed a madman by some of his parishioners, was hated by most Bostonians, and was sometimes spit on in the street. Then came a personal tragedy—his newborn child, a boy, was born deformed with an unnaturally twisted up intestine, part of which could be seen outside the body. That poor creature passed from life quickly. Folk who learned of it called it God's retribution; whereas, he insisted those knots had been tied by the Devil's Fingers. Soon after, he wrote and published a new treatise entitled: *Pillars of Salt*—hoping it would prove as popular as his *Wonders of the Invisible World*:

SUZY WITTEN

A history of criminals executed in this land for capital crimes, with some of their dying speeches collected and published for the warning of such as live in destructive courses of ungodliness.

It didn't.

The Nurse clan continued to prosper, and that family endures to this day.

Ben Nurse married young and fathered many accomplished children, numerous grandchildren and great-grandchildren, who each in turn sat upon his knee listening to his far-flung tales of an enchanted blue-eyed deer that was really a maid, and of a maid that was rescued from the gallows by a masked stranger, that same gallows on which their own Great Granny Rebecca Nurse was martyred by envy and spite for her goodness and wisdom, like Christ had once been on His Cross.

He'd achieved his every goal in life: substantial wealth and property, a pretty wife, hearty progeny, a respected voice in Commonwealth politics, and as a gentryman, no less. His swift rise to prominence was mostly through the influence peddling of his widowed childless friend, Joseph Putnam, the richest man in Essex County, who came often to dine at his table, and still preferred horsemanship to statesmanship. And who had, for many years now, let Ben Nurse fight the battles of his convictions.

And in this warmest of family circles, Joseph Putnam finally found his peace. Or, in John Bunyan's words:

> *One will, I think, say, both his laughs and cries*
> *May well be guessed at by his watery eyes.*
> *Some things are of that nature as to make*
> *One's fancy chuckle while his heart doth ache.*

The Afflicted Girls

EPILOGUE

A TOW-HAIRED BOY OF FOUR HAD BEEN CHASING a bright orange butterfly flitting from daisy to bluebell, snapdragon to buttercup in the soft highland grasses overlooking Henry Hudson's river. But now that indifferent creature fluttered out beyond the edge of the bluff, ending his game. He came running tearfully back across the hillside to his mother.

She was propped on her side on a rich-embroidered silk shawl her good friend, the sea captain, had recently brought her back from Lisbon. Hearing her child's cries, she closed her journal and laid down her scribing pen.

Writing was her profession now. Several works to date—three essays, two long-form poems—had been published. Another was rooting in these wild weeds today. Although she was yet years from writing her most prominent title: *Psychologia:* (she would one day coin that far-reaching phrase) *an account of the nature of the rational soul.* Arguing against and alongside Locke that Divine Mystery not merely exists, but shapes us and completes our human understanding.

Her future mentor, the English philosopher Broughton, whom she would encounter on a voyage next summer to Old England, would, in admiration of her intellect, publish her treatise under his own pen, since women philosophers were unheard of. But even were they not, radical rarified views such as hers would alarm Messrs. Bennet & Bosvile, the two old-fashioned academics, currently his London publishers.

During her long lifetime, only one other person besides her amanuensis, her Quaker captain, and her son would know the truth of her accomplishments: a promising young printer met on another ocean crossing, a visionary thinker, surname Franklin, a relation of her sea captain, who would become an enduring friend.

But these scribbled thoughts today reflected none of that exceptional future. These were remnants of her past. For last night, she'd dreamt vividly of the tragic events. It wasn't a nightmare. All her torments had ceased with the birth of her son.

> *Four years have passed, but still no one knows the truth of those happenings. Who it was, God or the Devil, wreaking wrathful vengeance in an uncaring place. While I suffer the sore no longer, to them that yet do, let them ponder this necessary question: "Would people turn so evil? Wound so evilly, and so easily . . . if not for either one?"*

When the cherub reached her, she smothered him with kisses. When that didn't console him, she picked a dandelion, offering, "Wish on it, Joseph." "No," he sniffled, with his usual stubborn pout.

She took a deep breath and leaned in toward that puffer, pursing her berry-stained lips, with her thoughtful eyes misting. "Then I wish—"

"No!" cried the little fellow, filling his chubby cheeks with purpose. He blew. A grin of wonderment appeared on his tear-streaked face seeing his puffer sail high up into the sky, even higher than his butterfly had flown.

Smiling, Mercy wrapped him inside her soft billowy silken sleeves. And now mother and son lay back in their garden to watch the summer breeze lift their wishes, like dancing butterflies, through an untroubled sky toward the sun.

AFTERWORD

When I began my research for *The Afflicted Girls* screenplay in the 1990s, like every layperson I understood how Salem Village's witchcraft craze and the outcries of the afflicted girls were a result of "hysteria" within a troubled community. Later, when a handful of historians began attributing those strange maladies to "ergot" poisoning, I considered that cause also (i.e., a hallucinogenic fungus, which can grow on wet rye—it has since been disputed that the Salem summer of 1691 was a rainy one). But I didn't embrace either explanation, for if it were "hysteria," how did Salem's youth suffer such deadly physical maladies? And if it were "ergot," why wasn't the entire population of Essex County sick, since everyone would have ingested food from the same moldy crop?

Then I came across three distinct references that turned my mind in a new direction. First was a mention by one researcher how the native shamans in South American Carib tribes during colonial times used the wild weed *Datura* in their rituals. (It grew throughout the Americas.) Second was a description of maddened colonial soldiers in Jamestown, Virginia, who accidentally ate Jamestown weed (i.e., "Jimson") in a salad. Third came a true revelation, my unique insight, which became the conceit of this book—that took shape as a spate of newspapers around the country ran stories about an epidemic of teenagers experimenting with Jimson weed, with most of them hospitalized and a few dying from their strange "afflictions." The symptoms were described.

I began comparing the symptoms of "ergot" poisoning with those of "Jimson weed," and discovered that it could only have been Jimson in Salem Village. This plant's attack on the nervous system corresponded exactly (unlike ergot's) to the written descriptions of the children's afflictions in the Historical Record of the Salem Witch Trials of 1692—a common-sense premise and conclusion by which a 300-year-old enduring mystery is solved . . . in this old story with a new twist.

Suzy Witten
Los Angeles, California November 2009

ABOUT THE AUTHOR

Suzy Witten's career spans more than twenty years in the entertainment industry: as a filmmaker, screenwriter, story analyst, and an editor for both film and television. She has also taught meditation. Currently, she works as a writer and researcher during disasters for FEMA (United States Federal Emergency Management Agency) Public Affairs. She resides in Los Angeles, California. *The Afflicted Girls* is her first novel.

8-5-10
17

LaVergne, TN USA
23 July 2010
190568LV00002B/9/P